the
STYLIST

Also by Cai Emmons

His Mother's Son

the STYLIST

A NOVEL

CAI EMMONS

HARPER  PERENNIAL

NEW YORK • LONDON • TORONTO • SYDNEY

HARPER PERENNIAL

HarperCollins books may be purchased for educational, business, or sales promotional use. For information please write: Special Markets Department, HarperCollins Publishers, 10 East 53rd Street, New York, NY 10022.

FIRST EDITION

Designed by Jan Pisciotta

Library of Congress Cataloging-in-Publication Data is available upon request.

ISBN: 978-0-06-089895-3
ISBN-10: 0-06-089895-X

07 08 09 10 11   OV/RRD   10 9 8 7 6 5 4 3 2 1

For my *habibi*, Paul

"And he wondered at this trick his mind continued to play on him, this constant turning of one thing into another thing, as if behind each real thing there were a shadow thing, as alive in his mind as the thing before his eyes."

—Paul Auster, *The Invention of Solitude*

Prologue

As a child, she was always seeking refuge, a small plot of cool blue faintly redolent of violets or eucalyptus, lavish in nothing except a great generosity of air. In winter she hid on the middle shelf of the linen closet among the cool cotton sheets that smelled of lavender sachets. She sat still as a dish in the brown darkness, listening to her sisters, Sophie and Cornelia, rummaging in their drawers, to Arleen and Mother transporting things from one room to another. It sometimes seemed to her that all adults did was carry things from place to place, seeking to satisfy some inscrutable sense of order. In the linen closet she was the eye of the storm, the pit of the plum, the anti-star of her own universe. No one had any doubts about what to do in her absence; life went on perfectly well without her.

In summer she sought refuge in outdoor places, usually beyond everyone's earshot. Under the arching branches of the mulberry tree light filtered through where human vision did not, and her mind dimmed easily so her body seemed to disappear, and she forgot her name. For unquantified stretches of time nothing about her or her brain was any more advanced than a prehistoric lizard.

Only worry lured her out. A sudden prescience of danger—Mother's presence could no longer be accounted for. A bristling coldness would come over her, a call to arms, and she rushed from her closet or tree and tore around the house scouring room after room until she found her, her beloved, her mother, stretched long and feather-light and seemingly translucent on the bed, all of her body, crown to toe, intact, holding a book, laughing in her soft reassuring way when she saw Hayden. Hayden's worry-heart was always galloping like some faster-than-cheetah species. "Don't look so worried. Everything is fine," Mother would say.

"I thought something was wrong with you," Hayden said. "I thought you might—" She said this, or some version of this, years before there was any reason to worry.

It was unbecoming in a child to be of such a worrying nature. Children are thought to have milky brows, unvexed hearts, souls with no intimations of darkness. They should not be seeking sanctuary, certainly not when they are loved and cloistered and live in spacious houses, are fed nutritious food, and surrounded by books and art, safe from the world's depredations. What more sanctuary could a child need?

Now she knows she was not so unusual. Women parade through her life daily—coworkers and clients—often speaking of how they were afflicted with worry as she was, from early on. They are women who move with more strings on their limbs than a marionette; women who slink through their lives preferring not to be noticed; women who try to shrink themselves to fit in small spaces; women who slip into public restrooms without any need to pee because inside a ladies' room there is a door to close, a legitimate way to say *no* to intrusion, a place to float in suspended animation and arrested thought, if only for a moment.

Until she found Pizzazz, she did not believe the world could deliver real sanctuary, not beyond the wishful thinking of daydreams. She and her sisters grew up as old-fashioned girls, readers, aloof from modernity; they kept their hair long, and regarded those who patronized beauty parlors as vulgar. Salons were part of some world others moved in, a world that included malls and Hollywood and fast food. In that world women bleached their hair blond and painted their nails red. It was a world Hayden was expected to revile. It was not her mother, the blue blood, who promulgated this notion that they should live at some remove from the rest of humanity; it was her father, the picked-up-by-the-bootstraps son of Irish immigrants. He was the one who looked down on popular culture and manual labor, the labor his ancestors had so dutifully performed for decades—no, *centuries*—to benefit him. Father was the one who put them through intellectual boot camp, who wanted them to know things and use eloquent words, who wanted them all to opt for a life of the mind, as if thinking were nobler than manual labor, as if it were not what it most clearly was—only another conceit of biology.

Few men fully appreciate the satisfactions a salon delivers. Men want, quite simply, a quick cut—in and out with efficiency and a reasonable payment. But women want so much more. They want to step away. They want to set aside the appointment book, the arrangements with babysitters, the soccer game, the meal about to be cooked. They want a gleeful shirking, relief from all that claws both inside and out. They want to begin to know the edges of their own bodies again, feel their legs without a toddler grabbing them, feel their breasts as their own. That is phase one: the reclaiming.

Then they want to trust: phase two. They want to trust their salon workers as they once trusted their mothers. They want to give themselves over to gentle, competent hands. They want to glance in the mirror and see someone smiling back at them and feel in that smile a great permission.

Phase three is the washing: a portal in. It begins in silence or light chat, but nothing that diverts attention from the gush of water flooding the head, warm as the amniotic sea, rich and slow as a good idea. A choice of shampoos—herbal or floral, no edible scents, please—and then the washing, fingers kneading the crown, the base of the skull, the top of the vertebrae, behind the ears. What ecstasy the cranium feels in finding itself alone, the brain on leave, recognized and released.

Phase four: the reluctant departure from the washbasin. Back in the chair with tea or coffee or wine, and the "work" begins. The fun is over, the client might think. But the good salon worker knows that the fun is never over. This is life's epicenter; there is always celebration here—women nerve-to-nerve, laughing, sometimes crying. Children and husbands and lovers and schools and diets and hair—nothing is more elemental than the sharing and comparing of details about these things.

Vanity, her father would once have said, but vanity be damned. How can someone be vain when she does not even see herself? The salon insists: *Look in the mirror. See who you are. See your loveliness, the undomesticated you. Rejoice. Think: No one begrudges birds their plumage.*

Women in salons everywhere sit in the thick of molting, surrounded by the susurrant roux of other female voices. Oh, what beauties they are: middle-aged women with hair like straw, the silky-haired young ones, the shagged, the shaved, the mulleted. She loves them all with an intensity she thought could only be evoked by children.

Around her, underpinning the chat, the sounds of consciousness rise to a boil. All those proto-selves becoming real ones. For men it might be different, but for a woman to come to full consciousness her story must not only be thought, it must be told out loud, not once but over and over until its shape is known, its swamps and pinnacles equally clear. And that telling begins in sanctuary where the sound of women's stories solidifying is so much more than mere noise.

Part I

Hoboken, New Jersey

"Some wild notion she had of following the birds
to the rim of the world and flinging herself on the
spongy turf and there drinking forgetfulness, while
the rooks' hoarse laughter sounded over her."

—Virginia Woolf, *Orlando*

"I am the swathed figure in the hairdresser's
shop taking up only so much space."

—Virginia Woolf, *The Waves*

Chapter 1

The Pizzazz Salon where Hayden worked was located in one of the few remaining shabby sections of Hoboken, on a block where, despite the fact that some adventuring Wall Street types had moved in and contractors were a daily sight, there remained, on certain days, an overpowering scent of garbage mingled with fetid Hudson River oils. Crumpled remnants of the *Hoboken Reporter*, torn bits of losing lottery tickets, clear plastic collars freed of their six-packs, all periodically blew down the sidewalk past the salon's front door.

Rena, the salon's owner, a fiftyish former hippie with extravagant hair and an optimistic personality, believed the neighborhood was on the upswing, and being in her employ it was hard not to believe along with her. But in the four months since 9/11 they had all been battling a generalized ennui that passed from woman to woman like a sneaker wave. They were an urban tribe of round-the-track, stand-alone, self-supporting women who all had in common strong noses for the seeds of fascism that resided in overzealous managers. They bucked under too much authority and appreciated that Rena let them run their own businesses under her umbrella. Their clients were women of all descriptions—middle-aged moms, a young arty crowd, a handful of

Wall Street go-getters, and even some blue-haired ladies who had been coming to the salon for decades, women with roiling curls and unbreakable habits of Wednesday salon visits followed by lunch at Dino's and afternoons of bridge.

Since early December there had been a vacant station, the one closest to the front door that served most of the walk-ins. They needed desperately to fill this station. From mid-October they'd been booked solid—a result of people trying to live as fully as they could for whatever time they might have left—and they had had to turn many people away. Rena had been interviewing for weeks—a series of bleach-blond, gum-chewing girls fresh from beauty school, girls with exposed navels and multiple piercings and bad attitudes to rival the Gambino family. Rena was looking for flexible people, women who had a few bones of maturity about them and would be able to service all types. As far as Hayden knew no one had been hired, so she wasn't prepared that early January Sunday when Emory Bellew made an appearance.

The weather seemed malevolent that day, the wind on a mad Machiavellian tear down the north-facing streets; the waters of the Hudson churning like sewer slop; the sky a glowering gray, regurgitating snow and hail with peristaltic regularity; the temperature dangerously low, sullen, so exposed skin was first seared then paralyzed. Staying out too long on days like that changed the whole nervous system, retarding and diluting its reactions, making the owner of those nerves feel as if she'd been aged and dumbed down.

Hayden was on her way back from Manhattan where she and Tina, one of her salon mates—a tall, tough, wry woman with a long face suggestive of an investigating aardvark—had gone for dim sum and a close-out product sale on Canal. Hayden was pleased to have found her favorite texturing gel called Chops. Afterward they had taken their ritual weepy walk through Battery Park, past

Ground Zero, then up through Tribeca, ending in the West Village. They had been doing this same walk, or a version of it, every Sunday for three months now, putting their feet to the pavement in solidarity with each other and the world, taking a stance against despair, letting it be known they had not fled the city and could be counted on should they be needed. A futile effort, they knew, but one they could not relinquish.

After they parted that day Hayden had stopped for a quick coffee before heading home. As she sat in the amber light of Starbucks, her mouth filled with airy latte foam, a guy en route to his seat squeezed behind her, jostled his own elbow, and lost half his cappuccino foam on her head so it dribbled past her earlobe and covered her shoulder like a snowflake cape. Her skin was not scalded, her hair and clothing could be washed—there was nothing to do but laugh, but when she did, the man, a few years older than Hayden—perhaps thirty to Hayden's twenty-five—thick-lipped, creamy-skinned, his black-rimmed spectacles suggesting a child doing dress-up, halted his apologies and looked at her with shock or curiosity or some amalgam of the two. "You think it's *funny*?" he said.

She shrugged. "Is there a choice?"

He shook his head in some obscurely rueful, almost parental way and looked her up and down, his eyes like slots verifying the authenticity of dollar bills. He made much of toweling her clean with a cloth handkerchief, took a seat near hers, and gazed for a long while at his remaining foam before eventually sipping. Then he looked up, reflections winking in his glasses, and told her she interested him.

It was, she thought, a silly thing to say. She was not the least bit interesting: Her mouse-brown hair was thin and slack; her chest was flat; her tattoos, nine of them, were mostly hidden; her

personality was retiring. She had schooled herself to be a profes-
sional chameleon, a watcher of others, a woman oiled to move
fast to new locations, preferring not to get stuck. Nevertheless,
she tried to receive his comment graciously. His name turned
out to be Saterious, which made her laugh again. He smiled and
didn't offer to explain. They talked for a while, flirting a bit, but
Hayden was a squirrelly flirt and knew exactly when she would
stop, and she felt dirty for playing along knowing things would go
nowhere. Everything she understood about men until then had
told her they were to be indulged but not trusted. So she drank
her latte, and chatted, and acquiesced to take the card he pressed
on her, and finally blurted her own number, hoping she wouldn't
regret it, but then her time was up, and she headed out into the
cold, tossing him the agreeable, open-mouthed, noncommittal
smile of an underling primate.

By the time she exited the PATH in Hoboken the air was so
cold it seemed brittle to the touch. She had to pass the salon on
the way to her apartment, so she stepped in briefly to warm up.
She stood at her station in semidarkness, pulling at each of her
fingers to coax blood back into their numbed tips. The salon was
closed for business on Sundays. The only regular Sunday visitors were Raymond, their weekly cleaner, and Rena, who came
in sometimes to do the books and straighten things and decorate
and generally prepare for the chattery, girly, chemical, confesso-
rial chaos that comprised their six-day work week. Hayden only
went in on Sundays for practical reasons—a place to pee en route
from the PATH train to her apartment, or perhaps to restock her
supplies—but Sunday visits were not the norm.

The salon was empty that night. She assembled the new products at her station, lifting their caps first to smell and confirm her
choices, beguiled in particular by an excellent freesia conditioner;

then she sat in the swivel chair and removed her low-heeled ankle boots, freeing her toes to squirm their way back into sentience. Rena's recently installed fish tank hummed and bubbled and cast a celestial blue light throughout the salon. The sound and pulsing light, regular as heartbeats, were comforting, though she preferred not to look at the fish themselves who hung among the bubbles like spooks. Outside dusk had taken the town in a tight fist and wedges of streetlight shouldered through the loose slats of the Levolors, strafing the floor and losing themselves in the salon's mirrored walls. Happy to exist in semidarkness, she waggled her digits and massaged her limbs and wondered, idly, who Saterious really was. She pulled out his card. *New York Times*, it said, a fact she registered with detached amusement.

Even with the lights off and not another soul present, the salon made her happy. She drew pleasure from the curvaceous, body-suggesting shapes of the shampoo bottles, each product line a different palette of earth tones or brights or pastels; and she drew pleasure from the scents of these products that unraveled in the air unpredictably, like loose skeins of yarn—a thread of calendula, a trace of lavender, a wisp of peppermint, aloe vera and gardenia, musk and vetiver, almond and bergamot, all knitted together and mated with the lingering molecules of patchouli from the incense Rena liked to burn, finally melding into some bouquet the nose could never accurately untangle. And she drew pleasure from the shimmery purple and teal capes they gave to their clients to protect their shoulders and necks from slivers of their own shorn hair. A different kind of pleasure could be culled from the accumulated stack of women's magazines peddling glamour to make it seem accessible, and commonsense advice under the guise of new discovery—you could lose yourself in those magazines, fall happily idle, slack-jawed, and worry-free as you waited for your styling, like a sated animal in the sun, doing what she was made to do. Hayden loved it all. She even loved the smell of ammonia and singed over-chlorinated hair, and the preposterous clutter, the overall visual and olfactory suggestion that this was a place that tolerated the unleashing of female fugues. She loved the swivel chairs with their adjustable backs and their cushioned leather seats. She loved the way her salon mates had all arranged their stations with photographs and personal effects—ribbons and cards from birthdays gone by, stuffed animals rescued from childhood, the paraphernalia left by old boyfriends, small bowls of their favorite snack foods. Demetria displayed her GED certificate, three bounced checks, and a stack of books she intended to read; Amber had a rhinestone tiara from her high school senior prom; Tina draped a Grateful Dead necktie on the faucet of her basin; Donelle prized a stuffed tailless monkey for anxious clients to clutch; Birdie's mirror sported a Yankees' banner courtesy of Billy.

What distinguished Hayden's station was a small bird collection, not actual birds but images of them: a pen-and-ink drawing of a feeding chickadee, a postcard of a haggard eagle wearing an Uncle Sam hat, a magazine cutout of a flock of migrating Canada geese, several postcard-sized copies of Audubon prints, and on and on. They were taped to the wall that formed a right angle to her mirror, not necessarily announcing themselves loudly, but there to be noticed by anyone who cared to look. Above her mirror hung the conical, glitter-flecked cardboard party hat that had survived from her twenty-fifth birthday (four months earlier, exactly ten days prior to 9/11), the hat's frayed edges and broken chin string a forlorn echo of some youthful state she couldn't hope to regain. And tucked behind her answering machine was the small laminated photo of Mother holding Russ, their three-legged dog. On the countertop were the usual appurtenances of her trade—

the combs, shears, razors, blow dryers, cream rinses, shampoos, mousses, detanglers, and myriad other gels and lotions, whose color and viscous consistency resembled body fluids.

Each of the stations was equipped with a basin for hair washing and functioned as a separate fiefdom where the stylist reigned with kindness, or humor, or honed listening skills, or raw hairstyling talent. Once Rena hired a girl and gave her a few ground rules, she let her call her own shots. They each set up their own businesses, recruited and booked their own clients, purchased their own products from whatever suppliers they wanted, and worked as many hours as suited them. Hayden had put in time enough at other salons (all in California) to know this was a better place than most, factoring in the inevitable irritants: the occasional squabbling of those who worked cheek-to-jowl, the rising and falling tides of the almighty dollar, and of course, with so many women, the shrapnel of hormones.

Into that column of lush, gynocentric contentment stepped Emory Bellew. At the time Hayden did not know who Emory Bellew was, and therefore she had no reason to believe this angular figure in belted black pants was anything other than a determined and knowledgeable intruder. Frozen, shadowed, Hayden watched the stranger who closed the salon's door, locked it, and proceeded to the empty station without the slightest hesitation or misstep or appearance of criminal furtiveness, but rather a preoccupied look, as if her intense familiarity with the routine freed her to look inward. At the empty station she knew just where the light was and she flicked it on, flooding the chair and console in a warm aureole of yolk-yellow light, transforming the area and its swivel chair into a tiny stage, while shoving Hayden into a deeper and more obscuring darkness.

The stranger laid down a massive black messenger bag, flung

back its flap, and began to remove her gear. It was now apparent that she must be the new girl, but Hayden said nothing and clung to her observing perch, in part because she was so stunned that Rena had neglected to tell them of the new hire, and in part because this woman herself was so unusual. Everything in her pressed black clothing and her angular movement suggested precision and control, but her head seemed borrowed from another woman entirely. Her hair was arranged in grapelike clusters of small blond curls, her face thickly painted with mascara and predatory red lipstick, the net effect being a garish version of Lillian Gish. She reminded Hayden of the child's book that had pictures of people sliced into thirds so the heads and torsos and legs could be mixed and matched to preposterous effect. But in real life Hayden had never seen such a mismatched human.

The stranger arranged her tools for ten or fifteen minutes, arms moving in and out of her drawers with purposive thrusts. Hayden's silence by now was a thing of note; to suddenly introduce herself from her pit of darkness would be tantamount to admitting that she had spent those minutes spying. She held fast to her silence and hoped she wouldn't be seen. The stranger began humming something low and almost Gregorian, not melancholy exactly, but chant-like, incantatory. Hayden was locked in stillness. Her limbs felt squirmy with their new influx of blood, and restlessness grew in her like panic. Soon she would have to leap from her cover.

Something stopped the intruder, snagging her attention so she leaned into the mirror. Hayden was certain she'd been seen. But the intruder only stared, taken with nothing other than her own image. She ran a finger lightly over her upper lip and along her cheek, and she tugged lightly at one of her drill-bit curls. Then, fingers splayed on either side of her head, she moved her hair, adjusting it to one side, then the other, until it was centered, as if it were a tea cozy, or a blanket, or a birdcage. Cancer, Hayden thought. One of Rena's famous charity hires. Another member of their crew who would take up temporary residence at the station near the door, only to vanish before they really knew her. Hayden closed her eyes, deciding feigned sleep was her only possible out. After another ten minutes or so she heard the stranger's heels tapping a path to the door; the locks made their satisfied sucks and clicks, and she was gone.

Rena interviewed new girls by having them style her hair. Relaxing into the role of client while they worked on her, she was able to get them talking and claimed to learn more this way than if they'd been sitting face-to-face. She also gained firsthand information about how they handled hair. If you could handle Rena's hair effectively, you could handle anyone's. Rena's coarse black hair, laced with a bit of gray, flew from her head as if she were being electrocuted. She liked to keep it shoulder-length so its sheer mass doubled the size of her head's silhouette. There was a time, she said, when she had changed her look every few months—permed hair, rainbow-colored hair, dreadlocks, braids, an upsweep, a shag, straightened hair, a crew cut with her initials shaved into it—but now, at fifty-something, she just wanted boring, a laughable idea for a woman like Rena who was always on the move, always in the grip of a new idea—a new business she wanted to start, a new charity case she wanted to take on, a new friend she wanted to reform.

The charity hires, such as Hayden deemed Emory Bellew to be, were not all that unusual for Rena. While seven of them had been nearly permanent fixtures at the salon for at least two and a half years—which, in the personnel life of a salon, was millennial—there was that one station that functioned as a round-robin for

Rena's risky but noble hires. There had been an ex-con who fell prey to her prior heroin addiction and began "borrowing" from other girls' tills, a "sex worker" who wanted to change her line of work but was hopeless with hair, a recently widowed grandmother who was always in tears and offended by the language some of the girls used, a paraplegic woman in an old wheelchair who was in the job market for the first time and not a bad stylist but intolerably slow due to the difficulty of maneuvering her chair. Eventually her regular client roster dwindled and died, and the walk-ins excused themselves to other salons. The most recent occupant of the station had been nineteen-year-old Laura from Tennessee, competent in all observable ways, risky only for her youth. She had been at the salon for three months and seemed reasonably happy, but one day she left work and never returned and Rena discovered her phone had been disconnected. But the failure of these experimental hires never deterred Rena from taking yet another chance. It was a mission with her.

Hayden arrived at the salon at ten fifteen the following day though her first client wasn't until eleven. She liked the extra time to finish her coffee slowly, get her station and tools ready for the week, and compare with the other girls the ecstasies and transgressions of their weekends. Tina had met a friend at a bar after Hayden left her and they had both drunk too much; Demetria's hot date had been too prudish to spend the night; Birdie had made a lasagna to die for. Monday morning bleed-down—they ranted and extolled, hemorrhaging feeling like the victims of quack surgery. They tried to contain themselves in front of the clients, but sometimes the clients themselves, especially if they were regular clients, got caught in the crossfire and joined in, volleying back with their own triumphs and horror stories and adding to the edifice of salon legend.

Birdie and Tina were already at work, Birdie with a familiar young motormouth actress/waitress who was going on an audition that afternoon and wanted to look like a "dazzling cop," and Tina (smiling hard through her hangover) with a pleasant-looking, middle-aged woman Hayden didn't recognize. Emory sat in her client chair reading a magazine, a somewhat anomalous sight in a place where the girls were usually standing, and when they weren't occupied with a client they swept or dusted their stations, or cleaned their combs, or replenished supplies, or stirred up conversation with the other girls, or took orders and went out to Finelli's for coffee and pastries. But the fact that Emory sat idle was the least of her oddity. She wore an entirely different wig from the one she'd been wearing the prior night. That morning's wig was an insurgent auburn, and it cut a sharp V at her nape. In front a forelock curtained one eye. It was an asymmetrical, modern, youthful, even hip style that flirted with the salon's lights each time she moved, making her entire head look strangely volatile and definitely at odds with her image of the night before though perhaps more synchronous with her streamlined body. Hayden read defiance in Emory's sprawled posture—heels perched on the handles of her cabinet's drawers, bottom slid forward so she was nearly reclining. Hayden also noticed in the harsh light of morning that Emory appeared older than she'd looked the night before—she might be pushing forty.

The salon smelled strongly of singed hair and ammonia, an odor Rena found repellent and was always trying to foil with several sticks of patchouli incense, which had the effect of complicating the scent but not masking it. Outside freezing rain tapped a scherzo rhythm on the expensive, double-paneled, weather-sealed windows. It was nasty weather and Hayden expected cancellations. She replenished her coffee in the small back room, a kitchen/lounge where Rena, clad in a red wool dress, was arranging red and lavender tulips in a vase, tugging at each stem to keep them from cleaving. Rena was committed to Atmosphere. She had painted the walls a deep mauve and installed recessed, rose-tinged lights that flattered face and hair; she played Enya and Windham Hill CDs at a low volume; and she did whatever she could to minimize the chemical smells that were unavoidable in the profession. And ritualistically, every other day, she bought fresh flowers that she displayed on a table by the entrance.

"Hey, Hayden," she said with an energy that seemed to promise she had something special in store.

"Tulips in January?" Hayden said.

"The most feminine flowers. Don't they remind you of vaginas?" Rena cupped one of the blooms and poked an investigative finger between the clenched petals so the tip came up powdered with yellow. "Aren't you freezing?" She stared down to the divide between shirt and waistband where a tattooed cat curled around Hayden's navel. Tattooing her flesh had been one of the ways Hayden had found back in high school to keep people's expectations low.

"I'm used to it," Hayden said.

"Have you met the new girl?" It was their prerogative, their pleasure, their rebellion and conceit to call themselves girls.

"Not officially."

"Well, let's go." Rena, vase of tulips in hand, started for the door, but Hayden gripped her elbow, forcing her to turn.

"What's with her?" Hayden asked.

Rena stood expressionless, said nothing.

"She has cancer?" Hayden pushed.

"Like all of the rest of us, she needs the work." Rena spun and left with her tulips.

Seeing Rena, Emory Bellew sat up straight and laid down her magazine, but did not rise.

"This is Emory Bellew," said Rena. "Emory, this here is Hayden. She's been around a while. If you've got questions you can ask her. Right Hayden?"

Hayden nodded. "Something like that." She felt stiff and stupid, unnerved by Emory's wig and by the noisy silver bangles on Emory's wrists, by her secret knowledge from the prior night, and by some strange sense of vertigo she felt in Emory's presence. Without a flicker of recognition Emory said her name in a voice that was quiet and low, like the faint rumble before a loud thunderclap. Her extended hand was dry, sprinkled with several long hairs, and more aged than her face, like the hand of an artist that has been in contact too frequently with paint and gesso and turpentine. Hayden was about to ask a few of those preliminary, getting-to-know-you questions, but she could see something remote and untouchable in Emory's eyes, and Emory kept glancing at her magazine as if she longed to be released from the threat of a conversation.

Hayden moved on to her own workstation in the crook of the L-shaped salon, where, with the benefit of mirrors, she could keep Emory in view. Tina lifted a comb in greeting, Birdie waggled a free forefinger, and Hayden settled into the day and its reliable salve of routine.

Hayden's first client that day was Mrs. Bella Cattori, an elderly, liver-spotted Italian woman who had lived in the neighborhood all her life. Hayden watched Bella approach from two blocks away, bundled and umbrellaed against the weather, negotiating the sidewalk cracks with aplomb and occasionally losing her balance, tottering then straightening, glancing around to see if anyone had noticed. At the intersection she stepped boldly into the street though the momentum of oncoming traffic did not favor her. She knew the furious, swearing drivers would defer to her seniority. She was eighty-three and her posture revealed that, but little else about her did. Every day she wore some small outward sign of her eccentricity, her Life Force, she said—a red beret covered with buttons bearing defiant slogans like Don't Push Me, or Women Belong on Top, a gauzy purple Isadora Duncan scarf, a pair of skintight leopard-skin pants with gloves to match, tights woven with glinting gold threads that caught the light, purple sneakers—all items that were barometers of her mood if you knew how to read them. She saw Hayden weekly though her hair grew so slowly Hayden often only pretended to cut it, her shears busily clipping at air as Bella talked, telling the entire salon about her cat, her young neighbors' parties, her dead husband's food preferences. For a month after 9/11 Bella wept through all her appointments and talked about going to work on the task of dying. She never went to Manhattan, but the fact that such a daily, rock-solid part of her visual world had changed on her so suddenly was unacceptable. Then one day in early November she came in and spoke of her new strategy. "In the morning while I'm still in bed I draw the towers in my head, just the way they were. Tall. Simple. A little ugly, you know. Then I go out, and I look over and—presto, there they are! Just like they were. Not a thing is different. Because I said so. You create your own reality, hon. You should try it." After that she was restored to her former ebullient self. Bella was a high-maintenance client, but Hayden loved her for her stamina, her defiance of aging.

"How's it going?" Hayden asked as she helped Bella into the chair and pulled a teal cape around her shoulders. The loose peacock feather parked behind one of Bella's ears flickered from the breeze of Tina's dryer. "What's up?" Hayden pressed, as she fastened the cape at the back of Bella's neck.

Bella sighed extravagantly, taking time to sweep in extra air and letting it go with the precision of a time-release capsule. The things that perturbed her all seemed to merit equal amounts of distress, so Hayden could never tell from her preliminary sighs if she was about to announce that a close friend of hers had died or the bakery had run out of cannolis.

"I *hate* my hair," she said. "I am *so* sick of it." Hayden laughed. How often she heard those words. How elemental was the feeling that hair was a litmus test for the state of psyche and soul. Bella pulled hard on the sparse pewter locks at the sides of her head as if trying to uproot them. Hayden could see Emory eyeing the two of them.

"What's wrong with it?" Hayden said.

"It always looks so—so flabbergasted. I want hair that makes me look like I can control myself."

"A new cut then?"

"I don't know," she said, making faces in the mirror. "Maybe a shave."

Hayden laughed. "Sinead O'Connor look?"

"Who's she?"

"Oh, just a woman. A singer."

Bella squinted and stared hard at her reflection, ignoring Hayden in the full grip of some interior self-assessment that the sight of herself in the mirror brought on. "Yeah," she said after an interval of silence. She nodded emphatically. "Yeah, I'll get a shave. Mother of mercy, a shave for old Bella. Bald and beautiful Bella." She closed her eyes, leaned back, and laughed savagely. "Maybe it'll make me look younger."

Hayden laughed too, uncomfortably aware of Emory's attention thrust squarely on her and Bella. She fluffed the hair of Bella's crown. "We could go shorter on the sides, a little fuller on top."

"A shave, girl. I said a shave."

Hayden walked between Bella and the mirror so she could look at Bella head-on. "Bella, it's January. It's arctic out there. You'll catch your death."

"Hats, my dear."

"Well, yes, but—"

"Go to it, I have a luncheon at twelve fifteen."

"If you don't like it, it might take a while to grow back," Hayden persisted. "Have you thought of that?"

"Girl, you spend your life thinking of the negative, you'll never do anything. Right now, hair is something I can do without."

"I don't know—"

"For Christ's sake," came Emory's gravelly voice, "the woman wants a shave, give the woman a shave."

Bella and Hayden both looked over at Emory who stared back at them, unabashed. Her auburn wig shot off a petulant gleam. *That isn't the way we do things here,* Hayden wanted to tell her. *I don't tell you how to handle your clients, and you don't tell me how to handle mine.* But, stunned by Emory's sudden intervention and oddly touched that she should come to Bella's aid, Hayden remained mute.

"Well, there you have it," said Bella after several silent seconds of readjustment. "I'm Bella. Don't think we've met."

"Emory Bellew," said Emory, her voice no longer confrontational.

They nodded and smiled at each other. "What do you know— Bella, Bell*ew*," Bella said to Emory, chuckling. "There's a song there." She turned back to Hayden, eager to get on with things.

Hayden was in the habit of using her razor on the backs of necks, occasionally around the ears, but she had not shaved an entire head since beauty school, when the students had been required to shave ten consecutive balloons without popping them before going onto the floor and shaving an entire head with the straight razor. After Hayden had shaved her requisite ten balloons, she had been assigned to work on the head of a woman with an advanced case of head lice. The operation was a repulsive one. First Hayden cut the hair as close to the scalp as possible, only to see the breeding grounds more clearly, clotted with larval yellow eggs and newly hatched young, and live excitable adult lice that hopped with taunting hubris around the straight edge of her razor. After she was done with the final pass of the razor and had shampooed and oiled the flaking scalp, she washed herself compulsively for days, checking every outcropping of head and body hair she grew, no matter how scant. Since that day she had never shaved a full head of hair.

Bella settled back into her chair, her body abuzz with the novelty and exoticism of her choice. She pulled the peacock feather from behind her ear and laid it on Hayden's countertop.

"No need for a shampoo," she said. Grinning and giddy Bella was, a mood Hayden tried to match. But Hayden's hands were already palsied and, though Emory had returned to her chair and her magazine, Hayden could still feel the close zip of Emory's attention.

Since childhood Hayden had hated to be watched. She hated how her father's eyes, when he wanted her to perform for him, would creep in and lay claim, appropriating something in her she had believed was her own and hidden to the world, stealing some part of her personality or soul that wasn't rightfully his. Didn't Emory have better things to do than watch her so shamelessly? Shouldn't she have clients? But maybe others felt as Hayden did, that someone ill with cancer should not be a hairdresser.

Asking one last time if Bella was sure—*utterly, utterly*—Hayden

laid her shears on Bella's thinning locks. Bella could not stop laughing, a dry, succumbing sound that made her shoulders bob, as her
gray curls made their silent, irrevocable voyage to the floor.

"Keep still," Hayden said, touching Bella's shoulder. "You want
to save any?"

"Naw, get rid of it."

When Hayden was done with the shears, she paused to let
Bella reevaluate. The remaining hair was less than half an inch
long, but its curl was indefatigable; 270 of its 360 degrees had
been lopped off so it was now a congress of small apostrophes.
A slight point in Bella's head had revealed itself, but overall she
looked fine then, neat and no-nonsense; it would have been perfectly acceptable and far less radical to stop there.

"You sure you want to keep going?" Hayden asked.

"Am I a backing-down kind of woman, Hayden?"

Hayden resumed work slowly, trying to still her shimmying
hand, trying to see, in Bella's ancient head, the fragility of a balloon, trying to hold a consistent razor angle while Bella giggled
beneath her. Hayden's focus was singular and the rest of the salon activity—the whir of dryers, the snip of shears, the slap of
freezing rain on the windows—all blurred to insignificance. As
soon as she had mowed a bare patch from the center of Bella's
forehead to the top of her vertebrae, Bella reached up to finger
her scalp, her thickened digits tapping with the skillful obser-
vance of the blind.

"How come it's so bumpy?" she said, cracks of worry criss-
crossing her forehead.

Hayden didn't need Bella worrying. "Scalps are always a little
bumpy. It's fine; it'll be fine. But get your fingers out of the way
until I'm done."

It would not look fine of course—it would look strange and

maybe frightening, and the scalp itself might be flaky, diseased, or even scabby, and much paler than the skin of her face. Bella would probably be surprised by the shape of her head, by its new shrunken size and by the way it joined onto the rest of her body. She might even be surprised by the sudden ambiguity of her gender. Hayden had seen people reacting in these ways, the sight of denuded heads stirring up childhood apprehensions, unnamable species fears.

Just then Amber arrived in a whorl of distress: Her son was sick, it had taken an hour to find a babysitter, the fridge was on the blink, the milk had soured, she had had to start her day without coffee, a grief with which they could all empathize. She brought her brouhaha with her—as they were all given license to do as long as it did not interfere with business—hurling the door open so wide a stormlet came with her, mist and a propulsive cyclone of wind penetrating to the center of the salon. The top bottle of Hayden's product pyramid toppled, but she let it go. They all shivered.

"Sorry guys," Amber apologized. As she shed her dripping paraphernalia—umbrella, two tote bags, hat, gloves, purse, and drenched raincoat—she began to center her stout short body. Her attention traveled to Emory, lingered for a moment curiously, and finally came to rest on Bella and Hayden. "Jesus—" she began, but stopped herself before saying something she (and Bella) might regret.

"Don't say it," warned Bella, still laughing.

"No, it looks good. I just— I wouldn't be brave enough, is all."

By now all eyes rested on Hayden—Tina's and Birdie's eyes, and those of their respective clients—and Rena had come out of the back room and she was staring too.

"Knock it off everyone. No comments until I'm done."

"Touchy. You on the rag, Hayden?" Tina said. "Or just hung-over?"

Hayden didn't answer. She wasn't on the rag or hungover, and she hadn't been particularly touchy until Emory had started giving her the hairy eyeball, but it was true she had a reputation for evenness and reliability and holding her tongue. She could feel them all peeling their attention away from her and returning reluctantly to their activities. Beneath her Bella had stopped laughing and her eyes, which Hayden glimpsed periodically in the mirror, seemed doubt-ridden as they followed the movement of the razor.

"It's okay, honey," Bella said to Hayden, stretching out her hand behind her to pat whatever part of Hayden's body was reachable and finding Hayden's hip. "I'm sure it'll look good and if not, it's my fault, right? I'm the one made you do it. Right, hon? I'm sure you're doing a good job."

"Thanks," Hayden said. "Close your eyes."

Dear Bella did just that. The truth was it would have been an easier job on someone other than Bella, but Bella's scalp, as she herself had felt, was stippled with lesions and moles. Hayden had to pay strict attention to avoid nicking or slicing these assorted bits of flesh. Inch by inch she proceeded, rarely more eager to complete a task, and in the severity of her concentration even Emory faded from her consciousness. When Hayden had shaved the right hemisphere of Bella's head to buck-naked baldness and was beginning on the left, she made a small nick at the back of Bella's head, behind her left ear where her cranium protruded unexpectedly in a small but sharp point. It was one of those tiny shaving nicks that in the making is not felt, so it was not surprising that Bella did not react. Hayden said nothing and used the edge of the teal cape to wipe away the blood. Still, Bella said nothing. Eyes closed, hands clasped placidly on her lap, she had drifted into a trance. The cape was too repellent to absorb the blood, and the cut went on bleeding, a slow but regular trickle. Hayden wiped again, hoping Bella would remain oblivious, but the bleeding continued. The blood was tracing a narrow creek bed down Bella's neck. Something more absorbent than a polyester cape was required.

"Excuse me a minute, Bella," Hayden said, hurrying to the back room for paper towels. Rena, still puttering in the kitchen, eyed Hayden's haste but said nothing.

Back out on the floor the atmosphere had shifted in a silent but nonetheless palpable way. Tina's and Birdie's clients had left, and they were cleaning up their stations. Amber thumbed through the Yellow Pages. But like bit players on stage, their attention never strayed from the lead actress, Emory, who had moved into Hayden's station—one of her hands pressed a dish towel over Bella's obstreperous cut, while the other hand resumed the shaving.

"I've done a million of these," Emory said.

"You can tell," said Bella, who had emerged from her trance, eyes open, effervescence restored. "She's good. She's got confidence."

Another person might have protested, might have shrieked curses, but Hayden, even at her most rebellious, had never been that kind of girl. Even in high school when she had had blue hair and begun getting tattoos, even then she had made sure her grades were good and her public behavior remained within the limits of propriety. At graduation she walked calmly to the podium and delivered her valedictorian speech in conciliatory tones, with nodding reassurance to parents, teachers, administrators.

Now she stood exiled at Emory's station, beaming nothing maladaptive, keeping a polite distance, her overt demeanor one of admiration and gratitude. She said nothing. *She owes me one.*

Hayden knew it was quite possible that Emory was thinking the same thing.

Emory's work was done. She was massaging Bella's scalp with a soothing, fragrant herbal pomade she'd taken from her own station. Bella's head lay before them, pale as lard, inert as stranded sea pork, cratered and rutted, something even a butcher would have cast off distastefully and sent to be rendered. It was like a new appendage altogether, not one you would like to present to the world.

But Bella, looking like a prematurely aged baby, crowed. "Maybe I'll begin a whole new life."

She stood up, laughing again and stroking her glossy pate, her roving fingers reminiscent of a tongue traveling the surfaces of newly cleaned teeth. As she was leaving she thrust cash on the table in the waiting area. "You figure it out," she said, gesturing to Hayden and Emory. Only a small bead of dried blood remained at the site of the nick, a red berry festooning a naked winter branch. Then she was gone.

"Hope you didn't mind," Emory said. "I thought I should step in before she got bent out of shape. You apply pressure for bleeding you know."

Hayden shrugged. "Of course." She tried to deliver to Emory a nasty look, but she couldn't forget that Emory might be dead in a few months, and then she would torture herself for every unkindness.

Sweeping done (their two brooms lunged greedily for every last bristle of hair), Hayden and Emory retired warily to their stations, like weary boxers recouping vitality for the next round of sparring. Bella's bills lay on the table untouched.

Chapter 2

Hayden had learned early in life about the volatility of hair. Once every two weeks Arleen braided Hayden and her sisters. Arleen always began at the temple, yanking the loose tendrils as if they'd been naughty, stretching the forehead skin so it changed the shape of their cheeks and their eyes. It hurt, but Mother told them not to cry because crying hurt Arleen's feelings. Hayden didn't think Arleen's feelings were more important than the pain that vaulted across their scalps, but Mother shamed them with her goodness so they learned to cringe in silence. The braids were French braids, tight and neat, and they could keep them in for two full weeks without having to be rebraided. Before they went to school they smoothed the stray wisps with moistened hands.

"Never in a million years could I do that," Mother said to Arleen. "What manual dexterity! You're a marvel, Arleen. A real hair wizard."

Arleen was pleased. She raised her upper lip in a smile that seemed to quiver. Later, the girls overheard her saying on the phone to her friend Marie: "I am a hair wizard." After that, when Cornelia and Hayden wanted to mock each other they would say: "You're a hair wizard—that's what you are."

Arleen was short and pale and pudgy, reminding Hayden of

the uncooked gingerbread man—or how he would look if he'd been a sugar cookie. She had come to work for them from a state institution. Cornelia and Hayden were not so young—though perhaps Sophie was—that they couldn't see clearly that there was something wrong with Arleen, something more than the dead brown front tooth that her smile exposed, a tooth that looked as if it were slathered with chocolate and made you want to check your own teeth in the mirror. A lady had brought Arleen to them in a black sedan with a state seal emblazoned on the door, the kind of car they knew you traveled in if something was wrong. The car drove up just as Mother was telling them that someone would be coming to care for them—a *normal* person, she said, to whom they should be polite and kind. But Mother's face, em-broidered with empathy, told them another story—Arleen would not be normal.

Mother showed Arleen around the house: the room she would sleep in on the third floor, each of the girls' rooms, the closets and cabinets where the linens and cleaning things were kept. Arleen wore a tight turquoise shirt of stretchy material and brown poly-ester pants that showed the line of her underpants and the exact shape of her squirrel-cheeked buttocks beneath. She stared out of an ominously placid face as if she didn't hear what Mother was saying.

"Isn't that right, Hayden?" Mother said, trying to keep the conversational ball rolling, hoping Hayden would chime in. But there was nothing to say, even though Hayden did feel sorry for her mother who was always unreasonably nice. Sometimes Hayden wanted her mother to be quiet for a while and let things wither into gloom. She didn't understand the point of Arleen. Arleen was supposed to be helping Mother take care of Hayden and her sisters, but for the first few months Mother was always around, showing Arleen how to do things: how to iron shirt collars and fold linen napkins, how the sponge mop worked and which cleanser to use on which floor. "Do you think you can do this?" Mother would ask and Arleen would grunt ambiguously. It would be easier for Mother to do those things herself, Hayden thought. Even Hayden could iron better than Arleen could, and she knew how to use the stove.

"Just precautionary," Mother said when she oversaw Arleen cooking a box of Rice-A-Roni.

Left alone with Arleen, Hayden and Cornelia teased her. "What's the capital of Connecticut?" Hayden said.

Arleen shrugged.

"It's *your state*—you've got to know," Cornelia said. "New Haven?"

"Yeah," Arleen said, her usually blank face beginning to twitch as she eyed Cornelia, then Hayden. "Either that or something else."

"Well, it's something else," Cornelia said.

"Hartford," Hayden said.

"Yeah," Arleen said. "Hartford." She sat at the kitchen table, panting slightly, the fingers of her left hand curling slowly around a column of air as if she were squeezing a lemon. When Mother came home they watched Arleen closely, checking to see if she'd tell on them. "Mrs. Risley?" Arleen said.

"Claire. You can call me Claire."

"Mrs. Claire, can I smoke?"

"Outside you may."

Arleen went out to the patio and lit a cigarette, and they watched her through the window from upstairs in Sophie's bedroom. The smoke accrued around her head in billows like gray cotton candy. "Maybe she's dumb 'cause she smokes," Sophie said.

"No, silly," Hayden said. "Smoking gives you cancer not dumbness."

Arleen was allowed to smoke and chew gum and watch TV, all privileges Hayden and her sisters were denied. It seemed unfair to them that someone would have those privileges if they didn't know the capital of Connecticut.

They weren't supposed to disturb Arleen in her room, but Cornelia and Hayden followed her up there one night. Arleen didn't hear them tiptoeing behind her, and she looked surprised to see them standing in her doorway. A roll of fat spilled over her waistband into a fold of her pink sweater. "Can we have some Chiclets?" Cornelia—always braver than Hayden—asked.

"I'm not s'posed to."

"Why not?" Cornelia pressed.

"Mrs. Claire says no."

They thought she should make decisions for herself, as they were encouraged to do, instead of following orders slavishly.

"What could one piece of gum do?" Hayden said. "It won't kill us."

"Your mother said—" She looked genuinely sorry. She sat on the edge of the bed, rocking back and forth.

Back downstairs in the living room Hayden could hear the laugh track from Arleen's TV. When Father was home Arleen had to keep the TV muted, but that night Father was away.

"How come Arleen gets gum and TV and we don't?" Hayden asked Mother.

Mother looked at Hayden with her head tilted, her eyes glowing. "Arleen has a beautiful soul, girls. A special soul. I want you to understand that."

Cornelia looked up from *Gone With the Wind*. "People with beautiful souls shouldn't yank hair."

"Tell her if she's hurting you, honey. I'm sure she doesn't mean to. You know that a quick brain means nothing really."

Cornelia rolled her eyes at Hayden and Hayden rolled hers back. They knew no such thing—of course brains mattered. There was little that mattered as much as brains. Sometimes at night Cornelia and Sophie visited Hayden's room and they pretended that Arleen had a doll's body, stuffed with cotton or mud. *Dumb as a dog. Dumb as a clam. Dumb as a tree. Dumb as a thumb.*

"A special, special soul," Mother repeated to them almost every day. "Put on earth to teach us," she said.

"Dumb as a rule, dumb as a tool, dumb as a fool," they quietly countered Mother at night. Hayden whispered when she said these things. What if she herself turned out to be as dumb as Arleen?

"What if we touch her and she makes us as dumb as she is?" Sophie asked.

"You can't catch dumb," Cornelia said. "It's like cancer."

They were all presumed to be sleeping when Hayden and Cornelia rose from their beds one night and tiptoed up the creaking Victorian staircase to the third floor. There were three rooms up there: a playroom they never used, its board games and baby toys gathering dust; a fly-strewn storeroom full of boxes of unused dishes and tarnished silver that made Mother sigh; and there was Arleen's room, decorated by Mother in a red and pink rose motif just before Arleen's arrival. Hayden coveted Arleen's room, which was not only the most private room in the house, but also the most luxuriously appointed, with flannel rose-sprigged sheets, rose-sprigged quilt and comforter, pillows of all sizes in pink and red and yellow, a deep-slung easy chair for reading, a picture of horses grazing and another of sunflowers and another depicting the fairies in *A Midsummer Night's Dream*. There was a white chest of drawers and an old-fashioned dressing table equipped with a seat and a mirror and rosy lighting that made people extra-beautiful. Then, of course, there was the TV and the big glass bowl of the sought-after gum. Once Hayden had told her mother she thought the room was wasted on Arleen, and Mother had looked at her hard, as if she were not Hayden's mother anymore, or wished not to be.

"Have you done something, Hayden, that makes you feel you deserve more than Arleen deserves?" she said.

"No, but—"

"Then let's not hear any more about fair and not fair."

The bedside light was on but Arleen was asleep, lying on her back, still wearing her pink quilted bathrobe as if sleep had blind-sided her and taken her down quickly. Her mouth hung open to her dead brown tooth and the black cave of her throat. Two turrets of her hair-sprayed hair jutted from her crown. She had placed her TV on a chair beside her bed and it was on, its volume turned low, its flickering screen sending wands of light across her flaccid cheeks. They crossed the threshold and stopped dead when the floorboards creaked. They stared at the glass bowl of gum resting on a lace doily on her chest of drawers. It had been recently restocked and was full to the brim with yellow packs of Juicy Fruit, two-packs of Chiclets, scored pink squares of Dubble Bubble wrapped in waxy two-frame comic strips.

They advanced at the rate of Arleen's breathing—one step with her in-breath, one step with the out. In sleep she might be as smart as they were, inhaling Father's know-it-all air. Perhaps she would awaken suddenly a genius, hot on their trail, their crime sensed through the alpha waves of her rest. They arrived at the bowl while she still slept, not safe but halfway there.

They reached in with hands like scoops, both at once, and they crammed the pockets of their bathrobes, exchanging the mute, knowing, guilt-ridden glances of accomplices. Out the open door they crept amid the din of shouting floorboards and Arleen's sleep snorts that sounded perilously close to the sounds of waking. As soon as they crossed the room's threshold, their fear turned to glee. Cornelia skittered back in and laid a ridged pink square of unwrapped Dubble Bubble on Arleen's broad forehead.

A nighttime household prevailed, quiet with the pretense of sleep. In Father's study his desk chair's casters bumped across a short stretch of floor. Cornelia and Hayden sat on Hayden's bed, the mound of contraband between them. They each took a piece, two pieces, three, and began to chew with the exuberance and abandon of confirmed sinners. They hadn't really sinned, Hayden reasoned—they had simply asserted their rights, taking what they had always deserved. Cornelia favored the Chiclets, Hayden preferred the Juicy Fruit. They both liked Dubble Bubble. They loaded it in, piece upon piece, until their tongues and teeth were too crowded to accommodate more. When the gum's sweetness dissipated they reloaded, removing the chewed wads, fat and pale as albino slugs, and sticking them on Hayden's bedpost. Cornelia gathered the strewn yellow Juicy Fruit wrappers and tried to re-create a chain she had once seen. Hayden invented a game she called "The Taxonomy of Gum": Chiclets were suitcase gum for their hard encasement, sticks of gum were McAdam gum for their resemblance to roads, Dubble Bubble was party gum for its festive pinkness. Hot-air gum was any gum with a minty-hot aftertaste.

They gave in to sleep side-by-side in Hayden's bed, wads of gum tucked in their cheeks. Furtive, opportunistic, the wily gum migrated to their hair as they slept, Cornelia's settling at the back of her head, Hayden's fixing on a lock near her face. They awakened suddenly, exhausted, sticky. It was a school day. They picked and tugged at each other like grooming chimps. The gum lodged in Cornelia's hair looked like an engorged tick that wouldn't pop or budge. The lump in Hayden's hair had turned eerily hard. The usual morning sounds were in full swing—a toilet flushing, Arleen fetching cereal bowls from the cupboards, Sophie rummaging in her closet for clothes. Father was certainly already installed in his study. Mother might have been anywhere.

"We need scissors," Cornelia said.

"No cutting," Hayden said.

"What else *can* we do?"

She was right, there was little else to do; the gum and hair were as firmly interlaced as the tough twisted sprouts of sphagnum moss.

Cornelia found, in Hayden's desk, a pair of blunt child's scissors that had been kicking around the house for years. They scarcely worked on paper anymore. The sharp ones they should have been using were downstairs. Hayden made Cornelia sit on the edge of the bed. Hayden knelt and went to work. Getting through Cornelia's thick, gum-clotted locks was like trying to scythe hay with nail scissors. Progress was slow. Sophie came to watch, transfixed by their predicament.

The door, already ajar, seemed to blow open without anyone's agency. Arleen stood behind it. Hayden had the distinct impression she had not walked there but had been lowered into place by a large crane. Her face was unresponsive.

"You got school," she said. Her voice was flat; her face was flat; she inhabited her flatness fully. "You in trouble?" she said. She entered the room and walked straight to where Hayden was kneeling on the edge of the bed. She touched the wad of gum in

Hayden's hair. "You got gum in your hair." She said this without surprise, without judgment, without discernible affect of any kind. "Lemme do that," she said, taking the scissors from Hayden.

She cut well above Hayden's tangle, easily severing the gum-mucked lock of hair. Hayden reached up to feel the strand, short and sharp as straw. Cornelia pointed sheepishly to the back of her own head and Arleen cut off her wad too. Both girls stroked their hair hard, as if they could coax it into growing back quickly.

"Where's yours?" Arleen examined Sophie's head, and Sophie looked as if she might cry.

"She's okay," Hayden said.

"Get dressed," Arleen said. "Breakfast is ready. I'll braid you downstairs."

Cornelia and Sophie dashed from Hayden's room. Hayden went to her closet for clothes. She could feel Arleen watching her. Hayden averted her eyes, flipping through her mental cata-logue of lies to see if any would hold up. She pulled a shirt ran-domly from the shelf; it was a deep cobalt color.

"I like blue," Arleen said.

Hayden knew a good person would apologize, admit to the misdeed. Arleen couldn't be dumb enough not to have noticed her gum supply was seriously depleted, not to have been aware of awakening with a piece of Dubble Bubble on her forehead.

"I like Juicy Fruit," Arleen said.

Hayden felt certain now that Arleen was unbearably smart and all along had only been acting compromised. Cornered, unnerved, she clutched the shirt. Arleen turned slowly to the door. Her body floated or lumbered; she had no other kind of locomotion.

Downstairs Mother was preparing a special breakfast tray to bring to Father in his study—hot popovers, brie, turkey bacon, fresh-squeezed juice, and coffee. She bustled around acting,

Hayden thought, too solicitous. The girls awaited their braiding, awaited the moment when Mother would notice their maimed hair. She usually noticed everything about them, but she was deeply in Father Zone and apparently saw nothing out of the ordinary. Hayden took her place in the braiding chair below Arleen, her head downturned, unable to meet Arleen's eyes. The lank short strand, still sticky, jutted accusingly from her temple. Power emanated from Arleen's deft hands. She took up the lock. She pulled it hard. Hayden closed her eyes, thinking this would be the moment when Arleen would pour hot oil on her, or maybe spit. Hayden tried to convey her contrition through stillness, but she had too much to account for. She was a supplicant at Arleen's altar. Arleen breathed heavily and started to braid.

"My, things are quiet," Mother said, returning to the kitchen with an empty tray.

Arleen laughed lightly and continued to braid. Hayden couldn't see Arleen's face but she could picture her lip rising, as it always did, to show off her dead tooth.

"Cat got their tongue," Arleen said. Her hand grazed Hayden's cheek. It was heavy and warm. It was doing what it had done dozens of times before. A hand that knew things.

Chapter 3

There was nothing overtly unpleasant about Emory Bellew. She wasn't noisy. She kept her station neat. She washed out her mugs. Her clients—the three Hayden saw that day, all of whom had appointments—seemed like reasonable people. But by the time the afternoon of that first day had reached its midpoint, she had vacuumed through so much of Hayden's psychic space that Hayden felt as if she herself had shrunk to the size of a tiddlywink, while Emory had moved quietly but impertinently into a castle of her own.

What was it about Emory that held Hayden captive? Was it the evasive auburn head? The force of her movements? She spoke to her clients in low, confidential, almost conspiratorial tones, suggesting she had known them for a long time, but with the girls she remained aloof, and Hayden marveled that Rena had hired someone so unsociable. Hayden yearned to ask the other girls what they were thinking, but the salon provided little privacy. It was understood that what was said on the floor was public material to which the other girls could be privy. If you didn't want something known by everyone, you didn't say it there. The back room with its kitchenette and squishy four-seater couch offered a degree of separation, but people came and went unpredictably there, so privacy couldn't be guaranteed. If you wanted absolute assurance of secrecy, you went out for coffee, or to a bar, or to the clandestine quarters of your own sealed apartment, but in the salon your mood, your clothing, your hair, your story, your life were all fair targets for comment.

In the past, when new girls first came to work, Hayden and her salon mates had immediately shared the stories that defined them. They were PR stories, based in truth but embellished to fit with the way they wanted others to see them and with how they wanted to regard themselves. Demetria would tell about how her Greek family had thrown her out of the house when she got pregnant out of wedlock, and how she'd had an abortion, and with her second pregnancy she'd decided to have the baby, but the baby had died of SIDS, and how for two years after that she had wanted to forget everything and worked as a belly dancer and a stripper. Now ambition had hit her; she had earned her GED and was looking to go to college. Amber, a single mom whose husband had left when she was pregnant with her second child, told about her kids, ages three and four, the crazy loveable tyranny of kids—how they had "given" her ADD, made chaos of her apartment, how she loved and hated it all, and expected to die when they left home.

Birdie claimed she was different from the rest of them because she was the only one among them—she said this winking, mugging, but still dead serious—who adored men, still believed in romance and femininity, in innocence and in the fundamental goodness of humanity. She believed men liked to see women wearing long hair and lace. And she knew that Billy, her boyfriend of nine years, intended to marry her. Tina relayed her hard-luck story of three rancorous divorces and years selling subway tokens in an underground booth, a tenure that had made her both jaded and fearless. Donelle told how it felt to be a 238-pound woman and of her plans to staple her stomach someday. Hayden told of the months after dropping out of college when she had driven west and slept for a month—voluntarily, though she never said that—under a bench in Santa Monica with a woman named Elva. They recognized each other's stories from many prior tellings if not from their own experiences; sometimes the details would change a little, but the fundamental message remained intact: *I am a woman who* _____ (fill in a single defining feature). Not that these stories told who these women really were entirely, but they served as adequate shorthand. And the new girl would usually respond in kind, offering her own defining story, serving herself up to her new workmates in a weave of doctored truth and mythology.

Not so with Emory. The day moved through its familiar beats, but no one offered a story, and Emory offered none of her own. She went about her work with unnerving, close-lipped determination. Hayden was pretty sure you couldn't work cheek-to-jowl with someone and reveal nothing about yourself. It was irresponsible. It was rude. The salon was too small for that.

By one p.m. it was a full house, clients coming and going, the sound of snipping and chatting and blow-drying akin to the fracas of a launching bird flock. And then, at three thirty, the rush was over before the post-work traffic began, and in the lull Emory was the only one left with a client. She was shaping a shag on some tiny woman with shiny flat red hair. The rest of them cleaned their stations.

"This morning I come out and she's chowing down on the candle," Amber said of her three-year-old daughter, Iris. "There's all this crumbly waxy shit in her mouth and she's looking at me like *What's your problem, Mom?* Last night it was a dry sponge— she actually swallowed it. It's not like I don't feed her."

"I've heard of that disorder before," Hayden said. "Everything's fair game—plastic, rubber, you name it."

"My cousin had that," Tina said, her long face flat and expressionless.

"What happened to her?" said Amber.

"She died." Tina smiled slyly down at the hair she whisked into her dustpan.

"Oh *God*." Amber clutched her shears like a tragedian.

"She's *kidding*, Amber," Demetria said. "Lay off, Tina."

Amber turned from her station to nail Tina's back with a glare. "You're a shit," she said, anger only half moderated by jest. "What really happened to her?"

"She's fine," Tina said. "A-okay."

"PICA," Hayden said.

"What?" said Amber.

"It's called PICA. Persistent internal cravings for—I forget. I think you outgrow it. At least I've never known any adults who suffer from it."

Across the salon, set apart, notably silent, stood Emory, proffering a mirror to her red-headed client, glancing over in the direction of the others and, for a moment, her eye caught Hayden's and they both froze. Hayden looked away, then had to look back and Emory's eyes were still there, direct and shameless as weapons. She had no humility—that was what irked Hayden most. Why hadn't anyone taught her some restraint? Didn't she know that some people hated to be looked at? Hayden might as well have been back on the couch in Connecticut, waiting for her turn to speak, made small by the excoriating beam of her father's gaze. A sliver of a thought, previously unconscious, swelled into certainty. Emory Bellew was a man. A petite man certainly, possibly effeminate, but definitely XY. The knowledge spread through

Hayden like a blush, carrying so much debris—embarrassment at her own blindness, annoyance at having been duped, uncertainty about whether the others knew, indignation that he had invaded their female fortress.

Hayden's face in its staring—lips parted, eyes bugged—began to feel moronic. She turned quickly away, assembling her combs noisily and fighting a quickening heart-rate. It was not that she had not seen such people—living in a large metropolis, of course she had—but not right next to her in her own place of work.

In the lounge she stirred her combs furiously in the jar of disinfectant. Back outside the other girls were still chatting. Didn't they know, or did they know and not care? The front doorbell rang, a client coming or going. Someone turned the music from New Age to country, a duet of twanging female voices that sounded like Dolly Parton and Emmylou Harris. She wanted him gone. He had no right to be here, puncturing their world, masquerading as a woman. Why would he even *want* to be here? She stopped her stirring and stood still, closing her eyes to restore her privacy for a moment. Focusing all the power of her thought into a point, she wished Emory Bellew away.

Chapter 4

This had nothing to do with hating men. Men were fine. Hayden had had occasional liaisons with men and had some as friends. You didn't get to be twenty-five without knowing men. At Harvard there was a guy she ate with a lot, Pitzer he called himself. They always happened to be there in the dining hall at the same time, standing in doleful indecision with their full trays, casting about for a safe haven. After a while it got to be habit, the two of them meeting in the corner of the dining hall farthest from the kitchen. It was dark there, like a separate room. Pitzer ate slowly and selectively, commenting on the colors and textures of the foods before he tasted them. He always kept a piece of dried orange rind in his pocket. He would pull it out from time to time to sniff it, long after it looked so puckery-old Hayden couldn't imagine it held much scent. In the other pocket he had pieces of an old cracked bay leaf. He sniffed that too, inhaling its odors not once but over and over until he seemed to be hyperventilating, and she could tell the smell held some meaning that he didn't intend to share with her. She wondered if these bits of organic matter went through the wash, or if he transferred them carefully to each fresh pair of pants. He said his nose was unusually sensitive for a man's nose. He said women had developed good noses because in ancestral societies they had had to be able to detect when food was bad, a skill that kept their offspring alive. Hayden had always thought she had pretty good nasal equipment herself, and she wondered if that was, obscurely, unconsciously, why the two of them got along. She didn't know if they ever would have slept together; her life changed too quickly to let her find out.

So men were fine—arrogant and obnoxious sometimes, but not necessarily any more arrogant and obnoxious than women. Still—you couldn't just toss a man into a salad of women and expect that things wouldn't change. Of course they would change. If her childhood had taught her anything, it was that women alone were different from women with men.

Men cared about silence, Hayden knew that. They needed silent households in which to write the books that would make them famous. As long as they were famous they could forget the indignities of their childhoods—too many siblings and not enough of anything, particularly attention, to go around. They could feel justified barking out orders. They could declare certain rooms off limits. They could command the attention of admiring wives. They could try to hone their children into intellectual giants so they, too, could one day be famous. Against these men, whose heads were filled to imperviousness with facts and ideas, feminism worked like so much gutter sludge.

Hayden and her sisters, their mother, and Arleen lived in two worlds: the world with Father and the one without him. Most of the time Father—Angus Risley, eminent author of essays, travel memoirs, occasional works of fiction, fifteen books by the time Hayden was fifteen—was away, traveling in foreign countries to research or write his books. When he returned from abroad—the Far East, the Near East, South America, God knows where—he would come home to their Connecticut house for a few weeks before heading up to Bartlett, Vermont where, ensconced in the bucolic silence of a country cabin, he wrote in solitude. A month might pass. Six weeks. Then he would return home to Connecticut for a stint of a month or two before he was off again. Hayden was too young to keep track of his comings and goings, but Mother would tell her, in soft confiding tones, when his return was imminent.

When he was home, everything was different. The house was quiet and clotted with worry. Hayden didn't understand whose worry it was that weighed the air down so heavily. She had heard Mother say Father worried about money, but it seemed to Hayden that they had more money than most people, at least they had a nice house on four acres of land. *If you've been poor you always worry about money*, Mother confided in Hayden, her eldest. The worry was Mother's too—Hayden could see it in her mother's torn cuticles and raddled hair. Mother worried that she would interfere somehow, mess things up for Father, and consequently for Hayden and her sisters. Finally it seemed to Hayden as if the worry was as much her own as anyone else's, because it followed her to bed like a pet, loyal and irksome.

Their meals were better when Father was around, because Mother cooked them, instead of Arleen. She made herbed risottos, roasted meats, garlic potatoes, sweet and savory soufflés, artichokes, fruit tarts, hundreds of delectable dishes that they rarely had the appetite to eat at Father's table. Hayden sat up straight, her spine inflexible as an alligator's, watching Father eat fast—impolitely, she thought. She yearned for Arleen's mac and cheese, and for a sense of ownership of the air. With Father at home a new cartography existed. The air belonged to him. So did the sofa, and the carpets, even their beloved climbing tree, a giant silver maple in the back yard whose branches arched capaciously, making a great green tent in summer. Not that he climbed this tree himself, he just acted proprietary about it—if the girls went near it he told them to be careful with its bark, that trees were living things too and deserved their respect. They had to go to the far end of the property, beyond the stone wall, to feel safe from the possibility that they might violate his spaces.

Hayden didn't like watching Mother during those dinners. She was a tall woman, taller than Father by a couple of inches, with a pale, ethereal look that turned into extreme fragility when Father was around. She was the only child of a well-to-do couple on Manhattan's Upper East Side. She had a PhD in art history, which she had not put to public use, and she had never been taught practical matters, so when Father was around she worried that things might not run smoothly: that the dinner would be a flop, that signs of lax domesticity would emerge in soiled linen or tarnished silver or bad behavior from the children. She sat at the table with her eyes on Father, like Hayden suddenly incapable of eating. She reminded Hayden of a too-tall, top-heavy tomato plant in need of shoring up.

And Arleen. When Father was away she cooked (Mother had taught her the basics) and they all ate together in the kitchen. Sometimes they sang or played games with the food. Mother didn't care—she thought it was funny. She played too, making whipped-cream mustaches or playing pea croquet with her knife. And Arleen was one of them then. Her dead tooth and low IQ meant nothing. Her laugh came easily, and on her way to the sink she touched the girls' braided heads as if she were their mother. But when Father came home Mother made Arleen wait on them. Arleen had to wear a white apron and serve each dish standing beside them on the left. *You should know this too, girls,* Mother had said when she trained Arleen. *Serve on the left; remove on the right.* Arleen did what Mother told her to do, but she seemed, during those dining room dinners, to slink around the table with her spine suddenly softened as if her whole skeletal system had turned into cartilage. Father never spoke to Arleen—to him she was as incidental as the chandelier. Taking their cue from him, Hayden and her sisters didn't speak to Arleen either, except to murmur the occasional thanks. Sometimes Hayden stole a look to see if Arleen was the same person, the one they mashed peas with and the one who braided their hair. Hayden saw Arleen mouth-breathing, as if the worry had gotten to her too, and had climbed right into her mouth, filling and clogging it. When she finished serving she would go back into the kitchen, through the swinging door; the sound of water running and the muted clatter of dishes came to them like faint conversational salvos from her exile.

After dinner they didn't slouch around on the couch with their feet up; then it was time to show Father what they knew. By third or fourth grade Hayden understood how important it was to know things. Maybe it was the *most* important thing. She tried to be good at knowing things, maybe even the best. She concentrated on keeping track of where all the facts were stored, each like a brain needle you wouldn't remember unless you felt it going in.

Miss Corliss wanted them to know things. She stood in front of Hayden's fourth-grade class in her floral-print dress, hips grown from her waist in the unlikely shape of elephant ears, her concentration gathered, hound-like, at the center of her face. She wanted them to know many things. The meaning of *lateral*. Who Florence Nightingale was. How many states there were. What stars were made of. She maintained a notebook with a frayed gray spine; in it was a page for each student. She made marks in the book, cryptograms based on how much each student knew. Sometimes she gave them gold stars they could paste on their foreheads. After she distributed them, she asked what *ignoramus* meant.

But no one cared as much as Father. Each evening when he wasn't traveling they recited for him after dinner. The three girls sat lined up along the edge of the red couch in order of age: Hayden, Cornelia, Sophie. Bright and ready as freshly minted pennies. Mother hovered nearby, clutching pieces of toffee to slip to them afterward. *What did you learn today?* Father would ask. Even Sophie, when she got to be three, was held accountable for her days.

"I found a frog," she might say in her chickadee voice. Always the pleaser, always the clown. "Frogs like water."

"They're *amphibians*," Cornelia added, lingering on the word *amphibian*, proud at age seven to know such a word. "They like water *and* land."

Father's mouth remained stern and his gaze strayed past Cornelia and Sophie, then meandered idly over the mantelpiece to the picture window which held a black rectangle of nightness. He didn't believe in nodding. He didn't believe in smiling. He didn't believe in letting them know if they were right. He simply sat with his lean legs crossed and his arms rooted on the arms of his leather easy chair, like some modern-day Irish sphinx, his pale lupine face refusing to move, refusing to tell them a thing. The only sign of life in him was his bobbing right leg.

Mother stood halfway between the couch where they sat and Father's chair. She towered above them, her eyebrows arched like short Venetian bridges. She tugged at her hair which, though it fell past her shoulders, was thin and wispy. Her hand moved rhythmically as an oil pump while her head rotated from Father to the girls back to Father. But no amount of pumping and tugging prompted Father to react.

It was Hayden's turn now. She hesitated, detesting the moment, but wanting nonetheless to say something Vesuvian so Father would leap from his seat, consumed with awe at the immensity of her memory, the incisiveness of her intellect. She made it her business to seek out obscure facts of history and science. That day she was versed in nematodes; this was not school material, she had discovered them in a zoology book on the top shelf of their home library. They had bookshelves in every room, most running from floor to ceiling. To get this book she had had to use a stepstool.

"Nematodes," she began, "are the next frontier in zoology . . ."

She spoke for a few minutes and when she was done Father turned his head from the night window to her. This she considered to be a good thing. He looked at her hard.

"Good, Hayden. That was good." He blinked. "I hear you lost your soccer game."

Hayden didn't confirm or deny this, but it was true they had lost. Out of the corner of her eye she saw Mother wincing. Father rose abruptly and left the room. Distracted? Annoyed? Consumed with thoughts of nematodes or soccer? They didn't know. They never knew. They had to resign themselves to not knowing. This was his way: these sudden shifts, this distractibility, the inner turmoil they knew of only through the flicking foot. Still, each day spawned hope for other responses.

Mother clapped her hands once to revive the girlish atmosphere. "Well, chickapiddies, let's look outside, shall we?"

They followed her mutely as she opened the French doors and, without turning on the outdoor light, she led them a few steps onto the grass and into the wooly night. Without her they would have been afraid, but with her there they were fearless.

"Close your eyes," she said.

They did as she said. It was November and chilly, but with a warm house so close at hand the cement-cold slats of air did not daunt them.

"He adores all three of you, you know. He just doesn't know how to show you. Lift your faces," she said. "Smell. A night like this is magical."

Hayden lifted her face, wanting to feel the magic, wondering how Mother knew which nights were the magical ones. Hayden smelled the musty scent of seasoned deadness—leaves crumbled, pumpkins past their prime. She felt the grace that comes when resistance to the inevitable is laid aside. The whole world was waiting, as she was, for the first snow. A hand stroked her cheek; something sweet slid into her mouth. She tried to think about Father loving them. Love seemed like a sheer invisible scarf that blew off too easily in the wind. Mother's long, gauzy skirt grazed Hayden's arm as she floated past to Cornelia.

"Oh, Mum," Sophie squealed when it was her turn.

"You are lovely girls," Mother said. "You don't need to know things to be lovely."

Chapter 5

Hoboken crouched against the Hudson River and glared at Manhattan with the wary insistence of a pugilist. This unfortunate geography of proximity conferred on the citizens of Hoboken an uneasy awareness of second-class status. They stepped from their buildings, walked a few blocks, and there loomed the great metropolis, irrefutable and central as the sun, her skyscrapers, her perennial lights, her wounded silhouette forlorn and beautiful. You could not live with the Manhattan skyline so close at hand, so omnipresent and unignorable, and not feel a need to justify yourself. Even the altered, cauterized skyline exerted its force. Especially that skyline. It did not matter that you had chosen for all the best reasons not to live in Manhattan—you couldn't afford it, you hated the crowds, you disdained the excesses, you reviled the city's overinflated sense of itself—still some small interior voice told you that you should be there, instead of across the river, in another state even. You could not help wondering if you had made the wrong choice, if you were living erroneously, if you had not received a large enough slice of the proverbial pie. And this feeling was compounded by Hoboken being a way station for many people. For the New Jersey Transit riders and the Erie Lackawanna riders Hoboken was simply a stop along the way, a place where you sipped a latte and perused a *Times* or a *Journal*, waiting for the main event. If you were a Hoboken resident these realities permeated your consciousness unwittingly, and if you lived there for long you eventually synchronized your sense of self with the town's geography. You had your list of the city's virtues, which you were proud to recite—Sinatra's birthplace, the place where baseball was invented, not far from the fatal duel between Hamilton and Burr, and, you said, lifting your chin with aggressive pride, *We have an unobstructed view of the Manhattan skyline*—but in your heart of hearts you knew how poorly these things stacked up against the Gotham virtue list. And finally, you accepted that there might be something about you yourself that did not measure up.

Nevertheless, after four years in Hoboken, Hayden was deeply ensconced there. She had come of age in Hoboken; she had been there when the hit happened and she went down to Pier A with other Hobokenites, some of her salon mates and multitudes of strangers, and they stared across the Hudson at the fire and ash and wreckage of buildings and people fleeing along the West Side Highway, all small across the river and too far to touch or rescue, and they all felt a terrible futility and an aching love and Hayden knew she was tangled up there in those two cities, she would always be hurtling between them, big city and little one, over or under the river; she would never—could never—leave. And every night since then when she left the salon and shopped for groceries on Washington Street, she could not help but glance east to Manhattan and she felt again that surge of inscrutable love you feel for the damaged, and she marveled at how she had started out a country girl, red-knee'd and dirt-loving, and she was that girl no longer.

She headed back to her apartment that January night with

three packages of ramen, a cabbage, and a quart of milk, thinking of love and dislocation and contemplating Emory. It seemed
to Hayden that the cold had bent her senses seriously out of
calibration. The cold was indomitable. A conquistador, it stalked
everywhere, changing the rudiments of things, making water
into ice, killing off exposed human flesh, making normally comfortable places—boats, park benches, bus stations, subways—
uninhabitable.

This terrible cold was the only explanation she had for how
she could have spent a full day in the salon without suspecting
Emory's secret. It was akin to not recognizing your own hand, or
your home, or your mother, akin to seeing a banana and thinking it was an apple, mistaking a dog for a cat, thinking snow was
rain. How could she now trust her senses to give her information
she could take for truth? And why were none of the other girls
disturbed by this as she was?

Her thoughts tornadoed like this as she mounted the three
flights to her modest apartment. She knew others might think
her place was squalid, but that was not how she felt about it. The
nicked walls, the splintering window frames, the bathroom door
listing on its single hinge, the battalion of roaches that made their
quotidian visits in search of leftovers—they all were to Hayden
like badges awarded for her resourcefulness and survival. Whatever inconvenience they created was far outweighed by the apartment's attributes: its solid and soundproof walls, a window from
which she could view the street, a fire escape that paired nicely
with a margarita for heat relief on summer nights, all this for the
rock-bottom New York metropolitan area price of four hundred
dollars a month.

The best thing about her apartment was that it reminded
Hayden she was capable of making a life for herself—*her* life, no

one else's idea of her life. It had been a long evolution. After the fiasco surrounding her mother's death she had cashed her tuition check, bought an old Honda Civic, and drove west, telling no one. She drifted here and there, stopping for a month in Texas, three months in Arizona, working occasionally as a waitress, cashing in on obsequiousness and good grammar. She ended up in Santa Monica, living outside for the hot month of September near the beach with a homeless former actress named Elva. It was true that Hayden didn't have to make that choice. She could have rented a place. She was not flush, but she had enough money to spring for a cheap room somewhere. But she wanted to see how little she needed to get by. Her life had been too sheltered. She wanted to toughen up. She wanted the wisdom of toughness. It seemed as if there was something to be learned from Elva's leathery, febrile smile.

Elva had come to Santa Monica from Utah and won roles in some detergent commercials and a few bit parts in TV series. But when she had earned a little money she spent it too fast, snorted too much cocaine, and eventually ended up by that beach full time, forty-two but looking sixty, not caring anymore about what she did or didn't have. Every day she tasted the ocean, wading ankle deep into the shallow water, crouching, with outstretched tongue. She was still limber and strong from the daily physical demands of urban survival, and Hayden could tell she had once been beautiful, but her face looked stiff as if it had mineralized and developed a crust as old snow does, in which holes had been cut just large enough to let through her soulful eyes and rutilant smile. Every evening as the sun set she and Hayden settled under a certain palm tree to watch the patterns of the volatile, colored sky, and Elva asked Hayden to play with her hair. It was blondish-brown, came halfway down her back, and was in need of serious washing. Hayden would comb through it with her fingers because that was all that would go through the tangles, and Elva would croon quietly, half in a trance. The setting sun, virulently red, and the sound of Elva's crooning, helped silence the assertive memory of Hayden's final fight with Father. This preening became a nightly ritual, necessary for both of them. It was Elva who eventually encouraged Hayden to begin training at the Institute for the Body Styling Arts.

After living outside and bathing in public restrooms, then living in a rented garage in Venice for a while, Hayden's one-bedroom apartment in Hoboken with all its tenement-like leanings was not only adequate, it was more than enough—it was a blessing for which she renewed her gratitude day after day. Even that night, when she returned home to find no heat, she was pleased to be in her little cocoon of a home. If she could have had a "better," more upscale, more thing-filled place, she wouldn't have wanted it.

She pulled the blanket off her bed, wrapped herself like a Bedouin, and set about fixing ramen. Later she would put in a call to Arnaux, her landlord, though she was pretty sure Mrs. Canaro on the first floor, who cared for her ailing mother as well as two young sons, must already have made the call. Arnaux, who owned buildings in Paramus and Passaic and lived in Tenafly, was a lazy old walrus. Most of the tenants' requests got forgotten or relegated to the bottom of his priority list so, while he didn't mean to be a slumlord, de facto he was one. The furnace had been out for five days in mid-November and some of the building's tenants had secured space heaters to tide them over, but Hayden didn't have the extra cash for a power-hungry space heater, so she had layered up as Elva had taught her to do and took lots of brisk walks.

The ramen was ready and she fried herself an egg to go with it. Too lazy to prepare the cabbage, she stowed it in the fridge.

Then she sat on the vinyl chair in the kitchen and ate, staring out at an icicle, long, pointed, and imperious as a bayonet, hanging from the fire escape and bifurcating the view. She couldn't get Emory Bellew out of her mind.

Without heat, bed was the only welcome harbor so, wearing wool socks, fleece pants, wool sweater, down vest, fleece hat and gloves, and swaddled in three blankets, she was in bed by eight thirty. She dreamed of her mother. Hayden, no bigger than a flea, was walking along Mother's body. She was stuck on a fingernail without traction, and moved with great care to avoid slipping. She wanted to be close to her mother's heat spots—her belly or her breasts—but ahead of her the knuckles were mountainous and Hayden realized it would take forever to traverse them.

Hayden had known her mother's body so well: her neck, long and bamboo-cool with deep culverts at the bottom which filled sometimes with rainwater when they went out on a summer night; the smudge of red on one side of her upper lip, where a cold sore often flared; the gauntness of her shoulders and chest; the wispiness of her hair even before she began tugging it. It was baby's hair, so gossamer-fine it looked as if weather or chemicals or hormones had never touched it. Everything about Mother spoke of delicacy. Even when Hayden was a child, a smaller person than her mother, she worried that she might hug too hard and her mother's ribs would crumble as easily as one of their pillow forts. When Mother lifted Sophie, a round healthy baby, Hayden worried that her mother's forearms, like dry autumn stalks, would snap. They were long and flat, tendons pulsing through their every movement, the blood vessels on their insides a prominent blue-green. These glimmers Hayden saw of her mother's body's inner workings appeared without warning, obscure announcements of complexity and vulnerability. Hayden saw these things long before the cutting, and she knew in her core that her mother needed her.

Chapter 6

Later she would wonder why it took her so long to see Emory clearly. How could she not have seen? What else was right in front of her that she could not see? She would review the elements of those days endlessly.

Her building still had no heat. The salon's air was silvery and cool when she arrived at seven, but not as cool as her own apartment. Even her makeup was half frozen then; the lipstick she wore, its color the ferruginous red of old fishhooks, crossed her lips like a surgical tool. Her customary black jeans were not warm enough for the punishing weather, but still she wore them. She sat in her chair and sipped scalding hot chocolate, watching ill-shod women outside on the street skittering over patches of black ice on their way to work. Traces of sunlight pearled the condensation on the window. As the salon warmed, some of the droplets oozed down the glass, wormy and lachrymal. For long moments at a time she was sure this was all she needed. Alone in the salon, the day's mood as yet unformed, she felt peaceful and powerful and sure she could see to the bottom of everything.

When Emory came in it was only eight o'clock. The serenity and solitude were smashed and Hayden felt like spitting. Emory puttered at his station, ignoring Hayden, but still Hayden felt intruded upon. Buttocks stiffened, she stood and turned on her radio to a news broadcast. The voices were pushy and abrasive, but now that she was not alone she might as well fill the room with sound.

Emory wore a black V-neck sweater that made it seem as if he had breasts. He touched the back of his hair gently, as women do, as if an infant slept beneath its layers. Hayden looked at him only out of the corner of her eye, but still she took in many small things about him. A few maverick hairs grew from the backs of his hands.

After their first greeting no more words passed between them.

When Tina arrived Hayden followed her to the back room. Tina, in her outdoor clothes, looked regal. She removed her fur-edged hat ceremoniously; she took off her long black coat and the scarf beneath it; she poured coffee; she examined her teeth in the mirror. She touched the irregular patch of unpigmented skin on her long neck. Her clothing, the parts of her body, she checked in with them as if they would remind her of who she was. Hayden watched and Tina did not seem to mind.

"What's with Emory?" Hayden said.

"What do you mean?"

"I mean she's not a she."

Tina laughed, turned from the mirror. In the dim light of the back room her toughness faded and she seemed almost pretty. "Oh, she's a she all right."

Donelle interrupted them. They couldn't talk with Donelle around—Tina bothered Donelle; Donelle bothered Tina; Donelle's religion and Tina's lack of it got in the way—and Hayden's first client was waiting on the floor.

Like some ailing locomotive the day chugged on, stopped, resumed chugging. It seemed endless to Hayden, like the long trip in a nightmare from which you will never return. Even the fish seemed haggard. Hayden tried to snag Tina again, to resume their conversation, but every time Hayden was free Tina had a client.

"Beer after work?" Hayden mouthed over the head of her last client.

Tina nodded. She was always good for a beer and a talk. What would Hayden have done without Tina? She was a cynic; nothing surprised her. She recast the world as if the two of them were the only rational people remaining.

They sat in a booth in the bar's dusty, red-tinged light. Demetria was with them, spelunking for peanuts in the pretzel bowl. The men at nearby tables, all over sixty, left them alone. The waitress knew them and brought a pitcher of beer without their having to ask. The first sip made them all sigh. The red light brought out Tina's steely melancholia, Demetria's restlessness.

"I got *two* bounced checks last week. *Two* in one week," Demetria said. "You guys never get bounced checks. Do I invite this somehow?"

"Hayden has something to say."

"Why aren't we talking about Emory?" Hayden said.

"We are. We are right now," Tina said.

"What do you think?" Hayden turned to Demetria. "He or she?"

"Are you kidding?" Demetria said. "Of course she's a she."

"An androgynous she," Tina said, chuckling. "But still a she."

"Don't laugh," Hayden said. "It makes a difference."

"Does it?" Tina said. "I never pegged you for a bigot."

Demetria found another peanut. "They're cheap with these things."

"I'm not a bigot. It changes things. You might not want it to, but it does."

Tina shrugged.

Hayden persisted. "He's got a beard."

"So do I," said Tina. "See here. I pull out hairs here every morning." She dragged her finger over some purported stubble on her chin, but it was too dark to see anything.

"She's a she," said Demetria. "*She* has a beard."

"A real five o'clock shadow."

"That doesn't make her a man," Demetria said.

"All I'm saying is what does it matter?" Tina said. "Why do you need everything to be this way or that?"

"Certain things I wouldn't say to a man," said Hayden.

"Like what?" Tina asked.

"I don't know, just some things—"

"This heat problem is getting to you."

"It has nothing to do with heat. Or cold," Hayden said. "I'm saying—" She couldn't go on. They all dropped it and fell to silence, their beer mugs thunking the table hard, intractable as trucks. After a few minutes Hayden excused herself.

"Ease up," Tina said.

Hayden stood at her station, clientless, dazed. She was thinking about Arleen, how it used to feel to be in the braiding chair with nothing to do but sit still. She used to think that the tugging hurt—that's what she'd always told Mother—but it hadn't really hurt. When the braiding was done Arleen would pat everything down and tuck back in the few escaped hairs. Her fingers, moving through scalp and hair, felt like the feet of nesting mice. Hayden tried to stretch this memory, make it long and resilient as a Chinese jump rope, but Emory was watching her.

"You have something to say to me?" Emory said. "Say it. I don't bite."

Hayden had no voice. Emory's feet were planted far apart. Her chest rattled like chain mail.

"Oh," Hayden said. "No," she said. "I'm just trying to get my body back after a bunch of nights with no heat." She picked up her whisk broom. She searched for dust on her countertop.

"Shitty landlord?" Emory said.

Hayden punished her clean surfaces, didn't look up. "He's a nice enough guy, but he doesn't lift a finger. I wore a whole closetful of clothes last night and I was still cold. Even now I can't get warm."

"Hoboken or Manhattan?"

"Here."

"My place is in Manhattan. A sublet on Fifth near the Bowery. There're a lot of Russians in the building who don't speak English so the landlord uses it as an excuse and doesn't do shit."

Hayden stopped sweeping. She had never heard Emory use so many words.

"Well," Emory said. "If it doesn't get fixed, I've got room. Nothing fancy, but you're welcome to it."

"I'm fine," Hayden said. She didn't need charity. She was perfectly fine.

She felt shamed into silence. She no longer trusted her senses and she couldn't concentrate. Her client, Melissa, was confiding in her about a boyfriend who had become distant. Maybe he was seeing someone else. What did Hayden think Melissa should do? Hayden had no expertise in these things. "Maybe you should talk to him," she said. That's what everyone said: *talk, talk, talk,* as if talk were some magical transforming pill. All they did in the salon was talk and no one's life changed much for it. Hayden strained to hear what Emory was saying to Tina but the bubbling of the fish tank made it difficult—something about coming from Florida, the white-trash-and-alligator state. Emory's father owned a small, low-budget motel in the Keys. He was a mild, sweet man, and an expert marksman. On his rare days off they went camping. He taught her how to shoot a rifle. They shot, for sport, anything that moved—birds, squirrels, snakes, once an alligator despite prohibitions against it. It was his hair she first cut because he hated spending money on such a thing.

"So you really think I should ask him point-blank?" Melissa said.

Was that what Hayden had advised? She couldn't remember saying exactly that. She wished she could silence Melissa but it was her job to be nice, to reassure, to soothe. "Yes," Hayden said. "Yes, I do." Melissa had used a styling product that smelled to Hayden like formaldehyde. The smell persisted even after shampooing. Hayden wasn't sure what she had said and what she had only thought. Maybe it was time to move on, find another salon, another city.

Emory's client had a mullet and an unyielding expression. They seemed to know each other. Tina kept nodding. "So where was your mother?" Tina said.

The reply was swept away by the updraft of Demetria's dryer.

At home Hayden phoned Arnaux. His machine was too full now to take her messages, so she called a city hotline and tried to make her way to a live person. Where were all the live people these days? She could withhold her rent, but she wouldn't be warmed by that. She lusted for sleep.

Back at the salon she worked on a new client, a thirty-year-old paralegal whose silence scared her. There were different kinds of silence and this kind seemed reproachful, merciless, testing, far too familiar. The woman had silky, lustrous hair she didn't appreciate. It was too flat for her. She wanted wiry hair that made claims on the world. No one wanted what they had.

"Damn." Someone had taken Hayden's favorite shampoo, the one that smelled like aloe and lavender.

"Hayden's pissed." Demetria always saw it first. A rill of light laughter spread around the salon.

"I'm not pissed. Who took my shampoo?"

It was Amber. She had meant to give it back but she forgot. She'd only used a little. "Sorry, sorry, I'm really sorry," Amber kept saying.

"Forget it," Hayden said. They weren't supposed to hold Amber responsible for anything because she had kids and was overworked. And because she was nice. Being so nice would be Amber's downfall. Hayden swept at Amber's apologies with a dismissive palm. She glimpsed the dark look in the eyes of the silky-haired woman in her chair. She saw malice. The woman would not come back.

Like any group they had their alliances and antagonisms, and there were certain melancholic days when everyone was on the rag. But they knew how to pull together when someone needed help.

It was a quiet, overcast day when Birdie arrived wearing dark glasses, emitting *don't touch me* quills. When she removed the glasses her face gave everything away. It was splotched and spongy, her nostrils flared. Her hair, usually a shiny cap of gentle curls, was pulled into a tight ponytail, for which her hair was too short and which spoke of haste. She returned no one's gaze.

"Hey girl, what's up?" Demetria asked.

"I'm fine." Birdie pawed in her station drawer.

"I know fine," said Demetria, "and I know not fine. And you're as not fine as they come. Did Billy leave?"

Birdie paused, her eyes piercing Demetria. "No, he didn't. And if he did it's none of your damn business."

"Ouch!" Demetria raised both palms and retreated a few steps backward.

"You can tell us, honey," Donelle said.

"We are fam-i-lee," Amber sang while she snipped the air behind her client's head and did a quick two-step.

"Leave me alone," Birdie said.

They took the message. They turned pointedly away. They chatted with their clients, those who had clients. Birdie blasted Endust onto a rag.

Hayden's next client was twenty minutes late, probably a no-show. She sat in the waiting area reading O, but only half reading. She could see what was happening to everyone: everyone's life was fraying. It was the kind of falling apart that didn't come in one dramatic ax-falling moment, but rather as a slow chipping, a gradual wearing away, the way a shirt developed holes or an icicle melted. When you looked closely you saw that the things in your life you thought were so solid had no solidity at all.

Birdie's body was taut and purposeful. Her voice had a businesslike clip. Watching Birdie exhausted Hayden while making her perversely calm.

"Makeover night," Rena announced in the mid-afternoon.

It was a regular tribal ritual. They would all stay after work, ignoring unmade dinners, undone loads of laundry, empty apartments. They would settle into each other's chairs and do what was called for: coloring, styling, washing, massaging. Rena supplied wine and snacks, and they all handled each other, giving themselves over to grooming, to tending and attending, to making things better.

Tonight Hayden would not stay. But she was curious about what Emory would do. Rena turned the sign from OPEN to CLOSED. The night made a cloistering tunnel around them. Emory was still at his station, neatening. Birdie put on her coat, zipped up her bag. At the door, Rena stopped her.

"You can't go."

"Billy's expecting me."

"This is *mandatory*," Rena said, pulling rank.

Birdie hesitated. "I don't need this," she said.

"It's not about you," Rena said. "It's for *us*."

Birdie stood not far from Emory's station and the way Emory was doing things you could tell he was all ears. The wrongness of his presence there chafed and clanged. Family quarrels like these belonged among the women. Hayden fled, ducking out the door past Birdie and Rena.

She had not made it to the corner when Tina came after her. "Get your butt back in there. Don't fucking bail on us."

"I'm not bailing, I'm tired."

"Things get a little unpleasant and you jump ship. Don't say you don't."

Hayden let herself be led back in. Tina wasn't usually coercive, certainly she wasn't self-righteous. Maybe she had a point. Back inside Hayden went to the toilet. Things would be better for her in a place that was warm—Arizona maybe, she had liked Arizona.

When she came out Birdie was sitting in her own chair, eyes closed, holding a Dixie cup of wine. "Okay, okay," she erupted. "You're right. It's Billy. He's talking about leaving. He saw some other girl—"

The tears began. Long, disfiguring sobs. She gulped air. She coughed. A highway wreck, she galvanized everyone's attention.

Emory broke the group paralysis. He stood up and slid behind Birdie's harrumphing back. He touched her shoulders with both palms, leaving his hands there for a minute or two before he began to massage. He kneaded slowly. Everyone watched. His fingers had the imploring sensuality of a cat's paws. They stretched and retracted rhythmically as they moved from shoulders to scalp. Birdie's sobs began to subside. Soon the only sounds coming from her were occasional whimpers and moans that were more suggestive of pleasure than anguish. Everyone was breathing along with her. Whirring like wind.

"You're putting me to sleep just watching," Amber said.

Hayden felt dizzy. Disgust, respect, envy, God knows. What was Emory trying to prove—that women didn't have the corner on sensitivity? Whatever it was, Hayden didn't need it. She was rotting in this Hoboken salon. She had to get out.

She sat in her chair, brittle, cantankerous.

"What shall I do for you?" Amber asked.

"I don't care. Whatever." Hayden closed her eyes. When she opened them she saw Emory sitting in Birdie's chair ready to be worked on, wigless. He looked diminutive, feminine, his face sharp and beard-shadowed. Who knew what he was. Birdie tugged at the short dark hairs that had been flattened by the wig.

"Let's spike it a little. What do you think?" Birdie said.

"Go for it," Emory said.

"You mind my asking. Are you a lesbian?"

Emory smiled. "You thought I was coming on to you?"

"I mean, not that I'd mind if you were. I just wondered, you know."

Emory glanced at Hayden, turned away, and whispered something inaudible. Hayden clamped her eyes shut.

When they left that night Hayden's hair had been shagged to silliness. She should have paid attention. Emory's hair was a pointillist's triumph of tiny regular spikes that looked not like a built-in weapons system but more like the timid, unexercised quills of a baby porcupine.

They had talked among themselves and they gave her an ultimatum. Hayden had to find a warm place to stay. Tina was their spokeswoman. Hayden was welcome to stay with any one of them, Tina said, or they would check her into a hotel and share the expense. It couldn't go on like this.

When had they talked? What an embarrassing thought that they had all gathered to discuss her. She thought she had kept her malaise to herself. She picked up a sponge and swiped her countertop. Was she really as difficult as they made her out to be?

The hotel was not an option—she wasn't going to let them pay hundreds of dollars a night for a hotel, she didn't need that kind of charity. But who had room? No one had room though they all insisted they did. Tina's place was tiny. Demetria kept unpredictable hours. Donelle, in western New Jersey, was too far away. Rena's place was a two-bedroom but she had a regular round-robin of overnight male guests. Amber had her kids. Birdie had Billy and all their attendant problems. Emory's place was an unknown but surely small.

It was dark outside and Rena had locked the front door. Demetria was fixing her hair in the mirror. Tina tallied her checks and kept glancing at Hayden, once, twice. Emory pawed through her messenger bag. Amber was on the phone, making arrangements with her mom. Donelle had already put on her coat and was emptying her pockets of Kleenexes and candy wrappers. Rena sprinkled some flakes of fish food into the tank, turned off the overhead lights, tweaked the front blinds. Insulated from the city, they awaited her reply.

Emory stood in front of Hayden, coat on, bag packed. "I already offered. And I'm offering again."

Hayden looked to one side so she wouldn't have to look directly at Emory. Her gaze latched onto the photo of her mother holding Russ. For a moment her mother seemed to wink, an oblique but encouraging message.

"Yes," Hayden said. "I guess so," she said. "Okay."

Emory's place was a fifth-floor walk-up in the East Village. A studio, predictably small, the bathtub in the kitchen hinged with a piece of plywood to double as a dining table, the bed separated from the rest of the living area by only a curtain.

Emory kicked off her shoes and laid her auburn wig on the bathtub's plywood cover like an actor sliding out of costume. Beneath the wig her black hair was a weed bed, each lock with a different idea of how best to grow, each possessed of a different texture and trope. She heated some oil in a frying pan, found some leftover rice in the half-size refrigerator, threw it into the pan. Hayden perched on the arm of the couch. It was unnatural to be there. The silence caught her like a labyrinth.

"Can I help?" she said.

"Nothing fancy."

Hayden looked around. The apartment was a shell, temporary, unclaimed. Like some army barracks in which anyone could have lived. Nothing individualized the space except for the inflated plastic flamingo that hung in the window's casement, a cardboard box spewing a jumble of colorful clothing, and a cracked full-length mirror propped against one wall.

The phone's ringing was obstreperous, alarming. Emory dove for it like an act of rescue. She grunted in answer. The grunt gave way to a wail. Then words. "No, I can't talk now. I'll call you . . . I don't know when. Maybe later tonight, maybe not. I've got a guest here . . . No, none of your business . . ."

She returned the phone to its cradle as if gluing it there. With a large cleaver she slashed at squares of soft tofu. "Old business," she said. Her voice was low and aimed at the cutting board. Anyone, then, could have thought she was male.

The phone rang again, louder than before. Emory diced the tofu to the size of pebbles. The ringing filled the room. Yell, stop, yell, stop, yell, stop. At the invisible end of the line lay a swill of need. The final ring burst like a hemorrhaging vessel. Emory scraped the mauled tofu into the pan and watched the oil spit. She lifted the phone and laid it on the window ledge. The dial tone turned to an operator's plea.

The phone had made Hayden stupid. "Why do you wear wigs?"

Emory's turning head looked mesmerized. "Trying things out. Getting and holding a job. It's a long story. How much time do you have?"

"I've got time."

They sat around the bathtub table eating jasmine rice and tofu from brown ceramic bowls. Emory, chopsticks side by side like a small lashed raft, ate with the grim perseverance of a mountaineer, holding the bowl a few inches from her mouth. Once she stopped eating to scratch her head with the tips of her chopsticks. She didn't speak. Hayden didn't ask. The lifeless wig lay on the table between them. Hayden looked at the dark stitching of its underbelly. It reminded her of the tough sealed scar of a once-open heart.

"A beer?" Emory said.

"Yes, a beer would be nice, thank you."

Emory laughed with a fricative "ha." "You've got some manners on you."

The brakes of a truck yowled off Second Avenue. The beer tasted faintly of blackberries.

"What's your thing with me? I'm trying to figure you out." Emory's apartment voice was distinctly lower than her salon voice.

"I don't have a thing."

The laugh again, short and disbelieving. "Okay. Have it your way."

Hayden drank her beer, ate a few more bites of tofu. It wasn't working out. "How long have you been here?" she said.

"Two months. Subletting from some friends I know in Florida."

"Where were you before that?"

"Miami."

Hayden had never been to Miami. She didn't think she would like it. "This is a good neighborhood. Convenient."

"Get rid of the students and it would be good."

"Yeah, the students."

"They suck."

The word *suck* silenced Hayden, shocked her a little. It seemed incongruous with Emory's age. "Yeah, they suck," Hayden said, trying the word in her own mouth and finding it unexpectedly pleasant. "You don't have too many belongings."

"I got enough."

The word *belongings* sounded strange too. *Don't forget your belongings,* people said. It brought to mind memberships, connections people wouldn't want to abandon. *Longing* was parked so centrally in that string of letters. What would it be like to be the mother or father of Emory, would you be unnerved by her androgynous state? Hayden thought about the cockatiel they'd had when she was a child. The pet store had said they thought it was male, but they couldn't be sure until the bird was mature. They called the bird Tillie for some reason—whose idea was that?— and used male and female pronouns interchangeably. Maybe if you were a bird or a dust mote it was okay to be indefinable, but if you were born into a species with language, you needed to name things conclusively.

They finished their rice. Emory did the dishes. They retired to beds within ten feet of each other. Hayden lay beneath the thick covers of her foldout couch bed and reveled in its warmth.

"You girls can be anything you want to be," Hayden's mother used to say. "You know that don't you? Absolutely anything."

The three girls stood around Mother, who sat at the dining room table. It was midsummer, mid-afternoon, the sleepy dreamy time of day. They were hot and bored. They needed to be told what to do so they hovered around Mother, touching her shoulders, her neck, her long bony back.

"My lovely anythings," she sighed.

"We're not *anythings*. Why do you call us *anythings*?" Cornelia said.

"Because who knows what you are? You must tell me when you know. Until then you will be my anything."

"Well, I'm going to be an international lawyer," Cornelia said. "So I'm not an anything."

"That's lovely, Cornelia. What about you, Hayden?"

The heat pasted over Hayden's brain. She wanted a pool. She wanted pistachio ice cream. The future had no shape; it might not come. "Nothing," Hayden said.

"Anything," Mother insisted.

Chapter 7

Sleep, long overdue, was medicinal. It pulsed under her toenails, was a healing poultice on her fingers and kneecaps. It prompted her hair to grow. The ambulances, the trucks snarling down Second Avenue, the drunks altercating, the hissing radiators, the insistent cabbies' horns—none of it mattered.

She woke slowly, unsure of what she was hearing. Running water. A body nearby. She was not used to waking up so near someone else. She kept her eyes closed and only opened them when the coffeemaker had begun to burp and clunk. Emory sat at the bathtub table with a mug, staring past the inflated flamingo, out the barred window. She wore tight-fitting brown houndstooth trousers and a collared polyester shirt in a pink and brown paisley pattern. The shirt was form-fitting, her chest flat. This day's wig was jet-black and ruler-straight with bluntly cut bangs that echoed the curve of her eyebrows. She looked robotic, draggish. It could have been a wig from *Star Trek*.

"Coffee?"

"Yes, please."

Hayden propped herself on the arm of the couch to drink. They drank without speaking, each in her private realm. They owed each other nothing beyond human decency. Their silence seemed contractual, almost companionable.

They crossed Astor Place, then over to Ninth at Broadway. The sidewalks were speckled with tiny frost flecks that glistened but did not melt in the sun's rays. A bank's digital readout declared the temperature was ten degrees. At the curbs people stomped while waiting to cross the street. They blew warm air into their gloves and brought their takeout cardboard coffee cups to bare ears. Hayden was bundled, but Emory wore only her customary leather jacket and neither hat nor gloves.

At the salon Rena said Hayden looked rested. The others kidded her. "You're one stubborn fuck," Demetria said.

"Sometimes," she agreed.

"No, *all* the time."

She was surprised her stubbornness showed so clearly.

"That's some get-up you put together, Emory," Demetria said. "You in a play or something?" Emory's flat expression germinated into a smile.

Rested, Hayden felt happy for the first time in weeks. There was nothing she desired. She forgot the fractal patterns of sorrow— her own or anyone else's—there was only the world of female voices, herbal fragrances, metallic wintery light. Her regular client Myra, gentle to the point of meekness, gave herself over as if Hayden were a masseuse. Her neck and shoulder muscles softened. Her scalp seemed to weep with the pleasure of touch. Whatever Hayden wanted to do was fine, she said.

How different all Hayden's clients were. Some arrived with photographs showing precisely what they wanted. Others knew only what they didn't want. Still others sat retracted in terror, incapable of speaking, hoarding secret desires. Once, a woman had reached out to slap the scissors mid-cut. Hayden powered through, intuiting as much as she could.

Afternoons were never as good as mornings. The day had a

cast by then that could not be altered even with coffee and sweet pastries from Finelli's. A mother came in dragging her daughter, Gabriella, a tiny young teen with a puffy lavender jacket and a rush of straight brown hair that fell past her rump. Under the salon's light the hair shone, gemlike.

"It's all coming off," the mother said.

Gabriella stood still as a building, gaze to the floor. She wore low-slung blue jeans, a form-fitting yellow V-neck shirt that showed off the nipples of her small breasts. Her chest sparkled with purple-tinged glitter.

"I warned you," her mother said. "Now get in the chair."

Gabriella sat, her eyes burning the mirror.

"Short," said the mother. "Three nights in a row she ignores her curfew. Thirteen years old and out *all night long*. It's all coming off. You brought this on yourself, Gabriella."

Hayden combed. She considered. Into her field of vision stalked the mother's stylish black boots. *Comb, comb, keep on combing*.

"If you're thinking of leaving it long I'll take her somewhere else right now," the mother said to Hayden.

"We have to shampoo first." Hayden held the hair. It seemed to her alive and powerful as Samson's tresses. How could she cut? She wanted help. She wanted rescue.

"What do *you* want?" she said to the girl.

The girl said nothing. Her eyes were dead.

"We don't have all day," said the mother.

Hayden floundered, but there was Emory in houndstooth and paisley, offering coffee to the mother. There was Emory in all her oddity.

"Seats are over there," Emory said, indicating the waiting area. The mother perched on a chair, sipped her black coffee, ignored the plate of cookies and the bowl of sweets.

"Shoulder-length?" Hayden asked.

The girl shrugged. "Whatever."

Time was no panacea, it would not fix a thing. The fish would keep on swimming. Night would come. The mother and daughter would go elsewhere. They would fight anyway.

Hayden made a loose braid. She cut.

Chapter 8

The phone calls made them a team, coming in as they did like snipers, impaling the air, raiding the silence, ruining all semblance of safety. A part of both of them was always devoted to thinking: *When will the next one come? How long will it last?* Emory had no answering machine, and though she could have lifted the receiver to sever the connection, she didn't. Hayden didn't question this—it wasn't her right. They endured together, on the first ring glancing briefly at each other, half-smiling like comrades before their faces camped on their usual platforms of grim endurance. A tightness set in around Hayden's eyes and forehead, the seeds of a headache. They found places to settle. Emory sat in a chair by the bathtub table, Hayden would lie on the couch or hustle to the toilet. Crouching was best, the safest way to survive all those rings. *Ten, fifteen, twenty.* You counted, you couldn't not count as the ringing bludgeoned you with its encrypted desire. It always reached a multiple of five before it stopped.

"Who is it?" Hayden finally asked.

"I'll get into it some time," Emory said.

At lunch each day Hayden checked her apartment. A six-inch snowstorm had left the walkway and front steps buried. The garbage cans wore columnar hats like frozen soldiers. Inside the pipes had frozen, and each day the apartment's temperature sank lower.

At the end of each workday Emory raised her eyebrows at Hayden. No words, just the inquiring eyebrows. "You sure you don't mind?" Hayden would say. "I can find some other place if—"

"Get over it," Emory said.

They made single-dish meals. Cheesy omelets with toast. Fried rice with vegetables. Black bean chili. After dinner they retired to their separate spaces. Hayden read *Newsweek* and wondered how long her life would be like this. Sometimes she read mystery novels, nothing too serious. She was picky about what she read. Very few novels. No memoirs. No books about travel. Informational works only; reading for solutions, for betterment, though she had no plans to better herself. Emory lay on her back, knees elevated, staring at the air. Hayden tried not to notice, didn't ask, avoided conclusions. It was enough that Emory, strange Emory, accepted her there.

A routine developed over nine days, but it seemed to both of them like far more than nine days. On the tenth night they emerged from the PATH train station. Traffic on Sixth Avenue hooted by on its uptown tear. The streetlights lit coils of their outgoing breath. They idled there for a moment in the crowd before consecrating themselves to their crosstown walk. Then Hayden noticed: one of the many women bearing parcels, this one taller than many and somewhat more chic, but not so different from the others—except for the hair. You had to admire hair like that—it was the move-over color of sirens and ambulances, of emergency and blood. It was darker now than when she was a child, not so orange. It took forever for Hayden to know what she was seeing. Corner by blurry corner she came into focus, feature by feature. A slow draw on the past. A glacial assemblage of parts. A developing photograph. Surprising, yes, but familiar as a catechism. Familiar as knuckle bones. Familiar as the odor of pea soup. Cornelia it was before her, two glossy shopping bags at her sides, her face complicated with disbelief.

"Cornelia," Hayden said.

"Hayden."

How begin a conversation beyond the utterance of a name?

Emory took measure, standing there watching, buffeted by thick-coated pedestrians. Who was this somebody, this affluent woman with shopping bags spewing pink and green tissue?

Cornelia seized Hayden, pulled her close. Her body was full, soft. "Jesus, Hayden, you *asshole*." They gripped each other hard, then withdrew.

"You might as well go ahead," Hayden said to Emory. "I'll be a while."

"I've got to catch a train," Cornelia said. She listed away from them.

Emory slipped into the crowd without a word. She was lost in the ruthless moil of pedestrians; it was too late to lasso her back. Hayden knew she'd been careless.

"Train to where?" Hayden said.

"North."

"*Where* north?"

Cornelia hesitated. "Scarsdale."

Hayden nodded, Scarsdale fit. What now? They stood uncertainly, a few feet from the roaring traffic. The exhaust, rank and particle-bearing, was lit to a viscous slurry by the streetlights.

"We should go somewhere? You want to get coffee?" she said.

Cornelia sighed. She pulled back her fur-cuffed sleeve to find her watch. "I guess I could get the 7:26." She looked around. "Where though?"

They walked a few blocks up Sixth to a Greek coffee shop. The glass door was fogged and inside they met a front of humid heat that seemed equatorial. They sat in a vacant booth still strewn with dirty dishes, remnants of pizza and falafel. Cornelia kept her coat on, scoured the table top with her gaze, said nothing.

Once, they had tromped side by side through meadow and mud, performed nightly recitations on the couch, plotted the stealing of Arleen's gum; now their eyes flew to each other like rubberneckers'. Withdrew, flew back. The awkwardness was palpable as bone spurs. They stared at sticky laminated menus.

"Just tea for me," Cornelia said. "I can't stay long."

The busboy cleared the dishes with his gaze out the window. "I'll get your waiter."

Finger by finger Cornelia peeled off her leather gloves. Her nails were manicured, one finger was heavy with rings of platinum and diamond. From a gold-clasped brown leather clutch she took a cell phone. She punched a button.

"It's me," she said. "I'm taking the 7:26. I ran into someone. I'll tell you later. Love you, honey."

The table was clear, their cups of tea too hot to drink, the space between them vast and empty, the years behind them thickly their own. Cornelia's eyes looked shellacked and brittle.

"You're married?" Hayden said.

Cornelia nodded. She was powerful, aloof. Even her silence commanded attention. Especially her silence. The red hair alone made you look at her. Only 2 to 5 percent of the population had red hair. Cornelia had liked to say that to people when she was a child. Even as a young child Cornelia had had the muscular personality common to redheads. She hadn't fawned as Hayden had, she didn't skulk around Mother's hiding places. She had never cared to see what Hayden saw.

"You're good?" Hayden said.

"Reasonably good." She unbuttoned her coat. Her belly pushed against her beige sweater like a cloaked soccer ball.

"You're *pregnant*?"

"Fat." She smiled.

"How can you be pregnant?"

"Is this a birds-and-bees question? Insert penis—"

"You know that's not what I mean."

"What *do* you mean?"

Hayden shrugged. "You're so young."

"Because I'm younger than you, you mean? You're the standard here?"

Hayden sighed. She was mesmerized by a stand of freckles near Cornelia's left nostril. She remembered those freckles. The freckles, unchanged, were a thin spindle to the past.

"What about Sophie?" Hayden said.

"University of Michigan."

Hayden tried to picture a grown Sophie, a Sophie all done with cartwheels and giggling, childhood and adolescence dissolved. Hayden's questions grew rowdy now.

"How's Father doing?"

Cornelia grimaced. "What is this, the Inquisition? The point here isn't *us*. *We're* not the ones who dropped off the face of the earth. The point is—what happened to *you*?"

"You didn't get my cards?" Hayden had always sent postcards, brief though they were. She had told them she was in Tucson, or Santa Monica, or Venice. She had told them she was okay. It wasn't as if she had left them wondering.

Cornelia snorted. "Yeah, right, the cards."

Hayden yanked the tea bag from her cup and sipped the still-hot tea. How could she explain herself in the waning minutes before Cornelia had to leave?

"I don't think you have time," she said.

"Probably not." Cornelia pushed her teacup away—she hadn't taken a sip. She gathered her things, gloves, shopping bags.

Longing guttered in Hayden. "Do you know what became of Arleen?"

"Arleen? She's still around. Life didn't stop, you know, just because you left."

"I thought Father hated her."

"Well, you thought a lot of wrong things."

"I saw things you never saw," Hayden said.

"How would you know what I saw? You have no idea. You weren't even *there*."

Cornelia stood, regal and slow, a female translation of their father, not point for point, but in some ineffable stateliness, some whispered emanation that turned heads and spawned envy.

"Can we do this again?" said Hayden. She heard in her own voice the fawning of a spurned lover.

"I don't know. You live here? How do you get by?"

"I live in Hoboken."

"What do you do for work?"

"I'm a stylist."

Cornelia frowned. "*Hair* stylist?" Incredulity and disdain mangled her face for a moment. "You've *got* to be kidding me."

Hayden shook her head. Yes, no.

"Jesus, Hayden. Is there a point to all this?"

"What do you do?"

"I'm in law school. I'm about to be a mother." She laid down a five-dollar bill and began to move to the door. After a few steps she turned back. "I take it you've seen Father's most recent book? It just came out."

"No."

"Here's a copy. You should read it. My card is in there."

Cornelia reached into her bag and pulled out a slim hardcover book. She dropped it onto the booth's table top and turned to leave. The moment felt choreographed, destined.

"When's your baby coming? How will you do law school with a baby?"

But Cornelia was gone, her hair like a beacon as she passed through the door and raised her arm, a gesture Hayden took to be a goodbye until she realized Cornelia was stepping off the curb to hail a cab. Even as she slipped into the cab the panel of red hair that fenced her cheek was visible. It lingered like an afterglow as Hayden thumbed absently through the book. She closed it quickly. It was her policy not to read her father's work. She thought of leaving the book for the waiter. A card had fluttered from the pages. She picked it up. Cornelia Risley Vandermeer.

She took the book. Maybe she'd read it later.

Chapter 9

She had a key but it seemed wrong to use it. She rang and Emory buzzed her up. The apartment was steamy and smelled of oil and onions. Emory, immersed in cooking, was de-wigged and her hair had been ruffled to haphazardness. Her face looked angular, her body a long wafer devoid of curves. Tonight, despite all Hayden knew to the contrary, despite all people said, indeterminacy tipped again toward maleness. At least at that moment. This world Hayden was entering seemed more mysterious than before, more concealing. It filled her with caution and a sudden awareness of her unwitting, unwanted power.

She laid her father's book on the table. Cornelia would be on the train by now, other passengers sneaking peeks in her direction, dazzled by her hair, understanding it to be an amulet of some kind, a jeweled crown, an important signifier. *Stunning*, they used to tell Cornelia when she was a child. *Fiery. Magical. It will age like a fine wine as your father's hair has.* Straddling two worlds Hayden felt a sudden weary longing for things to be more fixed than they were.

"Your sister?" Emory said.

"How did you know?"

"You're really asking?"

Hayden had never thought they looked alike. Especially now—Cornelia with her hair, her elegant manner, all the trappings of affluence. She looked like a person who made things happen, a woman whose life was full of forward motion and plans. She *was* that person.

The phone rang. They groaned in unison. Like sisters. As sisters should be. Emory pulled out the phone cord and Hayden did not comment.

"I always thought your name sounded rich," Emory said. She dropped diced carrots and garlic into the hot pan where they sizzled, their molecules of scent exploding into the apartment's sultry air.

"I'm not rich," Hayden said. "Maybe I could have been if I'd done things differently. Hayden Lucia Chase Armstrong Buchanan Risley. That's my full name."

"Blue blood."

Hayden shrugged, thinking of the color blue. A cold color. The color of blood without oxygen. Blue babies died. Who would want such blood? A death knell for sure.

"Not really," she said.

"It's just a fact," Emory said. "It only has whatever meaning you give it."

"I should have introduced you. But I—we haven't seen each other for years. I was flustered. I'm sorry."

Emory turned back to her cooking as if none of this made any difference, and in the silence that followed Hayden felt derailed, ambushed somehow, not only by Cornelia, but by all of her past, irascibly present inside her like some parallel life. She pictured her mother laid out cold and alone, looking so unlike herself in the long-sleeved, high-necked navy blue dress.

Emory set two bowls of soup on the table along with a long,

crusty loaf of bread and a round of yellow cheese. Hayden joined her without needing to be summoned. They accommodated each other like animals, wordlessly, but aware of bodily needs. It reminded Hayden of the way things had been with Elva.

"It's really okay, you know," Emory said as they began to eat.

"What's okay?"

"To be that way?"

"What way?"

"Blue blood."

"But I'm not blue blood anymore. I don't have a dime more than what I make. What I've got is a subarctic apartment in Hoboken and blood like everyone else's."

"Yeah, right."

They ate their soup. Hayden could only think now of how not-blue her mother's blood had been. A red so dark under the dangling cellar light it had almost looked black. The natural light from the window, stolen from a bright blue autumn day, had been dulled by its voyage inside and, bristling with dust motes, it seemed to smolder. The dots of dark blood sprang up like Morse code under the X-Acto knife.

Outside, the city screeched like a dissatisfied harem, but in the steamy asylum of their indoor cubicle they scarcely noticed. The sounds of their breathing and eating matched the sighs of the radiator. Hayden yearned for the phone to ring. She wanted the focus it provided, the sense of their being a team. She knew Emory wanted something from her, she wasn't sure what. Whatever it was, however much Hayden might want to give it, she knew she would come up short.

Emory's spoon crashed to the table. "Go on, ask. Say what you're thinking. Don't be so goddamn withholding. You want to get over your blue blood thing? Here's your chance." Her voice was too loud for the space, and it opened them up to the outside, inviting in the hollering traffic.

"Ask what?"

"You think I'm blind? These looks you sneak. What is it that bothers you? My mustache? My wigs? The fucking hair on my arms? Go on—find the words. Ask me, for God's sake." She paused. "Or was it my crotch you wanted to see?"

She was standing now a few feet from the table, legs spread to an invincible inverted V like the legs of a soldier. She shook her head, began clearing the bowls. Hayden tried to help but Emory waved her away.

Hayden went to the bathroom. She sat on the toilet and stared at the graffiti'd door. *Gunsmoke rocks. Girls need muses.* Water gushed from the kitchen faucet in a fulminating torrent that sounded wrong and was filled with the unspoken debris of Emory's inner life. It scared Hayden. She wondered if Emory was the kind of person whose anger would take on drastic forms. Would she do things she might later regret, or things the law would find actionable? It was time to leave.

She flushed the toilet, a warning. The faucet ceased its roaring. Footsteps. When she exited the bathroom Hayden saw Emory standing by the front door. Hayden gathered her things slowly, trying to figure. She remembered running through the house of her childhood, slapping furniture as she passed, sweeping books off tables, wanting to get out and get out loudly. A standing lamp had crashed in her wake. She had thrown open the French doors and headed outside, leaving the doors flung wide like hapless arms so wind could blow through the house. *Hayden, Hayden,* Arleen called.

Hayden, two feet from Emory and face-to-face, tried to thicken her body with bravado and wondered if she had what it took to fight.

"Say it," Emory said.

Hayden shook her head. There was nothing to say. "I'm going."

"No, you're not. You're talking. You've stayed here all these nights—you owe me some talking."

They both were breathing hard, as if something physical had happened between them. Emory's eyes had the unrelenting, coruscating power of the sun, dazzling, impossible to look into. Hayden looked away, to the floor where a cockroach was scuttling under the couch.

"You think I'm a weirdo, don't you?" Emory said.

"Of course not."

"Ask, damn it."

The radiator's hiss was reptilian. No question could be answered honestly, not from lack of will but because truths came and went so quickly, ungraspable as vapor.

"Ask me *now*," Emory commanded.

A loud truck honk subsided, leaving a vacuum of silence. "Okay. What are you? I mean are you really a woman?"

"I'm half a man," Emory said. "I'm on my way to becoming a man. Or I was—I'm taking a break now to figure things out."

Hayden nodded, an inadequate gesture. Emory relaxed her sentry stance, her armature. There was no shock by now, but dozens of questions. *Why the wigs? Why the act? Who has been calling?*

Emory reached out and removed the strap of Hayden's bag from her shoulder.

"You're staying," she said.

They were on the other side of something, but there was no relief in being there. Hayden lay awake thinking of her mother. It wasn't the fiasco with the animals that got things going wrong. It must have been long before that. Perhaps having children in the first place. Her first pregnancy was in the Bicentennial year when other women were gathered in living rooms, mirrors in hand, examining the luxuriant hot colors of their own vaginas. Women were dressing in trousers, eschewing makeup, purchasing hammers and briefcases, cropping their hair into the truculent shapes of power. They were marching out into the world. Claire, meanwhile, sat in a pillowed easy chair in a house in the middle of nowhere, thumbing through art books, pausing occasionally to hear the call of the mourning dove who strutted the driveway at dusk. She was wide and plodding and quiet in her pregnancy. The world had a weak hold on her. There was no call toward power or anger when you were growing a child. Her husband frequently away, she sat for days on end and stared at the Brownian motion of the silt-filled light.

Chapter 10

She dozed lightly and in her dreams someone was brandishing a fist. A toneless incantation came at her from a distance. Someone tried to shake answers from her.

Why become a man? *How* become one? Surely it involved horrific procedures. Cutting and stitching. She couldn't think of this. It was too barbaric and she was too besotted with thoughts of her childhood before people began trying to change themselves. Before Father's return in the autumn of her fourteenth year. Before she saw too much and hated herself for doing nothing.

The days dawned early without names and numbers attached to them, without duties accruing. In the morning the sun was white and they could feel its heat boxed inside a lingering night coolness. For breakfast Mother gave them orange popsicles and sent them outside. They were still in their nighties. They sat on the edge of the hammock blinking themselves awake, licking and slurping, popping dewdrops with their toes, tossing chunks of popsicles to a curious blue jay. It was just after the Fourth of July and everything—a lawn mower, a distant chainsaw—sounded like a world making ready to erupt in celebration. Summer stretched before them as long as their lives did—they couldn't imagine its downward slope.

Arleen had slipped outside too, and she watched them idly from her patio chair in the sun. She filed her nails and drank a Coke, squinting against the light. Mother eyed them from the picture window, her fleeting image a mirage in the window's reflection. Despite the heat she wore blouses with long loose sleeves and gauzy pastel skirts that grazed her ankles. She looked fragile, but she was game. She climbed trees along with the girls and perched in the high branches like a queen bird, graceful and colorful.

Bored, they cast their popsicles into the grass, rescuing the sticks for later uses. Mother brought her coffee outside and sat in the Adirondack chair next to Arleen. Hayden, on the cusp of adolescence and too big now for Mother's lap, sat on the chair's wide arm. She craved her mother's touch. She stared at her mother's ruddy fingertips. Traces of blood dotted the forefinger and thumb. A parade of scabs marched up the side of each nail. A few wiry threads of skin protruded from the cuticles. Ravaged hands. Mutilated. They exchanged glances, daughter to mother, mother to daughter. Mother buried her hands.

"I have an idea," Mother said loudly. "I think we should get some pets."

So many years, all their short lives, they had longed for pets. It was a longing that had come to define them—privileged kids, deeply deprived. Father did not believe in domesticated animals. The hubris of homo sapiens, he said, to believe animals could be owned.

"Pets!" Cornelia and Sophie shrieked.

They returned from the Humane Society with a menagerie: a three-legged beagle, an elderly gray cat weighing twenty pounds, a high-strung cockatiel that plucked herself obsessively.

Sophie appropriated the cat and lugged her from room to room. "Her name is Pretty," she said.

Cornelia threw a stick for the limping beagle and named him Russ.

In the kitchen Mother, Arleen, and Hayden were left with the bird. She was gray, with a plume of yellow rising from her head and orange spots on her cheeks. She regarded them with her head tilted, her eyes beady and wary and smart in the wily way of a gypsy. There was sweetness in her hesitancy and the questioning angle of her head, cruelty in the hooked beak. She swooped across her cage, alit on the fat dowel, squawked loudly, then lifted a wing and pecked beneath it hard, her squawk rising in pitch and urgency, like a knell of alarm for all the birds in the neighborhood. Mother and Arleen and Hayden stepped back from the cage. A terrifying bird, a dubious addition to the household. Nothing like what the name Tillie suggested. Surely Herod or Rasputin or Ivan would be better names than Tillie.

But Mother tamed Tillie. The bird willingly hopped onto her chewed red forefinger and skittered up her arm to her shoulder. They traveled contentedly from room to room, Tillie whistling, canting her (his?) head, hissing when others came near. Mother happied the bird as magically as she happied everyone else.

That summer, when they went out she wore a floppy pale green sun hat whose brim fell around her cheeks in a lazy parabola, hiding her eyes and making her look waifish. Back at home she often forgot to remove the hat and she navigated the house, bird on her shoulder, hat on her head, looking like an Ionesco character.

"Take off your hat," Hayden pleaded.

"I like my hat," she said.

The menagerie grew to include half a dozen goldfish, two parakeets, another cat, and, for a week, a sheep who would graze the lawn to baldness. Except for the goldfish, brought home in a plastic bag from the high-ceilinged discount store, all the animals were disabled in some way. Each parakeet was missing a wing, the cat had diabetes and required daily shots, the sheep was blind. Even the goldfish purchase was a sympathy call—Mother couldn't stand to see them displayed under the cruel fluorescents like another piece of merchandise, the only other life forms nearby being the careless teenage clerks who, responsible for stacking the shelves, created slurping tsunamis each time they moved the fish bowls.

Mother spent the better part of her days in animal care, cleaning cages and tanks, running off to the pet store for special tinctures and treats. Sometimes she coaxed Arleen into helping her, telling her to set aside the cooking, the cleaning, the hair braiding and whatnot. It was summer, the girls were fine on their own. Their hair flew out, long and wild, as they adventured in the fields and woods behind the house.

But Hayden that summer mostly dogged Mother, whose hands, when idle, always twisted a scant lock of hair, whose eyebrows had been plucked to scarcity, whose hairline was dotted with scabs that sometimes bled, whose head at the back held a saucer-sized area completely devoid of hair. She'd begun to wear a headcloth all the time, a hat or a scarf wound like a turban.

"You shouldn't deface yourself like that," Hayden said.

Mother ignored her.

When school started that year Father was still not home. Mother had been asked to give a lecture about Caravaggio at the local art museum. She never did such things, but she agreed. Caravaggio was her favorite painter and had been the subject of her dissertation. For three days in a row she was up all night. When the girls went to bed she kissed them forlornly.

"My three little bears. My three good little bears."

Hayden heard her in the middle of the night sometimes. She was downstairs pulling art books from the shelves, making herself coffee.

It was four in the afternoon, the day before her talk. Mother found Hayden in her room, reading on the bed. She closed the door, bringing with her the scent of lavender. She sat next to Hayden and brought a finger to her lips. "Don't tell your sisters," she said. She untied her scarf, letting it fall in dreamy descent to the carpet. Hayden slammed her eyes shut.

"Hayden," Mother said. "Tell me the truth. I look a fright, don't I?"

The damage was worse than Hayden had thought. There were multiple bald patches interspersed with sparse hillocks of hay-colored hair, no more than fuzz.

"I can't go before a group."

Of course you can't, Hayden felt like saying. "Just wear a scarf," she said.

"No, I can't do that." Mother moaned quietly. "How could I do this to myself?" She tilted her head so her scalped crown rested momentarily on Hayden's cheek. Hayden froze.

"I've got to call Alice and tell her I can't do it." She looked at Hayden with eyes large and wet as peeled plums.

"Don't be bleak," Hayden said. "You said so yourself. There's always a choice."

"Oh that." She laughed and wandered out of the room, fingering her uncovered head. Hayden stayed where she was, responsible, churlish, sure of nothing.

A week later Mother sat in the solarium with the door wide open to dusk's rustle. A breeze creaked the maple branches. Hayden, returning from soccer, tried to slink by unnoticed. Mother had declined to give her talk; Hayden knew she was responsible—with the slightest encouragement her mother would have gone through with it. Evidence of the interrupted preparation lay around the house—piles of thick art books with torn strips of paper marking significant pages, reams of handwritten notes on lined white pads. Mother patted the cushion beside her.

"Come here," she said.

"I'm too sweaty."

"Don't be silly."

Hayden sat and smelled the lemon and lilac scents issuing from her mother.

"Your father is coming home soon. Are you ready for him?"

"Of course not," Hayden said.

"We'll do the best we can, won't we? You must remember he loves us."

"How can you say he loves us? If he loved us he wouldn't always be away."

"He has his work, Hayden. We all have our work to do. It's our job to teach him how to show us his love."

"Why is that our job? Anyway, how could we possibly do that?"

"We're learning. Best foot forward. Chin up. Shoulders back. Make yourself higher than the Empire State Building—that's what my mother used to say to me. I did that during my orals. For a couple of hours I was taller than everyone in that room. It helped, I think."

On a gust of wind a few dry fall leaves, bright as blood, blew in from outside.

"You'll take extra care of the little girls, won't you?"

"Why?" Hayden said. "Why extra care?"

"Hayden, honey, close the door, will you?"

Hayden closed the door and returned to her post, the chill

wind freezing her sweat into a salty rind. She shuddered and her mother drew her close and put her face into the curve of Hayden's neck. Mother's warm breath tiptoed under Hayden's chin; against Hayden's cheek, the head scarf whispered.

"Don't worry, honey," Mother said. "We'll get through. We're feminists, after all, aren't we? We can conquer the world." They sat together quietly, thinking up ways to keep their small distresses from burgeoning into vast fields of dread.

In preparation for Father, they cleared the house of the animals. The cats, Pretty and Arabella, were confined to the third-floor playroom. Russ was made into an outdoor dog with a sleeping place in the garage. The sheep was already gone, the goldfish were moved into Sophie's room. Tillie and the parakeets were banished to the basement. Tears glowed in Mother's eyes as she carried their cages down the cellar stairs.

Still, if you knew what to listen for you could hear, in the hinterlands of the house, the muffled sounds of animal life.

Father returned in early October, weeks later than expected. A black limousine brought him up the quarter-mile driveway. Inside the women and girls stood at the kitchen's picture window, watching Father and the limo driver move around in the blue-gray dusk. The driver pulled luggage from the trunk. Father pulled bills from his wallet. The women said nothing, neither did the girls. Hayden felt the summer's habit of hilarity draining from them.

In the foyer the younger girls hopped up and down, and vined their legs around Father. Father's bags thunked to the floor. In the airspace above the daughters Mother and Father's exchanged gazes made a nearly audible fizz—the collision of love and strangeness, of familiarity and dislocation, of certainty and doubt.

Father's red hair looked thick; it was longer than usual and it gleamed under the tungsten light. His entire presence gleamed. He looked as Odysseus might have, or the prodigal son, a celebrated male returning to the fold.

Mother's turban was greenish-blue silk. Her scabs had been covered with some kind of makeup that shed dusty particles onto the collar of her blouse. Ragged brown lines were penciled in where eyebrows used to be.

Father kissed them one by one, but Hayden leaped back, flattening herself against the wall. "Hayden. Hayden," he said. He squinted, began to say more, thought better of it.

At dinner, he spoke of the Masai. "Beautiful, beautiful human specimens," he said. He stroked the stem of his wineglass. Hayden watched Arleen who served as quietly as she could, one foot on tiptoe, the other flat, her gait uneven. She bent low over the serving dishes, her mouth working in silent gyrations over her dead front tooth. Mother said her soul was lovely. If her soul was lovely why must she serve them?

Mother was wilted, Father cheerful and garrulous. He ate large slabs of pork loin, butternut squash, endive salad, kalamata olive bread. His hands were thick and asynchronous with his stringy body.

"Hayden," he said. "What would you think of accompanying me on a trip sometime soon? To China perhaps. Or maybe Brazil. It's time you saw the world, I think."

"I want to go to Brazil," Cornelia said.

"Hayden first. She's the oldest."

Hayden tried to picture herself in the Amazon jungle, she and her father alone. Minute after minute, meal after meal, all strung together with just the two of them. What would they say to each other, what would they do, who would care for Mother in her absence?

They gripped each other's eyes for an elongated second and his incandescence coursed over her, overwhelming any recognizable patterns of sweetness.

"Brazil?" she said.

The light of him flickered out for a moment. "We don't have to decide this now." He pushed back his plate. "Listen. I hear something."

They knew what it was—Russ the dog nosing at the French doors, lobbying to come in. Looks flew among the women and girls.

"A dog," Father said.

Mother rose, suddenly peppy. "Stay there, Angus. I'll see what it is."

"That damn Spofford dog, I bet. It's a complete mystery to me how so-called intelligent people can justify animal ownership."

The French doors opened. "No, doggie," they heard Mother say. "Go away." The doors closed. More muffled sound. Mother had gone outside with Russ. When she returned she stood under the archway that separated living and dining rooms, smiling hard against failing courage. Arleen kept clearing the dishes, making sound when none of the rest of them dared.

"Is that headdress really necessary, Claire?" Father said suddenly. "We're in Connecticut, not Senegal."

Mother swayed, lifted both hands to her head, and unwound the band of silk, pulling it free from her head with a flourish. "Ta-da," she said.

Arleen stopped working. Hayden hummed. Cornelia gasped. Mother's head was a wasteland.

"For God's sake, see a doctor," Father said as he left the table.

"Mrs. Claire—" Arleen said. She wiped her hands on her apron and went to Mother, whose eyes were closed and whose swaying drew wider and wider arcs. "It's okay," Arleen said again and again as she put her hand on Mother's scalp.

When the house was quiet Hayden crept downstairs, stepped outside. The night was caterwauling. Russ, cold and lonely, whined in the garage. She stepped out across the lawn. A sharp fraction of a moon illuminated her path.

Someone had beaten her to it. The side door was open, and she heard Mother's cooing. "Yes, boy. You're a good boy. A very good boy." Mother, canvas jacket over her nightgown, crouched, holding Russ's single forepaw on her knee, letting Russ lick her face.

"Mother," Hayden said.

"Hayden."

"Why didn't you tell him?"

"You know why."

"He'll find out anyway."

"Go back to bed, honey. You'll freeze."

"I can't sleep."

She nodded. "You need your sleep for school. Try to sleep."

"Tomorrow's Saturday," Hayden said. Mother nodded. "Are you really going to the doctor?" Hayden said.

"It's time for bed."

Hayden didn't move. "Don't let him rule you. Pretend he isn't here."

Mother and Russ wrestled for possession of his bone. "I rule myself, Hayden. Don't you worry."

Hayden blinked. Her tongue throbbed. Who was she to tell her mother she didn't rule herself?

"It would be good for you to travel with your father," Mother said.

She dreamed the animals had risen up; they had burst from

their exile and taken over the house. They roamed freely, eating from the pantry and the refrigerator, urinating and defecating on the carpet and quilted bedspreads. They were fractious and angry and would not be controlled.

The dream made her restless, gave her ideas. She would make her move, assist their escape. Wreak havoc. She opened the cellar door and crept down quietly. Halfway down, she stopped abruptly. In the corner by the window Mother sat on a folding chair between the two cages. She murmured to her audience of birds as she eased an X-Acto knife down her bare forearm. Blood sprang up, black as oil.

A bubble of sound formed in Hayden's throat and died there. She backed up the stairs. The stair boards whined. Mother turned. "Get out," she said, her voice guttural.

Hayden ran back up the stairs and whacked the door closed behind her. She stood with the small of her back pressed against the door handle. Where was her father? He should be there, helping. She ran through the living room, clomping, slapping furniture. Outside she ran across the backyard, over the stone wall, into the meadow. Behind her the world crashed, muffling the sound of Arleen's calls.

Chapter 11

She wouldn't go back to Emory's. She couldn't. There was too much weirdness there. Too many elusive strands. She returned to her hibernal apartment in Hoboken. Everyone had vacated the building. Usually a light burned in Mrs. Canaro's first-floor window, but even that was dark, and icicles big enough for city citations dangled like dares from the window ledges and fire escapes. She climbed the dark stairwell slowly. There was scarcely enough light to see the lock, but the key wouldn't go in anyway. Someone had stuffed toothpicks into the keyhole. She pulled them out and went inside. It was obvious she'd been robbed.

The table in the living room had been overturned and books had been pulled from the shelves. In the bedroom clothes had been dumped from dresser to floor, where they lay, heaped and sordidly inanimate, untouchable as the plumage of dead birds. The sheets had been slashed. Her anger ratcheted. *Junkies.* In the kitchen the window was wide open and winter had muscled in. Everything within a couple of feet of the opening was covered with crusty snow. But the electricity was still working and the stove still put out gas.

She wandered from room to room, picking things up. She listened to her phone messages. There was one from Saterious asking her out on a date. Needing distraction, she called him back.

"You want to go on a *date*?" he said, as if she'd asked him. He laughed through his teeth, as if he had pins in them.

"I suppose I could," she said. "I don't normally date, but I guess I could."

"Heck, I don't either. But if you'd rather not, we don't need to."

"We can," she said.

She made her way slowly to the West Village bar/restaurant that Saterious had suggested. She wasn't dating material of late. It was three days since she'd taken a light sponge bath in Emory's bathtub/table. And there was the sticky issue of her virginity. She wondered if she should have said something about that right away, though it seemed too presumptuous. He was approaching at the same time she was, and they stopped simultaneously under the bar's pink neon. He laughed and pressed her cheek with his large soft lips as if they'd met like this dozens of times before. An intimate gesture for a formal man. He wore black earmuffs that looked like complex headgear and he carried a black messenger bag like Emory's.

"This okay?" he said, glancing toward the front door, to the neon sign that said LIBBY's in cursive.

"Fine," she said.

It was dim inside, with dark oak paneling and niches of light subdividing the room like architecture. Saterious commandeered a table at the back. He assisted her with her coat, a Demetria hand-me-down with a faux-leopard collar.

"This can't be warm enough," he said, clucking maternally. He bent his attention on ordering and within minutes they stared at a tableful of international hors d'oeuvres—California roll, focaccia, stuffed mushrooms, hummus. The quantity was alarming. He ordered mojitos.

"Tropical drinks to make the night warmer," he said.

She nodded, she sipped, she ate a stuffed mushroom. She should have objected to his ordering without consulting her, but it would only have been theoretical—really there was something quite nice in it. She studied his face, looking for a gene pool. The features were strong—Eastern European? WASP?—but they were hidden by the heavy black glasses so it was hard to tell. His mouth was smooth and eager. It struck her as funny suddenly— the self-consciousness of it all, the way they both were trying to extract meaning from the smallest of gestures. She laughed and spat her mojito. He grabbed a napkin and gave it to her, knocking the California roll so it slid precariously close to the table's edge, kicking his bag so it spewed its contents. When he resumed his seat he chuckled along with her.

"I'm not usually so disarmed," he said. "I'm just not sure what to assume about you."

"Why assume anything?"

"Quite right. But your laughter confuses me—it's so private. I want to be an insider." His look turned quizzical. "What do you do for a living that allows you to dress like that?"

She looked down at her tight black jeans, at the black span- dex top which revealed a sliver of her dragon tattoo. "Stockbro- ker," she said.

"Uh-huh. Likely."

"Okay—if you must know, I'm a hairdresser. At a salon in Hoboken."

He blinked. His eyes trolled for truth. "Okay," he said. "It's not what I thought, but I'll try it on for size."

"What did you think?"

"Oh, actress, I guess. Dancer maybe. Something along those lines."

"I *am* an actress."

"Don't do this to me." He waved his hand as if erasing a blackboard. "You're only allowed to be more than one thing when you're a kid."

She drank her mojito. She hated being arch like this, untouchable. "You talk now. I'm messing things up." As she said this she was struck by the urge to confide in him. She wanted to tell him about the robbery, about Emory, even about Cornelia. He would listen. He might have words of comfort. She pictured him reaching across the table to lay his hand on her shoulder. Lovely and safe.

"I'm sorry," she said. She lowered her eyes and they fell on the spilled contents of his bag. Some pens and a red spiral notebook. A paperback Spanish-English dictionary and a hardback book by Angus Risley. The book Cornelia had given her.

"There's nothing to be sorry about," he said.

"I'm very, very sorry." She rose and put on her coat. "It's not you, I promise."

"What? Say what?"

She found a twenty, laid it on the table.

"Don't be ridiculous," he said.

From the street she looked back through the front window to see if she could see him. It made her sad to think of him sitting there alone at that table full of food.

Chapter 12

The stylus made a slow, deep line, leaving a trail of black ink, dark and permanent. Angela did not talk as she cut. At intervals she sucked air harshly through her mouth then held her breath for a long time before blowing it out her nose. Hayden smelled rubbing alcohol, Angela's vanilla Coke, her own burning flesh. She felt no pain, having morphed herself into a body that refused to honor pain.

It was a small bird on the bulb of her shoulder. A look of ferocious determination around the eyes and beak, wings thrust wide in flight. At school Olivia Broussard responded with satisfying theatrics of shock and admiration. She did not show anyone else. Not right away.

A few weeks went by. Arleen was about to mount the stairs to her third-floor room. "Come here," Hayden said. "Shut the door." Arleen sat on Hayden's bed. "Don't tell anyone," Hayden said. She peeled back her nightgown.

Arleen sighed. "Oh," she said. "Can I touch it?"

It was healed by then. Hayden nodded. Arleen stroked the bird with her callused forefinger. She sighed and pursed her lips as if she were holding something back.

Weeks later. Father was away and the house was beset with a deep-quarried stillness. Hayden lay in bed with a book on

Mesopotamian history. Her sisters were stashed in their rooms, soundless. Mother wandered in, clad in a billowing blue flannel nightgown.

"Are you sleepy?" Mother said.

"No. Are you?"

"Not in the least."

Hayden sat up, suddenly alert. "Look," she said and, surprising herself, she drew back her pajama top. A tattooed cat lay curled around her navel in a long comma of sleep.

"Oh my," Mother said. "When did you do that?"

"A while ago."

"It's beautiful," Mother said. "It's art really, isn't it?"

She put a finger on the cat's back. Hayden tightened and loosened her stomach muscles to make the cat move. She put out a purr from the back of her throat.

Mother laughed. "It would do nothing for me," she said. "If that's what you're suggesting. I'm not going to tattoo myself. We aren't the same, you and I. I am you and you're me—" She stopped herself, crossed her eyes, laughed lightly. "I mean the opposite of course."

It was a few weeks after Hayden had seen her mother cutting. Now they watched each other warily, playing catch with their burdens.

"Hayden, honey, come on a walk with me."

"No thanks."

"I'd like your help with something."

Hayden agreed to walk the length of the driveway and back. The gravel crunched under their feet like empty insect skins.

"I'm returning the animals to the shelter," Mother said. "We've taken on too much. I'd like you to help me explain this to your sisters."

"Because Father—"

"No, not because of your father. We just bit off too much."

"But you need—" Hayden said.

"What do I need? Surely not all those compromised animals. What was I thinking?" She laughed. "I will be perfectly happy without the animals." She laughed again. "So you'll help me tell the girls?"

Animal by animal the menagerie was dismantled. First Russ, then Pretty, then Arabella, then the birds. The fish were the last to go; though they did not come from the shelter that was where they ended up. Mother drove the animals away while the girls were at school. She had never been a good driver. She drove too slowly, was too enmeshed in her internal world to notice each stop sign or the line of impatient cars snaking at her tail. In the rain, sodden leaves fell on her windshield and clung there like slugs.

"We weren't pulling our weight," Hayden said to her sisters.

Cornelia said she didn't care. She was in debate club, she had other things on her mind. Sophie threw herself onto her pillow and sobbed.

"You can't take Pretty. I *love* Pretty," she wailed.

"You don't even know where Pretty is," Hayden said, feeling uncharitable.

Sophie lifted her wet face to Hayden. It was narrow and covered with freckles that seemed, in her righteousness, to glow. "I do so."

But she did not know that Pretty was already gone, already back at the shelter. Hayden wondered what would become of Sophie's love. Perhaps if they pretended that Pretty was still in the house the love would live on. Phantom love for a phantom cat. The love seemed like something formed and absolute, something that might outlive its source, a habit entombed in Sophie's heart, independent of Pretty herself.

Hayden cruised the house, clearing the desks, the cupboards, the shelves of all sharp objects. She gathered scissors, razors, letter openers, safety pins, a thin glass vase that might have been easily broken. What a minefield the house was. The kitchen was a particular problem because Arleen needed the knives for cooking. Hayden left the knives in place, but patrolled the kitchen closely.

Hayden dyed her hair blue. She earned straight As. She tattooed herself. She wasn't old enough, but when she flashed bills no one stood in her way. The menagerie they had let go reappeared on her body, a new animal every few months. The bird on her shoulder and the cat on her stomach were followed by another bird; a fire-breathing dragon on her chest; on her back a unicorn; a mouse and a butterfly in the crooks of her elbows; at the small of her back, a snake. She wanted animals everywhere, rascaling over her with abandon, leaving their numbed trails of pain.

Mother grew more secretive. She had developed a glance that reminded Hayden of her classmates, the ones who hadn't done their homework or the ones who came to class stoned. They looked at the teachers out of the corners of their eyes, guilty looks torqued with defiant anxiety. Mother no longer treated Hayden as one of a trio of daughters. She singled Hayden out. "Hayden, I know you have homework—you needn't rake leaves this afternoon." She released Hayden from nightly recitations for Father. She bought Hayden gifts. A new shirt appeared on Hayden's dresser, neatly folded in that fresh-from-the-store way. *Thought you'd look lovely in this. Love, C.* Not Mother, but C for Claire, as if they were friends.

Where was Father during all this? Father had deadlines. He was in his study with the door closed, writing, with earplugs in. What if he had not been writing? What if his study door had been open? What might have been said? And altered?

Sometimes Mother came to Hayden's room late at night. She wore floor-length gowns over her long spindle of a body. They were light-colored clothes that might be easily blood-stained. She would sit on the bed, smelling of lilacs. "Are you okay, honey?" she would ask. She stroked Hayden's arm with slow mournful fingers, up and down over the tattoos, her face narrow and sad, framed by her usual headscarf. The stroking made Hayden drowsy though she tried to stay alert.

"You should talk to your father," Mother said. "He thinks the world of you."

"Not now," Hayden said.

"Oh, I didn't mean now."

Up and down went the long lazy fingers, hypnotizing Hayden, making her beholden.

"He's under a lot of stress, but he means well. You know that don't you?"

Hayden's eyes were closed. "Yeah," she said.

"But you're okay?"

"Yeah."

"I'm glad we can talk, you and I," Mother said, drifting out of the room and leaving Hayden wide-awake.

By the time Hayden was a high school senior, she lived in a maze of predictions and arrangements. Certain things had to be done to preclude other things from happening. At night the faucets had to be checked. No dripping could be tolerated. None. The pregnant drop, the thick, mercurial bulge that grew slowly from chrome and fell with a deafening ping while the next one germinated—it had to be eliminated. Listening for the fall of each drop could drive a person crazy. And if Mother was awake, which no doubt she was (lying bug-eyed in the dark), this forming and falling of drops could derail her.

Certain phrases had to be said. Especially in the morning. *How are you, Mother? Did you sleep well?* Without these jovial greetings silence would etch itself into Mother's day, and as she and Arleen moved about the house doing their domestic tasks without the distraction of the animals, the silence would become like a rash itching and tearing at her flesh. When Hayden came home she had to say: *How was your day? Did you have a good day?* It was like buying insurance, small regular investments as hedges against full-scale disaster.

Still, despite her regimens, Hayden saw evidence in the bathroom—a bright spot of blood on the floor near the toilet, and in the wastebasket under the sink, dozens of blood-soaked tissues. Hidden, but not hidden well enough from Hayden.

When Father returned next time, she vowed she would go to him. She had to do something. *Go, Hayden, go.* She opened the door without knocking, sleeves rolled up. He sat at his desk, face thrust ceiling-ward, pen in hand. He twisted to look at her, his blue-haired, tattooed daughter.

"I'm working, Hayden," he said.

She drew breath for bravery. "Why aren't you doing anything?"

"Clue me in. To what are you referring?"

"You know what Mother's doing. Don't play dumb."

"Hayden, this isn't your concern. We've got things under control."

"How can you say that? Nothing's under control."

"I'm working now. We'll discuss this later."

Hayden snorted. She knew about the laters that never came. She wanted to hit his glittering red head. She left the room and, emboldened by anger, went to the bedroom where Mother lay.

"You have to stop," she yelled. "I know you're doing it again and you have to stop."

Mother lay unmoving, eyes closed, belly rising and falling in a perfect charade of sleep. Hayden barked, trying to arouse her. Mother slept determinedly on.

Hayden was huddled on her bed when Arleen found her. Arleen took Hayden's head in her lap. She rested her splayed hand over Hayden's forehead. The hand was heavy and warm, and it smelled of peanut butter and bacon. Arleen rocked back and forth in a rhythm Hayden knew, and Hayden rocked with her.

Chapter 13

Hayden had taken a day off from work and now she dreaded going back. Too many busybodies. Too many questions. And Emory would be there pretending nothing had happened between them. But she had to go back, of course, and she soldiered in there, thinking of Marmite, a teacher of hers in beauty school.

Marmite was a short, stocky, sadistic woman with a missionary insistence that her students were an inferior lot. They called her Marmite because of a slightly rancid odor she gave off. It was odd that she taught styling, because her own style was so notably uninspired. She wore plaid button-down shirts and belted denim skirts, and she clipped her long wiry gray hair in a red barrette at the back of her neck. She strode from table to table, berating the girls for their bad habits: *Don't you know what hard work is? Don't you ever bathe?* No one liked Marmite, but they all felt sorry for her. Before teaching she had owned a salon on Wilshire that had failed. They knew she resented her students' bright futures. But the most unusual thing about Marmite was her cache of obscure facts.

"Listen up, girls," she had said to them one day. "I'm going to tell you about the Spartans at Thermopylae."

"What's Thermopylae?" asked Linda Blake.

"What's Thermopylae?" Marmite stared hard at Linda, who

was a tiny, thin-lipped, thin-skinned girl with such white-blond hair she looked, though was not, albino. "Are you girls dunces? Is there something wrong with you? Do we have a learning problem here? Just because you're in beauty college doesn't give you a right to be a *know-nothing* about other subjects. Does *nobody* here know about Thermopylae?"

Hayden, it happened, did, but she was not going to cast her lot with Marmite by saying so. So Marmite, prefacing her story with a cantata of sighs, told them her version of the events at Thermopylae. The Spartans had prided themselves on courage and military discipline—*Surely you all know this*—but the Persian army they faced outnumbered them fifteen to one, which gave the Spartans a serious case of self-doubt. To conceal their apprehensions and put forth an image of insouciant ease, they passed the prebattle hours dressing one another's hair.

Really? That had not been part of Harvard's ancient history curriculum. But Hayden realized Marmite was probably right. That was what hair did for humans—it showed the world who you were and how you felt about things. Sometimes good hair could make all the difference.

Hayden slunk to her station, ignoring Tina's butt-goosing. "Okay, be that way," Tina said.

"No way," Hayden said, smiling insouciantly like a Spartan, "no way at all."

At her station she sat and listened to her messages, mostly from people she'd canceled the prior day. She stared at the rheumy trails of condensation traveling down the glass. She stared at the fish who hovered more than they swam, their eyes vacant, resigned, certainly nihilistic. Emory was unlocking her drawer and laying out tools. Wigless, she looked very masculine. She did not look at Hayden, said nothing either.

Hayden's first client was Felice Merkin, a real estate agent, always on the go, always talking loudly through a wide, lipsticked gash of a mouth.

"Booming," she kept saying. "Still booming. Booming despite Armageddon. Can you believe it?"

Usually when Felice came in Hayden enjoyed reminding her colleagues of the meaning of Felice's last name—a wig for the female pudenda—but not today. Today it didn't seem funny. Hayden nodded at Felice's monologue, produced the requisite yeahs and nos. Then she was face-to-face with Bella, Bella on tiptoes, bringing her soft wizened face to Hayden's ear.

"I hope you don't mind, dear, but I'm going to have Emory do my touchup. Emory was just so confident with the razor. I hope it's all right with you." She pulled off her skullcap so Hayden could appreciate the gray-white fuzz that had grown in. "Everyone loves it," Bella said. With a finger wave she twirled off to Emory's chair.

When Felice was gone Hayden went out. She had an hour before her next appointment and she couldn't stand to watch Bella and Emory in perfidious chitchat across the salon. Perhaps it wasn't directed at Hayden, perhaps it was. The February sun was wan. She wandered down Washington Street, thinking how easy it was for a single person to get dislodged from life. When you lived in a family you woke up daily and gazed into the faces around you and they reminded you of who you were.

In the hardware store she looked at space heaters. She asked the clerk about the difference between the seventy-five-dollar model and the hundred-dollar model. "Well, this one is much better," he said, pointing to the more expensive one.

"But what about it is better?"

"It's got more features."

"What features?"

"For starters it's not going to burn your house down."

"Never mind," she said. "I'll figure it out."

He walked away shaking his head. Hayden bought the cheaper model which was so big she had to cradle it in both arms. On the way back to Pizzazz she stopped at Finelli's, the Italian pastry shop she and her salon mates frequented. Vince and Stella, the owners, were sniping at each other as they moved up and down the counter, filling customer orders. Stella played the stoic, rolling her eyes at the customers for support.

"Vi-ince," she said, goading him toward the next waiting customer.

It was Emory, set to place an order. She read her list, a full litany of the bakery's offerings—cannolis, tarts, quaresimales. An order for the entire salon, no doubt. Vince shook his head, looked to the back of the line, and began assembling Emory's order with a disgruntled flurry of his arms.

"Move it," said Stella. "We're losing customers."

Vince grunted. "Orders for the whole Russian army."

"Move it," Stella yelled again. She grabbed the bag from Vince and raised it high. "Who's this for? It comes to $15.65."

"Jesus, Stella. Over there. For that—" He looked up now from where he wiped crumbs and stared assessingly at Emory. Emory, waiting for his next words, did not flinch. "For that *person*," continued Vince, "that *whatever*." His mouth curled in disgust.

"Who?" Stella said.

Emory held out a wad of cash.

"That *thing* in front of you," Vince said, his gaze digging Emory.

Emory's face stiffened slightly, became more resolute, it seemed to Hayden—more manly?

"Get over it," Hayden called out to Vince. "Leave her alone."

Vince shook his head. It was not clear if he had heard Hayden. But Emory had heard. She turned slightly before collecting her change then she ambled to the door in a stride led by shoulders not hips, the locomotion of a person who has power and time and wants to make a show of invincibility. The next person in line pushed up to the counter while Vince was still grousing.

"Go back to Manhattan is what I say. We got enough weirdos."

Emory was out the door. Hayden hefted her box and followed. Outside Emory was already crossing the street. Hayden almost hailed her, but then thought better of it and followed a judicious twenty feet behind. There was nothing more to be said.

Later, when the outdoor light had purpled and a jewel-like moment of near silence sneaked up on the salon, Emory came up behind Hayden. Hayden was working on Frances Demarco then, a retired schoolteacher with a watchful air about her.

"Oh my," Frances said, startled. In the mirror, a trinity of faces. They stared at one another, guarded by glass: Frances, Hayden, Emory. No one smiled automatically, the glass allowed that.

"I owe you one," Emory said.

"Big difference it made," Hayden said.

"Yeah, well some people are assholes. At least no one pulled a knife on me."

Frances frowned and looked discreetly away. Emory touched Hayden's elbow briefly and withdrew with her swaggering stride. Frances turned to watch. She was on the cusp of speech. She started, stopped, started, stopped. Hayden recognized the pronoun problem. "That person is new here?" Frances finally said and Hayden nodded.

Emory helped Hayden home with her heater. In silence they walked the quiet side streets back to Hayden's apartment, each carrying a side of the box. It was dark by then, and they traveled through pools of light and shadow, flat-footed for traction on the ice. They were tentative with each other again. They set up the heater in Hayden's kitchen and waited for the cold to slacken. The apartment felt safe once more. Hayden showed Emory around, told her about the robbery, how invasive it felt though nothing much was taken. Then she heated some pea soup and made buttered toast to go with it. They ate by candlelight. Hayden's respiration was off. She couldn't remember what she was supposed to apologize for.

Halfway through their bowls of soup the chill went off them.

"I was just bent because you're like me," Emory said. "You never learned how to talk. I know it's not your fault—you're a fucking blue blood. So forget it."

Hayden nodded.

"But your tattoos are lies. You know that don't you? They're misleading about you."

Chapter 14

Emory set down her spoon and kept on talking in a voice that was sepulchral, monotone almost. Hayden was seduced by that voice, summoned straight into Emory's brain, so the things Emory recalled felt to Hayden like memories of her own. Emory talked about watching the people who came to her father's motel, Frank's Motel, a blue-and-white building on the main road of Duck Key. When Emory got to be ten or eleven she would help her father out behind the front desk. While he wrote down registration information, Emory would fetch keys, maps, tourist brochures. She would lay these things on the countertop and stand by, listening for her father's next request.

While she waited, she watched the guests. They were couples mostly, sometimes families with kids, largely people from up north seeking warmth and rest, escape of some kind, people who had driven for hours through hellacious weather that kept them on high alert so when they arrived they had the gray skin and pouched goggle eyes of insomniacs. The motel was not fancy enough to attract people who took planes. They surveyed the place, wondering if it was really worth the drive, the exhaustion of travel. *Does that traffic ever die down?* they asked. *Is it always this humid?* They looked tired and prematurely old.

Emory squinted at them, isolating their body parts to test out her ideas. Was there something in that ear that made it a woman's ear? Was it smaller than a man's ear? Did it sponsor less hair? She would look at noses this way, and knees, and necks. The same questions always arose: What made those parts female? What made them male? Maybe an ear was simply an ear. She was startled by the variety she saw in ears alone. No two looked alike. Some had lobes the size of small pancakes; other had hardly any lobes at all. Some were ridged and wrinkled, others cupped like funnels.

If there weren't too many guests Emory and her father would go out to the pool at night. He threw pennies to the bottom, and she dove for them under lights that cast wavering shadows across the water and made her feel as if the pool were a miniature ocean, unknown creatures lurking at its depths. She always found the pennies. When she got cold she would get out and sit in her father's lap. He looped his heavy arms over her bare, goosebumped legs, and she could feel his belly and chest through the thin fabric of his shirt. His body was old (he'd been past fifty when she was born), and though his muscles were strong, the skin around them was drapey as rayon and jiggled with his movements. When he surrounded her with his arms, she felt how alike they were. She imagined their insides: the pink of their organs surrounded by the blue of veins, the red of blood, the white and yellow of fat. They matched inside, she knew—both a bit shy, a bit sad, happy to be left alone.

She couldn't talk to her daddy much, but she knew he loved her. She knew she made him proud when she swam two and a half lengths of the pool under water at age six (*Such a strong critter you are*, he would say); and when she learned to register guests by herself when she was eleven, asking all the right questions and writing the answers in legible block letters on the correct forms, he told her she was a smart critter. He was proud when she, without being asked, gathered up the palm fronds fallen from the trees in front of the motel and piled them in the big laundry basket, or when she swept the front office and tidied the map displays, made fresh coffee for the guests, and laid out more Lorna Doones. She hated to disappoint him. When the motel's front portico came down in Hurricane Agnes she helped him rebuild it. Every few weeks she trimmed his hair as he told her to, shears on the front part, razor at the back of his neck. *I don't know how,* she had objected at first, but he gave her a few pointers and soon she was good enough that some of the motel employees were asking her too.

She knew she could never tell him her secrets. He loved her too much to see how different she was. He did not see her at school, did not see how little she fit in with the other girls, how hard it was for her to rise to their talk. Everyone else saw it, she was certain—the other girls, the teachers—but it was not the kind of thing anyone mentioned (they wouldn't say anything to her at least, or to her father). She wasn't the only girl who kept her hair short and always wore trousers, but everyone knew that attire, while it said a great deal, didn't speak to everything. In eighth grade she was the only girl who could do fifteen pull-ups—the only girl, in fact, who could do any pull-ups at all—but even that was not essential. It was something less nameable that set her apart. It was how she rattled inside herself. To her, that rattling was a distinct sound, the horrible screech of he-parts and she-parts chafing against one another.

When she was a young child the boys had taken her in, let her play their games, valued her speed and agility. She felt she was one of them. A few other girls hung out with them too. But in the polarized world of junior high she lost her place. Once, in seventh grade, she took her cafeteria tray to a table of boys she knew. They were the Merson boys and Zack Gemino and Kevin Hooly, boys she had played kickball with that summer. Someone new sat with them, a boy with flat blond hair that covered his head like fabric. He had moved recently from California. He ducked under the table when he saw her approach. "Cootie smell," he said. He made gagging sounds and one by one, Kevin, Zack, and the Merson boys gagged along with him and joined him under the table. Emory sat alone, looking around like a felon, deeply humiliated, hoping no one had seen. She got up and walked away, leaving her corn dog and chips and the Dixie cup of coleslaw. She didn't care that she got a ticket that day for not busing her tray.

The girls' table she didn't even try to approach. They lived in a blizzard of talk. She couldn't churn out enough words to interest them, and she wore the wrong clothes. Girls her age were trying to show as much skin as they could and still get away with it. Emory wore T-shirts that hung in a flat plane over her burgeoning, still-small breasts. Small as they were, those breasts disgusted her. They were body parts that moved without muscles to motivate them. Sometimes she experimented with winding an Ace bandage across her chest, flattening everything. She took to sitting alone at lunch, head bent to her food, hating the other girls and lusting after them, wishing the boys hadn't turned on her, knowing it was unlikely to change.

It's not like you don't know this shit, she said. *You grew up along with everyone else. You heard, along with everyone else, what is and isn't normal. You know the rewards of normal, so you try to strike a balance. This I'll live with, this I won't.*

At the motel in the afternoons and evenings, everything was the same. She took on more and more work, helping with the books, regulating the pool's chlorine, repainting the walls in the office a light orange. By eighth grade she had met a guy on the beach who worked at the hardware store and who introduced her to marijuana. A few strong hits before school made everything more tolerable.

Was her father clueless, or just too loving to say anything? Some nights after the office was locked up, they would walk down to the beach together. Their strides were the same length (though his was a bit slower) and their hips the same height from the ground. In the semidarkness she felt their differences melt away. Sometimes she felt like telling him he was her best friend, but she guessed he already knew that.

Emory's story had a million possible endings, or perhaps none at all. Listening, Hayden finished her soup slowly and watched wax drool from the lips of the two squat candles. She watched Emory's shadow thinning and deepening on the wall behind her. Her silhouette was that of a person without maleness or femaleness. The heart, the kidneys, the liver—they had no gender, Hayden thought. Neither did the lungs or the intestines. Mice, she had read, shared 97.5 percent of their DNA with humans, bananas 50 percent, so how different could men and women be? Slight air currents blew the candle flame, so Emory's shadow wavered as if it were alive and separate from Emory herself. Hayden contemplated her own body parts—was there woman-ness in them or not? Did a female force oscillate through her entire person, or was it confined to one central place?

"Then Daddy died," Emory said.

She was living in Miami by then, was part of the gay and lesbian community. "That was before we called ourselves queer," she said. "I'm a lot older than you are."

She had a pool cleaning business and made ends meet with

occasional salon work. She didn't love hairdressing, but she knew how to do it and it helped pay the bills. She had a girlfriend named Peg. Peg was tall, broad-hipped, big-breasted. Her body was a marvel to Emory, as was her frothing emotion. Peg liked to examine every feeling she had. She laid them out like endlessly fascinating specimens, categorizing them and looking for patterns. This habit amused Emory; it made her feel strong and even. They had bonded quickly, she and Peg, taking easily to roles of butch and femme. They both loved swimming and they spent hours in the ocean, sometimes stroking with the full elastic reach of their arms, sometimes hanging in one place with legs drawn close, floating like fetuses. For a while, seven years, Emory had felt mostly right with Peg—though many nights she still dreamed of being a man, a particularly tall man walking down the beach with an exposed furry penis that everyone gaped at—but her daddy's death cast everything differently.

The motel in Duck Key was willed to her along with everything else. She closed the motel down and lived there without Peg through the winter months, traveling to Miami once or twice a week to keep her pool cleaning business alive and to maintain her salon connections. And to see Peg, of course, who was beside herself with missing Emory. It was tourist season and Emory remembered how hard she and Frank had always worked in those winter months. But that year things were unseasonably cold and the tourists bundled themselves for beach walks and did not look happy. She missed Frank so intensely that her other problems seemed minor. Most days she spent stoned, walking on the beach for hours. But after six months of willed numbness she felt the old rattling again. With Frank dead she was free to do what she wanted, make real the dream she'd held inside herself since she was a young child. Frank would want her to be happy, she was sure of it. She sold the motel, moved back to Miami, and went to work on herself. She was thirty-one; it was time. She began seeing a therapist and she opened up the truth of things, the long-sealed box. She couldn't believe she had put this off so long, had not even talked to Peg about the possibility; now that change was in reach, she wanted manhood desperately.

There's stuff you have to tell the therapists and the doctors and you have to say it right because they're the ones that have to sign on the dotted line. You say stuff about not feeling normal all your life, about having an inner man inside that doesn't match your outside persona. I knew what *to say of course—but not* how *to say it.*

Hayden tried to imagine the person you were, the person who everyone saw, not being the person you wanted to be.

You need reasons? There are a million reasons. I don't see things like a woman. I don't talk like women talk. I don't move like women move. I feel different things than a woman feels.

She loved women. She loved women as she might love rare orchids, or wild endangered cats. She loved their exoticism. For years she had watched them closely, considering whether she could learn to do as they did (no, she couldn't), and later, to understand why those things had been so difficult for her. She had taken note of the easy laughter of women, their perennial talk, the way they drew their hands nonchalantly over one another's backs. After a while she stopped feeling she should imitate them, but the cataloguing continued. She noted the way women flirted with sidelong glances, with secret, close-mouthed smiles, and the way a woman could laugh, implying she knew others better than they knew themselves. She saw that while women said a lot they rarely said everything they meant.

She watched men too, of course. She envied their staunch impermeable bodies and their impervious stares, like thick-walled tunnels, guarding their thoughts in darkness. Like them, she lived in the world of actions, not words.

She knew what she was, but not how to get there.

Peg hated all this. Every night Peg wept. Why wasn't being butch enough? Didn't Emory see that she would never be a *real* man, no matter what she did? Peg worked in an art gallery. Men hit on her all the time. She laughed it off. She didn't hate men, but she found them pathetic. Why would Emory want to be one of them? When Peg was anxious she would get up in the middle of the night and bake. She would wake Emory from deep sleep and force her to eat hot brownies or steaming pieces of blueberry pie. Peg herself would not eat—she would watch, trailing her long fingers across Emory's neck or shoulder or back, looking for some sure way in.

Peg was a lesbian. She had always been a lesbian. She wanted to remain a lesbian. She did not want Emory to change. If Emory became a man and Peg kept loving Emory, then Peg would no longer be a lesbian. It bothered Peg to think about this. All her friends were lesbians. Some of her lesbian friends hated men and would not associate with them. Peg herself had been known to feel hostile toward men. Not for anything they'd done necessarily, just for being men and carrying attitudes of entitlement. Emory assured Peg that she would be a different kind of man, a man whose sensibility was formed by having once been a woman. But Peg was not convinced. What if Emory's pheromones changed and Peg was no longer attracted to Emory? That was perfectly possible, wasn't it? The results of tampering with hormones were anyone's guess.

When Emory told Peg she planned to live in drag for a while, Peg didn't get out of bed for three days. Emory cut things off between them; she moved out of their shared bungalow. Her therapist had told her she needed to work among people. Pool cleaning was a solitary business in which no one noticed her gender. So Emory went to work part-time in a new Miami salon as a man, using men's rooms for the first time. She used the stalls and made sure her feet were facing backward. She fashioned a homemade, stand-up peeing system with a tube and a spoon. After a year she had her mastectomy. By then she and Peg had patched things together again. Peg was against the surgery, but even she—when she allowed herself to look—had to admit its success. The nipples sometimes came out uneven in these surgeries, but Emory's were perfectly spaced, and the scars accentuated the strength of her pectorals. Emory was careful to use vitamin E oil on the scars. Her surgeon was proud of his workmanship and thought the scars would fade.

Not long after the surgery she began injections of T. The first indications of change were subtle but certain. The muscles pulled together in greater surety. Hair follicles along the arms and chest and cheeks and chin pushed forth like germinating seeds. A few lonely dark hairs grew on each of her hands. Her stride seemed to lengthen, her back discovered an ancient strength. She had energy and heat and enthusiasm for everything. In the streets, in crowds along the beach, people seemed to clear a path for her. *Excuse me, sir*, she heard for the first time. They had not said *sir* before the hormones. She had not fooled people so deeply with clothing alone. Now it jarred a little, but pleasantly, and inside she smiled. But she never gave an answering look to the people who said these things. Like a man now she looked above, through, and beyond. The glue in other people's eyes that used to hold her was gone. She had achieved her father's cool-eyed distance. Her father was inside her now for sure; she felt it when she reached for things. The blunt outstretching of the arm.

A new decisive spareness of movement. And her voice was unassailable. It was deep and arresting. It made people listen.

But Peg kept railing, telling Emory every day that the project was doomed. *It's like me trying to become Chinese. I could have a million operations but that wouldn't make me Chinese. It's arrogant, trying to steal someone else's identity. Anyway, you're too delicate to be a man. And medical science is not equipped to build you a real penis. You already act like a man. Isn't that enough? Don't you have a good life? Is it power you're after? Fucking male privilege. You're deluding yourself. Whatever you're after is a mirage.*

Sometimes Peg would throw herself against the sides of buildings in public bouts of weeping. She would shout her objections so passersby, after quick shocked glances, would lower their heads in embarrassment and give Peg and Emory wide berth. It was the upcoming hysterectomy that upset Peg, more than all the earlier things Emory had done. *If you let go of your uterus you'll never have the chance to be a woman again.* As if until now everything had been provisional.

Emory had said everything she could say. She was sick of justifying herself. She wasn't intentionally trying to hurt Peg; it was Peg herself who was letting herself be hurt. *Does my love count for nothing?* Peg would say, her usually raucous voice plaintive. Emory, without fail, felt selfish and small, and utterly unmanly. Emory wanted to live in a world where she didn't have to explain herself daily, where she could settle into being who she was without hurting someone else in the process. She moved out again from the bungalow and got her own apartment.

When Emory had the hysterectomy Peg was furious, then depressed. She spent a month in bed, taking leave from her job. Every day after work Emory would stop by to check on her. Peg would tell Emory the details of her day, the state of all her body's systems. Her diarrhea was better, but her feet were still cold. Emory listened, dull and corseted. Peg had always been prone to ups and downs. Emory had seen her go from laughing to crying in the space of a minute. It was one of the fascinating things about Peg. But this had gone beyond normal. Each evening now ended in a bout of Peg's shouting or crying that made Emory restless to get home to her own place. Finally, to reassure Peg, Emory stopped taking hormones, put everything on hold. But Peg didn't improve. She ended up in the hospital, on a psychiatric ward. She was medicated for manic depression. She was a striking woman with a full head of reddish-blond hair. In the street people would turn to take a second look at her. She talked a lot and fast; in groups she was always the center of attention. There had been no way to tell from looking at her that she would turn out to be so fragile.

Peg was released from the hospital after six weeks. When she was somewhat stabilized Emory came to New York to float. The timing was perfect because Mel and Rose wanted out of their apartment for a while anyway. Emory wasn't sure how much more changing she could do. She'd burned through most of the money from the motel sale. Peg's despair had become her own, despite all her efforts at fending it off. She needed relief from Peg. Crazy as Peg was, her words and ideas had still managed to worm their way into Emory's head. Emory often thought about the sex-changing fish the trans community reified; they could change from male to female and back as procreation demanded. Maybe that really was a better way to be.

"Man, woman, who the hell cares—I thought maybe I could settle for something in between. I wanted to play with that idea." Emory closed her eyes. She looked used up, older. The candlelight excavated wrinkles the size of spider silk along her upper lip.

"Turns out there's no floating. In between doesn't cut it. People care what you are. They care even if you're a complete stranger. They can't stand not knowing."

"But—" Hayden said.

"No. Think about it. *You* cared, didn't you? You've been giving me that look since day one." She shook her head, fell mute, then stood abruptly and found herself a water glass in the cabinet. She ran the faucet but the frozen pipes rattled and yielded nothing. In the refrigerator she found a plastic water jug, and she drank from it greedily, filling the kitchen with the sound of swallowing. When the jug was restored she stood in place, and Hayden felt afraid in some elemental way for all the uncertainty in living a life, any life.

"Peg might be right," Emory said.

Hayden thought she should say something reassuring, but she had no idea what that would be. She had no particular wisdom to offer and would have felt silly offering platitudes.

Emory put her bowl of soup in the sink, only a spoonful eaten. "Don't say anything," she said. She stood still again by the sink, her gaze directed out the window at the behemoth icicle.

She left without exchanging any conventional pleasantries. Hayden stayed awake for hours—now a habit—thinking about Emory and what she had said. How alone Emory was with both parents dead, no siblings. Peg was no salve for Emory's brand of loneliness. Every once in a while Hayden dozed off, and in her dreams Emory and Cornelia merged; Cornelia stood in the middle of Sixth Avenue, hugely, almost absurdly pregnant, her hand aloft like an outgoing warrior, saying: *I'm a man. I think I'm a man. Do I look like a man?*

When Hayden and her sisters used to play the "If You Could Be Anything" game Hayden had always wanted to be a tree—a deciduous tree, a maple perhaps, some tree with broad leaves that would dry and curl and crackle in fall and appear again in the spring. Not alone in a field, prey to lightning, but on the edge of a wood where, protected, anonymous, she could gaze out. She had liked the thought of not having to go anywhere. She would let the natural forces—rain, hail, wind, snow—have their way with her. And if her limbs broke, if deer ate her bark, she would learn to accept those things. In spring her sap would work a slow path through her trunk and branches, increasing her girth, lengthening her many parts.

"Why a tree?" Cornelia said dismissively. "They can't even *move*."

"They don't need to move."

"There might be a drought and they'd need water from some other place."

Hayden shook her head. Stillness appealed to her. Being part of a forest. Standing your ground no matter what.

"And they don't talk either. They don't even have voices," Cornelia said.

"Maybe they *think*," Sophie offered.

"What would they need to say?" Hayden said.

She had loved the thought of wordlessness, of not having a mouth that people watched all the time while you thought of something to say. She loved the staunch blankness of trees, the fact that they had nothing to prove. Cornelia had wanted to be an international lawyer from a very young age so she could travel to other countries and tell people who and what was right and wrong. She wanted to save people and have everyone thank her afterward for having done the saving. Sophie never wanted to be the same thing twice: a clown acrobat once, then a zookeeper, then a "submariner." How far could they stretch? As far as they wanted? As far as their wills would take them? Hayden knew she wasn't going to be a tree, but she guessed that Cornelia might be an international lawyer. As for Emory, who knew? The purview and force of any human will seemed small to Hayden now, perhaps only an illusion.

Hayden thought of Cornelia shooting up Sixth Avenue in the warmth and safety of her cab. She was almost a mother. She talked to Father regularly, saw him regularly; she read his books. She had forgiven him, Hayden supposed. No, that wasn't it—she had never blamed him in the first place.

Chapter 15

It was late September when Emory arrived in the wounded city. The East Village apartment belonging to Mel and Rose was small and dark. They meant to come back eventually, but meanwhile they had taken all their things with them, leaving an empty shell, an unmarked space that said nothing about the people or person who might live there. The darkness suited Emory. The smallness suited her. Mel and Rose couldn't wait to get out of the city. They couldn't wait to get down to Miami to Emory's one-bedroom apartment, small by Miami standards but to them palatial, light, not polluted by hemorrhaging grief. For Emory, this was the right place to be. The city's mood matched hers and swaddled her in a sorrow that was so much larger than her own.

By day Emory walked the streets trying to neutralize the battleground of her body. She had tapered off T gradually, not for Peg but because Peg had said certain things, about self-hatred and self-love, about femininity and separation and connection and divisions between people, about divisions between self and body. Peg had said so many things Emory could hardly remember them all. Peg was not of sound mind. Peg had fallen apart, and been put back together but only partially. She still had a crack in her, like Humpty Dumpty. The depression, the hospitalization, it was all because of Emory, all Emory's fault. Peg was smart. Even from the depths of her craziness she had a way with words that Emory did not have. *Incisive* was a good word for Peg—her mind scissored through things. She left Emory thinking. Emory had often pretended not to take Peg seriously—Peg was so histrionic she was easy to laugh off. But finally, when someone who loved you said the things Peg had said, things that might contain truth, you listened. You might not respond immediately, but you filed things away for later examination. This was Emory's later.

New York's scarred geometry became her temporary home. She left her footprints on sidewalks still coated with ash. A strange, unruly time to get to know this city she had never known before, a place both bellicose and tender, deeply dysphoric. No one on the streets of New York noticed her. There was only the singular calamity, the unbelievability of it all. People wept openly on street corners, and a million small acts of kindness happened daily, like the two gangly boys, underwear showing above their jeans, who assisted an elderly man across the street, or the clerk in the cheese shop who gave Emory a free wheel of brie one day, for no particular reason. The parallels Emory saw were eerie—too many congruities. A strong city reviling its moments of weakness, understanding its altered sense of self. Emory's body had weakened too—since stopping the testosterone—and all the walking did nothing to change that. Her pectorals were softening, her biceps had shrunk. She looked spindly again, a bantam weight. Glancing at her reflection in storefronts she saw the ways she no longer measured up to manhood. But she had opted for this and tried to watch it with equanimity. Still, for so long she had trained herself to respect—no, worship—the integrity of categories. Without categories how could change be measured? Now she was testing, trying to embrace what remained strong in her, determined to find the force in bio-female. But the fact was she wasn't really bio-female anymore. XX perhaps, but little else. Womb gone, breasts gone. She still had some non-female facial hair growth, and some on her chest and arms. Just before Peg's breakdown, when Emory was exhilarated by the powerful forward momentum of transition, she had wanted to say something to Peg—something about how as a male she could see the strength in femininity, she understood how being female wasn't all about weakness. When she was an almost-full male there was no urgency to excise the feminine. Now, off T, sliding back, losing verve, she wasn't sure.

She had no work yet. Her work was thinking, sorting things out, living off meager savings. Mel and Rose weren't charging her rent—what true friends they were. Emory was still paying off the surgeries—in a couple of months she would have to find work and there was certainly not much demand for pool cleaning in New York. To conserve, she ate cheese and day-old bread. She spent more money than she knew she should in thrift stores. She had bought a couple of men's jackets, two new wigs, three miniskirts, a couple of collared shirts, a pair of orange plaid jeans, a neon-green crocheted sweater vest. Her growing collection brought comfort. It made her feel she could be anything. Some days she went out as a man, other days as a woman. Both felt like drag.

Every day Peg called, sometimes twice a day, maybe more—how would Emory know without an answering machine? The calls, answered or not, were torture: all that guilt, all those questions without answers. It was better not to speak.

She kept track of that year's tropical storms and enumerated them in her head. An epicene mantra: *Allison, Barry, Chantal, Dean, Erin, Felix, Gabrielle, Humberto, Iris, Jerry, Karen, Lorenzo* . . . Rage, big surprise, was now officially male and female.

She was afraid of getting fat. Fat was feminine, bad feminine. If she was fat the choice would be gone. Passing either way was easier when she was slight. So she ate one small meal a day. Occasionally she went to a bar on Second Avenue and ordered a bowl of soup and a glass of wine, eating and drinking slowly as she eavesdropped on other people's conversations. She was synchronized with this city in mourning, scarred and yearning. She did not even know what she grieved for most—for her father, for the old Peg, for the girl in herself, for the boy who couldn't get out. She grieved for some ineffable sense of wanting to arrive home somewhere, at least in her own body.

The city had been cut. Its look was not natural. Cutting was not natural. That was what Peg used to say. *How could you cut your own skin, your own genitals? If you revile your parts then you must revile mine too. Do you think I like the size of the ass I've got? No, I don't, but I don't cut it off. I live with it. I accept it. No—I embrace it. That's the challenge of living. Maybe some boys should live in the skins of girls. Maybe there's a lesson in that. Things are never perfect. The world is full of disjuncture, disharmony, amalgamations, things living within other things. The bacteria in our stomach, the mold in blue cheese. What is your fight anyway? I certainly hope you're not going for penetration. Whatever it is—let it go.*

Every Sunday in February and into early March Emory and Hayden went adventuring. Hayden told Tina she was too tired to go out. She felt bad bailing on Tina, but reasoned with herself that just because they had a habit of Sunday walks did not mean they had a contract for them. Tina and Hayden had been friends for a long time and Hayden was sure they would continue to be friends and she hoped that Tina would forgive her—because just then Hayden could not explain why she was so drawn to the enigma that was Emory. She did not understand it herself. She was not in love, but she was certainly hooked, intrigued, a little bedazzled. Emory's age cinched the hold.

Emory was eager to know the city and Hayden was an avid guide. Not that Hayden was so knowledgeable herself, having never actually lived in the city and having only lived in Hoboken for four years, but she still knew more than Emory. Emory had spent most of her early months in New York below Fourteenth Street and there were still plenty of streets she had never set foot on, plenty of major buildings she'd never eyeballed up close. Their routine was to meet somewhere near the PATH station around ten when the streets were still sparsely populated; most people were still inside, pajama'd and quilt-wrapped, sipping coffee and working their way through their favorite sections of the *Times*. Hayden and Emory felt such ownership of those barren Sunday morning streets. Sometimes they would walk right down the center of an avenue, dodging the occasional taxi, for the sheer novelty and rebellious pleasure of it. Emory wanted to walk everywhere. They were about the same height, but Emory was stronger and leaner despite being nearly fifteen years older than Hayden. Often Hayden had to jog to keep up.

Sometimes they would go to museums. Emory's favorite was the Museum of Natural History where she was drawn to the ocean exhibits. She was already very knowledgeable about fish and she would come alive explaining things. Long past the ocean exhibits, when they were passing meteorites or fossils, she would be blinking more quickly than usual and gesticulating and regaling Hayden with factoids about the sexual plasticity of most fish around coral reefs, or the bioluminescence of jellyfish.

"There's nothing very dramatic about one of a thing," Emory was fond of saying. "It takes a whole school of fish, or a flock of birds, or a cloud of butterflies to see their fundamental nature. One species member alone has no significance at all."

When they left the museum Emory would pause at the top of the steps, arrested by the sight of people streaming in and out of Central Park, by the panoply of homo sapiens whose fundamental nature she seemed to be seeing. "But the same is true in reverse—just because you know something about a species does not make it predictive for any given individual."

Hayden dragged Emory to the Metropolitan Museum of Art. Despite her mother's influence she had not grown up loving art, but now it interested her. She wondered what it was that made some people need to make art and others need to look at it. She didn't think she had ever been to the Met before, but as soon as she stepped into the expansive white lobby with its marble floor and impressive columns, she remembered a visit with Mother, long ago, when she was only eight or nine. They had gone down to New York on the train, just the two of them. It was a windy, sun-struck day in mid fall, one of those days in which the boundaries between things appear sharper than usual. Mother had taken Hayden out of school. Mother was mischievous and animated, her clothing a vivid, almost gaudy vermillion, her gaze flitting here and there like one of the wind-blown leaves. On the train going down she kept pointing out the window to the bejeweled, wind-whipped water, talking nonstop about the impossible beauty of things. It seemed to Hayden that all the business-suited commuters were looking at them, at this nervous gazelle of a woman clad in exuberant clothing, unleashing a fountain of words. But Hayden was excited too, and pleased to be out of school though it seemed as if they were doing something they really shouldn't be doing. At the museum they ambled randomly from room to room—*Oh, Hayden you* have *to see this!* Mother said of at least one thing in every room—finally arriving at a display of Caravaggios where she stood in front of one painting for a long time. Hayden quickly became bored. After trying to amuse herself with people-watching she began sighing and tugging her mother and begging her to leave. They went to the Plaza for tea, and Mother let Hayden eat two entire platefuls of pink and green petit fours.

It was astounding to Hayden that she had not remembered this excursion until stepping into the lobby with Emory. Of course she had to drag Emory to the Caravaggios. Once there, she easily identified the painting that had captivated Mother. It was *The Holy Family with the Infant Saint John the Baptist*, a work that depicted a toddler-sized Saint John looking longingly up toward Jesus, Joseph, and Mary as if he wished to be part of their family. St. John's arm was up-stretched to touch the buttocks of Jesus, and his hair, his back, the side of his face were all visible, but his eyes were not. Joseph's down-turned eyes were also invisible. Largely in shadow, gently corrective, he tried with one hand to remove John's arm from Jesus. Jesus stood on his mother's knee, clutching her neck possessively. Though his bare body was bright with light his eyes, too, were obscured. The eyes that could be seen fully, that drew the viewer's attention, were Mary's eyes. She was unequivocally the subject of the painting: Mary, the female, the mother, the still and silent figure who perched on the edge of a table gripping its edge. Her dress was a robust but cautionary red; a narrow ivory shawl, gauzy enough to reveal the red beneath, draped her shoulders and spiraled around one arm clear to the wrist, as if to restrain her there. Her brown eyes—bigger, rounder, and more inexpressibly sad than any eyes Hayden had ever seen—soared out at an angle and penetrated the fourth wall, staring at some imagined world beyond the viewer. She was not present in that moment with husband and son. She wanted to be elsewhere, unhindered, free, possibly childless. She was the picture of longing, of sorrow, of a woman caught in one world and yearning for another.

Emory had to drag Hayden away.

They shopped on Orchard and Canal Streets as Hayden had done with Tina. Invariably, Emory would find some odd second-hand item—a red leather necktie, or a purple paisley scarf, or a fleece-lined herringbone vest—to add to the collection of costumes she had only begun assembling since arriving in New York. One day Hayden bought Emory an answering machine to foil those phone calls from Peg. The clerk was a burly Hasidic man with clammy hands and trembling *peyes*, who, as he made the sale, angled his body away from Emory as if avoiding an allergen.

At three or four in the afternoon they were usually ready for a meal, and they would seek some place where Emory could get fish and Hayden could get eggs. Emory's favorite meal was blackened fish with salsa, black beans, and rice. What Hayden craved on those afternoons was a cheesy omelet with buttered whole wheat toast. They often gravitated to a small café just off Houston where they knew they could get those two things at that off-hour. When the fish and the salsa and the beans commingled in the right stinging proportions on Emory's tongue, bringing her to some satisfied center of herself, she would talk to Hayden most openly. She told Hayden about phalloplasty, about how penises could be constructed from the skin of an arm or a leg. It was a ridiculous thing to do, she said, mangling yourself like that, taking tissue of one kind and trying to transform it into a different kind of tissue . . . but she wanted a phallus . . . but, no, it was stupid, unnecessary, a waste of money, far too much money . . . but still she couldn't stop thinking . . . As Emory spoke, sometimes Hayden wanted to yell: *Why? Why? Why?* She half-agreed with Peg—hadn't Emory gone far enough? The cutting and stitching seemed not only unnecessary but truly barbaric. Still, it was Hayden's job on those afternoons to eat her eggs and listen.

Sometimes, passing particular girls or women on the street, Hayden would notice Emory giving them the once-over, starting with the face and traveling down, lingering on the breasts if they could be seen through coat or jacket, and then again on the hips and legs. A male ritual that both fascinated and embarrassed Hayden. How differently the women responded to being evaluated. Some of them would rearrange their spines, rising up to display fine firm breasts, or high cheekbones, or voluptuous bee-stung lips, gazing forward impassively in a way that said they enjoyed being watched. Some would hunch over, closing their bodies down for inspection, intent on concealing what they deemed to be flaws—breasts too small or large, faces without distinction. Others turned away entirely, defiant, demeaned, and angered by the bad sexual politics of those silent exchanges. Hayden felt at those times that maybe Emory really was already a man.

It certainly seemed that Emory, in very short order, had become a New Yorker. Despite what Hayden knew of Emory's background it was hard to imagine that she had ever really been a Floridian—her personality didn't seem sunny enough. Her dark coloring, her diminutive stature, her intensity, all seemed synchronous with the city, this city. After those Sunday expeditions with Emory, Hayden would often lie in the granulated dark of her Hoboken apartment and wonder what it had been like for Emory to come to New York not to visit but to *live* so shortly after the attacks. How could you take ownership of a mourning that was not your own?

She knew firsthand that it came to no good to take on someone else's mourning. There were things she had never told anyone. Once her mother had forgotten to pick her up from soccer and Hayden had had to walk home four miles in the dark under a misting rain, certain that each pair of oncoming headlights was her mother's Volvo. Each time the lights turned out to be not her mother's car, she worried about what she would find—or not find—once she got home. When she did get home her mother was on the couch with her Caravaggio book, looking up at Hayden as if she only half-saw her daughter's furious, rain-bedraggled body. The alchemy of anger and relief Hayden felt made her rush away as her mother came after her. *Ohmy-lord,* her mother kept saying, *I'msosorry.* Later, at bedtime, after Mother had basted Hayden with too many apologies and demolished every last one of Hayden's genuine feelings, she perched on Hayden's bed and said: *What was really wonderful about your day?* She needed to ascertain that something in Hayden's day had been wonderful. She looked at Hayden with her secret, coaxing, art-book gaze that saw so easily the two-sidedness of things. Her day's success was staked on Hayden's answer. Hayden reveled in telling her mother: *Nothing at all wonderful happened.*

There was nothing to conclude about that incident. It wasn't even a story she could remember the end of—there was only the image of her mother's face, blank, eviscerated, no longer seeming to know things about art or anything else. She must have drifted off to some other room, though Hayden didn't rightly remember. But now, thinking of Emory, it showed Hayden clearly the danger of appropriating someone else's mourning.

Chapter 16

Nothing about the city seemed scarred that night. The Manhattan moon, big and fat and healing, was solely devoted to them. They were on the roof of Emory's building in a forest of East Village water towers, swimming in the moonlight, drowning in it, drinking it in. Chunks of dirty snow that had been hunkering in the tar's divots for days, now sparked up at them, revitalized into crystals by the moonlight. Hayden had never loved a moon as much as she loved it that night with Emory. Even the lights of the Chrysler Building were outdone by that moon.

Emory did not wear wigs anymore. No lipstick, no female garb, nothing to mask the true strange being that was Emory. Hayden had taken to calling him "him." Tonight he wore a black flannel men's button-down shirt. His hair, short on the sides, longer on top and in back, careered from his nape like a dorsal fin. The moonlight had de-aged his skin, making him soft and irresistible. He closed his eyes and moved his slim hips to internal rhythms, an angular dance made up of many small measured movements falling into one another like the glass chips inside a kaleidoscope. Hayden could imagine someone falling in love with Emory without considering his genitals—they would simply love the precision of his jigging, moonwalking body and his inward-looking spirit.

A phone began to ring and, though it could have come from anywhere, Hayden knew it was Peg. Hayden had never met Peg, but she could feel the force of her—her petulance, her intractable opinions, the insistence of her ovaries.

Emory opened his eyes and inched to the roof's edge. Another few millimeters and he'd plummet six stories. "Watch out," Hayden said.

He knelt and lay on his belly, chin on the gutter. "Who cares what we are, right?" Emory said, peering down over the edge.

"You're scaring me."

He rolled lazily away from the edge, bump, bump, bump over the pimpled, black, snow-crusted tar, until he lay at Hayden's feet and she felt stupid for standing.

"A moon like this is almost as good as water," Emory said. "If we lived in water my life would have been different."

Hayden sat beside him, startled by the roof's cool rigidity.

"I'll show you," Emory said. "I haven't shown you yet."

He unbuttoned his black flannel shirt, thin bare fingers deft despite the cold. He folded back the shirt flaps with the steady hand of a cardiac surgeon. There it lay: a custom-designed chest, all his own. Pectorals definite and strong, rising with the elegance of an old mountain range, and beneath them two scars in the shape of loose Us, unmasked, unapologetic, a sure part of the plan. The nipples were more incidental than central, flatter and farther apart than female nipples. And all of it was scattered with sparse seedlings of hair.

What could Hayden say? There were no words for responding, nothing original to say. "Wow," she said stupidly. "Impressive."

"The guy who did this was damn good. But if I had grown up in water—or moonlight for that matter—I swear I wouldn't have needed him." He shivered and his custom-built chest moved as any chest would and he lifted his arms to stroke the air. "I'm getting squishy. I need to find some water."

Hayden had already heard about the young Emory—six years old and an ace swimmer, indispensable to her father. Hayden could picture the impish face of that girl, her inquiring look, the wiry body capable of anything. And the restless, giving spirit too. When you knew how someone began, how could you help but feel empathy?

Under water Emory had found herself. Hair, buttocks, breasts all plastered to flatness, she was sleek and sexless as a dolphin. Like the skin divers she'd seen on TV, clad so tightly in rubber it was impossible to tell man from woman. On land obstacles were too fixed, images were too sharp, sounds too resonant, everything required too many decisions about how best to maneuver. But water offered no resistance; she could glide easily through it, steering around obstacles without having to think. Under water sound was muffled and images blurred, providing extra clarity for the things in her head.

Emory had loved swimming off Miami's South Beach, a wide sweep of soft white sand where colorful circles of humanity gathered, sunning themselves, building sand castles, playing ball, watching and being watched. Emory and Peg would lay down their towels, chant "Three Blind Mice," and run into the water without testing it beforehand. They splashed wildly, lifting their knees, strutting like Lipizzaners. When the water reached hip-high they plunged in and stroked in unison, swimming out as far as they wanted. No one thought to stop them. They would look back at the denizens of the land and laugh, and Emory delighted in knowing she wasn't like those people.

Now, in New York, Emory was desperate to swim. He and Hayden traipsed around Manhattan, trying to find a pool that would meet his standards. They began on the Lower East Side where they descended two floors to a sub-basement. Behind the walls steam pipes clanked, suggestive of railing prisoners. The smell of wet insulation and old food permeated everything. But the pool itself looked good—or so thought Hayden. They crouched to feel it and the warmth of its aloe-colored water radiated to their faces. A group of seniors bobbed in slow motion like cooling atomic particles.

"What do you think?" Hayden said.

Emory didn't answer. He strolled assessingly past shallow puddles of splashed water along the pitted concrete deck. The air, close and stagnant, carried a strong smell of chlorine, a trace of urine. Emory stood at the shallow end, eyeing the pale green-tiled, gray-grouted walls. He drew a finger down the suppurating surface, dug into the grout with his nail. Beneath his scratch mark the grout was whitish; lodged under his fingernail was a worm of black dirt. Hayden saw the place through Emory's eyes now—the sedimentation of years, the way the fluorescent tubes made everything dull and dingy, how the water's green tinge suggested something festering.

Their next visit was to a pool in the basement of a small hotel in Midtown, a place one of Emory's Miami friends had recommended. It was a tiny square pool in a room with an exceptionally high ceiling. Five or six swimmers stroked lustily, making waves that crashed against the pool's edges and turned the incandescent light coming from above into sharp swords. High-energy dance Muzak was piped in and it made the small space feel more like a strobe-lit discotheque than a swimming pool.

A pool Emory had had high hopes for was in the penthouse of a new building near Times Square. It was said to be domed in glass and Emory was thrilled to have found a pool that was lit by natural light. There would be a steep fee, of course—all the pools in New York exacted fees.

But the building's uniformed doorman would not let them in. "Only for residents," he said eyeing the two of them, making Hayden wonder if it was Emory's dubious gender or her own exposed midriff that gave the clerk pause.

They stood near the TKTS kiosk. "We'll find something, don't worry," Hayden said. She had to get back to work for two more appointments. She didn't know what Emory was going to do, now or in the long run.

"Where's the fucking sky?" Emory said, suddenly looking up. He was right, the sky was hard to find. The horizon was nonexistent, blotted by buildings. Higher up, billboards minced the sky into fragments, and neon altered its color so you could hardly tell if it was day or night.

Hayden returned to the salon thinking about how different her life had been from Emory's, how surprising it was they'd become friends. Hayden didn't think she had ever been dissatisfied with being a woman. It was such a given, a premise for her life. Most people, she thought, took it this way. Man or woman, that was that, not something you considered changing, not beyond a passing fantasy. Maybe her own mother, though, had been different. Was it possible that her own mother might have been better off not being a woman? Was there a way to not be a woman and still not have to be a man? She thought of the look of the woman in the Caravaggio painting. Such yearning. Maybe that woman, too, was contemplating a life without the trappings of womanhood.

They hooked up Emory's new answering machine.

"It looks alive," Emory said.

Hayden laughed.

"Really. Don't those buttons look like eyes? I'll put money down that she won't call anymore."

But minutes later, as they were cracking the caps off beers, the first call came through. They froze as had been their habit. It rang three times—subdued, modest, imploring rings, as if the caller knew she was being watched. Then, the voice, one long uninflected seeping ooze of a voice. *I know you're there*, said Peg. Hayden had expected Peg to have a brash frantic way of speaking, not this slow, barely audible, almost ludicrous drawl.

"She's drunk," Emory said. "She doesn't usually sound like that."

Hayden felt a spasm of jealousy that surprised her. Why should she be jealous of Peg, reviled and desperate Peg? But she was.

In the salon everyone watched in horror as Emory attacked his hair with scissors. It was not an uncommon sight—one of the girls deciding on an impromptu self-styling—but it was not a styling method anyone relied on. It took talent to cut while looking at a reversed mirror image. It made you feel all thumbs. You did it when you were fed up with life and needed an instantaneous fix. All the time you were doing it you knew you might not like the results, but you cut anyway, because you couldn't stop yourself. Usually everyone would watch and laugh and offer unsolicited advice to the cutter, but with Emory that day they all kept quiet, sneaking furtive looks through their mirrors.

He cut in lunging strikes, quarreling his hair shorter and shorter. When he was done he had a military-style crew cut, undeniably masculine. He looked at himself in the mirror with a determined grimace, a prebattle impenetrability that bordered on rage. Hayden thought of the Spartans, how they looked *after* Thermopylae, done forever with hairdressing.

That night Hayden and Emory were the last to leave. "Why did you do that?" Hayden said. "Are you going all the way now?"

"It's just hair," Emory said.

"No, it's not. It's never just hair."

Emory turned his back to Hayden and threw his tools back into his drawers.

"You could start taking T again," Hayden said.

"It's not something you suddenly do," Emory said. "You have to have a team. Not just doctors, but friends. A place to come out."

"You have a place, don't you? Miami, I mean."

"Miami. Right." Emory collapsed into his chair, closed his eyes, and rubbed the top of his crew cut with a flat palm.

A whirring. Hayden thought it was the fish tank, but no, it came from Emory, a quiet nickering protest that rose from the back of his throat like compulsive throat-clearing; it began as a chirk, then mutated to a croak that threatened to grow loud and yowl-like. But he cut it off.

"I dream sometimes about being in a room full of men and being invisible. Not that they don't see me, but all they see is that I'm one of the guys. Nothing more or less. You ever have those flying dreams? It's better than that."

Hayden nodded though she knew Emory couldn't see. She was ejected into a thought flight of her own, but she was flying to a place she couldn't get to, a place whose location she couldn't find.

"I am nowheresville," Emory said. "I stick out like a sow in pajamas. It would be so much easier to just go home and be a kid again. If there were the home to go to. It was good to be a kid."

Hayden supposed she thought that too. After two years out west wasn't that what had lured her back east—some idea of retrieving things, returning to a life of supposed simplicity? But when she arrived in her small battered Honda, hobbled from its cross-country tour, she had found everything different. The house looked huge and stern and judgmental. She didn't believe it had always been so big. And it appeared empty too. It suddenly occurred to her that she had no idea who was living there. Cornelia was in college by then, but Sophie was still in high school. Was it possible that Father had sold the house and he and Sophie were living elsewhere? She tried the front door and found it locked. She wandered around to the back. From the patio she could see into the living room clearly. Someone was lying on the couch. Arleen, asleep. It had not occurred to her that Arleen might still be there. She had assumed that after Mother's death Father would have dismissed Arleen. Arleen had belonged to Mother it seemed, had only been with them at Mother's behest. But there Arleen was, looking exactly the same, her head balanced on one of the sofa pillows so a shaft of sunlight spread across her face, her lips partway open in the shape of a lazy kiss. She slept on, still and heedless. Hayden tapped at the window and Arleen woke slowly. She blinked and stretched then ran to the French doors.

"Hayden! Where have you been, baby?" she said. They embraced, holding each other for a full minute.

"I wasn't sure you'd still be here," Hayden said.

"I'm here. Where else would I be?"

Arleen looked at Hayden as if she was not to be believed. Her smile was different—her dead tooth had been fixed. It was white now, covered with a cap, and the alteration seemed to not only straighten her smile but also elevate her intelligence.

"Your tooth," Hayden said.

"Oh, yeah." Arleen touched it with her forefinger. "Your dad wanted me to fix it. It looks real good, doesn't it?"

"Real good," Hayden said. "Oh, Arleen." She felt unaccountably happy to see Arleen. "I thought maybe the house belonged to someone else now."

Arleen laughed. "No, it's ours."

"Where is everyone?"

"It's spring break. They're someplace warm—I forget where."

"Why aren't you with them?"

"I got to keep house. He needs me to keep house."

Hayden nodded.

"Your room is all ready. I've been keeping it up good. I just got to dust."

"I wasn't planning to stay," Hayden said.

"Why not? You back in college?"

"I'm going to New York to get a job down there. You remember when you used to do our hair? I'm a hairdresser now too. Now I can do your hair."

"Yeah, sure, you can do my hair." Arleen shook her head so her permed curls waggled. She laughed, frowned. "You're not going now are you? Not now. Don't go." Her amber eyes lost their light.

"Well, not this minute."

They cooked dinner together—omelets with lots of cheese. They had toast and salad and instant chocolate pudding for dessert. They laughed at everything—the way the eggs spread sneakily around the pan, the way the grated cheese curled like permed hair. They laughed at the fact that they both liked raisins in their salad and they both drank milk with ice.

"You're a good cook," Arleen said.

"So are you," Hayden said thinking of Arleen's mac and cheese. Their laughter was so easily ignited that Hayden almost wept.

Arleen suggested a sleepover in her room. They pulled a mattress from the storeroom and laid it out on the floor beside Arleen's bed. Arleen insisted that Hayden take the bed. Arleen, still in her clothes, lay belly-down on the mattress and succumbed quickly to sleep, drawing long snorkly breaths through her open mouth. Hayden lay awake for a long time, staring at the rose wallpaper of that room she had always coveted, marveling at how love could come over you, quick and disturbing as thunder.

Emory twirled in his chair. It had been minutes since either of them had spoken.

"You know what?" Hayden said. "Every morning for six years I have had to relearn that my mother is dead." Emory stopped swiveling and kept his eyes closed. The fish tank bubbled on. Hayden had never said this to anyone. How she used to awaken with an unspecified dread, a feeling there was everything to lose. Her belly was empty and hunger surged around ideas of buttered toast. She listened for song, not melody and verse, but the tuneless jumble that comes from a non-singer, a lover of life, a celebrator of this minute and this one and this one. She listened for songs like cirrus clouds—wispy, intermittent, suffused with air, vanishing and returning . . . *Oh my dear, oh my dear, oh what will you wear Jenny Jenkins?* . . . and then, in the manifold synapses of a few seconds she would piece together again the falling apart. It was a loss renewed with each breaking day.

She stopped speaking for a moment, watched the slow fisting and unfisting of Emory's hands before finding the courage to resume.

"Then one morning, for no apparent reason . . ." in the stillness of her Hoboken apartment, cradled in dark, she understood that the songless silence would never yield what she wanted. The gnawing hunger promised nothing but more hunger. The question that had floated through every night's sleep—would she be rescued—was answered. Why on that particular morning three months ago? She could not say. Maybe her body was finally ready to hold that knowledge, because there it was: the only door she could pass through. Now she awakened each day to a new world in which Mother no longer existed. A duller, colder world that held the theory of freedom, but not the feeling of it.

She sat in her own chair now, keeping her eye on Emory who did all there ever was to do for anyone: nod and listen.

It was one more night in a string of endless nights. Traffic bickered as usual. Two drunks had camped outside the building and their harangues breached the closed window. The phone rang and it was Cornelia, her voice interlaced with sighs.

Chapter 17

Vandermeer, Hayden said when she arrived at the pricey Midtown restaurant where Cornelia had designated for them to meet. The host led her to a table reserved for two. Cornelia was late and Hayden sat alone feeling jumpy, out of her element. The atmosphere was hushed, so she could hear the rarefied clink of crystal and silver cutlery. Two well-dressed, gray-haired, martini-drinking men sat at an adjacent table. They looked like titans of business leaning into the table as if the entire world existed between their two heads. Hayden had worn the only dress she owned, a green wool long-sleeved thriftshop purchase that was horribly itchy but concealed her tattoos. There had been something in Cornelia's voice that had made her want to present herself more forcefully than usual.

Cornelia, whalishly pregnant, wove through the tables. She looked puffier than when Hayden had last seen her, as if her belly's occupant had sent multiplying argosies to every outpost. She collapsed into the chair opposite Hayden without any formal greeting.

"It's brutal out there and I'm famished," she said. "I've been thinking about tenderloin tips all the way here." She sloughed her fur-collared coat and looked at Hayden with slit-eyed censoriousness. One of the businessmen glanced over at them and nodded, and Hayden felt too young to be there, as if she and Cornelia were only playing at being grownups.

"You look good," Hayden said.

"Don't butter me up," said Cornelia. "I know I look like shit. And I certainly didn't ask you to come here with the intention of pretending you've been anything other than an asshole. In fact, that's the point of this meeting—you've been an asshole and you owe us."

Hayden looked over at the businessmen to see if they'd overheard. It was impossible to tell. "Could you lower your voice?" she said to Cornelia. She wished she hadn't agreed to come.

"We are so far beyond anything to do with propriety." Cornelia drank her water with deep concentration. "It's one thing to nurse a grudge for all this time," she said. "But it's another thing entirely to nurse a grudge that no one even knows about. What the *heck* are you so mad about?"

"I'm not mad," Hayden said.

"You disappear all that time and you're not mad?"

Cornelia closed her eyes for a moment against some internal spasm. In the moment of respite that gave Hayden she understood how her sister terrified her. Cornelia had Father's force about her, a presence that made others compliant against their better judgment. And the pregnancy, the metamorphosis to motherhood, augmented Cornelia's native haughtiness. Hayden felt she might sink in the face of it—unless she came back full-bore.

"Okay, you put it on the table, not me," said Hayden. "Why did you and Father wait *an entire day* to tell me about Mother?"

"Jesus, is *that* what this is about?"

"That's small to you? It's not small."

She had never felt so young in her life, catching the train by herself from Boston to Fairfield, thinking how she had been motherless for a full day without knowing it. Someone should be coming to get her, she thought; she shouldn't have to make this trip all by herself. In the day since Mother's death she'd been doing such silly things in her ignorance—studying, having spinach lasagna with Pitzer, daydreaming in various easy chairs around campus—and all that time she should have been with Mother, even if she was already dead. She belonged beside her mother, calming her, chaperoning her, *she* was the one her mother needed.

"Why did he have to say it was an aneurysm when everyone knew it wasn't?"

"For God's sake, Hayden, it *was* an aneurysm. I was *there*. Why do you have to be such a drama queen?"

The waiter came for their order, and they fell into irritable silence. Cornelia ordered her tenderloin tips along with spinach and milk. Hayden had no appetite but settled on carrot-ginger soup.

"I saw it with my own eyes," Hayden said when the waiter was out of earshot. "Father saw too. He could have done something. We never did anything."

"Hush," Cornelia said. "I don't know what you're trying to prove, but you're wrong. And even if you were right—which you are not—do you have *any* idea what you did to Father by leaving like that?"

The lights in the restaurant's vestibule flickered. One of the businessmen dropped a knife as he was starting to eat, and as he reached to lift it his eyes skewered Hayden.

On the ride from the station to the funeral parlor—just Hayden and her father—he had laid out the events of the prior day as if briefing the press. Hayden felt she was getting the official, edited version of things. At the funeral home Mother was groomed and dressed and laid out for viewing. She didn't look one bit like herself. The dress she wore was not one Hayden recognized—it was navy blue, not Mother's color or style at all, and it clung, sheath-like, to her body and arms, making her appear severe and schoolmarmish. Her face had been pumped with chemicals that smoothed the creases through which she had expressed her personality.

Father stood in the doorway while Hayden went for a closer look. She touched her mother's hair. What little there was of it had been teased and sprayed to sticky stiffness; it was nothing like real hair, and it rose from her head in a helmet that gravity would never permit in the upright and living.

"I hate this," Hayden said. "This isn't Mother. Give her a scarf, for God's sake."

Father seemed not to hear. His eyes were closed. Hayden lifted one of her mother's hands. It was heavy and waxy. She tried to peel back the sleeve, but it was sewn tight. With two hands she tried to rip it. Father descended.

"What the *hell* are you doing?" He pulled her back, out of the room.

"I want to see the scars," she said.

"What scars?"

"That's why you put those sleeves on her, right, to cover the cutting?"

"Hayden, for God's sake, she's peaceful now. Do you have to belabor these things?"

Their dishes had arrived. Cornelia's tenderloin tips were a sanguinated red, Hayden's carrot soup a lurid orange.

"You hurt him a lot, you know," Cornelia said.

"What about *her*? What about *him* hurting *her*?"

"Stop acting like you're the only one that loved her. You act as if she belonged to you."

They ate with exaggerated concentration, not like sisters who had once had playful pudding fights.

"Is this why you asked me here?" Hayden said. "So you could yell at me?"

"Actually, no." Cornelia kept her gaze to her food. She chewed slowly as if eating were an important job that needed to take precedence over everything else. She wouldn't be pushed. "Father is in Costa Rica. He broke his ankle and he needs help getting home. He wanted me to come get him, but I can't travel this far into my pregnancy. You need to go."

"Me? Why me?"

Cornelia laid down her fork and stared at Hayden in disbelief. "You're his daughter, aren't you?"

"Cornelia—you know—"

"No, I really do not know. All I know is you ditched us."

"What about Sophie?"

"Sophie's in college. She's got too much going on. Don't you have one iota of family feeling?"

"I don't have the money for a trip like that."

Cornelia looked at her plate again and stabbed another square of meat. She chewed while looking at Hayden. "I'll pay."

Hayden sighed. The men had finished eating. Their table looked pillaged—they'd eaten what had appealed, tromped over the rest. "It's complicated," Hayden said. "How am I supposed to help Father when—"

"All you have to do is get him home. Look, I told him you'd be there."

"And he said—?"

"Fine. He's expecting you."

"He said *fine*?"

Cornelia cycled methodically from meat to milk to spinach.

Guilt fisted Hayden; she could not speak. She'd never been good at being good.

The waiter refilled their water glasses and asked them how they were doing. They nodded sedately. The ice cubes bobbed timidly against the glass as if they were trying to speak. Each one had a hollow circle at its center.

"Let me think about it," Hayden said.

"Don't take forever. Someone's got to get down there soon. "

Chapter 18

A slight thaw had brought people out on the streets again. It wasn't springy, but the few extra degrees of warmth were an assurance that winter wasn't permanent, that the snow really would soften and melt, that spring and yes, even summer, would definitely come again. Sometimes, in the nave of winter you could forget the way things changed—you could imagine this might be the year when winter would become a permanent condition.

It was night now, but still not cold. Emory crossed Astor Place heading east toward his apartment. A cabal of students exuding erratic energy hovered by the big black cube. Several young women dared the weather in spaghetti-strap tank tops; their shoulders were burnished, their cleavages blossom-pale. Emory sensed the things these young people wanted—to be entertained, to get drunk, to get laid. They wanted to find themselves at the hub of things. They wanted to define the hub. He read the anxious jitter of activity but was immune to it—it had nothing to do with him. He was glad to not be so young that every weekend night had to thrill him, and it comforted him to see others riled about things that were not his things.

He was thinking of Rose and Mel. They wanted to return to the city in May. He'd have to decide by then whether to go back to Miami. He didn't like the thought of returning, but saw no other choice. The life he had here was provisional. He had no community, no place to swim. All he had was a small, temporary apartment—too expensive for him without charity—and one friend. He had imagined it would be mentally peaceful to live here—this place where he knew so few people and certainly no one who would pressure him—but mental peace, he saw now, had little to do with place.

There was Peg to think about too. Even if they weren't lovers anymore he still felt responsible. The drunken calls from her were not reassuring. But Hayden—he couldn't leave Hayden. She had moved into his life without either of them intending it.

He steered around an arty crowd waiting outside Cooper Union. A movie, an exhibit, who knew what they waited for; he didn't attend such events even though they were on his doorstep. If Peg were here she would have made him, but without her he could do as he liked.

He crossed to the east side of Third, dodging cabs, skipping to the curb. A squawk. A hiss. Someone running. A thrown beer bottle. A bellyaching cab horn. The city's coloratura dizzied him: the vortex of St. Mark's Place, the headlights throbbing, the glittering ice melting into sidewalk fissures. The streetlight was gauzy and granulated with moisture. Surly scraps of paper blew out of reach. The whack of wet footsteps. The sudden shouts. Sinuous, he moved through it all. The pandemonium gloved him for the moment; the smoke trails of annoyance and worry that had been plaguing him drifted off into nothing. He was anonymous here, only part of the city's ripped rhythms, its jagged pulse, the celebration of sudden warmth.

He took the long route home down St. Mark's Place past the pizza parlor, the head shop, past the shop selling jewelry and cheap souvenirs, past the basement hair salon and Dojo's. On Second Avenue he turned south, then right on Fifth Street. He felt the sudden silence and vacuum that descended upon leaving an avenue behind. A group of five or six teenagers in baggy, low-slung jeans and backward caps sat on a stoop, passing a joint, swilling beers, exchanging insults. He took them in, their already broken manhood, then looked away and kept on going.

"What're you lookin' at?"

Emory kept moving. Timing was everything.

"Hey, I'm talkin' to you faggot."

To speed up would speak of fear. Emory kept his gaze on the end of the empty street, on the traffic zipping along the Bowery. Then they were in front of him, swaying, fisted, wearing their youth like prickly shirts. Their swagger was pathetic.

"Fuckin' faggot," one of them said. *Fuckin' faggot*, the others echoed. Their eyes were glassy. He wouldn't have taken them seriously except now they held him and tried to wrestle him down. One was lithe, stronger than he expected. The burly one kept watch. The other two leveled blows. Gut punches. Face punches. The sick flat slam of fist on skin. Adrenaline clawed. It needled his lungs. He called up dormant swimming muscles. He grunted. He weaseled out and dashed around them.

They didn't follow. Too lazy. Too weak. Too dull for a real confrontation. They didn't care anymore; they'd staked their turf, nailed him, then lost interest. *Damn this city. Fuck this city.*

He wore his Dolphins baseball cap, which cast a shadow on his face, but Hayden saw anyway. His left eye was half shut from the swelling, his left cheek was mumpishly swollen. He had used foundation to try to cover things, but a hard dark purple still shone through. He wore a short leather bomber jacket with the collar turned up and in its pocket was his Walkman, the volume raised so loud Hayden could hear faint tinny tunes even from her station. She knew about the sheltering value of a Walkman's clamor. She had used it herself.

Emory had three clients that day and in between each hour-long appointment he hurried out as if he had urgent business. Each time he returned with his hat brim pulled low, his Walkman blaring. Hayden tried to make eye contact, but there was no receiving on Emory's end. On one of her breaks she approached his station. He raised both palms as if erecting an air barrier between them.

"Don't," he said. "Just don't." He backed away.

He left at four. Fifteen minutes later he returned. He came straight to her station and stood there, radiating intent. She was picking auburn hairs from a comb; and waited for him to speak.

"Okay," he said. "I'm sorry. I didn't mean anything against you. I'm just fucked, that's all. I can't stay here. I'm going back to Miami."

She nodded, began sweeping. She had known it was coming so there was no point in being upset.

"The whole picture here—it just isn't working."

She nodded. She didn't look at him. *Just go.*

"Oh, great. What is this—payback?"

"You've made up your mind so what am I supposed to say? You want me to convince you to stay? I knew you wouldn't stay."

She could feel Tina watching them over the head of her client. She wished Emory would just leave. What did he want from her, pleading, tears? *Just go.*

The walls of Hayden's apartment looked different that night; they had a gray Stygian tinge as if they had sucked in too much winter weather. She didn't see how they could have gotten this way without her noticing. She took a sponge to the walls in the bedroom, but it did no good; whatever it was that was making that grayness had to be in her eyes. Exhaustion had gotten to her, sleep was the only remedy. She ate a quick bowl of viscous, lukewarm lima bean soup and took herself to bed, where she lay wide-awake, thinking how wrong she was to ever get attached. You never knew what affection could steal from you until it was gone and you found yourself bereft.

She had called Emory three times. Each time she got the machine. She didn't know what else to do. Should she go to Manhattan, to his apartment, and insist on entering? What then?

It was unlikely she could go from being nearly invisible to being forceful. Once you got rid of your force it was hard to retrieve. And even if you could—how could you be sure you would use that force to good ends? She sniffed the history of everything that night and nothing seemed evident. All she saw clearly was the slice across her heart.

Long ago, on that autumn day when she left for college, she knew that her branches and roots were wrapped too chokingly around the roots and branches of another.

Dry leaves clicked under a whorl of brassy light, light that made everything metallic, especially the reds and golds of Father's hair. Everyone but Mother had assembled outside. Sophie spun cartwheels in the grass. Arleen swayed back and forth, tonguing her dead tooth. Angus looked at his watch.

"Where's your mother? Hayden, go find her, will you?"

Hayden could not go into that house that smelled of old eggs and emptiness. She could not stand to call out and hear her plea spiraling through the rooms unanswered. She could not stand to come upon her mother wearing that liver-colored outfit with the

pumpkin cummerbund, spilling sorrow onto the couch then rais-
ing her eyes, those gray-green chasms that received everything
with bottomless receptivity, not just the nuances of line and color
in fine art, but in small gestures, finding everywhere, even in her
daughters, things that could hurt her.

But Hayden went in anyway because old habits die hard, and
she could not refuse her father's command. There was no telling
if she would ever come back out. Much as she wanted to leave
for college, she knew, looking at the house head-on, how knitted
she was there. From the small bathroom off the kitchen came the
sound of something falling.

"Mother?" she said into the resolute silence.

Hayden had no doubt her mother was in there, though now
none of her five senses could verify that. It was another sense
altogether that registered a fluttering through the stillness, her
mother's quiet movements pushing air so the molecules around
Hayden sensed it too.

"Mother," Hayden said more firmly.

There was a beat of silence, then a churning of limbs that
acknowledged Hayden's presence. "I'm fine, Hayden. Don't come
in please."

She always said this—*go away*—but Hayden, reading the
pleading eyes, knew *go away* meant *stay*.

"You know I'm fine."

Hayden didn't say anything for a while. She stared out the kitchen
window to the driveway. Her father leaned against the BMW and
marched his fingers nervously across its hood. Arleen stood where
Hayden had left her. Sophie and Cornelia patted the grass for four-
leaf clovers. Hayden was seeing everything as if she was already
gone. It was long before scientists knew how healthy plants, in the
presence of wounded ones, send messages for healing.

"Hayden?"

"Yes."

"I wasn't sure if you were still out there."

"I'm still here."

There was more rustling and then her mother emerged, closing the door firmly behind her. She smiled quickly. "How do you like my Harvard colors?" She spun so her long skirt billowed. It was a dark red and it matched the silk scarf she had used to turban her head. Her blouse was made of brown rayon flecked with tan and black, long-sleeved as always, and around her waist was the wide orange cummerbund that accentuated her small waist and overall fragility.

"Ready?" she said. She seemed composed again, full of her usual loveliness, no longer needy, ready to address herself fully to motherhood. "Are you all right?" she said to Hayden.

Hayden shrugged and started for the bathroom, but her mother blocked her way.

"Why must you?" she said. "You know I'm fine."

Why? Because she always had. Because Hayden was the one that knew how not-fine things were. Her knowing kept things in check and when she was gone—

"Okay," Hayden said. "You're fine. Let's go."

Sitting in class, or in the great hallowed hollow silence of Widener Library, Hayden thought too much of Claire. She could not stop trawling the house in her imagination for the presence of sharp objects, trying to picture how her mother could possibly be getting on without her. At night, in her dorm room, she was awakened by the slightest of sounds—a toilet flushing down the hall, the sound of her roommate opening a pack of saltines, giggles muffled by a closed door—and she was always sure, in that moment of waking, that her mother's hand had been on her shoulder, gently rolling her awake, needing something only Hayden could give. Only Hayden. Hayden was the one who had seen. She alone carried responsibility for this secret.

There it was, the same image all over again: the girl in the over-stuffed armchair in a dark alcove of Widener Library. Day after day she sat there, tugging at a forelock while she preened her blood on *The Canterbury Tales, The Aeneid, King Lear*. Sometimes her gaze strayed from her book and she looked around the library's whispery spaces at the porcelain-faced boys and girls—future surgeons and judges and cabinet ministers and business magnates—who sat just as she did, in cerebration, reading or writing, knowledge accumulating, silent as spores. But unlike her, their attention did not waver. They were going places fast, even in their stillness. They had neither time nor inclination to tarry, to wonder, to dream of sloughing. They tasted no bitterness in their stations; they did not hate where they were, where they'd come from, where they might end up. But she, in the delicate chrysalis of her adolescence, thought of nothing but deconstructing, unbecoming, becoming something else. Transfiguration. Shakespeare had shown her people passing from one life to another. Choosing. She liked Shakespeare. She liked acting. In high school she had played Rosalind in *As You Like It*. She liked sinking into the brains and skins of others.

This is what she thought: You don't need Revere silver . . . you don't need Persian carpets . . . you don't need Windsor chairs . . . or BMWs . . . no cars at all, in fact . . . no microwaves or TVs . . . no Rolexes or lattes . . . no cats or koi . . . no multivitamins or crème brûlée . . . no extra socks. Gather no moss. Slash your overhead. Unmannacle yourself. Take a teeny-tiny slice of the pie and let the metamorphosis take effect. Then, rove anywhere, unburdened, unnoticed, preying off of no one, inciting no one's jealousy or wrath.

Abdicate.

From the bottom of those dreams of burden and escape a call came in. It was a slushy winter afternoon near the end of exams. She was trying to read *Beowulf* while she worked her way through a two-pack of Twinkies. Her mouth was happy with sweet cream. Outside a powdery snow fell.

His voice was quiet and without modulation, like a digitized track. She heard the words clearly. They had meaning but that didn't make them true. He said things into the room's groggy silence as if he were there himself. She pictured the basement, black blood spilling in the dimness.

"No. Not that," he snorted. "An *aneurysm.*"

"Yesterday?" she said. A gust of wind blew the snow straight up. Her daze lifted. She stood up so books and papers tumbled from her lap and *Beowulf* squashed the remaining half Twinkie.

Hayden and Cornelia seesawed on fiber-optic silence. "I'll go on one condition," Hayden said. "I want to take a friend with me."

Part II

Oso Peninsula, Costa Rica

"Whoever you are, no matter how lonely,
the world offers itself to your imagination,
calls to you like the wild geese, harsh and exciting—
over and over announcing your place
in the family of things."

—Mary Oliver, "Wild Geese"

Chapter 19

This is what the brochures pitched.

Come to Costa Rica. We are different. We are not like the other Latin American countries, debilitated by poverty and political instability, plagued by disease and unsanitary living conditions. This is a country that bridges north and south, a clean hygienic place with a literate, landowning population, a stable and democratic government. You can drink the water here without misgiving, you can walk the Costa Rican streets freely. You need not fear. Nor must you feel guilty: nothing here will remind you of the exploiting tendencies of the First World. *Come—see how happy we are.* Travel in high style. Bring binoculars. Watch monkeys cavort in the trees, see birds and butterflies in every color of the rainbow, find giant turtles nesting on the beach. If your preference is for speed and adventure we have rivers to raft and waves to surf. For those with quieter preferences we can show you a five-star jungle lodge far from the madding crowd. We have food to match all tastes—for the all-American palate and for the international-style gourmet.

In traveling to Costa Rica, you need not step outside your comfort zone. Nothing about the journey here will demand that you alter any aspect of yourself.

Chapter 20

Hayden and Emory sat rump-to-rump with four other American travelers in the back of an open jeep. For two hours in airless heat they bumped along, through the parched Costa Rican countryside, over pot-holed roads, past brown fields, skeletal cows, tumbledown shacks. The two other women were bright-eyed and irrepressible, their enthusiasm for this country undimmed by the forlorn landscape they were passing. Their husbands, too, seemed amiable enough, confident that at the terminus of this challenging ride there lay a tropical paradise.

Hayden and Emory's luggage had been lost and Hayden, hot in her long-sleeved New York garb, was torn between sociability and silence. Glancing forward to the sinewy brown neck of the driver, she felt hopelessly out of her element, impossibly American. The task ahead—escorting her injured father home—felt daunting and she knew she was foolish to have taken it on, and it made her wish, as was her habit, for invisibility. She and Emory had not spoken much since they'd embarked on this journey—it had been a hard sell to convince Emory to come in the first place, just when he was poised to return to Miami—and now Hayden was wondering if her idea had been a good one. As they had walked through three airports and boarded three planes, Hayden had seen a new side of Emory. The recent beating had left its imprint; he moved amid crowds expecting trouble. He did not establish eye contact with anyone and kept his eyes strobing as if guilty of something. Hayden tried to see him as others might; with his jeans, tight turquoise T-shirt, and radical self-styled crew cut, he looked to her like a small man. Though there was something not wholly manlike in his hypervigilance and his poreless facial skin. Hayden tried to make peace with the idea that others, certainly the other two couples in this jeep, were no doubt regarding them as a couple.

"Where are you two from?" asked the more outgoing of the other two women. She was clad in linen, and her thick, light gray hair curled becomingly around her jawline.

"Hoboken," Hayden said. She waited for Emory to offer his story, but he remained mute. "She lives in Manhattan," Hayden said. She cringed at her unwitting word choice. "Although he's from Florida originally," she said, trying to make amends.

"Oh, Florida! We're from Massachusetts. The Boston area." The woman appeared unfazed, perhaps she had not heard Hayden. "Have you been to Tranquilidad before? They say it's lovely, one of the top ten eco-resorts. This is our first time."

"Yes," Hayden said. "Mine too."

"I'm Janine."

"Hayden. And this is Emory." Hayden looked over at Emory, trying to communicate an apology. He nodded slightly at Janine, then returned his gaze to the scenery.

"Good to meet you both. And what do you do?"

"Hair," Hayden said. "I'm a stylist."

"Oh!" Janine said. "How nice." She then turned pointedly out to the tawny fields in search of something noteworthy.

The jeep lurched to a halt at the crest of a steep rise where the dirt road ended. The driver hopped out, all smiles and solicitousness. They had arrived. A hand-carved sign posted by a breeze-way said: BIENVENIDA/WELCOME/ACCUEIL/BENVENUTO/EMPFANG/ HET WELKOM A *TRANQUILIDAD*. Behind the sign and the breezeway stood a large thatched palapa with dining tables and a bar and an observation deck that provided a view over the treetops straight down to the water. This open structure was circled by tall trees, their leaves spatulate and light-blocking. Three people emerged from the shadows almost instantaneously, and a mutter of relief spread among the two other couples, as if such alacrity made good on the promise of *resort*. A man in white with a name badge that said SERVIO, carried a tray of sweating drinks. Gustavo, the manager (whom Hayden had spoken to on the phone)—bespec-tacled, short and stocky but fit—stepped forward with a firm handshake for each of them. He smiled a tireless bright white greeting. "Welcome, welcome. We're so happy to have you," he said in impeccable English. Roberto, one of the naturalists, with safari hat and knee-high rubber boots, nodded diffidently.

Emory was whispering in Hayden's ear: "I don't belong here. Christ do I not belong here." Hayden shook her head. "You're here," she whispered back.

Emory watched the other passengers gathering backpacks and handbags. Unlike the rumpled, frazzled people who used to visit Frank's Motel, this was a well-heeled lot—you could see it in their shoes and their luggage and in the perfect fit of their tropical clothing. They were incurably Caucasian to Emory, in-curably American, people whom no other culture could touch. Emory was acutely aware of his still-bruised face, his white-trash origins—a terrible sense of foreboding came over him. He should never have agreed to accompany Hayden here. The offer had only been charity on Hayden's part anyway, and Emory detested char-ity. He'd been relying on it too heavily of late.

The driver made quick work of unloading the luggage while Gustavo inquired about the comfort of their travel. They all drank deeply of the offered lemonade. The naturalist wanted to speak to them right away and he directed them to the palapa's shade. As the group reassembled, necklaced with binoculars they had taken from their carry-ons, Gustavo touched Hayden's arm.

"Miss Risley, it is good to meet you finally. I'd like to take you to your father. He is resting comfortably now. He will be glad to see you." His gaze traveled quickly to Emory—who stood just behind Hayden as if trying to hide—then back to Hayden. "We have a room for your friend in our temporary visitors' quarters. I'm sorry—it is somewhat smaller than the bungalows. You will stay with your father. Come."

They followed Gustavo to a white stucco building not far from the palapa. Gustavo opened the first of a row of four doors. The room was white-walled and light and simply appointed with a queen-sized bed, a ceiling fan, a dresser, an easy chair. Gustavo parted the sliding glass doors and they stepped out to a small wooden porch with a view of a small sunlit clearing and beyond that dense forest—jungle, Hayden supposed—so close you could practically touch it. Emory looked pleased. "Hey look!" he said. He pointed to the branch of a nearby tree where an iguana lazed in a cone of sunlight. Back inside he roved through the room with a renewed burst of energy and interest. Then he lay on the bed grinning, oblivious to Gustavo's fussy presence.

"Will this be all right?" Gustavo said.

"Great," Emory said.

"We are working on finding your luggage."

"Thanks," Emory said. "Whatever. I'm good."

Hayden and Emory agreed to meet for dinner at the palapa at six. Gustavo and Hayden left Emory alone.

They headed downhill on a winding dirt path bordered on both sides with dense vegetation, its leaves shiny, suggestive of plastic, the flowers sporting rapacious, tongue-sized stamens. In some places the foliage had grown tall enough to canopy the path, and in other places there was a clear view down over the forested hillside to the bay, blue and smooth from that distance, an invitation to forget. Gustavo explained to Hayden what had happened to her father: He had chosen to walk alone on a steep path to the beach—a *very steep path*, Gustavo said—and he had fallen and damaged his ankle. They thought it was just a sprain, but it could be a fracture. He shouldn't be walking on it. A local nurse had seen him, and the resort doctor, who was visiting his mother in San José, had been summoned. Normally Dr. Estuvio was there full-time; he would return as soon as possible.

"It may need an X-ray," Gustavo said. "Dr. Estuvio will tell us for sure."

Gustavo stopped to look into Hayden's face, regarding her ruefully, anxiously, from behind his thick glasses. He seemed afraid of what Hayden might do or say. "Good," she said. "Yes," she said, surprised by his deference.

The neat white bungalows they passed were situated for privacy with fenced patios to discourage probing eyes. Everything was tasteful and designed for sophisticated international travelers who could feel confident that what they were seeing was unique and indigenous. They stopped in front of Bungalow 8. Gustavo turned to Hayden.

"We are very fond of your father. Very fond indeed." He bent his body forward slightly then snapped it back into place. "He is like family to us," he said. Hayden understood him to be saying that Father was a regular visitor here, a fact she had already surmised.

Gustavo knocked. "Mr. Risley! It is Gustavo. I am here with your daughter."

They heard a voice, but its words were indecipherable.

"We are coming in, okay?" To Hayden Gustavo whispered, "He is supposed to remain as still as possible."

Hayden gestured for Gustavo to go first, but he insisted she precede him. She moved forward hesitantly, composure melting with each step. The bungalow was cool and dim, its dark wood and bamboo still exuded earthy scents. Matchstick blinds had been lowered over the screen windows to keep out the heat. Two large beds, regally draped with mosquito netting, were the room's centerpiece, but there was ample room for a desk and two easy chairs as well. A sign of the resort's ecological orientation, there was neither TV nor phone anywhere in the room. Overhead a languorous ceiling fan circled.

Hayden and Gustavo moved tentatively across the room to where the doors opened out onto a deck overlooking jungle and bay. There he was: Angus Risley, the writer, the famous man—or famous in certain circles—who happened to be Hayden's father. He lay stretched out on a chaise, inert, a brimmed straw hat fixed squarely over his eyes, cheeks, and nose to shield his pallid Irish complexion. One leg was bandaged from foot to mid-calf with gauzy white cloth, the other leg jutted from his shorts looking lean, pale as marshmallow, and decisively not of this place.

"Hello," he said from beneath his hat. "I know you're here."

Hayden didn't say anything. She wasn't sure of what she was seeing. She could not see the parts of his face that were needed to mount an expression. She could not see how the years had treated him, how he might have aged. He was schematically a person—a Caucasian male for sure, roughly in the shape of her father—but the details hadn't come into relief.

"Is that my daughter, Gustavo?"

Gustavo bent at the waist and pushed out a genteel shout. "Yes indeed. Your daughter has arrived." Gustavo waited for them to greet one another, but Father said nothing further and neither did Hayden.

"How are you feeling, sir?" Gustavo finally asked.

"Baked, Gustavo. The sun is the only thing that keeps me still."

"Perhaps the shade would be better," Gustavo suggested. "Dr. Estuvio is on his way, you know. He has been detained in the city. I am hoping he might arrive tomorrow. The next day at the latest."

"Tell him not to worry. I'm not going to die of this. Right Gustavo? If I do die burn me and throw my remains in the bay." Twitches shuddered through him and, as he moved to a sitting position, his hat fell off his face to the deck, revealing a bald pate and thinning ringleted red tresses that were long enough to dust his shoulders.

"You'll be fine, sir, I'm sure," Gustavo said. "You're not going to die. It's probably only a sprain the nurse said and Dr. Estuvio concurs."

She stared at this new incarnation of her father, a Connecticut conservative—at least personally, if not politically—now re-emerged as beat poet or aging hippie, or red-haired Little Lord Fauntleroy. Sitting now, he angled his head to look at her, one eye fully closed, the other squinting against the sun. He absorbed her strategically, a little at a time. The tangle of her blond-streaked, shoulder-length shag; her tight-fitting black clothes; the two-inch platforms. Did he see shards of the daughter he knew, or only some derelict daughter? A clap of embarrassment passed through her, cut short by his familiar, assessing gaze.

The silence between them made Gustavo nervous. He cleared

his throat several times as if rust had collected there. He rubbed his hands together. "Your dinner will be brought down," he said. "Good afternoon."

"Wait—" Hayden left her father on the deck and followed Gustavo as he headed back inside to the bungalow's front door.

Gustavo turned. "Your bags? We are checking on that."

The bag did not concern her. "Are you sure," she said, "that there is no other place for me to stay? My father and I, we—"

Gustavo blinked and Hayden was filled with an image of his disdain. *What is wrong with you Americans? This is a country in which an entire family might live in such a space and you cannot endure a few brief nights with your father?* But all he showed was a placid eagerness to please.

"Yes, Miss Risley, we are working on that." He smiled with fully exposed white teeth and what seemed like honest goodwill, so she doubted the thoughts she had imputed to him. She lingered at the door, watching him move quickly back up the path, his upper body in apparent repose, his legs scissoring with ostrich speed.

She closed the door on Gustavo reluctantly, sweat rupturing from all her pores. What horrified her was the thought of them lying in beds a few feet apart listening to each other's breathing in the dark of a tropical night. Things happened at night: serpents rose, ghosts danced, big cats howled.

If she had had her suitcase with her she would have unpacked, but all she had was a small carry-on backpack with a few toiletries, a twice-read *Newsweek*, a hair magazine, and the copy of her father's book that she had thought she might read on the plane but hadn't. She gazed out to where he still lay on the deck, wondering what to do with herself. As if he could tell she was watching him, he raised his head.

"Hayden!" he called. "Come out here."

She stepped out onto the deck. He looked inexplicably smaller than he had a moment earlier, and it occurred to her she was not appropriately worried for him. His injury might be only a sprain, but what if it was worse? She had never worried about her father before and wasn't sure how to begin.

"Are you all right?" she asked.

He shifted slightly to look at her head-on. "What possessed you to come here?"

She stood in direct sunlight and suddenly felt dragooned by the heat. Her head throbbed, her limbs drooped, her whole being craved lubrication. "I'm here to take you home."

"But I don't want to go anywhere."

"But Cornelia said— She sent me here to bring you home."

"Ah, so you're not here of your own volition, are you?"

"No, I mean, yes of course—" Had he changed his mind since she'd talked to Cornelia, or was this some ploy on Cornelia's part? "Cornelia wants you back for the birth of her baby."

He laughed, reflecting quietly on some secret joke it seemed, and a lock of orange hair jiggled against his neck. "Come here and let me greet you properly. I won't bite. Not yet, at least. The heat has dulled my teeth anyway."

She went to his deck chair and started to crouch next to him. But a crouch seemed too intimate after so much time, too awkward, so she rose to standing again. He grabbed her palm and pulled it to his lips. "Where are you staying?" he said.

"Apparently here. Until Gustavo can find me another room. He didn't mention that?"

He ejected a brief rough sound in answer, half a laugh. "You've got that kind of money?"

"Cornelia is—" she said, but the rest of her sentence vanished.

"I'm pulling your leg."

If it were cooler, if she were not so exhausted from travel, if she had recognized him more clearly, her thoughts would not muddle so easily. Around them, in the trees, she was aware of rustling, a wild unruliness. At the deck's railing she peered out. There was all manner of wildlife living out there; the couples had been talking about it on the jeep—the monkeys they expected to see, the gorgeous birds—but from where she stood she saw nothing. Was it quarreling monkeys she heard? Insects throbbed, loud then soft, reminiscent of the rising and ebbing pain of an infected wound. She looked down at her hands; though it was March they were summer hands, bloated from the heat, lined with bulging veins. Apparently there was no real point in her being here. She supposed she should find that funny.

A knock on the front door. "Hurry," Father said, nodding to her to open it.

She passed back through the bungalow's interior to the front door, where a woman stood before her, holding a tray of sliced fruit—mango, papaya, coconut, guava chunks—and a thick white drink in a sweaty glass. The woman laughed inexplicably, her mouth open, her down-turned gaze declaring shyness and, Hayden thought, goodwill.

"Hi," Hayden said.

"You must be"—the woman said in confident but accented English—"his daughter?"

Hayden nodded, surprised the woman knew of her. She was a short woman with a knot of black hair at her nape and the kind of skin Hayden had always coveted—an even light brown with the smooth, moist self-sufficiency of a succulent. She wore a gathered cotton skirt with a red and blue floral pattern, and a short-sleeved white blouse of very sheer cotton, clothes that lay lightly on a body that looked to Hayden as perfect as a woman's body could be—unaffected by confining standards of thinness, by too much or too little food, by too little exercise, or too-tight clothing. Everything about this woman looked ripe and strong and unfettered, and though she was not beautiful by American standards—her face was too round, her teeth too prominent—Hayden was transfixed.

"Did we order this?" Hayden said.

Father bellowed from his post on the deck. "Tell her to come in." He did not sound like an invalid.

"Come in," Hayden said.

The woman hesitated. "Yes?"

"Yes."

Hayden ushered her to the deck where Father had discarded his hat and was uncrumpling himself from his former slump. He rearranged his disparate parts as if pulling apart a tightly wadded ball of foil.

"Your fruit," she said in her accented English. She handed him the plate and bent forward in a sort of mini bow that echoed Gustavo's, a nod to bygone civility that some of the hotel guests—Father himself—might have expected.

"Sit down," he told her.

She nodded but did not sit, glancing back toward the door, the path, the responsibilities that beckoned her. "I must—"

"Of course, but stay just for a minute. A minute won't matter. Hayden, get her a seat."

Hayden brought a chair from across the deck and the woman perched on the edge of it, smiling so hard her teeth caught the western sun and made a small quick glimmer like fleeting sardines. Hayden wanted to release her, hating the awkward power inequity between server and served.

"This is my daughter Hayden," Father said. "And this is my friend Manuela. Manuela's good to me, aren't you? Even before this business with my ankle."

Manuela looked bewildered and a moment of general awkwardness followed. Glances tried to land—Manuela to Father, Father to Hayden, Hayden to Manuela—but failed and instead bounced around the interior of the triangle they defined.

Father ate his fruit with unusual concentration, chewing slowly, closing his eyes as if later he would be called upon to describe those flavors precisely. Hayden and Manuela watched. Manuela smiled, awaiting his comments. Hayden tried to make eye contact with Manuela, but Manuela did not look back. After a while Hayden could not watch her father anymore. She stood up and went to the railing just as a pair of scarlet macaws landed in a fig tree. They announced their bounty with shrieks. Behind them, the sun blazed, silhouetting them, robbing their scarlet color for its own radiant report.

A few minutes passed. Manuela rose and offered her shy good-byes. Then, still without returning Hayden's gaze, she retraced her steps back up the soft, sun-struck earth to the top of the hill.

Chapter 21

Macaws are large, resplendent birds, prima donnas of the jungle, male indistinguishable from female, old and young equally bright. Why be a tree? Why not a bird instead? It wouldn't have to be a magnificent bird, any bird would do—barn swallow, sparrow, hummingbird, vulture.

Consider the bird. Light-boned and fleet, servant to none, the bird inhabits both earth and sky. It knows treetops intimately, and invisible currents of air interlacing the clouds. It knows how to ride those currents, how to harness them. The bird is equipped for relocation, for quick escape. Replete with an inborn sense of the poles' magnetic force, it guides itself to seasonal harbor. Even the ostrich, the largest of birds and incapable of flying, can outrun most other species.

Yes, the bird was a possibility.

Hayden and her father sat mutely and watched the macaws preening. The day had shifted to evening. The first pair of macaws had been joined by a second and all four squawked and jabbed at one another with raucous authority. They were too boisterous for this tranquil time of day. Hayden stomped her foot but they ignored her. Then, after a few minutes, all four took off of their own volition, soaring in blustery, haranguing flight, their tails dragging behind them like slackening kite strings.

In the quiet she wondered what Emory was doing. "Why don't you want to go home?" she said.

Father sucked a papaya rind for its final offering of flavor. "I am home. One of them, at least."

How was she to respond? His change of plans, her sense of having stepped into a vacuum—what was she to do with it? "I brought a friend, you know," she said.

"Cornelia told me. Where is your friend? Will I have the pleasure?"

"I said I would meet him for dinner. He has a room up the hill."

"Does he have a name?"

"Emory."

The sun had ripened to the color of mango flesh, and was so fat now that it looked as if it was begging to be peeled. "Dinner," Father said suddenly. "The fruit has whetted my appetite. I'm famished."

"They're bringing it down," Hayden said.

"No, we're going up there."

"They said—" He cut her off with a swiping of his down-turned palm, a gesture that brooked no resistance.

She tried to imagine the three of them dining together, Father reacting to Emory, Emory to Father. If she'd thought of such an occasion back in New York she might not have come. The chemical smell of the weatherproofed railing invaded her nostrils. In the distance she could see out over the jungle canopy to the bay, the Golfo Dulce. Its water was such a bewitching azure it didn't look real.

They were losing their light quickly so now was the time to move if they planned on moving. Father beckoned to Hayden and she had no choice but to go to him. She gripped his arm hard to help him stand. His hand was freckled and doughy, but strong.

She teetered a bit from his weight and the shock of his touch. Of course they had to have touched in the past, but if they had she couldn't recall those times. After he'd hoisted himself to a standing position, he leaned on her shoulder and together they proceeded slowly to the front door, Father hopping, wincing. It embarrassed both of them, the sustained body contact, the signs of his neediness.

On the path wood chips mingling with the loam crunched under her shoes. In some places log steps had been built and it took great strength for Father to hop over them, even with Hayden's help. Within a few minutes they were both panting and had to stop at a lookout where a bench had been situated with an unobstructed view down to the bay. They collapsed on the bench, scaring off a lizard enjoying a few final shards of sunlight.

There was no wind and the sky had turned a luminous blue-gray. The air temperature, no longer sweltering, still held an embracing warmth. In the trees and bushes nocturnal creatures were springing to life. A group of other diners overtook them on the path, and Hayden recognized the couples who had driven over with them in the jeep. They had joined forces with another middle-aged couple; all fit, they moved briskly but without extraneous noise, only the gentle thump of sensible shoes on moist earth.

"Evening," they said in nature-modulated voices. "Beautiful, isn't it?"

"Yes," Hayden murmured back. "Beautiful."

Father's arm vibrated; still hooked in hers, it swelled over her consciousness. She could not ignore its heat, its weight, its moist, rough skin. She wanted to disentangle herself from him, but the action would draw too much attention. With his free hand he took a small white tablet from his pocket. He popped it in his mouth and swallowed. She doubted if they would make it to the top of the hill, but she wasn't going to be the one to say so.

Two resort workers appeared as if summoned, though no summons had been sent. They carried a portable chair with a canvas seat and metal arms—a chair for the facile transport of people in distress. Father refused their offer of assistance at first, but they smiled and urged him into it, and their charm was so irresistible he finally acquiesced. They were slight men, but strong as sherpas, and they managed Father's weight easily, spiriting him uphill over the rutted path in the gathering dusk as if he were hollow. When the lit dining area under the palapa came into view he demanded to be let down, and he walked the remaining distance unassisted, rising up through the pain to his full height.

She searched among the diners for Emory, but could not find him. The atmosphere was festive. Lit torches had been posted around the palapa's perimeter, making a clear distinction between the wilderness and the domesticated area. On one side of the dining room pastel-colored drinks were being served to people at a high bar. Nearby, three tables of different heights served meat and fish, a variety of salads, vegetables and bread, fruits and desserts. Except for one long table occupied by a large family from Texas, the dining tables were mostly peopled with middle-aged American and European couples wearing simple linen evening clothes designed especially for the tropics. Their faces were serene and unblemished, and they smiled patiently at the Costa Rican waiters, who recited the specials in flawed English.

Hayden and her father were seated at a table with an extra place for Emory, and Manuela appeared almost immediately with plates of food for them, though the other diners were serving themselves at the buffet. She smiled at Hayden briefly.

"You're trying to humiliate me," Father said to Manuela with mock ferocity. "I can walk, you know. I'm not an invalid."

Manuela shook her head scoldingly. Her laugh was mellifluous, songlike. Father consulted with her on the wine. "That's a very good choice," she said. "Full body." Her smooth brown arms came and went from Hayden's field of vision. Father, by contrast, appeared all pallor and redness, his skin rough and variegated as lichen.

"Is everything all right?" Manuela asked after she had poured the wine. She looked at Father, not Hayden, and her gaze seemed to bestow promises.

"We are expecting a third. Am I right, Hayden?"

"I guess so." Hayden craned her neck to see if Emory might be loitering at the palapa's periphery. Now she hoped he wouldn't appear. Perhaps Emory and Father would not have to meet one another after all.

"Isn't that impressive?" Father said when Manuela was gone. "That a woman in this little corner of the Third World not only knows a good Pinot Gris, but she also knows how to be a sommelier. Really something." He shook his head in disbelief. "Am I really to believe in this boyfriend of yours?" he said.

"He's not my boyfriend," Hayden said. She was aware of being in his dominion again, and it made her obstreperous and passive as a child. She drank her wine, wanting its balm. Suddenly her father was distracted. He surveyed the other tables, as if looking for a specific person, or perhaps as if waiting to be recognized. He had removed his hat and she saw his right cheek had been badly sunburned. She turned to eating. In the dim light she couldn't tell what the dishes were, but they enlivened her mouth—fish with mango chutney, spicy beans and rice, baked plantains. Foods Emory would love.

"So you have a life of some kind, of course," Father said, attention returned.

She drew more breath than she needed. "Yes, I have a life." She stopped eating, stabbed a bean with one tine of her fork.

"You live where?"

She hesitated. She could say *Hoboken* and await his snort (he would be thinking of downtrodden, mid–twentieth century Hoboken, not its more sought-after, early-millennium, gentrified incarnation), or she could simply say *New Jersey* and elicit another kind of slightly more hopeful snort, a *possibly Princeton* look in his eyes. She was no fool—she knew what he'd hoped for her.

"Hoboken," she said.

There was no snort, only silence. "And you do what?" he finally said.

She moved her eyes from place to place: from the woman nearby with a hacking laugh; to Father's pale, day-old chin fuzz; to the small lit votive in a glass bowl at the center of their table.

"I'm a stylist. Hair stylist."

Father leaned back so the copper of his hair glinted under the lamplight. He sized her up. "That's what Cornelia said. I didn't believe her."

Hayden glanced around at the other diners. Still no Emory. Now she really needed him. At a table of four a man pantomimed with wild, wind-milling arms, inciting a hail of laughter from his fellow diners. Hayden wished she were on someone else's vacation. She drank her wine and felt it going to work quickly on her travel-weary body.

"Really?" he said. "She was right? Hair?"

"How many times do I need to say it?"

"What does your boyfriend do?"

"I told you—he's not my boyfriend." She felt the telltale tightening of her teeth, the collision course of adrenaline. She tried to breathe deeply, but it did no good.

"What did you say his name was—Emory? What does Emory do?"

"He's also a stylist. At least for now he is." She lifted her eyes from the flame for a moment to watch him react. But she couldn't read him, couldn't find the father she had known. Her wineglass was empty; she poured herself more.

"I thought I taught you better than to put so much emphasis on appearance," he said. "Hair is so inconsequential to devote a whole life to."

"It's not just about appearances—" she began. She tried to grasp onto the things she had always known about hair as a statement of identity, a kind of communication, but under her father's demanding gaze these ideas floated off into vagueness. They seemed lightweight and vain and ephemeral. Yet she had been preparing for this moment for close to six years; she had to start somewhere. She sucked up air.

"Okay," she said. She tried to look directly at him, but he wore such a supercilious smile she looked back down to the candle. "There's subtext in hair, I think."

"Subtext? In *hair*?"

"It's—" If her breathing weren't so ragged she would be more articulate, but how did you force yourself to breathe smoothly? As a child she'd never had trouble. Then she had rattled things off without a stutter. She sipped her water. She gulped her wine.

"I mean first there's the biology. The human body, on average, has five million hairs—not just on the head, but on the back and the forearms and the feet and hands, and the belly, and the genitals and—"

"These are things I need to know? Do we have Harvard to thank for this information? Styling 101?"

She sucked air; she drank wine; she willed herself to continue: "When a hair is touched by even a slight breeze the nerves around the hair's base are sparked. And sensations are set in motion. They're like weathervanes or mini antennae, bringing news of danger nearby—or maybe comfort. All those hairs are receiving silent but essential messages."

"Messages, eh?" Father had not touched his food. He squinted at her, sliding thumb and forefinger slowly up and down the stem of his wineglass. She saw a pulse under his eyes. Their clear light blue, a rare color, seemed to hold moral superiority. "What is the point here?" he said.

She finished her glass of wine, poured more. She was drunk now, or almost drunk, but she didn't care. What *was* the point? It came and went. Just when she felt she could describe it perfectly, it melted like a palmed snowflake. She looked straight at him now, jabbing him with her gaze.

"I just like doing it, okay. Isn't that enough?"

"If you say so."

"No, don't do that. Don't be so condescending." She wanted to growl. This was the jungle and she was an animal in it. "I help people transform themselves," she said. "I help women be who they want to be."

It sounded so simplistic. She wanted to describe to him the overweight, fifty-year-old, stay-at-home mom with the chicken-skin neck, the hirsute upper lip. She wanted him to see how that woman sat so expectantly in the swivel chair. She wanted him to hear the woman say: *Make me gorgeous.* Hayden could make that woman into anyone: a woman with clout, an actress, a Bohemian activist. Did he have any idea how every woman carried a million different people buried inside her?

"So you see yourself as some kind of therapist?"

Emboldened by the wine, she stared back at the challenge of his limpid blue eyes. No, she was not a therapist. "I'm a stylist, a hair wizard." The wine had done its work; she was brave now.

"Good God, Hayden. I sent you to Harvard for this?"

"Harvard, the be-all and end-all." She gulped more wine. She was speaking too loudly, almost shouting, and some of the other diners had turned to look. She didn't care, not one bit.

"Hayden—" He stopped himself.

"Look at *your* hair, for fuck's sake."

Those orange ringlets that bobbed against his neck when he spoke—did he really believe they were *accidental*? How could he fail to see that he was the perfect exemplar of her *hair as identity* credo?

"Hayden—"

"Hayden what? I'm embarrassing you? Your low-life daughter."

"Do you want me to pretend I'm not disappointed?"

His expression changed, migrating within seconds from disgust to softness, and Hayden noticed Manuela approaching. "How is your meal?" she said, standing over them.

"Divine," he said. "We're just slow. Lots to talk about, you know." He grinned at Manuela and rolled his eyes, referring to Hayden. Manuela nodded and left. "Are you aware of the scene you are making? Drink some water," Father told Hayden. "Eat something."

She was running out of steam. She breathed heavily. She rested her forearms on the table. Father kneaded his chin. Their eyes bristled over each other's faces. Silence beset them. It thickened to sludge. She drew her right forefinger slowly through the votive's flame as she used to do when she was a child, but her calibration was off and she did it too slowly and her finger came out red and sore.

"Stop that," he said. "What are you doing to yourself?"

She sucked her finger, eyes on the flame. When she began to speak again she spoke more quietly. "That's the thing with hair—you get to say who you are with it. Look around—"

She scanned the hairdos of the other diners. They had practical haircuts, each strand perfectly aligned. Seeking exceptions, she turned from table to table. Emory stood in the shadows by the front desk. Hayden snapped her head back to her father.

"I *hated* seeing Mother in the casket that way. Her hair all teased and sprayed like that. The person in that casket had *nothing* to do with who she was."

"That's it," he said. He rose, hurling his napkin down in a gesture Hayden remembered so well from childhood, and he pushed his chair back from the table so fast it scraped the floor loudly, prompting scolding looks from a few nearby diners. A waiter hurried over to assist, reaching out to Father's forearm, but Father brushed him off. Limping badly, almost falling, he negotiated an unsteady path past the other tables, grasping the backs of other people's chairs. A few pieces of silverware clattered to the floor. People turned in alarm. He bumped the wind chimes, so they nattered the dark. By the time he found his way out onto the path that led down to the bungalows, everyone—guests and servers alike—was watching him.

A few people turned back toward Hayden, their eyes scalding. She took in their chiding. Reeling, she closed her eyes. When she opened them, Emory was sitting next to her.

"What the heck was that about?" Emory said.

Hayden shook her head back and forth violently. She licked her burned finger.

"Sorry I'm late—I fell asleep. Is your dad going to be okay on his own? He looked sort of unsteady."

Hayden's breath was quick. She knew she should move. She rose.

"You okay?" Emory frowned. He started to rise along with her.

"Fine," Hayden said. "See you tomorrow." She left Emory alone, following the same path her father had taken, through the tables and out into the fomenting night.

Chapter 22

Hayden could tell her father was awake. She lay in bed fully-clothed only a few feet from where he lay, feeling his consciousness like a charge, positive hitting negative, negative hitting positive, atoms ready for fission.

She was too exhausted, too dizzy, too scared to apologize. Outside the night whipped up a fandango of sound—churning wings; foraging paws; some guttural, almost human croak. They had been told by the jeep driver that wild cats lived in the jungle, although he'd said they were rare. Still, when she looked in the direction of the dark deck she imagined she saw the yellow eyes of a nocturnal animal spiraling laser-like through the night. She needed to urinate, but did not dare. A blister was rising on her burned finger.

Through the night they each took sleep in brief snatches. Finally light seeped through the matchstick blinds, and Hayden opened her eyes for good. She had been awakened by a scratching sound, and when she was oriented she saw the scratching came from the adjacent bed. Father had propped himself up with pillows and was scribbling furiously on a large pad of paper. She heard in the pen's scribbling the high wind of his thought. She heard his deafening critique of her, an announcement to his reading public: *I have a hopeless daughter who has devoted herself to hair.*

Head aching, she peeled back the silky mosquito netting and stepped out of bed. Her feet were bare and soundless on the cool tiled floor. Eyes averted, she slunk past Father's bed, feeling the sticky nimbus of his toiling consciousness threatening to lap up everything. Neither of them uttered a word as she headed to the bathroom to pee.

She pushed out the heavy front door and stood shoeless on the soft loam of the path. On the western slope of the hill the sun was not yet visible and the lightening sky still held a gray cast. The air was delicious—a cool promise. Around her, coming from all directions, she heard scuttling wildlife, but she saw nothing. Perhaps she was too urban for the nature-watching talent the jeep driver had talked about.

She walked slowly uphill, eyes sealed to the ground, thinking of camouflaged snakes, of tropical worms that bore through feet. Separated from her Hoboken/New York life by only two days, she felt as though it had been months since she'd traveled on a jam-packed PATH train or crunched glass under her boots on a Manhattan sidewalk. She heard footsteps behind her and turned, moving off the path to let a white-clad resort worker pass. He moved quickly but without haste, long legs intimate with the terrain so he scarcely needed his eyes to navigate.

"Morning," he said as he passed. Then, *"Buenos días,"* so as not to insult her by assuming she knew no Spanish, though he would have been correct in assuming this.

"Morning," Hayden said. *"Buenos días."*

He disappeared quickly where the path rounded a bend and Hayden was left with the sense that he had fluttered by her, leaving no imprint. When the path made another turn she faced the bay. A trace of sun had cleared the trees and it reached out so a thin strip of water was ignited to a blazing, incandescent white.

The day was in motion. A man cleared debris from the peanut-shaped pool with a long-handled net. With each swipe he found waterlogged leaves, flower petals, small frogs whose bodies, swimming away from the net, stretched long as thick elastic bands. He tossed them all into the bushes, cleansing the pool of every unsavory, off-putting trace of the jungle, lest the tourists who had come to see the jungle would rather not swim with it. Intent on his task, he did not see Hayden.

The palapa was empty. In the kitchen someone sang quietly along with a Spanish radio broadcast. Dishes clattered lightly against one another and the smell of frying onions garnished the air. The kitchen door swung open and two dark-haired women emerged, hips swaying under trays stacked high with dishes. Hayden looked for a place where she could sit—and possibly sleep—unnoticed. The deck fit her needs perfectly. It was built out from the palapa on fifty-foot pilings and it offered a panoramic view out over the canopy and down to the bay. With the help of expensive binoculars provided by the resort and available for borrowing free of charge, guests could stand at the railing and see, in the course of an hour, nearly the full spectrum of Costa Rica's heralded wildlife. Not interested in wildlife, she sank into a wooden armchair with plush pillows and soon she floated on ripples of hushed, quiescent sound: bird calls, monkey chatter, the muffled clink of dishes. Images glistened among the sounds. Father in bed, writing with the concentration of Rasputin. Emory's chin fuzzed with a fine beard. The pink-white depths of a snake's throat.

When she opened her eyes, one of the women from the jeep was standing by the deck's railing, face welded to a pair of binoculars. She wore leaf-green, quick-dry clothing, sensible walking shoes with olive socks, and a hat so determinedly round it seemed designed to return her to girlhood. She looked tidy and patrician. Feeling the stroke of Hayden's eyes, she turned.

"Some lovely scarlet macaws out there," she said. "Eight of them in one tree." Hayden nodded, too sluggish to rise. "Would you like the glasses?" the woman said.

"No, thanks. I can see them," Hayden lied.

The woman returned to the view for a moment then lowered the binoculars and came to sit in the chair next to Hayden. "An astounding species. They're monogamous, you know, just like wolves."

Hayden nodded, trying to stay engaged, but fighting the fierce pull of sleep.

"Are you enjoying your stay here?" the woman asked.

"It hasn't been very long yet."

"I know. We were on the same jeep. I'm Janine, remember?"

"Oh yes, of course," Hayden said though she wouldn't ever have remembered this woman specifically. She looked like all the others, middle-aged, prosperous, naively eager.

"Pardon me for asking, but I've been dying to know. I saw you last night at dinner. Is the man you were with—your father, I'm assuming—is he Angus Risley, the writer?"

Hayden blinked and stared into Janine's enthusiastic face. Its planes were bunched as peony petals in anticipation. "I don't know who you're talking about," Hayden said.

Janine's face deflated. "You don't know Angus Risley?"

"I'm sorry," Hayden said.

"I thought you might be the daughter who—in his recent book, the one who—never mind." Her eyebrows worked like chopsticks. "He's a wonderful writer. Novels. Books about travel. He's so prolific. I brought two of his books with me. One is about the tropics—the flora and fauna, but even more about the tropical frame of mind, how living in the tropics changes your thinking in the most fundamental ways. He uses such lovely words—*flocculent, cupreous*. Who uses words like that? Divine. So when I saw you and your father in the dining room last night—well, I guess it was a case of wishful thinking because I literally *just* finished his new book—it would have been too much of a coincidence, I guess, wouldn't it?"

She turned to the hillside. In the distance the now-risen sun had illuminated the sea to a flat, silver wafer. *The daughter who, in his recent book* . . . Hayden shuddered to think. No wonder she hadn't read it.

"Lovely here, isn't it? I've been all over the world—the Great Barrier Reef, the Amazon, all over the Mediterranean, Machu Pichu, Bhutan—and Costa Rica stands up very well in comparison. The resort is beautifully managed, I think. Comfortable without being lavish. We must keep it a secret so it doesn't get overrun." She laughed self-consciously.

"Oh, heavens!" She eyed Hayden's long sleeves and pants. "You aren't hot in those things?"

Hayden looked down at her limbs, clad in sweat-soaked black. "My luggage was lost," she said. The focus on her body embarrassed her.

"What a shame!" Janine hesitated, looked out to the sea again. "Well!" As if she'd been poked, she took up the staccato tempos of more temperate climes. "I must be off." She leaned forward and whispered. "My husband, Perry, is still asleep—he's expecting me to awaken him."

She departed just in time to encounter Roberto, the naturalist, who strode through the breezeway, rubber boots flapping like ducks about to take flight. Janine pulled him aside and pointed out to the forest with a question. He listened with an inscrutable absence of expression and answered her in a low seductive voice that was almost a whisper. He turned once to glance at Hayden and the consideration of his thoughtful gaze made her feel conspicuously alone. She closed her eyes, lulled by the sough of their talk. When she opened her eyes again, Janine was gone and Roberto was heading back to the office. She drifted off once more and the next time she opened her eyes it was Emory standing in front of her.

"Breakfast?" Emory said. He looked vigorous and rested. "I'm starving."

They sat at a table adjacent to the large family of Texans. Emory ate eggs and tortillas and fruit, but Hayden wasn't hungry. She sipped her coffee and watched Emory eat and thought how right he looked here, less strange than usual. It helped that the bruise on his cheekbone was beginning to fade a little. He leaned forward, whispering.

"I had no idea how upscale this place would be. I feel bad. This is going to cost your sister a chunk of cash."

Hayden shrugged. "It was her idea."

"Rumba," said one of the Texans.

"Rumba, rumba, rumba," echoed another and they all laughed.

Emory spread jam on a tortilla and rolled it up like a sleeping bag. "I haven't had an appetite like this since I was on T. What happened last night? With your father, I mean?" Emory said.

"It turns out he doesn't want to go home. That's what he said yesterday, at least."

"You're kidding."

Hayden shook her head. "I'm not. Although it's probably not the end of the story."

"If it is though, we leave, right?"

"I guess," Hayden said.

"Not too soon I hope. I like it here." Emory grinned. "I'm catching a jeep into town this afternoon to get hold of a bathing suit."

"How did you arrange that?"

"Gustavo."

Hayden was surprised. "You're so entrepreneurial."

The Texan family was getting rowdy. All ten of them had different ideas about how to spend the day. "I don't give a shit about the monkeys," said one of the teenage boys.

"I would have joined you last night, but"—Emory paused, looked into his coffee for the right word. When he looked up at Hayden again he was smiling coyly—"let's just say you were making a *scene* and I wasn't sure if I should butt in."

"I was tired. The heat got to me, I guess. And the wine. He's not happy with me," Hayden said. "Then again, I'm not happy with him either. He's a snob and an egomaniac."

Gustavo came by their table to tell them that Dr. Estuvio was expected. He greeted Emory warmly as if they knew each other well. To Hayden he said, "We have a tray of breakfast for your father. Would you like to take it down to him or shall we?" He looked at Hayden as if she might hiss and she realized that news of the prior night must have reached him.

"I'll take it," Hayden said and within moments, it seemed, Manuela was there with a tray of fruit and rolls, slabs of white cheese, coffee. She did not look directly at Hayden, and Hayden felt once again ashamed of last night's performance.

"Time to meet the man," Emory said after Gustavo and Manuela had both departed. "Do you know the Muffin Man, the Muffin Man, the Muffin Man? Do you know the Muffin Man who lives on Drury Lane," Emory sang as they made their way down the path.

They found him still in bed and writing, wearing only a white T-shirt and threadbare khaki shorts. Between shorts and shirt was a visible band of hair-flocked midriff. As he looked at them, his face remained blank, no sign of annoyance or pleasure. It seemed to Hayden he did not recognize her. Or perhaps she was the one who did not recognize him. In the past he had always groomed himself scrupulously, fanatically, as if his failure to do so would plunge him back to his working-class origins.

"Are you ready for this?" Hayden said, indicating the tray.

Slowly his personality resituated itself in the idling body before them. "Yes. Yes, of course. Put it down. This must be your— Emory, if I recall right?"

The two men regarded one another as if the occasion were perfectly natural. Emory, smiling, hand out-thrust. "Good to meet you, Mr. Risley."

"Angus, please," Father said. He returned the handshake with equal vigor and smiled the glistening smile of a redhead, of a charmed and famous man. "Please forgive me if I don't get up. I've injured my ankle. I understand you two have come to steal me away from this place."

"But you don't want to go," Emory said. "I can understand that—it's beautiful here. I don't want to go either."

Hayden watched this conversation, encased on the sidelines, a place far away from her father or Emory. Father was treating Emory like a full-fledged man, speaking to him in hearty male parlance. It seemed to her they had both lost their memories. Of last night's fight. Of the struggle to be a man. Of life in the States. Some native moroseness had lifted from both of them, and Hayden didn't understand what had brought it about. She turned away and lifted lids from the dishes.

"Hayden, bring some chairs, would you?" Father said.

Hayden handed him a cup of coffee and a plate with a buttered roll and mango slices. She brought two chairs for herself and Emory. "We were discussing hair last night," Father said to Emory.

"And—?" Emory leaned in, genuinely interested.

Father grew chatty. "Do you think Don King was saying something important with his hair? Or Sid Vicious? Or the gal who used to shave her head—the singer?"

"Sinead O'Connor," Emory said.

"Yes. She. Do you think those hair statements had important political or cultural meaning?"

Hayden wondered if he was mocking her. She didn't want a repeat of the prior night. She felt a twinge of annoyance at Emory— could it be jealousy? She picked up a roll and took a bite.

"It depends," Emory said.

"Hayden would rather not discuss this. Am I right?"

"I didn't say that," Hayden said. Her mouth was full of spongy roll. She tried to swallow.

"I don't suppose you know this," Father said, his eyes on Hayden, "but they're using hair follicles now to grow stem cells."

"Of course I know that," Hayden snapped. "We all do. Ask Emory. She'll tell you. *He'll* tell you." She bit her lip hard.

"Well, I can see my remarks are not very welcome. No matter. I need to get back to work anyway. Good to meet you Emory. I trust we'll see more of you."

"Yeah, sure you will. I'm not going anywhere. Except to get a bathing suit, that is. I'm really into swimming." He grinned.

"I'm done with the tray," Father said. "You can take it." He had eaten only a bite or two of his roll and a forkful of mango. Hayden left his coffee on the bedside table and took the rest.

"I hope we didn't interrupt your writing," Emory said.

"Coleridge," Father said. "Delirium. Nasty bruise you've got there."

"Oh," Emory said, touching his cheekbone. "It's getting better."

At the door, tray in hand, Hayden paused. "Do you really not want to leave?" she said to her father.

He stared at her for a moment, his lips full and parted in a way that suggested streams of thought had arrived in his mouth, ready to be sent forth as words. His eyes had the squirrelly, panicked look of someone in captivity. "Save it for later," he said finally, and he waved them off.

"He's very sweet," Emory said as soon as they hit the path.

"Sweet? You saw *sweet*?" Hayden snorted and quickened her stride. Emory said no more.

Chapter 23

At the pool Hayden sat on a lounge chair with most of her body in shade. Only her bare feet and lower legs were exposed to the sunshine. Her head still ached, though less poignantly now. Mostly she felt used up. It was late morning and midday heat draped the resort like the loose skin of a cat. A muffling force. A silencing force. Everything drowsed.

Emory sat at the pool's edge, dangling his feet in the azure water, transfixed by the tarantella of light. He yearned to swim. He lusted for it. Water seemed better to him than food or sex or sleep. They had the pool to themselves, and if it hadn't seemed offensive, he would have dived right in with all his clothes on. But he was a guest here, staying on someone else's dime. He would try to behave properly, the way he imagined his hosts would. Thoughts of the beating kept coming to him in waves. It was their eyes he remembered. They were only kids, not more than fifteen or sixteen years old, but they had the glassy eyes of bigots, the eyes of people who had never been listened to. The primary puncher wore a flimsy black windbreaker. He grunted with each punch. As Emory ran away their laughter poured over him, and he smelled the rank odor of his own humiliation. It was good to be away from the city for a while, away from the salon's mirrors and storefront reflections, away from the sense of himself as a loser.

Behind him Hayden slept off a hangover. She was annoyed at him; she hadn't liked it when Emory said her father was sweet. But Angus *was* sweet. Eager to talk, eager to please. Most of all—absolutely accepting of Emory himself. Or so it appeared. Emory was curious as to whether he really had passed with Angus, or if Angus was simply being polite.

A small girl child eyed him from the other side of the pool. He didn't see where she'd come from. She had taken off her shoes and socks and dangled her feet in the water as Emory was doing. She did not look older than four or five, but she was not accompanied by any adult as far as he could see. When he smiled at her she smiled back. She had a pointed chin and articulated cheekbones that made her look like a small adult. Her dark hair was braided into two substantial pigtails that hung down her back.

Emory reached down and stirred the water energetically with both hands. The little girl watched him and followed suit. Emory used one hand to slap the water. The girl slapped too. Emory touched his nose with one finger. The girl touched her own nose. Emory laughed and so did the girl.

"*¿Qué le pasó a su cara?*" she asked.

Emory shrugged. "*Nada.*"

"*Dicen que no debo hablar con usted,*" the girl said.

Hayden opened her eyes just enough to see a blurred landscape through her lashes. Emory was holding an animated conversation in Spanish with a small dark-haired girl. They laughed and splashed each other across the pool. The little girl didn't appear to find anything strange in Emory. Hayden clamped her eyes shut again. *Sweet.* That was one thing her father definitely was not.

* * *

Emory convinced Hayden to go to the beach with him though she was not keen on swimming. It was mid-afternoon and he had returned from town with a bathing suit and shorts. The sun's heat was already on the wane, and the day was tipping toward evening. The path emerged from the woods and descended steeply over a rocky scree.

"Just grant me that you've only seen one side of him, that's all," Hayden was saying. "I never said he couldn't be charming sometimes."

A large smooth rock rolled out from under the ball of Hayden's leather-soled shoe and began a cascade of rocks that ricocheted off one another in speedy descent. Hayden fell hard on her tailbone. Pain oscillated through her rump, thigh, spine. Startled wildlife scurried into the underbrush. One creature remained—not two feet from her was a fat rope of a snake, pus-yellow, lying in loops and coils like a haphazardly discarded garden hose. He eyed her but did not give ground. He sized her up as posing no danger. She dared not move. "Jesus," she said.

"Move back slowly," Emory said. "Just don't do anything quick." Having grown up in Florida he knew a bit about snakes.

Hayden did as Emory told her to do, rising slowly. She held eye contact with the snake, who seemed to know exactly how his gaze, his bulk, his simple snake-ness terrified her. Emory was excited; he thought it might be an eyelash viper, but wasn't sure.

"You know the story about Teiresias?" Emory said as they continued down the hill. "He came across some snakes mating and he knows he's supposed to turn away, but he doesn't and Hera—I think it was Hera—turns him into a woman."

Hayden didn't remember this. She laughed. "You're thinking it might work the other way too?"

"That's not all—it *did* work the other way. Teiresias lived for a while as a woman and had sex with men and stuff, and then she ran across the snakes again. And they were doing it then too. Or maybe still doing it, I don't know. Anyway, she watches again, trying to figure out if they're the same snakes and—bingo, she's a man again. It was after that, I think, that he was blinded by the gods, because of all the stuff he knew by then about men and women and sex." Emory laughed and ruffled his crew cut. "So maybe I should go back and have a chat with that snake. The point is—I'm not doing anything so new."

"How do you know about this?" Hayden said.

"Trans stuff. It gets around."

Hayden wanted to mention that she had always hated snakes, but it seemed like such a girl thing to say.

They moved directly out of the woods onto a small beach protected by a spit of land reaching out on the bay's western edge. The sky was the muted pale blue of baby blankets. It demanded nothing. A light breeze blew in off the water.

"Is that Panama?" Emory said, looking across to the distant shore. "I think that might be Panama." Emory was opened up to the world and noticing things well beyond the boundaries of his own skin.

"I'm not sure," Hayden said.

She sat on a log, hermit crabs scuttling around her feet, and watched Emory swim. His arms sliced through the loose swells, rose high above the water, then disappeared beneath. Soon his head was no larger than a bird's. He bobbed in one place for a while, giving himself over to the waves' whimsy, then he lifted his arm to wave at her. She could see he felt good, and she wondered if swimming could impart the same centered feeling to her.

By the water's edge two boys—one little, one big, both still in the energized thick of boyhood—made a high-walled fortress of sand. They raced back and forth, scooping up crabs by the handful and dumping them into the walled arena. When the crabs tried to escape they poked them back with sticks. Farther down the beach a quartet of birders strolled near the trees. She thought of her father and wondered if he needed anything. She supposed she should check.

Emory moved from water to land as if the transition were seamless. He had no towel, but was happy to drip-dry as he walked. She tried not to look at the scars from his chest surgery. In the moonlight the scars had seemed inconsequential, but now, in the sunlight, they looked three-dimensional and they shrieked of abnormalcy.

Hayden walked beside Emory in a daze, listening to the soothing *tsk* made by the fabric of his newly purchased shorts. The path was dappled with shadow like a Dalmatian's back. After seven or eight minutes they reached the lowermost bungalows. Their west-facing walls sucked up the late afternoon sun like chromatography strips, and glowed an orangey pink. They stopped in front of what Hayden thought was her father's bungalow, but she was wrong. Approaching from the other direction had confused her. They heard a female voice inside singing softly in Spanish. No, this *was* her father's bungalow. The voice—Manuela's? She and Emory exchanged a look.

The deck was fenced with wooden slats angled for privacy. Hayden pressed her eye up close—all she could see was a thin rod of sky and leaves and below them slivers of the human form, like the waxy slices of a high school rat biopsy. A tenebrous bird nearby thrust out his song.

"See you later, I guess," Emory said. "At dinner." He continued up the hill.

From inside the dim bungalow Hayden had a clear view out to the deck. Father lay, belly-down, on the chaise, covered to his neck with a white sheet. Manuela, no longer singing, stood at the table, loading several bottles of lotion into a basket. She wore a full-length white apron over her blouse and skirt, and her hair had been expertly twisted so it lay on her nape like a complex root system. She looked up at Hayden nervously, caught off guard, her face wearing the wide-eyed look of someone emerging from a daydream. After a second she gripped a smile. Father glanced up, drowsy.

"She gives a great massage," he said.

Manuela laughed lightly, embarrassed. "I'm going now, Mr. Risley. You have a good rest."

"Mr. Risley?" Father laughed. "Who's he?"

"Would you like for us to bring your dinner here? Or up there?" she asked.

"Here," Hayden said quickly, not relishing a repeat of the prior night.

"We'll go up," Father said, as if she'd said nothing.

"Yes." Manuela reached out to touch his covered shoulder. "You feel good."

"Oh, I will," he said. "I do."

Manuela was gone, but her presence lingered, palpable as heat. Her floral scent clung to the air, permeating their nostrils, tickling the brain stem. The bird on the fence, the tenebrous one, said something. Hayden stood where she was.

"Your Emory is a good man," Father said, lifting his head a little, twisting his neck to look at her. *Good man?* Was he joking? Surely he was not thinking of Emory now.

"He's not *my* Emory."

"I'm trying to be cordial," Father said.

"So am I." But even as she said so, staring at his hair, whose color had been emboldened by sunset's last flecks of gold, irritation roiled. Could it be as she was thinking it was? Manuela worked here. She served him. She had to be thirty years younger than he. "I came here, didn't I?" she said.

"Yes, you came." He shifted a little and tried to roll onto his back. His shoulder got in the way, he winced and gave up. Hayden watched to see if he would try again. She went inside for a pillow and offered it to him, and when he tried to turn again she used her arm as a shovel under his upper back.

She leaned against the railing. "So I guess you're screwing Manuela, right?"

Her own words stung her and without waiting for an answer she went inside and lay stiffly on the bed. It was dusk now and they still had dinner to negotiate. Through one of the glass panes of the deck door she could see his bony bare foot. She should have waited for his answer. Maybe she was wrong. But she was not wrong, she knew she was not wrong. He was taking what he pleased, just as he'd always done. She thought of her mother, telling her to be nice. *Tap wood, clap thrice, spin*, Mother used to say at moments of uncertainty.

From the deck he hooted. "Dinner!"

Hayden rose and the sherpas with the portable chair appeared like magic.

Chapter 24

The meal was endless. Manuela waited on them, laughing lightly as she laid down their dishes. She was friendly but attentive to her duties. She and Father smiled at one another, but not necessarily in any particularly knowing way. Still, Hayden was convinced she was right about them. Manuela's white blouse concealed perfect brown breasts, neat as unbroken eggs. But her teeth were imperfect. Not as bad as Arleen's teeth had been, but still imperfect. It seemed unlike Father to be attracted to someone with bad teeth.

Hayden wanted to say something to Manuela, question her. She thought of asking Manuela to have coffee with her, but Manuela kept floating off to other tables, laughing with everyone despite her innate shyness, so the opening did not present itself. The laugh disturbed Hayden. Was Manuela flirting with all the guests? Hayden realized she would have nothing to say over coffee.

Emory and Father conversed in Spanish. Their lips and tongues vaunted the foreign syllables. They, too, convulsed in riddles of laughter. Who knew what was so funny, who cared. Emory had learned to speak Spanish as a young child. In Florida, in the tourist trade, you needed Spanish. He loved the language, he said.

"Yes," Father agreed, "a lovely language," throwing glances at Hayden, urging, mocking, she wasn't sure what.

Emory wore his red tank top and his black New York jeans. His body, refreshed from the swim, gyrated with controlled energy. Lit from behind, his growing crew cut was a bristly black corona, his skin white. The little girl at the pool was Manuela's child, he said.

"Yes, Manuela's child," Father echoed.

They ate roast pork with a piquant fruity sauce.

"Your mother cooked a good pork loin," Father said. But even as he tried to draw her into the conversation, he seemed to push her away. It was his aloofness that drove her crazy. He was present but aloof. His crackle was gone, his ire, but he had become, in her absence, a man who had moved past pain to the relaxed belief that life had served him well. What was there to grip onto with a person like that?

"Let's not bring Mother into this," Hayden said.

"She's here anyway. I think so often how much she would have loved this place."

"We're supposed to be talking about getting you home. Cornelia wants you there for her baby's birth."

"I'll see the baby. The baby isn't going anywhere soon. People always think of one moment as critical. One moment is never critical. It's the aggregate of all the moments that means something."

She stared at her father, remembering his penchant for proclaiming how the world worked.

Afterward Hayden and Emory, on their way to Emory's room, stood in a spray of lamplight near the parked jeeps. Two monkeys swung and squabbled in the trees high above them.

"They're fucking," Hayden whispered. She could almost hear the word trembling in the branches, disturbing the landscape.

"So?" said Emory. "She's quite fuckable, I think."

"Jesus," Hayden said. "Whose side are you on, anyway?"

"I wasn't aware there were sides." Emory looked up, trying to see the monkeys in the swaying trees. Something hooted. He had said the wrong thing again. Why didn't he know any better?

"He's thirty years older than she is," Hayden said.

"There's no formula where attraction is involved," said Emory. He turned his gaze to Hayden's face, her absorbent green eyes. He seemed to enter them.

"Are you saying you're attracted to her?"

He laughed. Attracted to Manuela? In Hayden's world he supposed that made sense. He wanted to pull her from that world, bring her into the present for a while. "No, of course not, but I see how a person could be. And him too. They're both interesting, good-looking, likable people."

"Likable," Hayden said. "There's a word."

"Aren't you being a little hard on him?"

"It's always on *his* terms. What *he* wants. No one else has a voice. It's not just this."

"You don't know she has no voice. You can't be sure of that." Emory was saying the wrong thing again. Why did he persist in saying the wrong thing when he could feel how it annoyed her? And annoying her was the last, absolutely rock-bottom last thing he wanted to do. He sighed. So often in his life words had gotten him into trouble.

"I doubt if she's highly assertive," Hayden said.

"Okay—I shouldn't say anything. My father's dead and I honestly can't remember a single thing about him that bothered me."

"It's true what they say about the good ones dying young. My mother—" She shook her head.

"Yeah, the dead ones always become saints. Well, at least we have a good reason to die."

Hayden looked in the direction of the trees as if she expected the jungle to deliver something malevolent. Her forehead was fretted like that of a much older woman's. If only she could let the heat and the landscape relax her as it seemed to be relaxing him. They were both in Costa Rica, but he could see it was a different planet to each of them.

"Sorry," Emory said. "I'll stop being glib."

"Why don't you ever mention your mother?" Hayden said.

"Do I hear you talking about yours?"

"There's nothing to say, just that she's gone."

Emory nodded. "That about sums it up." He reached out and touched her shoulder. "Hey, let's shut up for a minute. Listen."

They listened and all they heard was the absence of the things they had left behind—the sirens and horns and trucks and phones, the wrangling and fractious voices. Hearing none of those things, they mistook what they heard for silence.

Chapter 25

The moon made a slick hallucination of everything. It flushed out parts of the landscape Hayden hadn't seen before and made the shadows seem cavernous. She wished she had some other place to go, a room of her own where she didn't have to negotiate another person's body or temperament. Her father's body disgusted her now. How could she sleep so close to him and not be plagued by images of him pawing Manuela?

She slipped into the bungalow as quietly as she could. The lights were off and Father was lying on his back, bandaged leg outstretched, eyes closed. His breathing simulated the rhythms of sleep. Maybe he really was asleep. At least he was not talking. She dared not look over at his bed for fear even her look might awaken him. It was not a new feeling, this need to preserve her distance from him, but one of those tattered old feelings she had not had for a while and would rather shed. She remembered him coming home when she was in high school. When they heard the familiar tire-and-gravel rumble on the driveway her sisters would scramble outside to greet him, Sophie squealing, Mother at their heels, her pace more sedate. Only Hayden did not follow suit. She stayed in her bedroom. She watched from the window as he stepped from his car, taller and more of a personage each time he returned. Sophie did cartwheels in the grass. Cornelia badgered him for stories, her arm slung around Father's back as if they were colleagues. They shared oily laughs. Everyone hugged him. All but Hayden who hung in her room, not coming out, not giving in, not letting him off the hook. But watching, of course. *Hayden,* Mother would call. *Your father is home!* Her voice, strong at first, weakened with each utterance until the shouts curdled in the air, their sound and meaning no longer reaching Hayden's ears. Mother's mouth became a caricature of a calling mouth. It was large enough to fill half her face, and Hayden imagined the lips themselves reaching out to her like grasping but ineffectual fingers.

She tried to think of something else. She pictured the way Emory had looked swimming. It was just as he had described: when he swam, he became something else, something sleek and happy and not easily named. Thinking of this she fell asleep and dreamed of phocine bodies swimming around one another, close but not touching.

She was shaken awake, hard. She woke up thinking: *I'm sleeping at last, at last I'm sleeping.* In the dark, the white of her father's face shone down like a close private planet, milky and familiar.

"Hayden, quick. Right now. It's a full moon."

Hayden groaned.

"I have to show you," he whispered. He was pulling back the covers, rattling her out of bed. "Normally I wouldn't do this," he said, clumping slowly ahead of her, clearly in pain.

The full moon slid over the deck, silvery and dangerous as mercury. He laid his hand on her back. He hovered at her side as if to steady her, as if she were the one in need. She would have recoiled had she not been so sleepy. He led her to the railing.

"Look out there."

Once again that night she saw things she had not seen before.

Along the perimeter of the small grassy area was a row of stones and shells. Nestled in the bushes stood a small statue of a woman cradling a baby. Everything was still and opaline, and while the moon gave off no heat, it seemed to scorch the rust from her memory so scraps of images from the past crowded her head then receded before she, in her drowsiness, could grasp them.

"Wait," he said as she started back to bed.

"What?"

"Just wait."

It had to be three or four in the morning. Too late, too early. He tugged her arm, urging her to stay, and a fresh switchblade of annoyance sprang up in her, and she thought of Manuela, how she should warn Manuela, and she was about to say something sharp when out of the bushes a wild cat sauntered. Spotted like a leopard, eyes of gold, he loped to the center of the grassy area, the muscles of his thighs and back fluid and wet-looking, simonized. He seemed to know they were watching him because he stopped in the dead center of the lawn, his head held high as if he were posing. Sniffing, his nose twitched then his head rotated slowly around until he held them in his gaze, his panoramic vision narrowing from the wide scope of the jungle to include only them. The moonlight flowed like a viscous liquid into his eyes, excavating their depths so she felt she could see rods and cones and even beyond, all the way to his brain on which was etched the imprint of them, two humans motionless on the deck. She didn't know how much time had passed, but as she watched her mood eased.

Her father's body stood at the edge of her own. His hand rested on her shoulder. They were breathing at the same rate, as if to pass themselves off to the cat as one organism, not two. She wondered, suddenly, if her father knew this would happen, if the wild cat before them was what he had wanted to show her, not the moon. She couldn't speak. The cat shivered; the skin and fur of his shoulders and loins slid back and forth in a massive tectonic twitch. But his eyes stayed on them, and when his shivering was done he went still again. An active stillness, not a frozen one.

Then she could see his consciousness, she was sure—at the base of his eyes, his mind shimmied, formulating thoughts, considering ideas, deciding whether to stay, to leave, to attack. She felt his intelligence and the accuracy of his judgment.

"She looks like Claire, doesn't she?" Father whispered. "It looks to me as if Claire is inhabiting that body. I see it in the eyes." Not *your mother,* but *Claire.*

The remark lay between them. It accumulated weight in the hush. It was a stupid remark, Hayden thought. But the cat's presence was compelling, preeminent; it obliterated pettiness. Little by little, she saw it was true: The cat—was it a she?—held something of Mother in her gaze. It was not so much a challenging look as a curious one. There was expectancy in the eyes, a desire to be liked and considered. And the eyes were housed in a regal body, just like Mother's.

Time was elastic. Without a watch, without the sun, without the movement of her own body, there were no identifying markers for the passing minutes and her mind seemed to rove through the jungle on the back of the cat's mind.

Though the edge of her father's body grazed the edge of hers, Hayden was not concerned with him just then, except she knew they were together in seeing this cat, and they were breathing synchronously, and later she would have to ask him certain kinds of questions she had never asked him before. Fear dissolved, but like dissolved sugar it left a strong awakening taste, and she wanted to speak—to the cat, to Father, to the night itself—though she knew speech would offend them all.

Suddenly some membrane around them seemed to rupture and the cat's head swiveled away from them and she—*she*, yes, of course the cat was a she, how could Hayden have thought differently—continued her majestic lope across the grassy area, stepping gingerly over the rock and shell border and passing into the bushes and shadows with scarcely a sound. A mere crack or two of twigs. She knew the forest so intimately she could lay her padded feet just so, cruise quietly, invisibly, get just what she wanted.

When she was gone Hayden and her father remained there, watching the shadows to see if she would reappear.

"A jaguar," he whispered. "Every full moon. Like clockwork. The ancients thought jaguars were sacred. There's something to it."

"I thought they were so rare and so shy no one ever saw them. That's what the naturalist said."

"Rare, yes. But not unheard of. They choose everything. You can't tell Gustavo. Or anyone else."

"Why not?"

"They would shoot her. They have a business to protect. It would scare people. They want wildlife, but not roving through their backyards." His whisper crackled, intermittently strong then weak.

"How many times have you seen her?" Hayden said.

"Dozens."

"She knows you?"

"Maybe."

"How did you know she'd come tonight?"

They were leaning on the railing but no longer touching one another. Still steeped in the aftermath of the cat's visit, they stared at the spot where she had stopped, as if something palpable remained they might lay eyes on. Father turned to look at Hayden's face.

"You read the signs," he said. Like the cat, he held his gaze on Hayden, taking careful measure, reading whatever signs she herself was giving off. "Were you frightened?" he whispered.

"Yes," she said. "At first. Were you?"

"I'm used to her."

"You're not easily frightened, I guess."

"Some things frighten me."

"It's hard to imagine," Hayden said.

"Your mother always frightened me."

A conversational cork. A fly ball. Nostrils flaring, she left him there in the moonlight. This was *her* topic to raise, not his.

Back in bed. The room defined stillness. Each molecule listened to every other one. The moon's sheen licked the white sheets of Father's empty bed. The drone of one lone mosquito arose from the dark like an underworld echo. Outside, Father shuffled slowly across the deck boards. Hayden did not get up. She looked around the room and saw all the objects—the lamps, the ceiling fan, the bamboo chairs—waiting, holding their collective breath for Father's return. What could be more ridiculous than thinking Mother was in that cat? Did he truly believe that? Was it consolation to him? Did it exonerate him to believe such a thing? And why, if she were a cat, would she possibly want to come here to witness Father's betrayals?

Outside Father clung to the railing, the chair, the bungalow's outdoor wall. Then he lurched through the door frame. Once inside he followed the room's perimeter, palm on the wall, unsteady in the best of circumstances, but especially in the dark. Tottering across the last few feet of open space, he made his way back to bed. He tried to move the mosquito netting and ended up lying partway on it so it separated from its frame and hung down in baleful folds. Prone, he breathed heavily and Hayden felt ashamed and furious. She wondered how Manuela could like him, how Mother could ever have liked him.

The night kept going, much to Hayden's dismay. She cursed herself for not deciding to crash with Emory. She yearned for her mother and tried to sleep.

Father's breathing had slowed. His voice startled her. "I suppose it is a quality of the young to think they have a monopoly on pain."

Outside something hooted and it lured their attention to the jungle again, silencing them for a while.

"You need to know, Hayden, that I was never unfaithful to your mother. She is no longer with us—should I not have a life?" He rearranged his pillows and shifted his body to the side of the bed that was close to her. He made himself laugh in a brief controlled eruption that seemed emblematic of the atmosphere of her childhood.

"I know I behaved badly when your mother died. Leaving you girls alone with Arleen. I couldn't stay still. I couldn't see my own shoes. I'm not proud of how I was."

She thought of that long horrible spring when she and Arleen had slogged around the house, taking forever to do the chores. In the late morning they would make instant butterscotch pudding and hot chocolate, and after eating they would fall asleep on the living room couch under quilts, the heat cranked high.

"Look, I'm not going to lie to you and tell you your mother stopped cutting herself after you left for college—she was cutting fairly regularly and seeing a therapist and all—but she died of an aneurysm, pure and simple. I wouldn't lie to you about that. And I didn't meet Manuela until afterward. So rest assured."

"I didn't come here to talk about this. I'm supposed to be helping you out, but you don't want help apparently."

"There are certain things you need to know."

"Maybe," Hayden said. "Maybe not."

"What the hell happened to your curiosity? Your empathy, for God's sake. Your mother wasn't always happy, but she was happy often enough. And she wanted to live. If for nothing else, for you girls."

Hayden felt like Peg then, wanting things to be different and knowing they never would be. "I'm going to sleep," she said, rigid as a horse, worlds away from sleep.

"I know you didn't like what I said out there about your mother being in the cat. But she never got over having to part with all those animals of hers, so it would make sense that her soul might have migrated to an animal, don't you think?"

"You knew about the animals?"

"Of course I knew."

Hayden sorted memories, trying to recall him knowing about the animals, but all the sure facts fell away from each other like a deck of slippery cards. Had Mother returned the animals because Father made her?

"Listen, can you understand I adored your mother? I worshipped her. And I was terrified of her too. Her elegance. Her sensitivity. Her background. Her money. She could be superior sometimes. But things worked between us. I had my things to do and she needed her autonomy. She liked to have me gone sometimes. She was nervous when I was around too much. She functioned better without me. You could see that."

He was gone because she had wanted him gone? That wasn't what Hayden remembered.

"But when you girls were young and she had her anxiety attacks, I was there for her. A hundred percent. Arleen was too."

Hayden tried to construct an image of what he might be talking about, an image of an anxiety attack Mother might have had, an image of him being there to help. Outside the rustling became louder—maybe the jaguar was back.

"You mean the cutting?" Hayden said.

"No, I mean when she hid in her room and wouldn't come out and wouldn't eat and wouldn't take you girls to school."

"She always took us to school."

Father cracked his knuckles, a sound as loud as breaking bones. Mother used to take long naps sometimes, but she always came out, she never didn't come out. She came out and sang and happied Hayden and her sisters in every way she knew how. She fortified them for future encounters with Father. She came out and fed the animals and fed the girls and made their girl-world glow. They lived just beyond the bus route so they had to be driven to school. Mother would drive slowly along the country roads, commenting on what they passed, making them look outside at the patterns of a flock of migrating geese, or at the saturated Titian blue of the sky. When she dropped them off in front of the school she squeezed their knees or shoulders as they left the car. *You're all queens,* she told them. *Be kind queens.*

"You're wrong," Hayden said. "I was there. You weren't there."

"I did what I could."

"You should have told me about Manuela."

"Would you feel better if I were unhappy now?" he said.

"I don't have any idea what you are. Happy or unhappy—I don't know you."

"I suppose I could say the same about you. I could tell you how I've been trying not to mourn for the Hayden-child I knew. I know she's still there somewhere. I may be a bit different from when I last knew you, but I am only more fully myself now and I suspect you are too."

Silence.

"I'm not perfect. I never was perfect. And your mother and I, we couldn't live with each other easily and we couldn't live without each other. We didn't do everything right, but I never stopped loving her. And I believe she loved me."

"So this is what you do—come down here and fuck the natives. That's your way of showing your love."

Hayden's words lay pasted across the dark as if she'd scrawled them there. Now they would be there for keeps, tainting every night.

"Hayden," he whispered. "Hayden. Your palliative was hair. Mine has been this place. Its rhythms. Manuela."

Hayden said nothing. She felt hard and stiff, head and heart split.

"Do you know the Heisenberg Uncertainty Principle? From physics. You see me, you change me. The more you try to measure what I am, the less likely I am to be that thing. I'm no physicist, but you get the idea."

She could almost hear the grandfather clock ticking and smell the hot wax and tiny strings of smoke from the recently snuffed dinner candles, and see the congealed roast beef fat on the dinner platter Arleen was taking to the kitchen. She saw the three of them on the couch in schooled eagerness to recite; she saw Father leaning back in his leather chair, legs crossed, hair aflame with tungsten light. She closed her eyes on that image, trying to return elsewhere—the salon, the jungle, anywhere else.

"Hayden?"

"What?"

"You want to tell me I'm an asshole? Go ahead and tell me. I don't dispute it. I try not to be, but I have been. Your mother often hated me too—I'm sure she told you." The next breath he took was long and jagged and within seconds, he wept.

Chapter 26

The tropics are hard on the hair of most North Americans. The sun, the ocean salt, the chlorine all burn through the cuticle and leach out moisture so the hair dries and breaks and takes on the frayed look of an old whisk broom, or a piece of stiffened burlap. Around the follicle humidity causes dandruff to coagulate into an off-smelling paste, a spongy fertile ground for dormant spores to develop. Skin conditions erupt—eczema and psoriasis—and it's hard to curtail the itching. With their hair maligned, beginning to resemble commercial carpeting, people take to wearing hats and scarves.

But the Ticos have adapted, and they grow resilient hair that is impervious to the climate's rigors. Dark hair, it gleams in the sun; it is soft to the touch; it sings of health.

Chapter 27

Febrile with energy, he rose early, when it was still dark. Morning sounds drifted from the palapa, dishes clattering in the kitchen, someone singing. Manuela was just arriving to work, her daughter in tow.

"*Buenos días.* Your name is Emory, right?" she said. "And you have met my Arista?"

He answered her in Spanish, and she laughed. He told her he and Arista had played together at the pool.

"*Sí, sí, Arista lo menicianó. Lo pasó muy bien.*"

"*Yo también. ¿Te gustaría jugar conmigo, otra vez, Arista?*"

"*Ah, sí. ¿Puedo jugar ahera, mamá, hasta que empiece la escula?*"

"*Sí, esta bien. Su tía Rosaria la lleva a la escuela en una hora. Muchas veces me acompaña en la mañana, cuando se porta bien.*"

Manuela laughed again, an easy laugh, sweet and nourishing. Emory would learn to laugh like that. He would make regular laughter his mission.

"*Qué bueno que usted haya podido venir. ¿Ha conocido al señor Risley?*"

"*No, nunca. Es buena gente.*"

"*Ah, sí, muy buena gente. Pués, ya tengo que trabajar. Soy muy habladora ¿verdad? Usted habla español bastante bien. Pocos huéspedes hablan español asi. ¡Usted ya puede entender nuestros chismes! ¡Suerte, hombre!*"

As she left she laughed her sweet laughter again, the laughter he wanted to learn.

While Arista used the bathroom he signed up for a guided nature walk and an evening lecture about reptiles. He stood idle in the breezeway watching the day lighten, and he found himself singing again. "My honey lamb and I, sit alone and talk, and watch a hawk, making lazy circles in the sky . . ." He'd been singing a lot recently. For years he had not sung songs, thinking all the songs belonged to other people's lives. But did it really matter what you sang? It was the singing itself that mattered. He thought about what a narrow life he had lived for the past decade. Maybe all his life. How could it be that in the space of a few short days things felt so different? Was it the landscape, the heat, the country itself?

Manuela was setting tables with her sister Rosaria and one other woman. They chatted quietly as they moved from table to table. It looked like a dance to him the way they moved, swaying their hips under the weight of the laden trays. The day stretched ahead of him, vast and full of possibility. He would play with Arista. There would be the nature walk, some swimming at the beach or the pool, talk with Hayden and her father. He remembered the way Hayden's translucent green eyes had looked the prior night, how he had wanted to pull her into the present and excise her trouble. Perhaps now he would be capable of soothing her.

Arista, dressed in a neon-pink, two-piece bathing suit, made her way through the dining area to where Emory stood. He offered his hand to her and, after a moment's hesitation, she took it.

"Aren't you cold?" Emory said.

The sky was light, but the sun was still too low for heat. Arista giggled and jumped into the pool's aqua water. "Watch me!" she called to Emory. But Emory's eyes were on the male resort worker who was stowing his skimming net in the shed under the trees. He was a stocky man who went about his work with assurance, with ease, with neither sluggishness nor haste. The white shorts of his uniform were still clean at this hour, and their bright spotlessness did not seem to faze him though it was a good bet that he'd be sweaty and dust-tinged by the end of the day. Surely he worried about some things, but not about being a man. Born a man, why would he question it? If he'd had questions they would have been visible. When there were questions it was always written on the body. The body had a million ways of trying to conceal things, but it always told the truth. Oh, the beauty of a body that moved so confidently in the world, the beauty of a body that accepted itself. "Look!" yelled Arista. The resort worker tipped a smile at Emory.

"I'm looking," Emory said.

Arista dove underwater and shot forward, a blur of pink and brown, minnow-fleet, frog-deft. The ripples blurred the outlines of her body to a mirage. Emory thought of himself at her age, every bit as nimble, but far less sure of things. The resort worker watched for a moment too—he must have a child. When he left he smiled and nodded again, as if he and Emory shared a secret.

Emory thought back to the days when he had spent so much time studying men. He used to go out explicitly for that purpose, with his friend James, a genetic man. They made a project of it, positioning themselves on crowded beaches or in heavily trafficked cafés. Starbucks was good, everyone went to Starbucks. Policemen parked their cruisers outside and sauntered in with the imperious eyes of conquerors. High school boys came in, ganglylimbed and baggy-panted, their undulating Adam's apples making Emory touch his own neck. "You know you'll never have an Adam's apple, don't you?" James had said. Emory knew. But the male voice could be had, the refusing-to-pander-I-know-what-I-want rumble of a man's voice, yes, that could be had, and so could the active pores that sent up daily whiskers and the dense fulminant muscles that pressed up under the skin like glacial eskers. A lot could be had. Emory was sure it would be enough. If you made yourself study, as he was doing, the rest would come. He memorized the postures of the stiff-backed businessmen, the way their forearms scythed the air. When men's bodies moved it was with a unity of motion governed by the upper body; men's bodies weren't like women's bodies which seemed to have hundreds of parts that fell, with each movement, into a new arrangement. Men's bodies were cased in a form that held them together, nothing scattered, nothing wasted. Always prepared.

James had grown up a man. What he needed to know had been there all along: a kit, ready-made, all parts included. "Watch me," James would say to Emory. "I'm going to walk over to the counter and order myself more coffee. See the expression on my face when the woman behind the counter says something. Watch the way I pull out my wallet." Emory watched James's face, its no-expression, its topography flat as a Texas plain. James said things to the clerk—friendly things—and kept right on being a man. He never, in action, lost any parts of himself, never let go of the one-thingness of being a man.

Arista was standing beside him, dripping onto his knees, shivering, gasping for breath. "Twelve times!" she said.

"Amazing! Pretty darn amazing." And he laughed and reached for a towel and took her into his lap.

Chapter 28

The cool of early morning. The clamor of birds. No one was around but Gustavo, puttering at the front desk. She stood in his inner office listening, waiting for the ringing phone to make a connection on the other end. She could almost feel the brash pulse shivering along the wires in the quiet morning, winding precariously through the jungle rot and above the parched pastures, then rising over the mountains between the resort and San José, pushing out even farther, across the lowlands of Central America, through the trammeled border villages of Mexico then into the United States with all its metropolitan cacophony. How far that ring had to travel—it exhausted her to think. Through the wide, plate-glass windows she could hear birds flapping noisily, a sloth lounged on the thick branch of a tree. Any wild creature could make its way into the palapa if it wanted, but no one seemed to worry about that. The faint ringing went on and on. Could Cornelia be up and out of the house already? Her thoughts drifted to the image of Father weeping the prior night. His face had looked mangled. His tears had been soundless and now seemed to flow in her own sinuses. Through the open door she could see Gustavo straightening papers at the front desk, trying to look busy. She didn't care if he listened.

The answering voice was gluey with sleep.

"Cornelia, can you talk?" Hayden said.

"Who is this?"

"It's me. Hayden."

"Jesus, it's not even seven o'clock. What're you doing calling so early?"

"I need to talk."

"You couldn't wait a couple of hours?"

"I'm sorry. Shall I call back later?"

"No, I'm up now. Hold on, let me go to another room."

Hayden heard Cornelia getting out of bed and shuffling down a hallway, her gait compromised. She sighed as she settled. "I'm sorry," Hayden said. "I know you have stuff going on."

"Can we get our terminology straight here—I don't have *stuff*, I have a baby about to be born. Is it hot there? It's freezing here."

"I have to ask you something—did Father really tell you he wants to come home?"

"Yes, why?"

"Because now he says he doesn't want to. He wants to stay here. I feel like I've come all this way for nothing."

"He has to come home. He said he'd come home for the birth. I've only got another month. And it could happen earlier. Get him home, would you?"

"How can I get him home if he doesn't want to come? I can't exactly *force* him. Do you remember what he said?"

"He said he'd hurt his ankle and he asked me to come."

"But maybe the part about getting him home was your idea, not his. Maybe he wanted help *down here*."

"No, I'm sure he said he would come home. He's got to see a doctor, doesn't he?"

"Apparently there's one here he can see. And he says this is his home—or one of them. You know about what he's got going on here?"

"You mean the woman?"

"So you know about her. Manuela."

"Yes. But I've never met her. Have you?"

"Yes."

"What's she like?"

"Not like Mother."

"Duh. You wouldn't want her to be like Mother. The point is—do you like her?"

"I guess so, but—"

"What?"

"I don't know. For one thing she's probably thirty years younger than he is."

"Get over it, Hayden—Mother is *dead*. Hold on." Cornelia fell silent, listening to something. "Arthur's getting up now. I've got to go."

"Wait, I have to ask you something—did Mother always take us to school?"

"Yeah, why?"

"Did she ever just stay in bed?"

"Sometimes, don't you remember?"

"Really? Tell me about it. Did you worry?"

"Of course I worried. You did too. Don't you remember how she would just check out for a couple of days and not let us in her bedroom and then Dad had to do household stuff he couldn't do very well? Or if Dad was away Arleen had to do everything and since she couldn't drive we sometimes had to skip school. Why are you dredging this up? It was years ago—let it go."

"I can't believe I don't remember."

"Well, don't bother with remembering—your job now is to get him home. How is his ankle?"

"Fine. Painful. I don't know. No one knows. The doctor hasn't been here yet. But he's weird, Cornelia. He's not like I remember him. He cried last night."

"He's in pain, you just said so. And he's had a lot to be sad about. He has a right to cry. Just get him home, okay?"

"I'll try."

She hung up and stood in the office for a long time, forgetting for a moment who she was and waiting to feel she was in the right skin. Gustavo poked his head around the edge of the door frame.

"Everything all right?" he said. She stared dumbly at his myopic eyes in their quick blink-a-blink behind the thick lenses. He had to be something other than obsequious, but she didn't know what. She supposed he loved people, perhaps he had a family somewhere. Just because Hayden hadn't seen them didn't mean they didn't exist. A breeze blew through. The wooden chimes in the breezeway chortled. She caught a sudden whiff of herself and the rank clothes she'd been wearing for several days straight.

"Did my father say he was leaving?" she said.

"Oh." Gustavo paused as if he were adding numbers in his head. "No, he hasn't mentioned leaving."

"Really? The whole reason I came here was to take him home."

The blinking ceased for a moment and Gustavo frowned. "That's not my understanding. My understanding was—" The phone on the outside desk rang, and he hurried to get it. He exchanged only a few words with the caller and returned to Hayden.

"I have good news. That was Dr. Estuvio. He will be here later this morning. He will examine your father." He cleared his throat. "As for leaving, your father has mentioned nothing about leaving." He cleared his throat again. "Is there anything else I can help you with?"

Hayden realized she was being dismissed.

The sun had just lipped over the horizon. It shot through the palapa and snagged a few green and blue bottles above the bar, making excitable prisms against one of the palapa's thick wooden pillars. Hayden wanted to wake Emory and tell him about last night—the jaguar, the tears—but it was too early.

At the water cooler she downed two full glasses of water. It wasn't even six o'clock yet and she was already sweating so much that her shirt was clinging to her belly. She should have gone with Emory to town to get clothing. Her dark, stench-ridden long pants and long-sleeved shirt had become an embarrassment. In the kitchen someone was whistling. Gustavo had retreated to his inner office. He would have scissors she was sure.

It turned out he did have scissors, but they were the kind one finds in kindergarten classrooms, hopelessly blunt, rounded at the tips, with blades no more than two inches long. "Nothing bigger?" she said. No, he had nothing bigger, so she took what he had to offer, pocketing the scissors and thanking him.

In the bathroom, under inadequate light, she tried to cut through the pant leg of her black jeans. She jabbed the scissors just above the knee, but the rounded tips skated over the denim, making not the slightest tear. She returned them to Gustavo who bent monkishly in thanks.

Behind the kitchen's swinging doors she found Servio, the lone worker. He looked up from his cutting board and grinned at her in surprised recognition. He was slicing onions with precisely the kind of knife she needed.

"Hello?" he said as she approached him. She was not sure of his English. "Knife?" she said, pointing.

He nodded enthusiastically. "Yes. Knife."

"Could I borrow?" she said.

He frowned, unsure what she was asking.

"Could I borrow a knife?" She gestured the act of cutting and pointed to the knife. Bewildered, he handed her his knife, still wet with onion juice. "No, no, not *this* knife. Do you have *another* knife?"

He frowned and shrugged. Did he not understand? She looked around the kitchen, a giant, high-ceilinged space, all sparkling white and chrome surfaces, with two six-burner stoves, four refrigerators, countless shelves and drawers. She could start searching for knives herself, but in Servio's mild presence it would surely feel rude. Nodding and thanking him, she sidestepped out of the kitchen, carrying the knife which felt uncomfortably like a weapon.

She went to work in the bathroom, removing her pants, stabbing a hole in one of the legs, then sawing around the circumference. Within a few seconds she had half a pair of shorts. She was just beginning on the second leg when the bathroom door opened. Manuela took a few steps towards the sink, registered the oddity of the situation—Hayden half dressed, the kitchen knife she wielded—and without a word, she turned to leave.

"Wait," Hayden said, but Manuela was already gone, leaving only a wisp of fragrance. Hastily Hayden finished her job and threw the amputated pant legs into the wastebasket where they lay, half in and half out, crossing one another like discarded prosthetics. She pulled on the "shorts," hurried out of the bathroom. In the kitchen she found Servio and returned the knife to him, pointing to her severed pant legs by way of explanation.

"*Gracias,*" he said. "*Gracias.* Thank you," as if the knife were a strange and unexpected gift.

Embarrassed, she fled the palapa in search of Emory. He grounded her, she thought. It was odd that he grounded her.

He was not in his room. He would be at the pool—or the beach. And yes, there he was at the pool in his neon-green shorts and electrified crew cut, scooping leaves from the water's surface with a long-handled net. When he looked up and smiled at her she felt a great flood of warmth and relief and connection. So focused was she on Emory and what she needed to tell him that she scarcely noticed his scarred bare chest, and it took her a moment to realize the little girl was there too, already wet from swimming, playing with her doll by the side of the pool.

"Have you met Arista?" Emory said. "Arista, Hayden—Hayden, Arista."

"Hi," they both said and, while Hayden wanted to be friendly, she felt disappointed. She had wanted Emory all to herself.

"Arista was telling me about her special doll," Emory said, "with long yellow hair and a hand-painted face. It's a very expensive doll. Her uncle gave it to her."

"That's nice," Hayden said.

"Hayden doesn't speak Spanish," Emory said. "But Arista speaks beautiful English."

The little girl smiled down at her doll privately. Hayden dangled her legs in the pool, assessing their ghastly ghostly pallor. "Ah," she said, "my legs love this water."

"Nice-looking shorts you've got there," Emory said.

Arista had laid her rag doll on a bed of round leaves. Now she was allocating a handful of seeds into a row of nutshells. She stopped what she was doing and regarded Hayden in silence for a moment, pulling her lips inward, thoughtful and prim as a scholar.

"They're funny," she said. "They don't look like shorts."

"I made them myself," Hayden said.

Arista began to sing in a low tuneless way, as if inflating a bubble of privacy around herself, as if to say *leave me alone*. Hayden was arrested by the sight of such self-sufficiency, this evidence of Arista's inner world. She forced herself to turn away.

"I need to tell you about last night," she said to Emory. "My father cried, it was terrible. I don't know what to do."

"Why was your father crying?" Arista said.

"Oh," said Hayden.

"Later," said Emory to Hayden.

"I don't have a father," Arista said.

"Everyone has a father," Hayden said.

"Well, that's not entirely true," Emory said.

"Well, I don't have one," said Arista.

She resumed her singing and Hayden watched, mesmerized now.

"Teach me your song," Emory said, but the little girl was beyond hearing, already immersed in feeding her rag doll. Devoted to the moment, she was too busy for smiling, for chitchat. Her movements were precise and targeted, not the frenzied movements one expected from children. Thinking back to her own childhood Hayden remembered her limbs flailing out of control, knocking things over.

Sun cracked over the tops of the bushes, drenching the pool in electric light. The pool's ripples sparked, the back of a fleeing red frog glinted like a sequin, so did the swaying leaves. Arista's song went on and on, coating the landscape. People on the path heading to breakfast glanced over at them and Hayden, despite her uncertainties, despite the burden of the prior night's tears, was dimly aware of being in possession of a moment that was fleeting and lovely.

When Arista disappeared for school Emory brought a breakfast tray to the pool. Hayden laughed at the bounty—eggs, beans, tortillas, mango slices, yogurt, coffee, juice.

"I'm already gaining weight," Emory said, "but I don't care."

"More weight might make you look more manly," Hayden said.

"I don't care how I look," Emory said. "I really don't. I love it here." He paused in his eating and watched the water. It shone like some toy he had wanted as a child. It had the unnatural color and brightness of a child's toy. It made him inexplicably happy. Hayden had broken a tortilla into tiny pieces. She ate a small portion, then forgot to eat, ate a bit more then forgot again. He could see she was only halfway grounded here, in the sun, in the sensuousness of water and food, in the idiosyncrasies of children. He watched her ponderous green eyes as she began to tell what had happened. She paused and held her upper lip between her teeth. Then she told about the jaguar they had seen—her father had said it held her mother's spirit. "Say more," Emory prompted.

She told him again that her father had wept. She paused, rubbed her forehead, covered her eyes. Angus had told her things about her mother she didn't believe.

"What things—?" Emory urged. He needed to hear more to understand.

Hayden couldn't say more. In silence he watched her. She lay on her side on the lounge chair, face in the shade, back turned to the rising sun. In everything about her he saw the tension of contrast and polarity: the way her long body was all balled up inside; the way her sleek white legs emerged from the hacked black shorts. She tried to present herself with a veneer of vulgarity, but her delicate, honey-haired, green-eyed beauty did not disappear. He felt so much older than she. Not old enough to be her parent, but almost.

"Now Cornelia makes me feel as if nothing I thought I knew is right."

"Ain't that the truth."

"Really," she insisted.

"I know. I'm not joking."

He had not seen her so clearly in the salon, not appreciated her fully. Now merely watching her made him happy. Talking to her—distraught as she was—made him happy. He had never, not since early childhood, been as happy as he was here in this land-scape. He felt like a well-watered plant, stroked by heat, leaves unfurling in the prismatic light.

She rolled onto her back and he thought she might speak again. He rose and sat beside her on the edge of her lounge chair.

"Don't move," he said. Her head was angled to one side and her eyes were closed. Her layered uncombed hair looked waifish. He brushed a lock of it from her cheek. Such beautiful skin, poreless, coursing with youth.

"Do you mind?" he said.

She opened her eyes wide, but her head hardly moved. Her eyes held no answers. They looked at first like the blank eyes of the preoccupied, but the more he looked into their faceted greens, the more he saw they were taking in his entire face.

He kissed her forehead. He was slow and careful as he could be. Only his lips made contact, nothing more. Not wanting to make noise, he held his breath. She held still, eyeing him, inquis-itive, passive. He let his breath out slowly. He kissed her nose.

"Don't move," he said again though he did not expect her to move. Years ago it was Peg who had made these moves; now it was Emory's turn. He knew what he wanted.

Her lips were softer than he expected them to be. They parted slightly. A faint onion smell wafted to him. Her body remained still as the constellations of a clear night sky.

He lifted his head to see her whole face. Her eyes were closed again. From under the neckline of her shirt he saw the edge of her dragon tattoo. He wanted to trace it so as to learn its shape, but he held himself back. If he wanted anything further to happen, he had to tread carefully, allow her room to come to him.

The sun was not yet harsh, it strummed them both like the tender, haunting melodies of a balalaika. He placed his lips on her forefinger where a firm white blister had risen.

"Don't worry," he said. "Please don't worry."

Chapter 29

She was back. For the last six years he had imagined this so many times and now, finally, she was here, a hairdresser with her strange flyaway hair and her odd posturing shoes and her androgynous companion. At moments he thought he saw glimpses of the old Hayden—the tenderness her eyes had always held, her eagerness to please. He thought of how good she had always been with Claire. At night Claire would go to Hayden's bedroom and the two of them would talk.

Someone was rapping hard on the door. "Come in!" Angus called out, thinking it was Hayden. "It's open."

"No, sir, it's not." The voice had a British inflection. Dr. Estuvio. Angus had not spoken to the man directly, but on earlier trips he had seen him from a distance, ghosting the resort with his disparaging, erect demeanor. He looked to Angus like a man who disapproved of the human body and all its appetites.

"Who is it?" called Angus.

"Dr. Estuvio, sir."

"I don't wish to see you."

"It won't take me a minute, sir, to have a quick look at your ankle. I really must."

Angus said nothing. The man was unbearably persistent. "It is my body, doctor, and I say *no*."

"Your choice is not wise, sir. The damage could be permanent."

Angus fell to silence. The whole thing galled him. No one understood why he would not accept help. Truth be told, Angus himself did not fully understand it. He sought a kind of mastery over his body—or was it yielding he sought? They were opposites and yet they now seemed to him so similar. He could not find words for the way he was trying to be, but it was definitely something this country and Manuela embodied.

The man knocked again. Silence was the only weapon of resistance Angus had—eventually Estuvio would have to go away.

He did not go away. Angus could hear him shuffling on the bungalow's steps, making his presence known. Every couple of minutes he resumed his knocking and his nasal *Please sirs*. Angus tried to return to writing, but his concentration was shot. Had Gustavo set Estuvio to this? Angus had always considered Gustavo a friend. But it was true he had a business to run and he might worry about being sued.

Angus roused himself slowly from the bed. The pain sang out to him, remote and friendly. As quietly as he could, he shuffled out to the deck. From there Estuvio's knocking was subsumed by the jungle's purr. Angus sank down to the deck flooring and leaned against the bungalow wall. He closed his eyes and tried to clear his mind, and after minutes—or was it an hour?—he heard Estuvio's smart military stride barking up the path.

Chapter 30

She hit the path at a run, Emory a phantom in her wake. They had parted with few words—what words were there? She couldn't look at him. She had let it happen. She had tasted and savored the tenderness. She had almost enjoyed it, hadn't she? Something must be wrong with her.

Her face burned. She leaped down the path, keeping her eyes on her feet. This place was a landmine beneath its sunshine and torpor. There was something wrong with a climate like this. The glare, the heat, the snakes, the tears, the unwanted revelations and kisses. So much that had happened to her here would not have happened in a temperate climate. Mostly she blamed the heat. Its weight came from all sides, above and below, boxing her in, stealing her light-boned, birdlike qualities. She needed to get her father away from here, away from Manuela, away from whatever it was about this place that made people crazy. She needed to get herself out of here, too, before the heat imprisoned her and made her acquiesce to a fate that was not hers.

Bungalow 8 was decidedly empty. "Father?" she said sharply, trying to flush him out. No one answered, the room gave back nothing. The blinds had been raised and the deck door was open. "Father? Where are you?" Light breezes answered, but there was no human respiration, strange how she could tell that for sure.

She checked the bathroom, the deck. She looked out over the railing to make sure he had not fallen. The bushes and trees were not forthcoming; the wildlife, usually so active, rebuked her with silence. She searched all the closets, heart cantering. His writing pad, scrawled with hieroglyphs, lay on the nightstand next to his empty coffee cup. The bedclothes had been cast aside, and no one from the resort had come to straighten them yet. She stood in front of the bungalow and tried to decide which direction would draw him. He couldn't have gotten too far on his own.

"Father?" she said, taking a few steps down the hill. "Father?" No one responded. Two butterflies scorched her vision in a quick fly-by.

"Over here." Her father's voice it was, but so faint and without directional clarity that she couldn't be sure it wasn't a voice in her own head.

"Here," he said more audibly.

He lay on his back just off the path, one chalky shin visible, torso and head mostly hidden in greenery, head and shoulder sloping downward, hands laced over his belly in a posture of repose.

"Jesus Christ," she said, "what are you doing here?"

"Resting," he said. "By the way, I'm your dad. Would you mind calling me Dad?"

"You're supposed to stay still."

"I am still."

She crouched beside him. He was gazing up through the mesh of leaves and branches that tented him. "What happened?" she said.

"Look at the ants. They think I'm landscape."

A line of leafcutter ants, each toting a bit of greenery, had charted a path around his foot. He looked planted in this place,

as if someone had dug a hole for him and laid him in it and replaced dirt and leaves around his edges so he could grow deep,
strong roots.

"You need to get up. You can't just lie here."

"I'm safe here. Dr. Estuvio can't find me."

"Yes, he's coming, Gustavo told me he's coming."

"Not to see me he's not. He already tried. He was pounding
on my door a little while ago like the Gestapo. He's horrifying, a
Nazi of caregivers. I don't need to see a man like that. Or anyone
for that matter."

"But aren't you in pain? And you need an X-ray."

"Do you know I used to dream of the conversations we would
have when you were an adult? I imagined you becoming my intellectual partner."

"We'll talk about this later," she said.

"When I asked you things you always knew the answer. I
never imagined you would stop trying to please me."

"Later, please," she begged.

The rims of his closed eyes fluttered as if he were dreaming. A
lock of his hair lodged under the dirt was serving as a ramp for a
bright green beetle. He started to make a noise; quiet and monotone, it sounded to her like moaning, but his face was tranquil.

"Humming helps," he said. "It eases things."

"Where is the pain?"

"I don't much believe in pain. Not anymore."

"I'm going to get help. Don't move." *Don't move, he had said
as he kissed her.*

"Don't go," he said. Alarm cycled through his eyes. His freckles stood out, dark and scary as nails. She didn't dare leave. She
placed her hand on his forehead to feel what she could.

"Think about it," he said. "Lying here until you decomposed."

"You're not decomposing."

"But it would feel so lovely, wouldn't it?"

She stayed crouched beside him, not knowing anything. Imperious Dad she knew how to handle, but this— She touched him lightly, resting her hand on his elbow. She wouldn't leave. She would say to the next person who passed: *Would you mind sending help?*

But no one passed. They waited in silence. She had no idea what to say. With her eyes closed she still felt Emory's lips on her face, prompting the return of old memories, not of sex, but of things that brought comfort. Sweat trickled down the creases of her folded legs. She wondered if Manuela would come looking for him. From the treetops came the plangent descending note of a bird. She opened her eyes, thinking how her father was not a force field anymore. At least not at that moment. She was accustomed to hating him but now, for the time being, she didn't hate him.

"I used to wish I could be a tree," she said. Saying it aloud now she could still inhabit that yearning.

A smile burgeoned over his face like a slow flash of heat lightning. "Maybe I should have become a woman."

"Emory used to be a woman," she said. She had thought this would be hard to say, but it was not hard to say. She did not say it meanly, or to score a point, it simply slipped out.

"Yes, I know," he said.

"He told you?"

"I surmised. All my life it's been women who have meant things to me: my mother, Nora; Claire; my daughters. It is beyond me why anyone would want to become a man. I'll stay what I am, but it's not because it's better than being a woman would be."

The sound of footsteps. She looked to the path. A woman was coming up the hill toward them. Seeing them, she stopped. She was a middle-aged woman with a soft body, long gray hair, and a face so motile it suggested a long history of compliance. She was dressed less elegantly than most of the other guests, in a white T-shirt and baggy sweatpants. She regarded them with her face slightly averted, not wanting to intrude.

"Is everything okay?" she said.

"Dandy," Father said. He rose to a sitting position.

"Could you send someone down," Hayden said. "His ankle is hurt and I can't move him myself."

"Nonsense, I'm fine." He pushed himself to kneeling with a grimace, but seemingly agile enough.

"Father," she said, "Dad," gripping his arm, "you shouldn't move." He ignored her and stood. He stepped from the bushes onto the path.

"I know I'm a mess," he said. "Call me an animal. No one cares what animals look like." He brushed dirt and bugs from his shoulders.

"Are you sure you're all right?" said the woman.

He was walking now, hobbling, doing all he could to keep the weight off his ankle. But he was quick despite the pain.

"Keep Estuvio away from me. Will you do that, Hayden?"

She nodded. She was scared by his smile which held the gorgeous intensity of a pollution-driven sunset. She would have given him anything just then. He kept on moving, slow but hardly incompetent. He brushed her off when she went to his side to help.

Hayden and the woman exchanged glances. "He's made up his mind," Hayden said.

"He belongs to you?"

Hayden paused; the woman's question was strange. Did he belong to her? "I guess," she said.

The woman followed Father slowly, making sure not to overtake him. Hayden watched them, mesmerized, bewildered.

Consider all the polarities. Fish and fowl. The things that wings or gills might offer. Consider beaks and claws and teeth and fur. Consider Mother and Father and Emory, exotic species of their own.

She brought him his writing things, a fresh glass of water, a book. She was reluctant to leave him alone, but he said he wanted to work. His eyebrows were bushy as caterpillars on the verge of metamorphosis. His hair spewed across the pillow like seaweed. He hardly looked like a father. Not her father.

"Don't go anywhere," she told him. "Give your ankle a rest."

"Don't give that doctor a chance to get at me," he said. "Lock the door." She promised to keep the doctor away if he promised to stay in bed.

"Yes, yes, of course," he said.

But with him, she knew, you couldn't be sure.

After she left he could not get to work. His ankle throbbed from his fall and his ear was cupped to the sound of her return. Every clicking leaf and foraging bird, all those sounds with which he was so familiar and he knew had nothing to do with her, made him turn to the door. He had her back, but did he really? He didn't trust this provisional return of hers. So volatile she was, so packed with anger, so invested in her déclassé self-image. He remembered teaching her to swim in Miller's Pond, and after she'd been doing beautifully, paddling all the way out to the raft and halfway back, she'd been stricken with a fear of sharks. There were no sharks in fresh water, he tried to assure her, but her mind was set. She clung to his shoulders and neck, inconsolable, while he stroked slowly ashore. He still liked to recall her small birdlike utterances, her taut almost strangling grip, the strength it gave him to know how much he was needed. She lived inside herself now and he could not touch her. If only he could trust that she would not leave again.

When Estuvio's knocking resumed Angus closed his eyes and plugged his ears with his fingers, willing it to go away. His body would heal perfectly well on its own. He could move through the pain. He had overcome blows to his heart that were far more painful.

Chapter 31

Hayden sat high on the beach under the shade of the she-oak trees. Most of the resort visitors were too active for beach-sitting, or ocean-gazing, or sun-soaking. They wanted activities with more concrete purpose: challenging hikes to see the marvels of Nature, followed by lectures and gourmet dinners. If they swam they used the pool for laps. Fine by Hayden—she had the beach to herself.

High tide waters were always deep due to the sand's sharp slope. Today the incoming sea was especially roisterous, and at this proximity it looked more brown than blue. Her eye fixed on something floating; at first she thought it was a person, but then she decided it must be a piece of driftwood, or maybe a clot of seaweed. Each new wave engulfed it and then, seconds later, it emerged again, bobbing about in exactly the same place, holding its own, but still unidentifiable. If Emory were here he would dive in to investigate, but to Hayden the idea of swimming in swaggering water like this—reaching out and touching God knows what—was downright terrifying.

She dug a groove for herself in the tepid sand and lay curled on her side, head on her arm, tempting sleep. An image came to her of her father flat on his back sinking into the soil millimeter by millimeter. She kept trying to dig under him and prevent him from going deeper, but the soil was claylike and resistant to her efforts. *I love being a woman*, he said as he sank and when his neck and belly were entirely covered she noticed he had breasts—two symmetrical mini volcanoes saluting from the center of his chest. It wasn't a dream, she was fully awake, but it wasn't an image she could control either. She opened her eyes and watched a passel of hermit crabs skittering every which way. Their movements looked random and desperate, but no more desperate and random than her own efforts had been recently. When she closed her eyes again another image descended: She and Emory had a drawerful of breasts and penises, all different sizes and shapes, and they were trying them on in different combinations, as if they were accessories like scarves or jewelry. She popped her eyes back open—she didn't want to be thinking these things. *She* wasn't one of the ones who'd been so insistent on changing. It was everyone else—not just Father and Emory, but all the salon girls too—no one was content to stay themselves while she went on being the same old Hayden.

She thought of her sisters and yearned for them. Cornelia, in adulthood, seemed to be insistently herself, with the same sense of entitlement. Perhaps Sophie had remained the same too. They weren't always nice to her, but she was used to their foibles; what a good threesome they had once been. She thought of how terrible it had been immediately after their mother had died. She had brought out this memory on and off over the years, toying with it, loving and hating it both.

At night she and Arleen would put her sisters to bed. They tried to act like mothers. Hayden usually went to Sophie's room first. She was thirteen then, but in bed she still seemed to be purely little girl, not teenager. Her gymnast's body wriggled under the sheets as she watched Hayden picking up the stuffed bears—Snickers and Avery and Mr. Riddle—and Zealous the Pig, from the floor where Sophie had flung them in restless sleep the night before. Hayden went through these motions slowly, without saying much, simply transporting the animals to their rightful places on the bed. She didn't have a mother's vocabulary, the *sweetie pies* and *darlings*. She wasn't even sure how to comfort herself. She tucked the animals around Sophie's shoulders and neck and face. She remembered her mother doing this. Sophie liked to have the softest bear, Mr. Riddle, on her chest. He was a foot-long, golden-haired creature with doleful, deep-set eyes. As Hayden laid him there she felt Sophie's need welling up in her face like a cold mist that could chill you to the bone if you had no protection against it. *I can't sleep,* Sophie said. *You haven't even tried,* Hayden told her. *I never sleep,* Sophie said. *Of course you do,* Hayden insisted. But Sophie did not sleep. Hers was a hummingbird body, lithe and dithery like Father's, not born for relaxation. It lived by leaping and gyrating, its spring-wound muscles firing, fluttering, firing again, defying the slow rhythms of night. When Hayden checked on her every so often in the middle of the night she had to look past the nest of twitches to see if Sophie really slept.

Read to me, Sophie said, the refrain of a much younger child. Hayden chose from the bottom shelf of tattered picture books, soothing stories with regular cadences which had been read over time to all three of them: *Goodnight Moon, Runaway Bunny, The Gingerbread Man.* These books turned back time, away from the recent sorrow. The Isabel book was Sophie's favorite—the one about the girl who roared at her fears and sent them running. *Boo to you!* Isabel yelled into the bared teeth of her monstrous night terrors. *Will you sleep now?* Hayden said when she was done reading. *Maybe,* Sophie said. And Hayden would tell her good night and Sophie made sure she got her three kisses—Eskimo, butterfly, and what they termed "regular old," a lip kiss.

Then Arleen and Hayden would switch rooms, and Hayden would go to Cornelia whose back was always a bastion. Hayden knew Cornelia wanted her there because if she tiptoed back out without saying anything Cornelia would call out, asking Hayden to fetch water. Cornelia was in high school, seventeen, mad at Hayden for having left for college (not knowing of the more formidable leaving that lay ahead), but unable to find the words to say so. She hated to grant Hayden her extra two years of living. She had always wanted to know more than Hayden knew. Hayden would get the water and Cornelia would say that the temperature was wrong. But she drank it anyway. Hayden stood by, tethered by some force Cornelia put out, the elusive power she had that made Hayden want, in spite of everything, to please her. Cornelia's drinking glugged on, the only noise in the house, a sound that suggested clogging and impasses. Hayden knew Cornelia had more to say. She always did. One night she said she was getting a D in physics. She was lying on her back with her eyes closed, and Hayden thought maybe it wasn't true. Hayden tried to think what their mother would have said from her cache of comforting words. Nothing came. Hayden thought of telling her, as Mother used to, that they were lovely girls, that getting a D did not unlovely her. But Hayden also wanted to pinch Cornelia out of pretending, or challenging, or whatever it was she was doing. *So what?* Hayden said.

Cornelia rolled over. She told Hayden to go away and Hayden knew from the stunned, concave look of Cornelia's cheeks and mouth that she was not pretending, it *was* a real D she had gotten. A Risley girl had gotten a D. Hayden could almost feel Cornelia's blood flowing faster in its longing for Mother's touch. What a poor surrogate Hayden felt herself to be. *What did Arleen say?* Hayden asked. But Cornelia's back was a fortress by then that no words could penetrate. Hayden tiptoed out, tromping on the wavering shadows made by the bubbling night light.

The memory weighed on Hayden now, and sleep finally came, and when she awoke, sand in her mouth, she longed for Cornelia. She longed for Sophie, too—the old Sophie or the new one, she didn't care. This longing was a bequest of the beach. Beaches, with their unending stretches of sea and sky, always brought longing; they reminded you of everything that could never be attained.

She left the beach, needing to see Manuela. She wanted to tell Manuela some of these things, ask her about Father, talk to her woman-to-woman. She was starved, suddenly, for the solace that only another woman could bring. She searched everywhere, but no one knew where Manuela was. They sent Hayden to the kitchen, to the laundry. *Not here*, they said, *no, not here. She might have gone home*, someone suggested. *Sometimes she goes home if she has the afternoon off.* She lived in the lowlands, a half hour walk away. It would be rude to seek her out at home, Hayden thought, they scarcely knew each other. Still, there were things to say and maybe comfort to be had—

She started down the path that led, she'd been told, to the enclave of houses at the base of the hill. The path took her away from the resort. It was steep and root-strewn and required concentration to keep from tripping. As she walked she tried to think what she would say to Manuela. They were women, such conversations among women were supposed to be easy, but this did not feel easy. If only she knew Spanish. If only she could consult with Emory first. But how could she talk to Emory without acknowledging their kiss? And that she was not about to do.

Immersed in thought, Hayden nearly collided with Manuela, who came bursting up the path, legs strong, ablaze with purpose.

The two women looked at each other, startled, dismayed. They stood two feet apart.

"Oh. Hello," they said simultaneously. They laughed a little in awkwardness.

Manuela frowned. She opened and closed her mouth.

"I didn't mean to scare you," Hayden said.

"No. I am looking for you."

"I was coming to find you, too," Hayden said.

"I want you to cut my hair. Will you come to my house and cut my hair?"

Manuela's hair was a prize: full, fervently straight, it begged to be touched. It was the black of panther fur, it gleamed white in the sun.

"Cut your hair? But it's so beautiful. Why would you want to cut such beautiful hair?"

She held the tip of her fat braid skyward. "Too much," she said. The hairs spewed thistle-like from their cloth binding. "Please, you must. I have time now. No work tonight."

Manuela's eyes pleaded, her eyebrows arched in hope. The blush of the afternoon sky accumulated in her face. She rubbed callused thumb and forefinger together, glanced up the path. It seemed to Hayden she was more nervous than usual.

"Your father says you are good," Manuela said.

"He does?" Had her father really said such a thing? Here in the jungle she hardly felt like a stylist anymore. "It will take forever to grow back," she said.

"No matter."

"But I don't have my scissors or combs."

"I have scissors. I have comb. I will pay you of course."

"Of course not," Hayden said. And that was the same as agreeing.

Chapter 32

In the kitchen of the pink and green house Hayden watched Manuela squeezing fresh lemonade. The clacking palm fronds had settled, an indolent sea licked the sand, the scent of the lemons sketched the air, and the day winked gold around them. Outside the heat hung on like lint, but in here it was cool. She thought of the kiss again with desire and dread commingling. Manuela's dry hands pressed the lemon halves hard against the Pyrex juicer with a force of personality Hayden had not seen before.

"Someday I would like to study in the United States," Manuela said. "Maybe I will go to college. I would like to do that. Your father says I do not need college."

"He has no business saying that."

Manuela laughed. She diluted the lemon juice with ice water and sweetened it with syrup from a lip-red bottle. They sat together and drank. A potent bath of sweet and sour jetted through Hayden's system.

"Your father and I," Manuela said. "We—"

Hayden nodded. "I know."

Manuela exhaled relief. "Oh, good. I wasn't sure. He is a dear, but sometimes—"

On the table lay the tools Manuela had assembled: scissors,

two combs, a brush. Arista's bright crayoned drawings taped on a near wall drew Hayden's gaze. The word *dear* did not seem right.

"You need to be careful with him," Hayden said. "He's selfish. Don't you find him too old?"

"I don't care about that. Age is nothing." Manuela took the empty glasses to the sink. In the middle of the kitchen she unfastened her braid, and the black hair sprang over her shoulders and back like a live thing too long in captivity. She sat in the chair again, back to Hayden, presenting her bounty of hair like a challenge.

"Here are your scissors," Manuela said. Waiting, she laughed, a quiet private sound.

Hayden stood still, gazing at the hair, Manuela's laughter rinsing over her. She picked up one of the combs and drew it down from Manuela's crown. Never had hair seemed so intimate. It felt wrong for Hayden to be touching this hair, let alone cutting it. Hair her own father had touched, it was imbued with his sexuality, his life force. Foreboding purled through the sunlight. Even without Father the hair would have been inviolable. It was not hair just anyone could grow.

"I can't cut, Manuela. Your hair is too beautiful."

Manuela waved her hand. "Yes. Cut. I want you to cut. It will grow back fast."

Hayden lifted the shears and exercised them on the air. They were blunt, kitchen-style scissors, not good for styling hair. She laid them down again and continued combing.

"You do not believe me?" Manuela said. "I want to get rid of this hair. Make me look American."

"Oh God no, you don't want to look American."

"I wait on tables and I ask people where they are from. They whisper: *I am from the United States, but do not tell anyone.* I tell them: *Be proud where you were born. Be proud.*"

"You should be proud of this hair."

Manuela rose suddenly. She went to a bright blue plastic radio on the counter and turned it on. Zippy guitar music played. She resumed her seat.

"Now—" she said.

The music was insistent and it moved inside Hayden. She thought of her father seeing the two of them here. He would not want Hayden to cut. Without this hair Manuela would be nothing. She had crooked teeth. She was short and fat. Without the hair, he might not like her.

Hayden picked up the scissors again. This time she cut. She cut in a straight blunt line. The hair fell in black swirls across the blue linoleum. If she was defacing Manuela it was not her fault—she'd been asked to do this.

A quick change in the body is rare. Growth is slow, weight loss is slow, but hair can be altered in a minute or less, and it changes the weight of the head, the way the head balances atop the spine. After a haircut a person looks out on the world differently. That is the appeal of cutting hair: the chance to achieve an almost instantaneous transformation.

Manuela giggled. Hayden liked cutting gigglers. The people who delighted in change delighted her. Soon it was all on the floor, a great mass of branching black. They both looked down. Manuela fingered the shorn tips.

"Will you make layers?" she said.

"Is that what you want?"

"Yes, layers."

Hayden finished the work with water, comb, and scissors. They stared into the bathroom mirror. Two faces, Manuela's at the bottom of the mirror, Hayden's above it. It reminded Hayden of being in the salon where much of the world was seen through mirrors. Manuela's eyes dazzled. Hair flounced playfully around her jaw and ears. She was different and exactly the same.

"Thank you so much," she said. She turned around and whispered to Hayden. "I must show you something now. Come."

She pulled Hayden back to the kitchen. Once there Manuela stood in the center of the room frowning at the floor where the ropes of her hair still lay. Hayden had no idea what was happening.

"Your hair?" Hayden said.

"No, no." Manuela shook her head fiercely, still looking down. "No, no." She pointed to the wall where Arista's drawings hung.

"What?" Hayden said.

Manuela inched closer to the wall and pointed more specifically at a grouping of snapshots. Thumbtacked among the photos of Arista was a picture of Hayden and her sisters. As Hayden bent to inspect it Manuela removed the photo and handed it to her. The photo was one Hayden remembered. She and Cornelia and Sophie were lined up on the patio with animal ears in their hair and long tails pinned to the backs of their shorts. They were generic animals. They stood at an angle so the camera could capture their tails which had been made by stuffing Mother's stockings with Kleenex. Hayden must have been about ten in the photo, which would have made Cornelia eight and Sophie four.

"Why did he give this to you?" Hayden said. Her eyes scraped the photo for more details of that day. Who had taken the photo, Mother or Father? She couldn't remember. It bothered her that she couldn't remember.

Manuela sighed. She took another photo from the wall, a recent shot of Arista standing on the front stoop of the pink house. She handed it to Hayden. Arista smiled up from the photo, pigtailed and pert. Hayden could feel Manuela bursting with intention, waiting for Hayden to react. Being watched like that made Hayden feel dense. Her eyes were useless. She looked out the window and saw the palm fronds move with a sudden huff of wind—the look of cold, but it wasn't cold. A shiver rearranged her. When she looked back at the photos the room had filled with knowledge. She held the pictures side by side. Now there was no mistaking the resemblance. The pointed chins they all had, the heart-shaped faces, the arched eyebrows Sophie and Arista shared. How could she not have seen this earlier? She handed the photos back to Manuela.

She went to the sink. She drank water. She rinsed the comb. She had proof now. Manuela, still frozen at the center of the kitchen, watched everything. "I told him he should tell you but he would not tell you," she said. "*Not yet*, he would say. *I will tell her but not yet*. He was afraid. I had to—"

She came to where Hayden stood at the sink. She touched Hayden's arm lightly and whispered, "Arista does not know. She thinks he is just a good friend—she calls him Uncle Angus. When he comes here he brings her beautiful gifts."

Manuela brought a doll out from the bedroom. The doll's hand-painted face was pink and white; the lidded eyes were hazel-blue; the clothes, hand-sewn, had taken someone hours to make. This was the doll Arista had been telling Emory about. Hayden reached out. The blond, fairy-princess hair fell in crenellated waves, indistinguishable from real hair, even for Hayden. She had never loved dolls, but she could see this was a special doll. She felt dead inside, listless. He hadn't loved anyone right.

"How often does he come here?" Hayden said.

"Two or three times a year."

"Why haven't you told Arista?"

"She cannot know yet because— Talk to him please."

Hayden nodded. She couldn't look directly at Manuela.

She stepped outside. It was late afternoon and the day had changed; the heat was easing and the bay had turned pink and breathless. Blue-gray clouds filigreed the horizon. Manuela stood at the door, her wave like a rattle, worry brawling across her brow.

"Talk to your father," she said.

Chapter 33

He went on the nature walk to distract himself. He stood with Roberto and the three other partici-pants (Janine and an Australian couple), and they watched granular afternoon sunlight sifting through the dense canopy, drifting into diaphanous pockets on the forest floor and parsing itself among the vines that corkscrewed around dead logs like filaments of hair. Chips of light and emerald shade, draperies of moss, the smell of rich rot, and everywhere, Hayden. A bird with a silver throat flew by, a butterfly, neon-blue. The capuchins sparred, and the quetzal belted its swooping song, and still no noise could touch the overarching hush. And still, Hayden.

Following the walk Janine invited him for a margarita and he surprised himself by accepting. He had never talked with anyone as super-straight as Janine, except maybe long ago, when he had his pool cleaning business. She sat on the bar stool next to him and leaned forward, weight on one arm. "I hope it's not rude of me to ask," she said, "but—" She laughed awkwardly. *Tell me about your weirdness,* she would have said if she hadn't been con-strained by manners. It was not chitchat; he could tell she was serious. He laughed and took a long drink. When he came up for air he said, "Am I male or female?" "Well, yes, I suppose that is the question." He laughed again. "Drink and tell," he said. He lifted his glass and clicked it against hers and she laughed too because what else could she do. He wondered if he would ever have a short version of his story. "Once upon a time in Florida," he began. He went from there. "Oh," she kept exclaiming. "Oh my, how interesting."

Soon he was done with the novelty of telling his story to Janine. And he was drunk, not out-of-control drunk, but noodle-loose and brave as a pit viper. He had to find Hayden. He had to tell her what he'd seen: the many shades of green and the jungle's trickery with light, it all reminded him of her. He had to tell her these things while his courage lasted. The bartender had put on some salsa music, and Emory excused himself and thanked Janine for the drink. He did a solo dance among the tables. When he got to the path he realized one of the Texan teenagers was watching him. He smiled at the boy vacantly, knowing he was being judged and not caring a bit.

He didn't know where Hayden had gone, but the bungalow was a good bet. He would ask her to go swimming with him. She could swim in her bra and underpants, no one would care. They would float together in the bay under the glow of the waning day. He would touch her under water. As the sun set he would speak of his desire.

No voices came from Bungalow 8. Emory knocked.

"Who is it?" Angus called.

"It's me. Emory."

Emory heard Angus hobbling to the door. "I had it locked because of that damn doctor. He won't leave me alone. Come in, come in." Angus beckoned emphatically. "Quick, before that man comes back."

He looked eccentric to Emory with his unkempt ringlets and his bald spot, his casual T-shirt and shorts, the brusque veneer that did not conceal his undercurrent of sadness. Emory had never seen a man quite like him and could not tell if this look of his was intentional or simply who he'd allowed himself to revert to.

"I don't want to bother you. I'm looking for Hayden. I thought she might want to go swimming."

"She's not here."

"Do you know where she is?"

"I honestly don't. But please come in. I imagine she'll be back soon and meanwhile I'd appreciate your company." Angus's rueful look made Emory feel he couldn't say no. Reluctant, he followed Angus into the deep shade of the room. Angus sat on the bed beside several books, legs outstretched.

"I'm under strict orders from Hayden not to move."

"Yes, you shouldn't move. How is your ankle doing?"

"Nothing to worry about." He made a sweeping gesture that told Emory he preferred not to discuss it.

Emory nodded. He felt awkward being there without Hayden. He wasn't sure where to park himself, and he did not feel interesting enough to sustain a conversation with Angus all by himself, especially when he had just been so centered in his body's desires. He wanted to be back outside feeling loose and drunk and watching the sunset on the beach with Hayden, ardent but wordless.

"Are you sure I'm not interrupting you?" Emory said.

"Not at all. Bring up a chair."

Emory pulled the desk chair closer to the bed and he sat himself squarely on it, knees spread wide, suddenly intent again on being read as a man. He hoped he did not smell of alcohol. He wanted to rise to this situation and give Angus what he wanted. He could feel Angus's intelligent blue eyes on him. Hayden and her father did not look much alike, but there was something similar in their eyes. They reminded Emory of the prized, striated marbles he'd had as a child. Color laced through their clear parts and made them seem deeper and more dimensional than most eyes; they fixed on people with an unusual mix of wariness and sincerity.

"Well, are you enjoying yourself so far?" Angus said.

"Definitely. It's great here. I love the heat and the sun. The nature. I meant it when I said I don't want to leave."

"Tell me truthfully. Don't you find my daughter a bit hard?"

The question startled Emory. He had not expected Angus to speak of Hayden so readily and so directly. Angus was so different from the way Emory's father had been. Frank had been taciturn, not a poser of questions.

Emory answered carefully. "Self-protective maybe, but not necessarily hard."

"Has she told you of our history?"

"I know you haven't seen each other for a while."

Angus snorted. "That is one way of putting it." He shook his head and gripped the back of his neck with both hands so his elbows stretched on either side of him like scaffolding for wings. He stared at the ceiling fan and poked his chin forward, stretching out his throat so he looked almost reptilian.

"I don't suppose she told you about how she disappeared on us?"

Emory shook his head.

"She was supposed to be back at college—that's where we thought she was. But one day a woman from Harvard called and said Hayden was missing. Apparently her roommate had been asking where she was."

He paused, turned as if about to pose a question. His eyes were solemn and their gravity centered Emory. "Go on," Emory said.

"I didn't believe this woman. Mrs. Dusseau her name was, and she had the most god-awful syrupy voice. I kept telling her: *Of course my daughter is there*. But she insisted that Hayden really was gone. We exchanged a couple of calls like that, this Mrs. Dusseau and I—I kept telling her they had to look harder. Then—I can't say why—there was a moment when I realized she was right, Hayden truly was gone. I'll never forget that moment."

Angus paused, closed his eyes, and resumed speaking. "The light looked odd, and the dust motes remained suspended where they were for a long time, motionless. It felt as if time itself had stopped."

He went silent again. He scratched the side of his head furiously and it seemed as if he was about to cry. Emory felt out of his element, panicked. It was one thing to be around a crying woman, but a crying man embodied everyone's futility.

"I'm so sorry," Emory said.

Angus nodded. Trying to continue, he cleared his throat again and again. "My imagination failed me. I couldn't picture anything but her death, her body worked over in some back alley. I hired a private investigator but he was useless. All he came up with was a car she had bought and registered with the tuition money I'd given her. Can you believe it—this is supposed to be an age when people can't disappear, but she had outwitted us all."

"So— What did you do?"

"We fell apart is what we did. We all had our own private breakdowns—me and Hayden's sisters, Sophie and Cornelia. They're younger than Hayden and they seemed even younger without her around. I hardly saw them for a while—they were always away at the houses of their friends. You see my wife Claire, Hayden's mother, had died nine months earlier and it was too much loss for all of us."

Angus's forefinger rubbed his clavicle absently and his face went blank, lost in remembering, a look that brought back so clearly Emory's months of walking on the beach after Frank died. Stoned and empty.

"And Arleen. Arleen worked for us, but she was a member of the family by then. She had always been so jovial, but after Claire died and Hayden left she became almost sullen. She slept endlessly. And I drank heavily—it's lucky I didn't go spiraling down like some of my relatives did. I could have so easily—because the fact was Hayden had simply dissolved into the ether."

"How terrible."

"Terrible. Horrible. Abominable. Unbelievable. Choose your word. Your daughter is gone—dead maybe, but you don't even know—and you never, *ever, ever* stop thinking about it." His hands lost their grip on his neck and fell hard on the bedclothes.

"It got worse though. We started getting postcards from her after a while. She was somewhere in Los Angeles, but she wouldn't tell us where she was or how to get in touch with her. She just sent these chirpy little postcards telling us she was fine and not to worry. *Not to worry.* How the hell is a parent not to worry?"

"Of course you would worry. Anyone would." The tension had stiffened Angus's bare feet. *Listen,* Emory told himself.

"But when those postcards came something else happened to me—I got angry. Anger eclipsed the worry. The postcards were such clear evidence of how little she cared." He looked at Emory with his chin protruded again as if it had a life of its own.

"She probably didn't think what effect the postcards were having."

"Precisely, she didn't think. She didn't care enough to think." Angus sighed heavily and continued to stare at Emory, testing to see how much more he should say.

"Until you two appeared a few days ago I thought I had put all this to rest. But now she's back, right here in the midst of this new world of mine, and everything is fresh again. As if it all just happened."

"Maybe we shouldn't have come?"

"No, no, of course not. The thing is, to look at us—me and Hayden—you would never think we are the same people we once were. I have my life here with Manuela and she has her hair involvements. She has you. We have both changed in so many fundamental ways, I'm sure. But those same old dejected people are in us somewhere too, still staking their turf. I'm both the contented man I am today, and I'm also still the forlorn and angry one I was back then. And she— God knows—"

Emory thought he heard thunder in the distance. From where he sat he couldn't see the sky. His body was relaxing; the muttering thunder and Angus's words melded and entered him like a potent serum. Angus was so trusting. His own father had never spoken to him so openly, no man ever had.

"Have you told her this?" Emory said.

"She doesn't want to hear these things. If I say them, she'll leave again."

"I don't mean to defend her or anything, but maybe she— I mean she's still young and—" A concussion of thunder interrupted him. The storm was moving in. They listened as wind and echoes of thunder circled the bungalow; loud at first and filled with churlish, strident emotion, the sound then tapered off to a rhythmic whisper. It took several minutes before it was gone altogether and the first few drops of rain began to fall. Angus chuckled.

"The tropics," he said. "You never know what to expect here. Enough about me. Tell me about yourself. Hayden told me you used to be a woman."

Emory nodded, uncomfortable with the light being turned on him. He wasn't used to being candid with people about this subject. So few people asked. And now, first Janine, then Angus. In the context of the story Angus had just told him, his lifelong preoccupation with manhood seemed almost trivial.

"What is it you prefer about being a man?"

"It isn't a question of preferring. It's a question of feeling I've always been that. You know—from when I was really young." He was aware again of how he was sitting, of how his shoulders and pectorals looked. It had been foolish, wishful thinking to believe he was beyond worrying about such things.

"Have you fully left off with being a woman? Aren't there some good woman things you had to part with?"

"I don't think I ever really was a full woman so there wasn't much to part with. But maybe having been some kind of girl makes me a better man, a more informed man at least. I guess I'm kind of like you—you know, the old Emory and the new Emory. My past isn't going anywhere, that's for sure. Sometimes I'd like to get rid of the past if I could, but then I'll remember a bunch of good stuff."

"It fascinates me— I myself have always found women to be superior."

"Oh, yeah," Emory said. "I do too."

Angus's laugh cracked through the room, as startling as the thunder had been. Emory smiled; he supposed it *was* funny.

"I guess most men feel that way," Angus said. He shook his head. "I wish my daughter would talk to me as you do."

Emory wished it too.

The rain was warm and lazy and it made a complex polyphony on the bungalow's roof. They fell silent again, listening. Being with Angus made Emory miss his own father with an intensity he had not felt for years. The memories came back to him with unexpected vigor. He thought of his father's robust physique, his velvety drawl. He thought of their nightly walks on the beach, the two of them hip to hip, waves tonguing the sand. On hot weekend mornings they swept the pool deck together, paced by the radio's Top 40 songs. He thought of the endless hours of clerical tasks they did behind the front desk, sharing observations about the guests' idiosyncrasies. He missed Frank; even after a full decade Emory missed him.

Someone was knocking. Emory hoped it was Hayden, but it was the doctor again. He was a short man and exceedingly thin, with a narrow face that looked as if it had not recovered from a tight birth canal. His black hair was greased into place so you could see the comb's furrows.

"He won't see you," Emory said.

"It will only take a minute." The doctor's posture looked stiff, antagonistic. Emory could tell immediately that the doctor didn't like him.

"I don't think it's a question of time," Emory said. "He just doesn't want to be seen."

"If it's broken and isn't properly set there will be permanent damage."

"Yes, he's aware of that. I don't think he cares."

"I don't care!" Angus shouted from inside the bungalow. "And I'm not going to sue. So leave me alone."

"You see," Emory said.

"What is he trying to prove?" Estuvio said.

"Don't answer that question!" Angus yelled.

Emory said nothing. Dr. Estuvio remained on the doorstep for a long time trying to stare Emory down. Emory could feel the doctor reading him, disapproving of him, trying to gauge the depth of his manhood. Raindrops rolled off Dr. Estuvio's slick hair. His suit jacket was soaked. Emory, a good sentry, stood his ground, solid and justified.

When Emory came back inside Angus was dozing. Emory was surprised that Angus had settled into sleep so quickly after having his anger aroused. There was a slight rasp in his breathing. His white T-shirt was frayed. His lean bare feet had relaxed but the tendons were still visible. Seeing Angus asleep reminded Emory of the times he had watched his own father dozing off in his chair behind the motel's front desk, snoring, eyelids flickering, exhausted having worked too many hours, but always wanting to be roused should he be needed.

Emory didn't dare leave Angus alone, but staying here was strange too. It was almost dark and the rain came down hard. He had signed up for tonight's reptile talk, but given the way things were going he thought he might blow it off. He hoped he had not done anything to upset Angus.

He lay on the bed that was Hayden's and yearned for her return. He thought of the things he'd been planning to say to her and wondered if he still, though no longer drunk, had the bravery for saying them.

Chapter 34

The rain crescendoed. It slapped the trees, it slimed the path, its live wet fingers tapped Hayden's neck. The sky had turned a nasty yellow, like the yellow of too much industrial zeal.

Hayden did math problems. She calculated the years. Arista was five. Mother was six years dead. She remembered how she and Arleen had stumbled around the Connecticut house after Mother died. Father was gone much of that spring, she hadn't known where. They had phone numbers for him, but she didn't pay attention. He would call occasionally to check in, but mostly they had been on their own. Whether Father was in mourning was anyone's guess.

At the palapa the rain had brought the guests inside. They stood on the observation deck by the easy chairs, looking out and taking stock. Sun hats doffed, they shivered as dogs do. The rain had caught some of them unaware and molded flat dark caps of their hair. *How long do you think it will last?* they asked one another. *We were told it never rains in March. Do we get a rebate?* someone said in jest.

Janine separated herself from the group and came over to Hayden. "Oh my word, look at you! You're drenched. It's good I brought you something."

She handed Hayden a canvas bag. In it were clothes—shorts and shirts in tropical fabrics, all in muted colors of khaki, olive green, ivory. Clothes in which the rich roughed it.

"It's okay," Hayden said. "I'm fine."

"No, take them. I always bring more than I need. And we're about the same size."

Hayden took the bag. She hesitated, looking at Janine, thinking she should return the favor with conversation. "I have to get down to my father," she said.

"Yes, of course. Go."

The rain came down now with prehistoric force. It cascaded from the gutters. Workers unfurled plastic sheets from under the eaves and lashed them to the palapa's posts. They moved chairs and tables to the dry center of the dining area. Hayden looked out at the gray wall the rain made. She remembered the lightning storms of her childhood. She and her sisters and her mother would stand behind the house with their faces raised to the sky, imbibing raindrops, waiting for the next flash, which would come as a thin line, clean and quick and alarming. With each explosion of light, fear tornadoed in your chest; your cheeks and kneecaps fluttered; you knew you were on the brink of annihilation. And then, after the flash was gone, your insides were vacant as an empty breadbox; you had no personality and you were desperate to be filled up again with the intensity you now knew you lacked.

Gustavo accosted her. "I have a bungalow available for you and your friend," he said.

"Oh," said Hayden. "Thank you. But can I look at it later? I have to go see my father now."

"Take an umbrella," he said. "And please, encourage him to admit the doctor."

"I'm fine," she said, refusing the umbrella. She stepped into the downpour.

Father lay propped up in bed, a book on his belly, his head turned to the door as if he knew she would be arriving. The room was dim, its air dense and stale. Emory lay reading on the other bed. He looked over at her slowly, as if she were a great distance away and he scarcely recognized her.

Emory felt trapped there, far from the door. Outside the rain was obstreperous, the world too loud. He was an intruder here now; he should leave Hayden and Angus to talk together, but he could not move.

Hayden's clothes hung heavy as trawling nets. Her usually pale face was florid. She dropped her bag. Rainwater streamed to the floor.

"You should have told me about Arista."

"Manuela told you?"

"I can't believe you didn't tell me."

"You didn't want to hear," Angus said.

"I had a right to know. And she does too."

Angus tried to raise himself higher on the bed. Hayden, in her soaking clothes, had begun to shiver. Her hair clung to her scalp. This place had stripped them down to bare essentials.

"Hayden, Hayden," Angus said. "It's Manuela's choice not to tell Arista. She doesn't want Arista to think of her father as someone who comes and goes."

"Hah," said Hayden. "It is what it is."

"Take that attitude if you must. But things are never as black and white as you might want them to be."

"I think some things are," she said.

She picked up Janine's bag and went into the bathroom. She toweled herself dry and changed into fecal-colored linen shorts and a rumpled, off-white camp shirt. She was not herself in these clothes, she was not herself even without the clothes. It was appropriate for her to look discarded, because she had been discarded. Her father had other priorities now. He had a daughter for whom he bought dolls.

Hayden tried to catch Emory's eye as she was leaving, but Emory would not look at her. That morning's kiss, whatever it had meant, was long gone, an unsettling remnant from the past. Taking her toiletries and Janine's bag of clothes, she went back out into the rain to find Gustavo.

They listened to the rain's clatter for a long time after Hayden left. Emory was hungry and he thought it must be close to dinnertime, but it seemed crude to mention food at a time like this. He tried to focus on what Hayden might be thinking—the shock of Arista's parentage. Was it any more shocking than the relationship with Manuela? Emory supposed it was, but he could not get a fix on why. Should Angus be blamed for coming here, for having sex after his wife was dead? People satisfied themselves as well as they could, trying not to hurt others, didn't they? Angus was a difficult man certainly, but had he hurt Hayden any more than she had hurt him?

The knocking was faint, muffled by downpour. He was sure it was Hayden and was surprised to find Servio offering a covered dinner tray.

"For Mr. Risley."

Emory took the tray and thanked Servio, who scurried back up the muddy path without umbrella or jacket, bedraggled but unmoved by the rain. Emory laid the tray on the desk and lifted the cover. It was the usual impressive display: fish, rice with a confetti of vegetables, black beans, yams, salad with walnuts and cheese, fruit salad, coconut cake, a small carafe of white wine.

"What would you like?" Emory said, wishing the tray had been made for two.

"I'm not hungry," Angus said. "If there's a roll there, I'll take a roll."

Emory found a roll wrapped in a napkin, still warm. He buttered it and handed it to Angus, and Angus thanked him with quiet gratitude. Hayden's sudden appearance and departure had changed things. Emory was not only Angus's confidant now, but something else. At this moment Angus seemed to need him. Much as Emory craved dinner, craved to know what Hayden was doing, he couldn't leave. He stood by the dinner tray, plucking a fingernail while Angus chewed his roll.

"I would have told her," Angus said. "It was only a matter of timing, you know."

"Yeah, of course."

"Manuela and I are planning to marry. We would have told Hayden about Arista before that. The time simply hasn't presented itself. There has been so much to say and so little time in which to say it."

"Of course."

"You don't need to humor me. I'm just thinking aloud."

"I'm not humoring you." Emory sat in the chair again and focused on Angus. "When you're married will you stay here?"

"Possibly. I don't know yet." He put his half-eaten roll down on his lap and it rolled among the bedclothes. It stayed there, inert and forgotten. "Don't tell Hayden about the marriage business— I'll tell her myself."

"Sure," Emory said.

"Parents are not supposed to have favorites among their children, and if they do they are certainly not supposed to say so. But Hayden was always my favorite. I shouldn't say it, but that's God's truth. And look at how we've treated each other."

Emory nodded. He wondered if he should tell Angus about his own feelings for Hayden. It was odd how just when you thought you'd expunged all your secrets more seemed to accrue.

"Did you—" Emory stopped himself. He thought his curiosity might appear rude.

"Did I what?"

"I was wondering if you raised Hayden like a boy. Naming her Hayden. Sending her to Harvard and all. Did you ever wish she was a boy?"

"No, of course not."

Emory expected him to expatiate, but instead Angus seemed irritated; he'd withdrawn into a private realm and Emory was glad he had not said anything about his own feeling for Hayden.

"Help yourself to that food," Angus said. "I have no appetite."

"Really?"

"Absolutely."

Emory settled at the desk and dug into the trayful of food. The fish was a moist whitefish and it parted like sedimentary layers under the fork tines. He took a single layer and combined it with rice, chewing slowly to identify the seasonings. There was some hot spice there, but not overwhelmingly hot. He also tasted cumin. The salad greens were garnished with candied walnuts and blue cheese in perfect proportions. The wine was crisp and fruity, and it reminded him of the loose carefree feeling he'd had earlier that afternoon. This was possibly one of the best meals he had ever had in his life, and he was ashamed of the strength of his appetite at a time when others were distressed. Eating took him out of the room for a while. He was thinking of the meals he and Hayden used to have in the café off Houston. They were usually the only ones dining at three on a Sunday afternoon. They always sat at the same table, and they always ordered the same things. It must have been there over her eggs, his beans, their open talk, that his ardor for her was born.

His back faced Angus, and they did not speak for quite a while. The rain kept coming and Emory wondered what the animals did with themselves in a storm like this. After a while all the plates were empty.

"I signed up for the nature lecture," Emory said. "But I guess I'll skip it."

"No. Let's go," Angus said.

"Really?" Emory said. "In this weather?"

"It's stopping. Listen."

Emory heard no cessation in the downpour. He said nothing. How could Angus possibly negotiate the slippery path?

A murmur of greeting popped up among the guests when Angus appeared at the palapa, borne like a pasha in the portable chair Emory had arranged to be brought down. Angus nodded back to them. He would have preferred not to make a stir, but the resort was small and news traveled fast in places where people ate together. After people had been here a few days they learned, inevitably, that he was a known writer.

He and Emory sat together with a dozen other guests and listened to Roberto talking about reptiles and snakes, one of seven or eight talks he commonly gave, all of which Angus had heard before. Roberto tried to avoid a sensationalist approach to nature, but tonight he had promised to talk about poisonous snakes. Angus's ankle throbbed, but it was a tolerable pain and, like a string around a finger, it reminded him of things he should think about.

It was good to have a new chaperone, a protector of sorts. Hayden's boy-man/man-boy/former girl was an easy, stabilizing presence. He was a good listener, this spiky-haired mite of a man, and intuitively smart. Angus liked him, though he preferred not to entertain thoughts of any sexual activities Emory might be conducting with his daughter.

Emory's companionship, however, was no replacement for what Angus had lost. He could not forgive himself for the hardness he had bred in his own daughter, for her inability to step into anyone else's shoes. Her life path eerily echoed his own: his hubris, his determination to go it alone. He had bequeathed her these things so unwittingly.

A slight breeze jiggled the slide screen now and then so the pictures wavered like dream images. None of the details of Roberto's talk were new—in terms of factual information Angus could have been giving it himself—but Roberto discussed the wildlife here as if he were speaking of his family members. His low even voice conveyed infinite wonder. Equally appreciative of mammals, birds, reptiles, insects, he was fond of coaxing the wildlife to walk over him as if his body were no different than some rotting log. Once Angus had seen Roberto cradling a three-toed sloth, and the look on his face at the time was one of true rapture. If Roberto were truly following his heart, he would have been living in the jungle himself, watchful, resilient, mute.

Most people came to Costa Rica for the birds and monkeys, but Angus had always had a fascination with the reptiles. An iguana camped regularly in the fig tree off Angus's deck, sucking up his daily dose of sun. Angus had grown fond of the fellow—his sleepy eyes and dispassionate mouth, his forefeet bent like the arms of an old man, his back fringed with spines like one of Arista's dragon drawings. The restraint and economy of energy interested Angus. The iguana appeared to be terrifyingly smart. He had the same outlook as Angus's youngest brother, Michael, the quiet one who had become a priest. Michael watched things pass by him with that same skeptical demeanor, biding his time, waiting for the best moment to speak his mind. The return of Hayden had made Angus think so much about his brothers. Six of them—or four if you didn't count the two that were dead—and Michael was the only one he had spoken to over the last twenty years. Perhaps the others were dead now too. His mother he still spoke to on and off. She lived in Weehawken, not far, ironically enough, from where Hayden now lived. Hayden knew nothing of these relatives. Kevin, the plumber. Sean, the trucker. Kyrie, who owned a bar. Alex had died in Korea and Joseph in a motorcycle accident. These were the people Angus was supposed to love, yet he had thought of them as pathetic people. He had never wanted to be around them. They drank beer and watched TV and he was ashamed of them. He shouldn't have been, but he was. He had hated bringing Claire around them, though she had never been anything but gracious. Angus's whole life had been devoted to making himself different from them—richer, more educated. And now Hayden had done the same thing—she had figured out how she could make her life as different as possible from the life he had hoped for her.

The wavering screen made the snake appear to be moving. A fer-de-lance, the most dangerous of Costa Rican snakes, it was depicted rearing up in striking S position. It was the so-called two-step snake: the mythology persisted that if bitten by the fer-de-lance, you could take only two steps before collapsing.

"It is not quite like that," Roberto said, "but certainly it is a snake to avoid."

Angus scanned the dark perimeter of the palapa, looking for Hayden, but she was not in sight. He hoped she had found some shelter from the downpour. Tomorrow would be sunny; the days always bloomed sunny and blue after storms like this.

Night, suppurating from the rain, squeezed around the palapa, dimming the lights and delivering them all to each other's custody.

Chapter 35

Gustavo showed her the new bungalow, Bungalow 11. It was a short walk down the hill from Bungalow 8. She stared at the two beds, the empty hugeness of the place. She had nothing to fill it with. Outside, rain thrashed the deck. Inside, turbulent air thrust the matchstick blinds noisily against the window frames. She took the key and thanked him.

After he left she sat on one of the beds, shrinking to a tiny hangnail of loneliness. She wanted Emory with her now. She wanted him to stroke her hair again. She wanted him to lie with her and hold her through this.

She was hungry but she did not want to go to the dining area and face whoever was there. Dinner was probably over anyway. She tried to forget Arista. She would fly home, back to Hoboken, and erase Arista from her life and her mind. She had already proven herself to be an expert at erasure.

She had never experienced such monumental rain, it wouldn't stop; it was the kind of rain that swelled rivers and washed out roads; it had the power to change landscapes; if you let it thrash your skin who knew what it might do. She had a fleeting image of the rain gouging bloody wounds on someone's bare back. Even the sound, an irate drumming, unnerved her and made her feel tiny. The outfit from Janine was soaked, her skin was soggy and chilled. She could have taken a hot shower, but she had no energy for it. Pulling the covers over her wet clothes, she tried to get warm. At least now she knew she'd been right to leave. Why stay in a place where you were not loved. Or where the love you had for others did no good. It had certainly been a loveless household after her mother had died.

She and Arleen had tried to keep things afloat. Arleen was schooled in the habits of caretaking and Hayden had tried to learn from her. They threw themselves into food. They made Rice-A-Roni with extra-sharp cheese; they coated minute steaks with salt and Worcestershire sauce; they soaked raisins in orange juice so they bulged and popped their juices into the coleslaw. They ate bowl after bowl of popcorn. Sophie and Cornelia were wary of the foods they made, but Hayden and Arleen shared the same taste for extreme flavors—lots of salt, sugar, spicy heat—and for foods that required chewing—nuts, popcorn, jerky—foods that occupied their mouths completely and removed them from the sodden atmosphere of the house.

Hayden rose from the bed. She needed something to eat. In her backpack she found a bar of dark chocolate. She found the hair magazine. She found her father's book. For the first time she looked at the book head-on and read its title: *Gone: A Father's Memoir.* The book's jacket was a dusty red and gray, with two silvered lines of light that directed attention to a distant horizon where a girl, back turned, looked into an abyss. The girl was only half an inch high and vaguely rendered, but she was undeniably central. It was partly the dab of red suggesting her dress that drew the eye; the red was shiny, almost garish, with orange tints that contrasted with the dusty matte finish of the rest of the jacket. The jacket's edges were fringed with small tears caused by

Hayden's having carted the book from place to place. She opened the book and read:

When my daughter left me, vanishing to a place I knew not and could not find, I mourned until it was unseemly. I had other daughters, but they were not present to me. They were too close at hand to fully see or appreciate, but The Absent One, her disappearance echoing the recent loss of my wife, devoured all my attention. She was my firstborn. Her disappearance—death? desertion?—was, in time, the only truth. Life was altered irremediably. This is my story—one man's story only, a father's story—of how I began to remake myself in the face of unfathomable loss.

Chapter 36

Emory found Hayden on her bed at the new bungalow, weeping or having wept. The sight of her so bedraggled, so bereft, so tear-streaked and pale, scared him. For a moment she looked the way Peg used to look, hair spinning out from a body flattened by sorrow.

"Don't be crying," he said, knowing how stupid it sounded. He wanted to touch her hair but didn't dare.

The book lay open beside her. He sat on the edge of her bed, wondering what he could do for her. He had learned in his time with Peg that he wasn't much good at comforting.

"Come with me," Hayden said after a while. "I can't go alone."

They went uphill from Bungalow 11 to Bungalow 8, where Emory had already installed Angus. He sat up in bed reading, glasses perched halfway down his nose.

"I read your book tonight," Hayden said. She couldn't look at him. "Well, not all of it," she said, "but enough." She wanted to park herself in the shadows where her voice would be the only conduit of her thoughts.

Angus watched her. "Ah, the book," he said. "When you first arrived I thought it was the book that brought you here."

She shook her head. "I read it only just now. I came here because Cornelia told me I had to. She made me feel guilty."

"You didn't appear guilty."

Hayden shrugged and moved across the room to the door that led to the deck. She kept her back to her father. Even before reading the book she'd been shrouded with guilt, blinded by it. It had covered her like Spanish moss, like an insistent, choking ficus. How could he not have seen?

Emory sat cross-legged on the floor near Angus's bed and leaned back against the bungalow wall where he wasn't looking directly at either one of them. He was their chaperone, he now saw. They needed him.

"I guess I should say something," Hayden said, "but I'm not sure what to say."

She couldn't even think anymore about what had been going through her head at the time she left. She had thought she was being resourceful, saving herself in an original way, or perhaps the only way she knew how. But to say so now sounded lame.

Angus spoke as if in a trance, looking at the bedclothes, his voice low and without inflection. "I'd like to know what has made you so hard. What made you hate me so much?"

"I didn't hate you." But even as she said this she remembered just the opposite. She saw herself sitting in Angela's Body Art, sick with the smell of burned flesh, the stylus waspish as her own heart. "I left because you kicked me out."

"I kicked you out?"

"You told me to go back to school."

She would never forget seeing the tuition check on her dresser. There had been no discussion about her return to school. Why hadn't he said something rather than speaking through his check? She marched to his study, check in hand. The door was wide open but it had taken him a moment to register her presence. When he finally looked up she felt as if they had already concluded the conversation.

"Are you serious?" she said, waving the check.

"You have to live your life," he said. "Go."

"But they need me. Cornelia and Sophie and—"

"They'll get along without you."

"Oh? Like Mother got along?"

"Hayden, you've got to put this behind you. You have big fish to fry."

"I don't have fish," she yelled. "I have no fish whatsoever." She was moving then, moving away, down the hall, down the stairs, out the door, almost gone.

She opened the door to the deck. A breeze came in and clawed her wet clothes so she shivered. Light glowed in one of the other bungalows where a different conversation was taking place.

Angus sat up straight and dangled his legs over the side of the bed. The pain was back full force and for a moment it seemed intolerable. There had to be something to say that would bring them both peace. He, the patriarch, should know, but he knew nothing. Wasn't there something good he could tell her, some words to hold out like the white flag of truce?

"I adopted Arleen," he said softly. "She's not a ward of the state anymore."

"How could you do that? She's a grown-up."

"No matter. It was only paperwork. She was already a member of the family in every other way."

Hayden leaned against the wall, laughing to herself. Her hand rested on the side of the table and in the lamplight he saw how her skin had been puckered by the rain.

"Sisters," she said. "All these new sisters I keep discovering I have. Emory, you might as well be my sister too. Sister, brother, whatever."

Angus glanced to Emory. His face betrayed nothing. He held his lips together around a straight line, and Angus saw him balancing this and that. He looked back at Hayden. Her hand was trembling, rattling the table ever so slightly. From cold surely, not from fear. He was the fearful one. He would never understand how his own daughter could scare him so much. He tried to remember when he began to be afraid of her. Was it in high school when she and her mother had seemed to form a secret bond? Or was he scared of her before that—scared of the wit she displayed early on, of the eerie sense she saw through him? Certainly now that he knew how she could hurt him his fear seemed justified. But hadn't she always served as some litmus test for his success or failure? It could be said that most women scared him. Claire had scared him, Manuela scared him. Even little Arista was developing an uncanny power to set him off balance. When these women came into their own they seemed to take something away from what he himself was. How could you ever love without this double helix of fear and love, in which fear always threatened to take the upper hand?

Perhaps he shouldn't have written the book; perhaps there might have been other ways to survive and work things out. But the problem was he didn't know them.

He spoke into his lap, ruminative and slow, and his voice sounded old and scarcely audible even to himself against the sounds of the jungle's wetness, but he forced himself to keep speaking.

"Arleen held me together after you left. A lot of the time she and I were the only ones in the house. I would always have my ear tuned to her whereabouts. I loved hearing her heavy tread coming down the attic stairs. I wanted the distraction of her. She would poke her head into my study. *Everything okay, Mr. Risley? You want some soup?* What a terrible cook she was, but I loved it when she got me things. She hardly ate anything herself, but she would bring trays of food to my study. Soup, or cheese and crackers, or dishes of instant pudding, or Jell-O. It was all the things she knew how to make that I had never liked before. But I ate it all. I even liked it.

"She would watch me eat. Sometimes she just stood there, waiting for me to ask her to leave. But I didn't want her to leave. I told her to sit down and she would perch on the edge of the easy chair and rock a little as I ate, still at my desk, the tray next to the computer. I remember eating slowly. My chewing rate was militated by the rhythm of her rocking, as if we could expunge all the bad things that had happened."

He didn't lift his head. Why was he saying these things? What good did it do for him to remember, or for her to know? But he spoke in a quiet gentle voice that was unfamiliar to her and it made her feel she'd missed out on the best of him. Would they always be here, wallowing in all the awful things they'd done to each other? She turned her face out to the moist darkness. She shivered again, violently this time, but it pleased her to feel so wracked by a physical sensation. She took a few steps onto the deck and she let out an experimental growl. It felt good to growl. She growled again, more loudly. When she stopped growling she listened to the erratic dripping of the leaves.

After a while she turned and looked back inside the room. Emory and her father sat in grim silence like men. They hadn't moved and they weren't acknowledging each other. It occurred to her that they needed her in there with them.

She went back inside. "Just one thing and then I'll shut up. Why didn't you call me for a full day when Mother died? A full day."

"Was it that long?" he said. "I suppose it probably was. I've done unforgivable things," he said.

He stood up. He limped to the doorway and continued through it without glancing at her. Out on the deck he went all the way to the railing, disappearing into darkness. She and Emory stared at each other. Emory wore no recognizable expression. Still as he was, he could have been part of the furniture.

She thought of how her mother had always managed to see things as lovely. How did one come to see things that way? The book had detailed precisely how unlovely Hayden herself was. She was a public pariah now, unnamed perhaps but known nonetheless. The loveless, thoughtless, childish things she had done were no longer private. Even her mother would not possibly see the girl in the book as lovely.

She stepped onto the deck. Her eyes, dilating quickly, ached. Her father's hair in dark silhouette looked like a hood. She posted herself a few feet from him.

"Am I as horrible as your book makes me out to be?"

"Oh, Hayden—"

"No, don't answer that," she said. "Are you really not coming home?"

He was silent for a long time. Whatever he answered she would not fully believe him.

Later that night, back in Bungalow 11, she and Emory, sleepless, lay on their respective beds without speaking. It was hotter than usual, a dense, implacable, mosquito-ridden heat.

"Can I touch you again?" Emory said, his voice tremulous.

The kiss seemed so long ago, the activity of another life. "I thought you hated me."

"Of course I don't hate you."

"I didn't mean to run away like I did," she said. "I—"

"You haven't answered me."

"Oh, Emory, not now," Hayden said. She was too weary to do anything but lie there and think. Anything else required too much concentration. "Maybe some time," she said. "Maybe later."

Emory didn't say anything more and Hayden felt bad. She was not a nice enough person for Emory. She liked Emory so much, but as with so much else, she would never understand him.

Chapter 37

n the stillness of morning, on the palapa's deck, under the fringe of Manuela's worried gaze, Hayden and Arista played tiddlywinks. Emory slept; Father slept; except for the kitchen workers, nothing moved. The red and yellow tiddlywinks flew through the air with the pleasing startle of morphos, strumming the currents with a silent calypso, ticking as they fell. Hayden studied Arista's face, her pointed chin, her look of concentration. She was absorbing Arista and taking her in as family. Arista's navy plaid school uniform was clean and unwrinkled, her braids tight and even. She stacked her tiddlywinks in precise columns. She was nothing like Hayden and her sisters had been.

"Tomorrow I have no school and you and Emory will take me swimming at the beach."

"That would be fun," Hayden said, amused by Arista's orderliness, her confidence, her certainty about the way the world worked.

Manuela laid condiments on each of the breakfast tables. She stopped to check on them.

"Everything's fine," Hayden said. She raised her eyebrows pointedly: *Don't worry, I haven't told her.*

Manuela moved off with her tray, reassured for the moment.

The breakfast tray held far too much food: sunset-colored mango chunks; rounds of kiwi and banana lined up like the beads of an abacus; curling slivers of coconut; a yeasty, conch-shaped roll; a nutty apple muffin; two rolled crêpes with powdered sugar for dipping; scrambled eggs and black beans. A few unadorned tortillas were included, in case nothing else appealed. Hayden knew that her father would have been content with only the carafe of coffee, but Manuela and Gustavo and all the kitchen staff liked to pamper him.

Manuela's brow rippled when she handed the tray off to Hayden; her mandible churned. Something still worried her, she wouldn't say what. In worry she was still self-possessed and beautiful in a way that defied all the usual algorithms of beauty. And her shorn hair, bouncing around her neck, lent her a feisty youthfulness.

Hayden carried the tray, weighty with dishes, gingerly down the path. With each descending step the dishes clattered a little, and a leaf fluttered into one of the coffee cups, but she arrived without dropping a thing. He had gotten himself out to the deck where he lay in one of the lounge chairs, contemplating the morning's perfection. She set the tray in a small quadrant of shade under the eaves and handed him some coffee.

"What else would you like?" she said, seized with shyness.

"We've been through something, haven't we?" he said, holding her in his gaze. "It's made me famished— I'll have everything."

She handed him a plate filled with a little of everything. He ate with a concentration that made her think back to all the meals she had shared with him, sitting at the dining room table in stiff-spined hypervigilance. She still had trouble eating in his presence. She drank some coffee, gnawed on a muffin. Was this forgiveness to be eating in silence like this? Or was it only truce? She would be leaving in a couple of days, no doubt without him.

She watched sunlight climb up a shiny leaf on the other side of the railing and felt the dull ache of defeat. How could she make amends if he didn't come home? She could feel him watching her with his so-familiar stare.

"You look so much like your mother these days, the way she looked when I first met her." Remembering, he smiled. "When I was courting your mother she lived in a slovenly little apartment that didn't befit her. It was near Central Square. With all her money she could have lived anywhere, but she chose that little place with its warped linoleum and stained carpeting and cubicle kitchen. It always smelled terrible too. Of spoiled French fries from the greasy spoon a few doors down. She spent most of her time sitting at an old red Formica table in the kitchen with little scraps of her research scattered across it, trying to make sense of her notes. There were all these ripped and wrinkled pieces of paper she had scribbled on—bits of paper toweling, old grocery receipts, pieces of brown paper bags. And a few dog-eared Caravaggio prints would be taped to the refrigerator. That was her doctoral research. Unbelievable, isn't it? She never used a proper pad of paper—it jinxed her she said. A blank pad expected something from her and she didn't want expectations. And she wrote in pencil so much of it got smudged and was almost illegible. I helped her type up some of that research and—"

He paused to drink his coffee and handed Hayden his empty plate. "Go on," she said.

"Well, the one real asset of that little place was a small courtyard with a flower garden. She had an Adirondack chair out there and before we were lovers, but knew we were going to be, she would sit in the chair and I would straddle her lap lightly. God, I could have crushed that woman with my weight—you remember how slim she was—and I would lean into her and steer her bony shoulders as if she were my sled and we would ride into the night like that.

"We left behind all the things that bothered us, soaring over my array of nasty low-level teaching jobs and the dissertation that was depressing her. The smell of her lavender soap would waft up to me. What nights those were, soaring like that. No skin touching yet, no exposed genitals, but the shared dreams— how often does that happen, when you know someone is thinking the same thing as you?"

"How did you know you were thinking the same thing?" Hayden asked.

He let some time pass. "I just knew," he said.

The sun was ascending into its pulverizing position. Soon they should move, or put on sunscreen. Hayden liked and hated knowing these things about her parents. Knowing them opened up great gulfs of possibility, great fields of unknown-ness.

"For all the difficulty of this, Hayden," Angus said, "I'm glad you're back."

She nodded. She wanted to tell him something deep like the things he was telling her. "Cornelia will never forgive me if I don't bring you home," she said. "Please come."

Emory and Hayden lay on the beach, too lazy to swim. Emory had his eyes closed. When he kept them open too long it seemed as if his irises would be sliced by the sharp edges of things. The rain had washed the landscape to unnerving clarity then ceded its power to the sun. All morning light had busied itself on the water beads in the foliage and the bay was a regular jewel-box of rainbows and prisms, and the brilliance of it all hurt his eyes and dizzied him as crowds of people sometimes dizzied him, and it felt as if these things were all vying for his attention and trying to impress upon him something essential about their souls.

He had come here for no particular reason beyond a break in the routine of doubt and worry, and now he felt there had never been any righter place to be than here, with Hayden and her father and all their difficulties, with the bright macaws and the fat sun and the lisping breezes, with all of his doomed but fervent hopes.

Hayden dug in the sand. He could feel her browning skin emanating heat a few feet away from him. He could feel the spin of her mind as it sorted all its new information. He had not thought of Peg for days.

He spoke with his eyes still closed. "There were times when I was growing up I would have killed for a family like yours. Your sisters. Your delicate mother. You had parents who loved each other."

"Yes—"

"Okay, so it wasn't the usual blueprint for love, but your father— He adored her. And I bet it went both ways."

"Maybe," Hayden said. "Tell me about your mother."

"I never knew her. She died when I was born. Growing up I didn't think mothers were necessary. I had my father."

"Was he enough?"

"He seemed to be at the time." Emory opened his eyes and watched Hayden's thin fingers sift the sand. It was an hourglass to him, a reminder of time running out.

"And now—?" Hayden said.

He sat up and stared out over the water at the strip of land he thought was Panama. He had never been to Panama. It was so close now, the divide between north and south, but he realized it was probable he would still never get there. In his peripheral

vision he could see Hayden's ear and a few strands of hair flickering on a breath of a breeze. How could you say what was enough?
One week of pulsing, single-sided desire, was that enough? If
you could remember what it was like to feel so alive perhaps that
would make it enough.

"Probably not," he said.

"Did Peg mother you?"

Emory nodded. He closed his eyes again so he could picture
Hayden reaching across the short distance between them to
lay her fingers on his knee. Or his arm. Or maybe his hair. He
felt noticed, breathless. He pictured them entwined like koalas,
teleporting themselves from the beach they sat on now over the
light-loving bay and its underwater secrets, to the blue-green of
Panama. There would be more jungles there, more landscapes,
more seascapes for uncovering. How did anyone do it, negotiate
what the world wanted them to be and what they really were?

Chapter 38

They seemed to live at the eye of a bonfire. The day kindled slowly, but it already held the certainty of stupefying heat, a sun hot enough to subsume all intention.

"Tomorrow we leave," Hayden said as she handed him coffee.

"I wish you would stay," he said. "For a while at least. There are still things to discuss." He hated to have her learn things scrap by scrap as she had been learning them of late.

"I doubt if we can change our flights."

"I'll pay," he said.

"Please come with us," she said. "Come until you're healed at least. It would make Cornelia happy. And me, too, of course."

She spooned scrambled eggs onto his breakfast plate. He could see contrition in her bent head and quiet voice. She was beautiful and fragile as her mother had been. Sometimes she appeared frightened as a gazelle. Cornelia took after him in looks and manner, but Hayden had always been her mother's child which had made him gravitate to her and expect things back.

"There's the matter with my ankle," he said.

"But you keep saying that's no big deal."

"It's getting better, but not for carrying bags and walking through airports."

"We'll carry your bags. And get you a wheelchair." She stopped working and stood to full height. How he cherished her. "Will you come eventually?" she said.

A light tapping interrupted them. Behind the bungalow door Arista's pixie face shone.

"We're swimming today," Arista said. She carried a bag with a corner of pink towel flapping out of it. She exuded purpose.

"I didn't expect you quite so early." Hayden smiled over a prick of envy.

"I have something for Uncle Angus."

Arista moved into the room without a hint of timidity. Hayden saw how her father drew energy from this little girl; he sat up straight in bed, looking whole and content and happy. He beckoned her closer, and she laid a drawing across his lap.

"I made this for you," she said. "This is me, and this is Mama, and this is Tia Rosaria. Mama said you would like this."

It was a picture of the little pink house adrift in flowers, three people standing on the steps in front. Father held the drawing at arm's length and regarded it solemnly for a long time without saying anything, his eyes combing every inch of the crayoned paper. Hayden watched the two of them, faces focused on the page, and she worked hard at trying not to compare. But she compared anyway. She could not restore him to vitality the way Arista did. Uncomplicated love between Hayden and her father was now beyond reach.

"What a fine artist you are," he said finally. "You have covered the paper with color. This shows you have great artistic instincts."

Arista hung her head, smiling at the floor.

"Might I have a kiss?" Father said. "Perhaps a 'regular old' kiss?"

He did not turn his head, but his eyes darted to Hayden, needle-quick. Or had she imagined it? Arista hesitated, then dove forward and touched his lips with her own pooched-out, Manuela-derived lips. When she pulled back she regarded him seriously.

"Uncle Angus?"

"Yes."

"You need a haircut like Mama had."

"I do, do I?"

"Yes, your hair is too long. You look like a girl."

He smiled and tugged on a lock. "Well then, maybe Hayden can do the honors?"

"Yes," Hayden said. "I will. Of course I will." She would comb his hair for a long time before deciding how to cut. When she cut she would know for sure she was cutting the right pieces.

"We are going to the beach," Arista said to him. "Will you come with us?"

"Oh no, you two go without me. Have fun."

Abruptly he took up his book and immersed himself, done for the moment with talking.

At the beach Hayden and Arista and Emory swam. They made a small driftwood house with stick dolls to go in it. They made mud pies. They buried each other in sand and pretended to sleep. Breaking out of their holes, spackled with sand, disguised, they made faces at each other. They sang songs in English and Spanish. Each engorged with a different kind of love, they played hard and made use of everything.

When Servio came down the path in a mad tear, through the trees and over the last stretch of hillside that gave way to the beach, and he slipped on the gravel and slid to his bottom, they laughed at him, not knowing what had happened. *Silly Servio,* they said to each other.

"*¡Ay, Servio, eres tan chistoso!*" Arista called out.

Chapter 39

His sleep was short-lived. He awakened with the torment of the invalid and the sure, distorted perception of regained strength. Confined too long, he needed to rove; he needed to strike out; he needed to join his daughters playing together on the beach.

He threw off the covers and the shrouds of mosquito netting. He threw off the curse of needing help. His own will was better than help.

As soon as he began walking—slow, galumphing—a calm fell over him. Light poured from his head and arms. The jungle was more peaceful than he had ever seen it. He thought of his daughters on the beach. They would be swimming and playing. Surely laughing. In front of him a snake lounged on a high branch, the crack of his wide mouth locked in a smile. Even the snakes were alert and gracious today. Usually snakes were such bashful, ornery creatures. He rarely saw them. He smiled back at the snake as if he were greeting a lost child who craved human connection. "Come here, Snake," he whispered. The point of his finger sent out a wand of coaxing silvery light.

The snake leaped from the branch above like an errant animated vine. A hallucination sent from the ancients. It descended with the flash and surprise of aurora borealis, its body the fierce improbable yellow of dominance, like lions and suns. He saw the snake's mouth opening to the size of a dungeon, but his ankle was peevish with pain and he could not move fast enough for escape. He saw, in that split second, his hubris, his fall. A seething, a snap, the yielding of skin, his neck exploding. Then a descent into the warm-cool-green of the jungle, all his faculties receding.

He stared past the winding ficus to the great black hole in the tree where the snake usually hid. For the first time in his life he felt no fear. He was fulfilling his destiny on the forest floor, nothing open for further dispute. He palmed all the fears he had carried from childhood and rubbed them to a fine powder, and then, to nothingness. Was it too late to teach others this talent? Hayden and Arista could make such good use of it. If they would only come to him he would whisper everything he knew. *Please come*.

When Janine and Perry found him he was scarcely moving, and the wound on his neck had swollen and yellowed and gave off a terrible stench. Janine went for help while Perry kept watch.

He stood above Angus Risley, staring down at the writer's larval eyebrows. He trained his binoculars nervously on the surrounding vegetation in search of the perpetrator. Not a leaf breathed, not a branch creaked; Perry's ears found only an extravagant silence that made him—a former tycoon of business—uneasy. Not scared, but distinctly uneasy. He thought he should do something—suck out the venom? slice it with his pocket knife?—but he wasn't sure what was right so instead he did nothing. His bowels churned. Soon he would have to relieve himself. Could he do it here? What if someone came? But no one came and time—fast one minute, slow the next, erratic as sparking fireflies—had no meaning. After a while, worn down by solitude and time's unreliability, he eased his 230-pound body down onto the path's soft dirt. He stretched his legs out alongside Angus's legs. He lay his head near Angus's head. His bowels still boiled, but less urgently now. Remembering the comfort his mother's singing used to bring, he tried to remember the words to a song, any song. *Take me out to the ball game,* he crooned quietly. He hoped no one would find him this way; then he decided it didn't matter.

After some time the maelstrom in his bowels demanded action; he rose and stepped off the path into a grouping of ferns. He unzipped and squatted and defecated and tried to clean himself off with wadded fronds. Then he stood and stared down at his output, amazed, ashamed, relieved.

Janine blasted back to the palapa. At the empty front desk she called for help in a voice that was hollow and deep and did not sound like her own. No one responded. How could that be? There was always someone there. She made herself scream, grabbing at the scary feeling in her chest and neck and turning it into a shrill, unsociable sound. After the first scream she found she could do it again more easily, and it felt powerful to see how people hurried from different directions as if they had been waiting not far away, poised for a summons. One of the Texan men came, the one who wore madras shirts, and Gustavo came, and so did the friendly homely waitress called Rosaria. In their hurry they seemed to flap like birds, disturbing the air with a small wind. Janine tried to explain things clearly, quickly, but she felt as if she was saying the wrong things, leaving out what was most important. But what point was there other than the felled body of the writer and the certainty of the snake?

Gustavo went straight to the phone, but his muttering did not sound urgent enough. She did not know for sure if Angus Risley would die, but she thought it was likely. She felt as if she was part of a great human drama, an important tragedy—*she* had been the first to find the famous stricken writer, *she* was the one who went for help.

Things should have been moving quickly, she thought, but

instead everything was soupy, irritatingly slow. The Texan in the madras shirt kept asking her what kind of snake. How would she know? She hadn't seen it. It was already gone by the time she and Perry arrived. She wanted this man with the lazy tongue to shut up. What did names matter? Help was what mattered. Speed was what mattered. She tried to describe the wound: its puffiness, its smell, how she had known instinctively what had caused it. It was as if she had lived a life in which snakes were a present danger, a life in which you checked your shoes in the morning to make sure no snakes lurked there. Why did she know these things—such as how the wound's color meant no good? It was funny how a crisis crystallized the things you knew. The Texan doubted her. The doubt made his face look square and ruthless. Rosaria brought her water, as if she, Janine, were the suffering one.

A stretcher appeared, borne silently by slight, dutiful men— how strong these Tica men were despite their diminutive stature— and Janine led them to the place in the jungle, scurrying to stay ahead of them, determined not to cry, dedicated to offering assistance so essential that the seesawing of life and death might be tipped. She had never felt this way before, invited under the dome that housed the hub of human life; she had never witnessed such a shining, urgent, grievous moment in which every detail was rich and tangible and permanently inscribed in her mind. She was certain her participation in this experience would map her place in human history.

The look she found on Perry's face she had never seen before—it was the wide-eyed look of a young child unsure of what would come next. He smelled bad. His silver hair, what little there was, flew up as if he had sprouted antennae. His back was covered in dirt, but she left it there because it would seem trivial to brush it off.

No one knew if Angus was alive or dead when they lifted him from the ground to the stretcher. They did not take a pulse. The two dutiful men and Perry and Janine all helped. It was a lean body, but in slackness it was surprisingly heavy. Janine was assigned to one leg, the one that was bandaged at the ankle. It seemed to jut out at an odd angle, and that wrong angle called everything into question.

Back at the palapa they laid the stretcher in the hastily cleared office and covered him to the neck with blankets. With scarcely a word the other men departed, leaving Janine and Perry alone, presiding over the unmoving body. Janine did and did not want to be the one who saw death happen. Her husband was like a stranger to her, and she had never felt closer to him. They exchanged helpless looks. Seeing Perry Janine knew that no matter what happened their lives would not be the same after this. The jungle's fearsome possibilities, the expression on Perry's face, these things you could not eradicate no matter how strong the plea of denial and retreat. *Where is the daughter?* Janine thought. *Someone needs to notify the daughter.*

The daughter in question was on the beach, acquiring a sister, picking off burrs of doubt and finally pulling her close. They were swimming and laughing and the daughter was remembering her own childhood, how for long periods when she was in the woods or meadows the past and future would hold no weight and the swath of the moment was everything. Servio found them. The daughter, feeling the cold blood of ignored premonition, overrode Servio's offers and piggybacked her younger sister herself. They all ran up the steep rocky path together, and the daughter did not notice the protests of her muscles and lungs.

At the palapa Rosaria appeared and whisked Arista away. Gustavo, wordless, hand at Hayden's elbow, took her and Emory to the back office, where her father's stretcher lay on what had once been a desk.

"A snake," Gustavo said. "An eyelash viper."

Hayden looked at the puffy wound and saw what everyone before her had seen.

"Oh Hayden," Emory said. "Oh Hayden." He pushed his body up close to Hayden's back so they leaned on one another.

A hasty effort had been made to transform the room to a medic's station. Files and stacks of paper had been shoved aside; pencils and brochures had fallen to the floor. A white sheet had been spread over the desk and a medical kit—a large blue plastic box with a red cross on its side—sat on the window ledge in readiness, next to a half-drunk cup of old coffee. The room smelled floral and fungal and not the least bit antiseptic.

Hayden stared at the waxen pallor of her father's face. His eyes were closed and their lids were tinged with a lichen-green. She wondered if he could feel her presence. If she spoke would he know what she'd said? She touched his forehead, his shoulder. His inert body exerted a magnetic force. No words seemed more important than any other words.

Janine and Perry stood whispering just outside the office door. Beyond them other guests assembled, muttering questions. *What happened? Is he dead? Was anyone with him?* These questions wouldn't be answered, but they bolstered the askers nonetheless.

"What do we do now?" Hayden asked Gustavo. Her face felt soggy.

"We wait," Gustavo told her. "Dr. Estuvio has gone for the antivenin. He should be back any minute now."

"There must be something we can do," said Emory. His voice pushed Gustavo, needled him. "Why don't you have anti-venom here already?"

"There are many different kinds," Gustavo said. "If you don't have the right one—" He blinked rapidly, sweating, aware of the limits of his command but wanting, against abundant evidence to the contrary, to appear in control.

Manuela was nowhere in sight, Hayden realized. *Shouldn't Manuela be here?*

Hayden floated. She almost forgot that Emory was there, and when she felt movement nearby, a rustling, she was shocked to turn to one side and see such a vibrant presence beside her—the black of his hair, the red of his tank top, the green of his shorts.

"It'll be okay," Emory said.

Hayden shook her head. Of course it would not be okay. She ignored the itch on her shoulder, the terrible thirst. *There had to be something to do.* Would she feel such terrible helplessness back home? There was only one thing to be done and it was staying just where she was, holding her position as precisely as she could. She could not reach out to scratch or drink water; such actions, small as they were, could change everything—they would move air, which would move his skin, which in turn would move his blood (and the venom streaming through the blood) closer to his heart, thereby inching him toward death. Hayden was not responsible for everything, but staying here, still—this she was equipped to do.

But with some things there was never enough. Never enough time, never enough help, never enough words. She watched the changes in his face and neck. She saw his thin lips lose color. Time circled around again and again to the same moment until she was sure she was a fossil, embedded here, a perennial witness.

At some moment she became aware that Emory was no longer by her side. She could not imagine where he had gone, or why. Shortly after that, time came to a full stop. It was the same sensation she had when a subway train stopped in a tunnel between stations, the feeling that ordinary things might never resume and you might be stuck there in that dingy, ill-lit limbo for the rest of your waking days without understanding the nature of the malfunction, without knowing who was in charge. She looked around for Janine and Perry, but they were gone too. She looked at Gustavo who, like she, had not moved, and she saw that he knew the same thing she knew.

She had never seen anyone die before and she could not say how she knew he was definitely dead. An animal instinct she had? An aura his deadness evinced? Nor could she say how the fact of death was communicated throughout the resort. She never heard the word *dead* enunciated, but everyone seemed to know almost immediately. The news worked its way around Tranquilidad the way mist climbs a shoreline: clandestine, ambushing, chilling the air. She could hear heightened activity in the dining area, where people had convened in small groups as they do in crises, needing species solace, wondering if their own lives might also be threatened.

She continued staring at her father, doubting now that he really was dead. All those things they had never said. All the fierce, unspoken love.

Gustavo had not left her side and now he touched the point of her elbow lightly.

"Shall we cover him?" he said.

Why? she thought. What was there to hide but the fate of them all?

An ululation shot up from behind her. Involuntary. Shrill. Manuela. Accompanied by Emory. Dropping her drawstring bag of groceries, Manuela hurtled past Janine and Perry, past Gustavo, past Hayden, and she spread both arms like the proud wings of a falcon to encompass Angus's blanketed midriff. For a moment it looked to Hayden as if Manuela might try to lift him, but instead she lowered her face, moaning into the white cotton blanket, rising for a moment to shove the blanket to the floor, then lifting his white T-shirt and finding the flesh of his belly which she kissed loudly between moans and belching sobs. *No te me mueras, por favor. No te vayas, mi amor.* Gustavo touched her shoulder, trying gently to pull her off, but she, without turning her head, batted him away and he quickly backed off, stepping back a few feet to where Hayden, too, had withdrawn. Gustavo looked at Hayden, probing her reaction.

"I'm so sorry," he whispered.

Hayden felt Emory's sinewy hand squeezing her shoulder. "Tell me what you want me to do," Emory said.

All they could do was watch, Hayden and Emory and Gustavo. Manuela's chopped black hair was a wilderness, her back an ocean swell that grew tidal with her heaving. They could not see her face. From behind, draped over Father, she looked dilapidated as a wet carton, prohibitively private. The sound of her keening lofted through the open window, the door, filling the palapa and the jungle, accosting and scrubbing the sky. There was no room for another grief alongside hers. She was bent on palpating Father's soul. From the eye of her hurricane she did not notice Hayden at all.

Gustavo swallowed many times in a row. He worked the insides of his mouth. His heavy glasses rose with the wrinkling of his nose. He turned to Hayden as if she, too, might erupt.

"Miss Risley, I must speak to you."

He took her to an anteroom adjacent to the office. Emory came with them, shadowing Hayden, bolstering her, his face brewing.

Gustavo laid a hand on Hayden's arm, an attempt to console her, though it was clear he had little practice in this department and was not sure what to do with the hand on her arm, or how long to leave it there. His feet were spread apart as if he had to reinforce his stance, and he brought to mind a neophyte surgeon whose first patient has died on the operating table. Manuela's weeping swirled around them and made it difficult to concentrate, a locution that soared like an aria, each note delineating to Hayden her own emotional deficiencies.

"Miss Risley, I am so sorry. He was like family to us, you know." His eyes moved like gnats under his prismatic lenses. "I am sorry about—she—they were, uh, close you know, and it is the practice here to—" He glanced toward the other room, raised and lowered his eyebrows in futility. He was like a man ill-prepared to tell his daughter the facts of life, and Hayden worried they might be stuck there for a long time, she drowning in Manuela's sorrow, he perseverating with sorrys.

"It's okay," Hayden said. "It's not your fault." A lizard sizzled up the wall by the unscreened window.

"It's not okay," Emory said.

"I never—" Gustavo said. "Even Roberto has never seen this, a bite like this in the daytime. They're nocturnal snakes. It is not advisable to walk alone— We do have warnings—"

Hayden shook her head. "It's okay," she said. She tried to shiver his sodden hand from her arm. Did he think she would sue? She wasn't going to sue.

Gustavo looked out to where servers laid tables for yet another meal. "We need to decide what we will do with— Your father's remains. We can't— This is the tropics, and bodies—" Each sentence listed toward unpleasantness and the words got stuck and he cleared his throat instead.

"There is already—" he began again. He sniffed and frowned and Hayden and Emory sniffed too, but Manuela's sobbing subsumed everything and Hayden could not smell a thing, nor could she concentrate on what Gustavo was saying; she knew only of the scuttling lizard, and the sunlight glinting off Gustavo's glasses, and Manuela's oratorio of grief.

"It is not hygienic," Gustavo said, "especially when we are serving meals so close. So we must decide. We will help you out with whatever you decide."

"No one's deciding anything right now," Emory said. His face was smudged with redness, dented beneath the eyes. The bruise which had been starting to fade was rising to nastiness again.

From the office came a descending note like the quetzal's call. A whimper. Silence. Semi-silence. Manuela was moving about, pulling something from her handbag: she laid a rosary across Angus Risley's chest.

"We must act quickly," Gustavo said. "We could fly him to San José— Our expense of course. I know a good funeral home there. That would be the best place. Or we could bury him here in the village cemetery. It is your choice, of course. But we must decide quickly."

Hayden watched Manuela. She was quite sure a rosary meant nothing to her father. "Burn him," she said.

Gustavo blinked.

"Cremate him," Hayden said.

"That is not common practice here, you know," said Gustavo. "I would have to find out—"

"We don't need to decide this minute," Emory said. "Please give us some peace."

"Cremation is what I want," Hayden said. "I'm sure that's what he would have wanted too." She knew she was right—he'd *said* it was what he wanted: a quick dispensation of his body; a low-impact, no-frills death. An abrupt movement skewered her attention, and she looked to the office where Manuela had heard her through the now-intermittent drone of her weeping. She stared at Hayden as if Hayden were the devil's mouthpiece. The virulence of Manuela's eyes matched the virulence of Hayden's. Manuela walked calmly through the door and knelt before Hayden, head bowed.

"Please do not burn him," Manuela said. "Please do not."

Her hunched back in its white cotton serving blouse, now dirty and wrinkled, stretched before Hayden like a stepstool. Gustavo, resembling a shrinking mammal who had now reached rat size with a rat's furious heartbeat, divided his glances between Hayden and Manuela, and the rising action in the dining area. The light coming through the square window had shifted in color from yellow to noontime white. Gustavo linked his arm in Hayden's to tug her away from Manuela.

"We must decide, you see, or the health department—"

A breeze choked up, piggybacking a stench Hayden had never smelled before but knew at once to be the stench of death. Manuela gazed up at her, eyes dull, pink, unreadable, arrested in pleading.

"We were going to be married," she said. *"Me amaba."* She hung her head.

Hayden's nostrils crawled with the death scent, a scent so strong it seemed to have its own killing power. If only Gustavo would stop peering at her, waiting for her to decide things; if only Manuela would get off her knees; if only Emory's face did not have that wounded look. If only she had said all the things she'd intended to say before it was too late. She turned and fled. Gustavo and Emory came after her.

"We will take your father's body to the jeep," Gustavo said. "Yes?"

"Whatever," Hayden said.

"Here, take this. You will need this." He pressed a cell phone into her hand.

"Leave us alone for a while," Emory said to Gustavo. "Please."

People drew back from Hayden in her tear across the palapa; they cleared a path as if she were a queen or a pariah, something outside the usual. They did not want their fates intersecting hers. She could feel Emory, loyal Emory, rushing in her wake.

It was noon and the resort was comatose. An apathetic sun monopolized the sky. Still. Stagnant.

Hayden stumbled down the path.

"Slow down," Emory said.

Something lay on the doorstep of Bungalow 8: two small black bags, battered and dirt-covered—their lost luggage. They stared down, trying to make sense of the timing of this arrival. Surely it signified something. Neither one of them said anything. They left the luggage on the stoop. Inside it was cool and quiet.

"We can go somewhere else," Emory said, looking around at the mayhem.

Hayden's eyes adjusted slowly to the dim light. Books and odd-ments of clothing were scattered everywhere, as if the room had been ransacked. But she knew what she saw was the aftermath of her father's own eruptions. What had possessed him to go out as he had, walking on a leg that would not support him? She could picture him doing it—stubborn as he had always been—but she could not imagine the *why* of it. Why court such pain? Why risk falling and incurring deeper, more intractable damage, let alone venomous snakes? This jungle love, this second family—didn't he have so much to live for? An incalculable trajectory.

She picked up one of his T-shirts from the floor. Its neckline was frayed; its spidery, dirt-darkened threads, up close, looked delicate as Belgian lace. She stood there, T-shirt in hand, alert as a lounging lizard, discerning as a prowling jaguar, still as a tree. Then she saw Emory weeping.

He had not meant to weep. He had meant to be a man about this. He didn't presume to own this grief as Hayden did, as Manuela did. He bolted to the deck, hoping Hayden had not seen his tears. Unlike him she had not cried yet, and her restraint made Emory feel knifed. He wanted to take her in his arms and swallow all the sadness she had boxed away. Why was it that women were so beautiful in sorrow? It seemed to Emory a regressive thing to feel, and yet he felt it, so drawn to Hayden in crisis, so desirous of comforting her.

Everything drooped to idiocy under the apathy of the midday heat. At this hour the sun seemed malicious. To survive, you had to commit to stillness. Emory moved under the slight protection of the eaves and leaned against the bungalow's exterior wall.

It was foolish to feel like this—after all, he had only known Angus a few days. But they had spoken, confided, and now sadness and longing swooned over everything—over Angus, and Frank, and Hayden, and himself. So many of the people he knew kept running up against that place where the world refused to deliver, refused to change, refused to conform to the way they knew it should be. Sometimes you tried desperately to change yourself when really all you wanted was for the world itself to be different. That, really, was the saddest part. Despite what he and Hayden and Manuela wanted, nothing would revive Angus now.

A sloth in the shade of a tree sized him up with do-nothing eyes. Others were watching him too. Exceedingly silent birds. All manner of insects. Perhaps even Hayden's jaguar was out there somewhere crouching under a shrub in expert camouflage.

Emory's eyes seemed to salivate—he didn't remember this ever happening before—each wiped tear was quickly replaced by a new one. He had never been prone to crying even as a child, and on T no one cried, at least not many did, certainly he had not. But now—

He tried hard not to think this way, not to be trapped in the notion that life's difficulties and mysteries were coiled exclusively around gender, because he could see since he'd arrived here and from the way grief lurched over him now, what was perhaps a deeper truth—that sorrow, like so many other things, pierced to the bottom of things, touched all chromosomes, impersonal and impervious. Of course they were all sad, he along with them.

Hayden sat on the bed, clutching Gustavo's phone, ears still suffused with Manuela's wailing. The memory of it boiled over her like an accusation. It was a sound that immured Manuela and kept her apart, not only from Hayden, but from everyone else as well. How could you talk to a person who wailed like that?

Outside on the deck she spotted a triangle of Emory's neon shorts, his lean, knobby shoulder and upper arm swaying. Unlike Manuela's, Emory's sorrow was soundless, but he was definitely weeping, that much was clear. What was wrong with her that everyone wept for her father and she did not? She coveted their tears. If she could have tears and wailing like theirs she would not have to feel the giant hole in her middle, getting bigger and bigger, eating up to her chest and down into her pelvis. If it kept on going she would soon amount to nothing at all. She had lived so long without her father, how could it be that now she felt he was all she had ever needed? He was the magnetic north to which she had calibrated her compass even as she had moved away.

She needed some ballast, some weight in the world. Without weight, or more forward motion, or more will, she might float anywhere—out to sea, or up through the canopy, or into the churning vapors of the clouds. Insubstantial as she was, it seemed as if even the smallest leafcutter ant might heft her away to an underground nest. She flipped open Gustavo's cell phone. It seemed too flimsy to be the conduit of any real connection.

"A snake?" Cornelia said. "I don't believe it."

And Cornelia wept too. The conversation foundered, stopped altogether. From such a great distance there was no way to staunch the flow of Cornelia's tears.

"You need to come down here," Hayden said.

"I would—" Cornelia said between sobs, "but I can't. I'm not allowed to travel. I've told you that. Not this far along." Her words were tiny fragments that sculpted sadness into sound.

"What should I do then?" said Hayden. "With his body, I mean?"

"Bring him home. We'll have a funeral here."

"But how?"

"Hayden, you're there. I'm not there."

Hayden heard wind, or Cornelia's sobbing—over the thousands of miles she couldn't tell the difference. "Please come," Hayden said.

"I would, but you know I can't. My doctor has absolutely prohibited it."

"Do you think Sophie could come? Do you have her number?"

They hung up mad, wrecked. Hayden missed Cornelia in a way that she had never imagined a sister could be missed. She called Sophie's number but it was a dorm phone and it rang and rang without yielding any answer. Trying not to think, she sat still. After a while she bit a hole in the blister on her burned finger and clear fluid ran from it. Gustavo and Manuela were waiting for her to decide things. Outside the light of midday looked impossibly strident.

She called the Connecticut house—she needed Arleen. And there was Arleen, *sister Arleen*, reliable as always, answering the phone, as always, as if surprised. But instead of giving comfort

Arleen sobbed as everyone else had, sobs that fell over one another, an avalanche of boulders crushing Hayden.

"It'll be okay," she told Arleen, but her heart was not in these
reassurances.

After she hung up she went out onto the deck, into the tortur-
ous heat. Emory was leaning against the wall, eyes closed but no
longer crying. She was so glad he was here. She went to him and
took him into her arms, remembering how soothing it used to
feel when her mother had stroked her arm or leg, or when Arleen
laid a warm hand on her forehead. Emory stayed limp for a few
seconds while she squeezed him. Though he was so much older
than she, for a moment she felt like his mother and the feeling
rose through her and imparted an unexpected power.

"I'm okay," he said. "Don't worry about me. How are you doing?" He hugged her back with a motion that was brief and fierce
and made his body feel dense and so much different from hers.

She hunkered against the wall beside him, out of the sun.
"What should I do?" she said. He would know—he had fifteen
years on her; he had life under his belt, wrinkles to prove it.

"Your call," he said. "But you have to make a decision soon."

"Do you think it's evil to burn someone? After they're dead, I
mean. Cremate them."

"I don't know the first thing about evil. But it's only a fucking
body, for chrissake. It's not *them*. A body is just like—you know,
the surface. That's all. It's not what matters. It really, really, really
isn't what matters." He had stepped away from the wall and was
breathing hard as he said this. "You know what I mean?" he said.

Hayden nodded. She thought she agreed, but it didn't make
sense, coming from Emory. He was all about bodies mattering.

"They were planning to marry," Hayden said. "Why didn't he
tell me?"

"In time he would have."

She saw in the way Emory said this that he knew things she did not. "You knew they were planning to marry?"

Emory nodded.

"He told you?"

Emory nodded. He leaned against the wall again and let his back slide down it so he crouched and his sunburned knees jutted prominently from his shorts. He sighed.

"I'm sorry," he said. "I fucked up. He told me not to tell you. He said he'd be telling you soon. I thought I should respect that— I wasn't sure—"

She swallowed this information. Another humiliating fact. But what did it matter now? She would never, even with open eyes, know more than a sliver of truth.

"If Mother were here, she would know what to do," Hayden said.

"Imagine she is here," Emory said.

Hayden lay on the chaise in direct sunlight and closed her eyes. She was dizzy from dehydration. Her popped blister stung. *We're feminists, aren't we?* she heard Mother saying. *We can go up there and decide what to do.*

A family of noisy macaws landed in their favorite fig tree. After being here almost a week she didn't need to open her eyes to know what species they were. She continued to lie there, stagnating, will-less. *Go decide something,* said the voice of her mother.

Hayden sat up. Everything was out of focus but she could tell the seemingly soporific jungle was teeming with quiet activity.

"Are you okay?" Emory said.

"We have to go up there," Hayden said.

Chapter 40

A body devoid of a heartbeat does not last long in the tropics. Necrosis sets in; heat and humidity accelerate the breakdown of tissue; blood pools in the lowest elevations of the body. Free of muscle constraints, urine and feces gush. The internal organs, decomposing, emit gases that course through the body, bloating the abdomen and limbs drum-tight. Bacteria, hitherto confined to mouth or foot or vagina, now migrate and multiply and amalgamate into virulent new bacterial cocktails. The eyes dehydrate and shrivel, retracting back into the skull like hibernating pebbles. A green color sets in, mottled and marbled and shaded with black. Throughout this process, the mouth, unhinged, hangs open in what first appears to be the shape of a shout, but a second look reveals the jaw is stretched far wider than any living jaw will stretch, wider than a howl, imparting to the physiognomy an aspect of terrified self-mockery. If the body is moved the mouth expels air in a sudden vocalization, a suggestion that life is still making its last-ditch appeal for continuance. Bacteria ride on the warm wet air of that utterance. Eventually, the skin begins to fall off, temporary as wrapping paper at the points where it's touched. Then there's the smell. No one can describe death's smell, though even the uninitiated recognize it. It holds chemicals such as uric acid and putricene, caustic molecules that the noses of the living instinctively revile. Mephitic. More than an olfactory experience, the smell of death reminds you of how you, too, are only one more set of molecules in the biochemical heap. This is how the unraveling goes—mucous membranes first, then organs, genitals, skin, muscle, ligaments, tendons. The last to go—bones and teeth and hair.

Only two things can retard the decomposition process: embalming and refrigeration. In the long run, however, both are temporary. Nothing will restore a body to its former, pre-death state. Nothing will repair the tissues. Nothing will jump-start the blood flow. No sharp rap to the buttocks or back will recalibrate the organism and summon back the spirit of life.

Nevertheless, you hope for such miracles: Hayden had hoped for such a miracle when her mother died and now she hoped again. She and Emory sped uphill over the now-familiar path in the vertiginous heat. Hayden was sure an idea would come to her. She would do things right for once and maybe she could recover a little of the many things she had lost. The sun had darkened to yellow and tipped off its apex.

Some of the Texan women were parked by the pool, holding pastel umbrella drinks, wearing bikinis. Seeing Hayden and Emory, they froze, tight smiles haunting their faces.

The shaded palapa was empty. They had been gone long enough for Dr. Estuvio to have brought the antivenin and found it to be too late; long enough for lunch to have been served and cleared; long enough for the voyeurs and disaster-mongers to have returned to their bungalows and beach walks; long enough for a priest to have been brought up from the village. Even the kitchen was quiet. From the employees' cabins came the sound of a strumming guitar. Activity was afoot on the grassy area where the resort jeeps were usually parked.

Halfway across the palapa Hayden and Emory were stopped by a tremulous sound—Janine, in an eddy of personal pandemonium, rushed toward them from the couch near the observation deck. Everything about her was disheveled: hair uncombed, face dirt-smudged, blouse stained with underarm sweat.

"Thank God," said Janine. "I've been waiting for you two. There have been some developments."

She seized Hayden's wrist and, finger to her lips, she led them across the palapa, stopping near the bathroom where they were sequestered in dark shade. She directed their attention to the activity outside. A quartet of people—a priest, Manuela, Gustavo, and Rosaria—surrounded Father's stretcher which had been laid on the back of one of the resort's jeeps parked about thirty feet away. Father was blanketed to his neck, but his head was visible with its flotsam of thinning red hair. The robed and collared priest, his back to them, stood to one side of Father; Manuela stood on the other side, gazing down. She had pulled herself together since Hayden had last seen her. She now wore a pale blue skirt and a fresh white blouse; her hair was combed and decorated at the ears with gardenias; and she held in both hands a modest pink and white bouquet. The priest was speaking in Spanish, pausing periodically to make the sign of the cross in the air before him. Last rites.

"I didn't know what to do, where to find you," Janine said. "I think they're getting *married*."

Hayden glanced at Janine to size up her statement. "But—" Hayden said.

"That's what I mean."

Emory listened intently, trying to make out the Spanish words spoken by the priest.

Could it be possible they'd had it wrong? Was he really with them again, intact and breathing, asserting his tenacious ability to survive? Manuela's hair was afire with the syrupy afternoon light, her expression a hologram of doom and radiance. Every once in a while she glanced at the priest, whose stream of hushed words was hypnotic, but mostly she kept her eyes on Father who lay still.

"What are they saying?" Hayden asked Emory.

"I can't quite hear."

Hayden thought she should join them, but a membrane of privacy surrounding them kept her at bay. Manuela leaned over and kissed Father's lips. Could he still be alive? Could Manuela have breathed the life back into him with the revivifying strength of her love? Hayden leaned against the cool wooden wall, thinking she might faint. Janine and Emory both reached out to steady her.

Manuela laid her foil-bound bouquet on Father's blanketed belly. She reached across him and from under the blanket she brought forth his left arm. Once a lean spindle, it was now a Polish sausage of an arm, heavy and inanimate and swollen to eliminate any evidence of underlying muscle or bone, purplish on its underside, mottled greenish-gray on top. Manuela placed the arm awkwardly beside the flowers. Then Rosaria handed her something—rings, two silver bands. Manuela slipped one on herself and the other she wedged, with some difficulty, over Father's bloated left ring finger. She leaned down and kissed him again before restoring his arm beneath the blanket. Tears began to stream from her now, traveling with the eerie silence of shooting stars across her fawn-colored face. She nodded at the priest.

"*Qué Dios los bendiga en santo matrimonio,*" said the priest. He looked up to the sky, then down to the ground, concluding the ceremony.

"They're married," Emory whispered.

Janine gaped. Hayden gaped. The quartet involved in the ceremony shook hands, embraced. Gustavo handed a paper to the priest and the priest signed it against the side of the jeep. After a minute or so of muted congratulations, the priest raised his hand to hush them again.

"*Es la hora de despedirnos.*"

They resumed their positions and the priest, standing directly over Father now, made the sign of the cross. He chanted more words, his voice louder.

"*Qué Dios le conceda la paz eterna.*"

Everyone fell quiet and crossed themselves and the priest drew the blanket over Father's head. Manuela stood tall, eyes on the priest, fingering her ring, married and widowed all at once.

"Shouldn't we do something?" Janine said.

What was there to do? thought Hayden. *Tap wood, clap thrice, spin. Above all breathe in unison.*

Janine clutched Hayden's arm, squeezed hard.

"Fuck," whispered Emory.

Rosaria linked arms with Manuela while Gustavo and the priest huddled together in discussion, forehead-to-forehead like butting bulls. Manuela, with Rosaria's assistance, began to walk slowly away from the jeep. She was invested with new stature, a dignity Hayden had always sensed in her but not yet seen fully manifested. As Manuela passed into the palapa's shade, she and Hayden locked gazes. Manuela's eyes were dark shafts.

"He's still alive?" Hayden said.

Manuela shook her head. "We looked for you. We could not find you."

"You married him?"

Janine and Emory sidled away, coaxing Rosaria to go with them. Rosaria resisted a little until Manuela nodded her off.

"Yes. I am married to him now."

"But he's dead."

Manuela nodded, refuting nothing, hiding nothing.

"Why?" Hayden said. "You can't marry a dead person. It's not even legal."

Manuela's eyes worked Hayden's face. She sighed heavily. One of the gardenias fell from her ear, giving off a fragrance as it brushed the air between them.

"He would not tell you," she said. "I told him he should tell you. Many times I told him. And now—" She blinked and kept her eyes closed several beats longer than usual. "He was scared."

"Of what?"

Manuela hesitated, then spoke so softly Hayden could hardly hear her. "You."

One of the resort's jeeps drove up to deliver a group of worn-looking hikers, a picnic hamper, another hamper of binoculars and cameras. The hikers moved toward the palapa cautiously, knowing already of the death that had happened in their absence. Their driver hurried straight to Gustavo who had retreated with the priest to one of the dining tables for a glass of lemonade. In a quick tête-à-tête something was decided, and the driver returned to his empty jeep and sped off.

"I'm not scary," Hayden said when the people had dispersed. "I'm the least scary person I know."

Manuela touched Hayden's arm and smiled faintly. A confirmation that Hayden *was* scary, or *was not?*

"Why would you do that?" Hayden said. "Why would you marry a dead man?"

Manuela shrugged the question off to the corner, to the place where questions go to gather moss when there is no easy answer. Hayden had not thought a great deal about marriage up until that point though she believed that for most people it was a mistake.

"I don't mean love," Hayden said. "I know you loved him."

"Until now I have no family here. Except Rosaria."

Hayden nodded. She did understand a little. She understood that Manuela had laid claims on her father, that she wanted him to be hers. She understood that Manuela had married the father of her child. She wanted not a dead lover but a dead husband, someone whose picture she could proudly display, someone who was part of her official family tree. Was it possible she wanted other things too: his money, his work?

Hayden went to the jeep which was now unattended. The stench had ballooned like flatulence. It stained the air and interpenetrated the foliage and it latched onto the fibers of her clothing. How would such a smell be eradicated? Surely it would always be here, putting visitors on alert, warning them of the dangers of the place, ruining business. Hayden sealed her nose and pulled back the sheet covering her father. In the few hours since she had last seen him he had been ravaged by necrosis. The lids of his closed eyes had sunk back into purpled sockets. His skin was a mottled gray-green. But under the late-afternoon sun his hair still glittered.

She wanted to seize him and shake him back to life. How could she immolate this body? How could she bury it? If bodies had no meaning, why couldn't she part with his?

An idea came to her. She hurried back to the palapa. No one stood behind the front desk, so she went behind it herself and rifled through drawers. When she found some scissors—the same blunt kindergarten-type scissors Gustavo had loaned her a few days earlier—she returned to the jeep.

She stood above her father's head, looking down the full length of his covered body. She was glad someone had closed his lids as she would have had trouble looking into his eyes. She touched his forehead with two fingers. It felt like cool vinyl. She drew her cupped hand lightly across the part of his crown where there was no longer any hair. She wondered what she would have said to him next if he'd kept on living. Behind her, high up, some monkeys were taunting each other and rocking the trees, shaking down organic debris which sounded for a moment like rain. She combed his hair with her fingers. It held so many colors—shades of red and orange interlaced with threads of gray. It reminded her of marigolds, and peach skins, and the variegated crimson shells of pomegranates. She found one of the longest coiled locks. She cut it with the blunt scissors and put it in her pocket. Then she covered him again and returned to the palapa.

Manuela stood where Hayden had left her, speaking in Spanish to an agitated Gustavo. Gustavo beckoned Hayden with a commandeering move of his head. Dutifully, Hayden went.

"We must decide," Gustavo said. "You see, don't you? We can't—"

A distant breeze tickled the wind chimes and their pock-pock echoed over Hayden's forehead like a doctor's mallet checking reflexes. The sepulchral hum of the jungle rose and abated. She fingered the ringlet of hair in her pocket. Manuela, mother, widow, stern and loving, poured her presence into Hayden.

"Okay," Hayden said. "We'll bury him here."

Chapter 41

Janine accompanied Hayden and Emory back to Bungalow 8. "You sure you're okay?" she kept saying to Hayden. Hayden thought Janine was the one in need of soothing. The day's events had disarranged her. She had a feral look about her, as if she'd gone days without grooming. Her tropics-ravaged hair bristled up from her scalp as if a wire armature held it there. The dirt on one cheek and the absence of her usual pale pink lipstick made her face appear lopsided and either older or younger than she had looked the day before.

"He was lying there on the path as if—" Janine sighed and shook her head. "Looking like—"

Why was it, Hayden thought, that all these strangers had come to be so disturbed by her father's death? Did their disturbance itself make them no longer strangers? Would she always know Janine?

Emory hadn't said anything for a long time.

They could have gone to sleep in the other bungalow but they had come here instead, to the place where Angus had lived, the place still strewn with his things, the place where the air still held his body's smells. They looked around the room, confused for a moment about their purpose there. Hayden felt defeated by the sight of her father's objects—assorted pieces of clothing, books and writing materials, shells and pieces of driftwood he'd collected, small plastic bottles of lotion on the nightstand. How was she to tell which of these objects had held importance for him?

Janine fondled a blue fountain pen that had fallen to the floor under the small desk. "This could be valuable," she said. "You never know—he was a famous writer, after all."

Under the bed Emory found a small empty straw basket that looked indigenous. They examined these objects as if they simmered with information, as if they might reveal essential facts about the deceased.

"What was he working on?" Janine said.

Hayden had no idea. The pages of scribbling she found were illegible.

"Do you mind if I stay with you two tonight?" Janine asked. "Perry's all right on his own and I need female companionship."

Emory sighed.

"Oh dear," said Janine. "I'm sorry. I didn't mean anything by it. I just need the kind of companionship you two provide."

Emory put up his palm. "Don't worry," he said. "I'm used to these things. You don't need to get balled up in my weird choices."

"They're not weird," Janine said.

"We can push the beds together," Hayden suggested. She was an orphan now, mother and father knitted inside her. Life went on and you still had to figure out where and how to sleep.

"I'm going for a walk," Emory said.

"Really?" Hayden said. "Is that a good idea. At night? Alone?"

"A short one."

"You promise you'll come back? You won't just go off and—"

"Don't worry. I'll be back," he said.

She couldn't stop him. She knew better than to try.

"I'm sorry," Janine said after Emory had left. "I hope he didn't take offense. He's a wonderful person. A very sensitive listener."

"Yes," Hayden said. "I agree."

She and Janine went to the bathroom both at the same time like schoolgirls. They washed their faces, synchronizing the soaping and rinsing so they didn't bump heads. Hayden peed while Janine gazed at herself in the mirror.

"I aged today, I think," Janine said. "I'm fifty-eight, not that much younger than your father was. I could be the next to go. Or Perry could. Perry is too big for living, you know?"

Hayden nodded. Perry was big in a prehistoric way that promised early extinction. Janine was easy to be with. She said things without necessarily expecting a response. Hayden was reminded of her high school friend Olivia Broussard, a busybody, but an amiable one.

They pushed the beds together and lay down without covers, outside the mosquito netting, wearing only their underpants. Janine's small breasts flopped off the sides of her chest like Hacky Sacks. Hayden hoped Emory was okay.

"I've known about you and your father all along, you know," Janine said. "I did a little research. But I didn't want to intrude. I could see there were problems."

Hayden thought of saying there were no problems, but why would she say that? Janine had read the book. Lying there half-naked in the hot dark she felt an intimacy with Janine, a stranger over twice her age. Deception seemed shabby.

They had left the light on in the bathroom and it bled into the rest of the bungalow, softening the night to gray and reflecting off the bright white of Janine's underpants. Earlier it had seemed to Hayden that Janine might have a perfect life, but now she could see the things Janine might worry about: getting old perhaps, and dying.

"I never had any children," Janine said.

"Did you want them?"

"I was scared of having them. They seemed too chaotic."

Hayden had no answer to this, though she felt she should have one. Amber was the only woman Hayden knew who had kids, and Amber's life was certainly chaotic. But most days she came to work happier than the rest of them, fueled by the chaos like a person who loves to stand on a cliff in a buffeting wind.

"Why does Emory want to be a man?" Janine said. "He told me about it, but I still don't understand why."

"It's hard to explain," Hayden said.

"I'm sure it's complicated. I've never met anyone who wanted that before. Do you envy men? I don't really. Perry's life is much harder than mine is."

"I used to," Hayden said. "But not anymore. I think I feel sorry for them."

They lay in a pocket of silence for a while. The fan circled lazily above them, but it did nothing to alleviate the heat.

Emory walked down the hill without a particular destination. It was lucky he had come to know the path well because once he had passed the lowermost bungalows the path entered the trees and darkness surrounded him. Still, he moved forward at a steady pace, sensing the path's curves and centering himself between the faint silhouettes of the flanking trees. Overhead a confetti of sharp stars helped guide him. He was not frightened out here, not as he had come to be frightened in New York. He had come to trust this landscape as he had once trusted the Floridian waters. The disturbances he felt now were all inside. He couldn't let go of thoughts about Frank. Memories he hadn't thought of for years were washing over him again. When Frank died and Emory moved back to the motel he found Frank's dentures lying at the bottom of a glass on the bedside table. The sight was unspeakably awful.

Teeth had suddenly seemed to Emory to be the center of a person, more central than the eyes or even the heart. Teeth were, after all, the defining feature of a skull. Teeth lived on, long after flesh was desiccated and decomposed. So it seemed as if the enduring things about Frank had to be squatting in those teeth, even if the teeth weren't real. Emory couldn't bear to do anything with the teeth. He didn't even want to touch them. He packed the glass (teeth still in it) in newspaper and stowed it all in a cardboard box.

Later, when he moved back to Miami, he showed the teeth to Peg. By then they seemed to have lost some of their power. Peg asked if she could have them and, though it was a peculiar request, Emory saw no reason not to part with them. He certainly had no plans for them and their sentimental value had faded. A week later Peg presented Emory with a necklace she had made. She had separated the teeth, drilled a hole in each one, and strung them on a piece of black leather twine. It was macabre, truly macabre, like something intended for voodoo or worship. Worse, it gave the teeth importance again so Emory had to keep it. He stuffed it in the back of a drawer and hadn't looked at it for years.

Movement in the bushes caused him to stop. Some low animal skittered across the path, and though Emory couldn't see what it was, he knew it was a mammal.

His thoughts moved to Hayden, smooth-skinned, rumple-browed Hayden. He thought of her talking intimately with Janine and felt a stab of jealousy. If he were there with them he would have been sidelined; he'd never been good at talking as women did. Still, thinking of them—two intense, small-breasted women, whispering, bonding—he felt forlorn. Stupidly lovesick. He saw himself wanting Hayden in the way some young girls wanted to be princesses. It was laughable and unrealistic—she didn't want him in return. Not now at least, and possibly, probably, never. They could be friends, yes, but friendship seemed pale. The silhouettes of the trees shimmied like hallucinations. He shuffled slowly down over the loose gravel. A new thought pumped through him. For so long Peg and transition were the only two subjects he had thought much about. They had wrangled with each other, and jangled him, for as long as he could remember. But for almost a week now he had thought of other things. He'd been, in fact, *consumed* by other things. Other passions, other people's pain. He'd been interested in the flow of life and all its external pleasures. It might not be Hayden he really loved. Maybe Hayden was only a stand-in for the new focus he needed, something other than Peg and transition. The path was sandy now and the trees delivered him onto the beach, opening in front of him like a proscenium curtain. He had made it here unharmed. Though it was night and all color was absent, everything seemed improbably light: the strip of white beach sand, the flat gray water reflecting clusters of stars. A stillness he would not have thought possible graced everything so he almost seemed to be looking at a photograph except that there were not only three dimensions but the feeling of a fourth too. The vastness out there, the endless exhilarating uncertainty of space, reached out to touch him.

"I used to get depressed every few months for two days," Janine said. "Then it would go away. That's not too bad, is it?"

The dark was translucent. "No," Hayden said, though she had no idea about bad or not bad.

Something scurried across the deck. They had left the door open to cool things down. Hayden hoped nothing would venture inside, ignoring human boundaries.

"This marriage thing," Janine said. "Aren't you horrified? Perry and I are horrified. He thinks it's actionable. *Some* sort of report should be filed. Does she really think she can pull it off and get his money and the rights to his work?"

Janine turned on her side, making the bedsprings tremble. She wanted Hayden to feel as she felt. Hayden had known so many women who wanted others to feel as they did. But Hayden knew there was so much else inside Manuela—Arista and love and legacy.

"I can't really think about that," Hayden said.

On the wall near where she lay something slithered. She flipped on the light and a tiny, harmless-looking brown lizard stared at her. Not a snake, thank God. But who could say the lizard was harmless? Maybe he, too, shot fatal venom. He was cute, though, and he surveyed her and took in all her parts. Love and fear intermingled.

"It's only a lizard," Hayden said. "Sorry I'm so skittish."

"Of course you would be. It's only natural."

"I'm worried about Emory."

"Don't worry about me." Emory was coming through the door. "I'm fine," he said. "I got out there and I thought: *What the hell am I doing out here while they're in there?* So I came back." He smiled. He looked perfectly unscathed. In his bright green and red clothing he fit here, Hayden thought.

Emory hadn't expected to find them half naked. He didn't want to embarrass them, but it was dark and except for the bright white of their underwear he couldn't see much. Hayden made room for him, moving to the center of the two beds and patting the empty space. Grief had made her brave. He lay beside her, keeping his clothes on. He had only been on the beach for a while before he realized he wanted to be back inside with them. There was no point in being solitary; the three of them should draw together and generate something. He felt stitched to these two. Just because he was a man didn't mean he had to be solitary. Peg had never liked his streak of independence; she had always sought to close the distance between them. *Move halfway toward me, then halfway again, now another halfway.* There was always more empty space.

His arm now was only a few millimeters from Hayden's arm. He left it there, resisting the yen to close the gap. Though his infatuation might be a stand-in for something else, he still wanted to make love to her. If she would have him he would be happy to make love to her right then and there, even with Janine present and watching. He would make love to her from the body of Emory, skin and follicles and hormones all Emory, opened up and unidentified Emory. This was the tropics; they had experienced death together; they could see and feel things now they could never have seen and felt before. Out of the corner of his eye he could see Hayden's long throat and the slight rise of one small breast. The impulse would have to come from her, but he was there, he was ready.

In the end, they found sleep. Hayden slept amid a river of images: coils of hair; hands patting the ground for four-leaf clovers; baby snakes, ostensibly dead, lurching alive and starting to grow again. She dreamed she was swimming and sick with fear. She rode her father's back, eyes closed. Her cheek lay on his freckled shoulder; her fingernails dug into his chest but he didn't complain. She wanted to be inside him, safe in his belly, away from the snakes. When she opened her eyes she saw the shoreline, far away. She hoped they would make it but worried they wouldn't.

Janine shook her shoulder, trying to awaken her. It was morning again, another hot one. Hayden tried to remember where she was. Pixels from all her former living spaces jittered kaleidoscopically in her brain. Janine and Emory both had the look of people who were deeply familiar.

When they arrived at the palapa breakfast was being cleared. Manuela, Arista, Rosaria, Gustavo, and Perry hovered around the jeeps, fresh and expectant. They were scheduled to meet the priest at the cemetery at ten. Angus's body had been transported down to the village the night before so they could do whatever they needed to do to preserve him and find him a coffin.

Gustavo waved to summon them, but Janine had other ideas. She was managing everyone. Earlier she had outfitted Hayden in the bathroom of her bungalow with a navy sundress. *You can't wear shorts to a funeral*, Janine had said. *You want to outfit me in a dress too?* Emory had asked. Janine blushed. *If you'd like—* she said, then realized Emory was joking. Now Janine strode to the kitchen and returned with coffee and rolls. They had not had dinner the night before.

"You have to eat something," Janine said. "Both of you."

Hayden and Emory downed their rolls like people on the lam. Janine took her time, refusing to acknowledge Gustavo's impatience. Arista made her way to their table and watched them eating as if she disapproved of their appetites on such a somber day.

"Hi," Hayden said.

Arista nodded. She was dressed all in white against which the brown of her skin and the black of her hair took on new radiance; she carried the porcelain, yellow-haired doll Father had given her.

"Uncle Angus died," she said.

"Yes, I know," said Hayden. "He's my father."

"No, he's my uncle."

"He's both. You can be a father and an uncle at the same time."

"This is my church dress. Only grown-ups have to wear black. I'm sad. Are you sad?"

"Yes."

"You can be sad about someone dying even when you don't see them very much. Mama is sad."

Hayden nodded. She wanted to silence Arista, who seemed to be on the verge of articulating trenchant, scary wisdom.

"Mama says we might go to the United States now. She wants to go to school like me."

Hayden nodded, fighting the urge to pull Arista on her lap. She was not the sort of child you did this to, not without asking.

"Mama married Uncle Angus because he was dying. She thought it might make him feel better. She was going to marry him anyway and then he would have been my father."

Janine had stopped eating. She and Emory shared a look. Hayden stayed focused on Arista. Her sister was talking to her. Her sister had things to say. It was Hayden's job to listen.

Manuela sang out. *"Vámanos. Ya nos tenemos que ir."*

"She wants us to come," said Arista.

Gustavo, Perry, Janine, Emory, Rosaria, and Arista went in one jeep; Manuela insisted that she and Hayden travel alone in the other.

Hayden took the passenger's seat nervously. Manuela—tiny, black-clad, witch-tough, her bobbed hair knotted—drove. She was a terrible driver. She waved Gustavo's jeep into the lead then she followed, lurching over the hill's blind lip in a burst of speed, jamming the brake, stalling. She shot forward once more, braked suddenly, stalled again. Finally Hayden offered to drive and Manuela acquiesced.

"I am sorry," Manuela said. "I do not drive much."

"Do you have a license?" Hayden asked.

Manuela shook her head. "I do not have a car. I have no need."

"Just tell me where to go," Hayden said.

The jeep had power and an unforgiving clutch. It took some time to gauge how much gas it needed—not much—and how much brake pressure—a lot. But there was no traffic at all, and Hayden liked driving a vehicle that was open so they could feel the wind jousting around them as they tore through the countryside.

The drive on dirt roads would take them forty-five minutes, Gustavo had said. They drove out of the trees into the parched meadowland. Gaunt goats and cows gazed listlessly at them as they passed. Manuela said nothing. Hayden's anxiety drifted off.

"How did you get to know my father?" she said. "What drew you to him?"

Manuela laughed softly, privately, sending a mutter of envy through Hayden. The mysterious moment Manuela was recalling had taken place during a time when Hayden had had no presence in her father's life except as a fat blot of sorrow and anger.

"He made me laugh," Manuela said. "Strange things, you know. One day he ate pie—" Remembering, she laughed. "He put his face in the plate and he ate. No fork. So messy."

She laughed again then glanced at Hayden and suppressed her laughter. "And he wanted to know about me and my country," she said. "His mind was full of ideas. So open and eager to learn."

Hayden punched the accelerator. She supposed she had seen this, yes. In the last week she had seen this.

"And at first," Manuela went on, "he was so sad. Your mother. You. I was sad too. Living here, away from my parents. It was hard. Your father and me, we made a puzzle, you know?" She fumbled in her handbag and pulled out a piece of textured yellow paper. "See," she said.

Hayden was driving and could not look. "What is it?"

"Look," she said.

Hayden pulled over to the shoulder and looked at what Manuela held. A wedding invitation, printed in Spanish. *Angus Risley y Manuela Ortiz*, it said at the top, and just beneath, *Arista Ortiz Risley . . . quisiéramos invitarlos . . .* Hayden stopped reading, except for catching the date, April 7, a week hence.

Hayden thought of all the things her father had said to her in the prior week, the things she had not wanted to hear. So why not this? Marriage had not been some future plan—it was already in motion, imminent. Manuela waited for her to say something. Hayden's eyes traveled along a stretch of barbed wire that restrained a couple of cows, and her thumb absently rubbed the corner of the invitation. It was printed on cheap paper and was not engraved. It held her father's name. Its cheapness made the love more evident. And the mention of Arista in print made it official—they were a family. Hayden was the add-on. She handed the invitation back to Manuela and began driving again.

Everything in the landscape was brown and etiolated, suffering from too much use. She already missed the green of the jungle. Someday scientists would find a way to see love and measure it. Then it could be controlled and allocated equitably, and more could be made with new compounds. Then there would not be the problem of too much, or too little, or the wrong person having it. Maybe Father had loved Mother as much as Hayden herself had. Maybe that love could be stacked right next to his love for Manuela. Maybe he had loved Hayden as much as he loved Arista. And maybe Hayden herself had loved him, not just now but all along.

Houses were appearing by the roadside, shacks really, that looked like dubious protection from the elements. This was the same road Hayden had traveled from the airport to the resort, but coming from the other direction she only recognized small stretches of it. A woman hanging out laundry waved to them and

Manuela waved back. Hayden wondered if they knew each other but Hayden didn't bother to ask. Signs of the village began to accrue: outdoor cafés, bodegas with neon promoting *cerveza* and Coke, small stucco houses with tribes of young children spinning in their yards.

Manuela directed Hayden to turn and turn again. They drove through a main street of the village, the road still unpaved. Hayden felt desperate to say something conclusive before they joined the others. The street was made of compacted dirt that sent up fine silt. People sauntered by on foot, carrying cardboard coffee cups and loaves of bread. One man carried a squawking chicken while goosing a small, bare-footed girl with his big toe. The somnolence of early morning had not yet faded and, steering the jumpy jeep through it all, Hayden felt distinctly out of place, as if her entire person held wrong, stepped-up rhythms that made her too visible and, if not unwelcome, at least strange.

"I told him many times not to be scared of you," Manuela said suddenly. She was a small black hole beside Hayden, willful and kind and full of controlled turmoil and sadness. Hayden felt she could be sucked up by the vortex of Manuela.

"You said that before," Hayden said. "But *why*? *Why* was he scared of me?"

The jeep stalled. A man walking by slapped the wheel well as if to push them out of the way. Hayden thought the gesture was hostile until she saw him smiling. Manuela laughed—at what Hayden wasn't sure. Hayden turned the key and the jeep leaped forward; a boy skittered out of their way; a man in front of a nearby bodega emptied orange soda into the dust. Hayden couldn't tell the right way to look at things, just when it seemed imperative to look at things right.

"Are you scared of me?" Hayden asked.

Manuela shifted her body, a shrug perhaps; Hayden couldn't focus, couldn't step out of the commotion. People ambled in front of the jeep and she tried not to hit them.

"He said you judge people. I don't say that—he did. Turn right down here. He was afraid you would leave if he said too much, or the wrong thing."

Hayden could see the cemetery already and the other jeep, and it was too soon. Too many things were yet to be said, but what were they exactly? Who was the blamer and who was to be blamed? Who was afraid and who was to be feared? They couldn't bring this jumble to Father's gravesite. They couldn't haunt him forever with these uncertainties.

The cemetery was a small grassy area with several large shade trees. It was set apart from the village by only a low brick wall. Hayden saw headstones with crucifixes and a mound of dirt, a yawning hole, a box that held Father. She pulled up to the grassy area where the other jeep had parked. The cooling engine continued to huff. The priest stood alone near the mound of dirt, head bowed. The others were making their way to where he stood, but Arista broke from the group and ran toward Manuela and Hayden. Hayden stared into her lap.

"God, Manuela," Hayden said. "I'm not scary. I'm really not. At least I don't mean to be."

"I'm not either," Manuela said.

"I hope he wasn't just scared of me. I hope he knew I loved him."

"He knows," Manuela said. "I am sure he knows."

When Hayden looked up Manuela was smiling, her face newly tear-streaked. She looked like a child-woman, a collage of innocent and wise, much like Arista but balanced differently.

"You will forgive me?" Manuela said.

"I don't think there is anything to forgive." Hayden thought of something then. "I guess you're my stepmother."

"Yes. You obey me."

They laughed in a series of reports that rose and fell and rose again, each of them finding joint and private amusement in the command. They laughed until Arista arrived at the jeep and curled her hands around the passenger door.

That was how Angus Risley left the mortal coil, disappearing into the Costa Rican soil under the shade of a magnolia tree. Radio music and smells of oil and charred peppers drifted over them from down the street; small boys interrupted their soccer game to peer, sharp-eyed and quiet, over the low wall, respectful until play reclaimed them; a mangy goat wandered through the open gate and went to work cropping the grass. Nothing was suspended due to Angus Risley's death, but the people close to him stepped out of time for a bit, while one moment evanesced to the next, and the priest's mesmerizing Spanish, reassuring as song, anointed them all with a temporary touch of holiness. In time, when his flesh was worn away and his coffin disintegrated, his red hair, too, would crumble and merge with the bright moldered plumage of macaws and quetzals, and its color would be indescribable, but it would invest the surrounding soil with a certain ineffable shimmer for those with the heightened sensitivity to notice.

Chapter 42

They stood on Hayden's rooftop on a crisp September evening a few days shy of the full moon. It was also a few days before Emory's metoidioplasty. The following day he would fly to San Francisco where he would have the surgery that would move him closer to manhood. They would cut the clitoris free from its hood, and use the labia minora as additional girth and protection. This was as much as Hayden understood. The main point was: Emory would end up with a small but credible penis. Cut from the same tap-wood-clap-thrice mold as Hayden, he had scheduled the procedure to coincide with the full moon. Tonight they were celebrating, commemorating, inaugurating, preparing him under the generous blue-tinged lunar light that seemed bent on changing things.

The sirens were more plentiful than usual. The garbage cans by the building's front steps glowed in the moonlight like shy women preparing to dance. Someone in the building had put on opera and opened a window as if wanting everyone to hear, and the baritone's recitative punctuated the rock music that played on Hayden's boom box. The moon, tarrying in its rise, hovered next to the Empire State Building. Sometimes Hayden found herself painting the comforting specter of the absent towers in her mind, just as Bella had instructed her. She remembered seeing the moon from her Hoboken side of the river, small and stuck between the two buildings like a pinball about to be jettisoned.

Once, Emory had despaired, but now he had no end of hope. He began to swim through the air to a Michael Jackson tune, careless of his water-loving body. He was unique and malleable. Watching him, Hayden tried to imagine how he would be after the surgery; she pictured him like Virginia Woolf's Orlando: defiant and fearless, a relentless time-traveler, cycling for the remainder of his life from male back to female, then to male again, then back to female, a continual embracing of transformation until death, the final change. Every change after that would be handed off to nature.

This was a moment of pause. In the six months since Angus Risley's death events had been galloping. There had been the birth of Cornelia's baby, Angus Jack, which Hayden had attended. There had been the event they had staged in the backyard of the Connecticut house, which included a smorgasbord of ceremonies: a wedding for Arleen and George, the tree man; funerals for Angus and Claire (who had never had one); and a "welcome to the world" for Angus Jack. There had been the meeting of Arleen and Manuela on the front driveway—Manuela technically Arleen's stepmother by then, though six years her junior. And there had been the meeting of Cornelia and Sophie with Manuela and Arista. Many new family configurations and the mind-bending mental adjustment that accompanied them. There had been Emory's return to Florida and Hayden's visit there and Hayden's offer of money for the surgery which Emory refused at first, and then, after a harrowing sleepless night, decided to take. There had been Hayden's introduction to Peg, a big sad proud woman who still adored Emory. She greeted Hayden with a crushing handshake and imperious, compulsive laughter.

Then there had been Hayden's visit to her father's mother, Nora, in Weehawken. Hayden sat by her grandmother's bedside and held her hand. Hayden wanted to ask about Angus, but Nora's hold on life was too tenuous for questions. Ten days after that Nora died. Hayden did not think she had anything to do with the death, but she worried that she had.

But now, in the slithery holographic moonlight, the moments lapped over one another, calm and endless. The night offered up to Hayden and Emory the illusion of permanence. What was before them was all there was. All there would ever be. They took it gladly. The roof. The moonlight. Manhattan draped before them, altered and humble and strong, the very model of resurgent hope.

Acknowledgments

Many people helped bring this book to life; I extend heartfelt thanks to all of them. To all the people at Panache Hair Salon, especially Kelly Loughary, who told me stories and answered all my questions and delighted in watching it all come together. To Sunny McHale and Ryan Powell who were both so generous in sharing their experiences as transgendered people. To Liz Reis who taught a wonderful class about gender. To all the friendly and open people at Seattle's 2004 Gender Odyssey Conference. To Dr. Ken Singer for talking me through some medical choices. To Laurie de Gonzáles and Andrew Rothgery for helping me cheerfully and tirelessly with Spanish. To Brad Childs of Musgrove Family Mortuary who schooled me on cadavers. To numerous astute readers: Liz Reis, Mary Wood, Ruth Knafo-Setton, Andrea Schwartz-Feit, and Kim O'Brien. To Claire Wachtel, Lauretta Charlton, Sean Griffin, and all the others at William Morrow/HarperCollins, who cared about the details. Thanks to my most splendid agent and cherished friend, Deborah Schneider. Finally, unending gratitude to my *habibi*, Paul Calandrino: reader, editor, hand-holder, soul mate.

Insights,
Interviews
& More...

Meet Cai Emmons

Rob Fraser

I GREW UP IN LINCOLN, MASSACHUSETTS, a small suburb about fifteen miles from Boston. When I was growing up, there were only about four thousand people in the town, and its population isn't much bigger today. I lived there until I went to college, and the life of that town has shaped me deeply. It was a "liberal" community, a place that valued reading and books, that valued the natural world. Although I have lived on the West Coast for many years, I will always consider myself a New Englander. Another special thing about that town was that there were a number of writers living there— the poet Philip Booth, and the fiction writer Jane Langton among them. I revered these grown-ups. I aspired, from a very early age, to be like them.

I began to write in fourth grade. My teacher, Stephen Vogel, had us write daily compositions. They were short creative pieces inspired by something he put on the board: a picture, perhaps, or an opening line. We could write whatever we wanted to write, and we were never graded. We did this all year long

❝ I began to write in fourth grade. ❞

2

and I loved it. After that I was hooked. I've written ever since.

In college I began to write plays and had some of them produced in New York, but I knew I would never earn a living by writing plays, so I decided to go to film school. I spent the next decade or so writing (and directing) film stories, and although I did have some success, I never felt very comfortable in the medium. When I began writing novels, I had a profound feeling of arriving at the place I belong as a writer. I am driven, in part, to write novels because I have always most enjoyed reading them. I love the scope of novels. I love that they allow me to explore the inner world of characters, which is so much harder to do with either plays or screenplays.

Like most writers, I have a huge number of favorite authors. My first favorite book, when I was a child, was *The River* by Rumer Godden. It's the story of a girl living with her family in India. She's dealing with a lot: growing up, being a younger sister, feeling ignored, wanting to be a writer, and having her brother die of a snakebite. I found it so lyrical, so sad. After I'd written *The Stylist*, I realized that certain things about *The River* had made their way into my own work. I have fallen in love with so many writers and books since then. When I was a teenager I loved the work of John Fowles (*The Magus*, *The French Lieutenant's Woman*, and *The Collector*). I adore Virginia Woolf (is there any female writer who doesn't?). How did she dare write a book like *The Waves*?!? Alice McDermott and Michael Cunningham are among my favorite contemporary writers, as well as Kent Haruf. The structure and language in McDermott's *That Night* dazzles me, and how did Cunningham inhabit Woolf's voice so accurately in *The Hours*!?! And I ▶

admire the compassion of Kent Haruf and his simple, lyrical style. I love Russell Banks's masterful book *Continental Drift* and Michael Chabon's *Amazing Adventures of Kavalier & Clay*. I adore Faulkner, Fitzgerald, and Cheever. I keep James Salter's novel *Light Years* under my bed so I can reread sections of it easily. Marilynne Robinson's *Housekeeping* is also within easy reach. I love lush language. I love to be gripped by story. I think we come to reading to both lose and find ourselves in story.

I like to write as soon as I can after waking up, so that I'm still near a dream state. I have a coffeemaker in the bedroom. I drink a cup of coffee in bed, and then I get to work right there, propping myself up with pillows and writing longhand on a lined pad. I like writing in bed because no one can interrupt me there—it's a completely private sphere. I don't answer the phone; I don't check e-mail; I don't answer the doorbell until I'm done writing for the day. It's very escapist, I suppose, but it seems to work. Eventually, of course, I type what I've written into the computer. And I have learned, the hard way, not to let too many pages accumulate before I type them in.

Over the years I have found a few readers (many of them also writers) who are so much in tune with my work that they are excellent critics for me. My best reader is my partner, Paul Calandrino, who writes plays and is so astute about fiction that I'm awestruck. I almost always take his suggestions.

Right now I am involved in two projects. I have just completed the sixth or seventh or eighth draft of a novel whose working title is *The Twenty-ninth Bather*. Because it is too long, I am about to do a page one rewrite. I also

> 66 I keep James Salter's novel *Light Years* under my bed so I can reread sections of it easily. 99

want to broaden the point of view. It is a story that takes place in a small, New England town very similar to the one I grew up in. A white Unitarian minister and his black wife move to this town from California, and various things are set in motion. I can't say too much more because there are some odd (not wholly realistic) things that happen in it, and I don't want potential readers to have preconceived notions. While waiting for feedback on *The Twenty-ninth Bather*, I wrote about a hundred pages of my fourth novel, *Pilgrims with Families* (or maybe *Continuous Travelers*). It is the story of a retired couple who have sold their house and all their belongings, and purchased an RV, becoming what the Oregon DMV terms "continuous travelers." The story begins when they have to take responsibility for two of their grandchildren because of a derelict (addicted and incarcerated) mother. With four people in such tight quarters, you can imagine that things don't go smoothly. I still need to do some research, in the form of my own RV traveling. ∾

> " I wrote about a hundred pages of my fourth novel.…It is the story of a retired couple who have sold their house and all their belongings, and purchased an RV, becoming what the Oregon DMV terms 'continuous travelers.' "

"The Probing of an Obsession"
On Writing *The Stylist*

I AM RECLINING in a chair at Panache Salon, head back, eyes closed, having my hair washed by my hairdresser and friend, Kelly. For the next hour no one can disturb me; I have no responsibilities other than sitting still, chatting a bit, laughing, and allowing Kelly to position my head and chair as needed. She applies a rosemary-scented shampoo and massages it gently into my scalp. The warm water, the herbal fragrance, the soothing touch of her fingers, the light laughter coming from the other room all conspire to put me in a trance, almost more delicious than sleep. When she's done we move to her station. She brings me tea, and after some discussion about how short I want my hair, she starts to cut. I coax her into telling me stories about beauty school. They learned to shave heads, she says, by using a straight razor on a balloon. After the requisite number of balloons, she was assigned to shave someone with an advanced case of head lice. Her description of the process is agonizing— she knows I'll later purloin this story for my book—and we're both laughing. We always laugh. I'm far too relaxed to do anything else. Having my hair cut here, at Panache, by Kelly, is one of my life's real pleasures. It wasn't always this way; it took me many years to find a salon like this. In the past having my hair cut was awkward or humiliating—or downright dangerous.

When I was a child I had extremely short hair, often cut by my mother. It was so short in nursery school that once, when I was doing

> **66** I coax her into telling me stories about beauty school. They learned to shave heads, [Kelly] says, by using a straight razor on a balloon. **99**

some hammering during a Father's Day event, another father said to my father, "Your son is pretty handy with a hammer." This story was always reported by my parents with pride, though it didn't seem to affect me one way or the other. However, by the time I got to high school, I was sick of short hair and wouldn't let anyone get near me with scissors. I allowed my hair to grow and grow, wore it long and unkempt and wild. I loved it and was attached to it in the way I imagine Samson was attached to his hair. But in my mid-twenties when I moved to New York for graduate school, I decided it was high time to get my hair styled. A friend recommended a salon on the Upper East Side. So off I went to Pipino Buccheri to get my locks shorn into some more fashionable shape. Coming from the Lower East Side, I was completely out of my element. The place was filled with wealthy matrons, who I imagined were women of leisure. As the hairdresser and I discussed what I should do with my hair, I mentioned its current *style*. She hushed me with a dismissive wave. "Honey, you don't have a style." For the rest of the session I remained silent and tried not to look in the mirror. When I emerged I definitely did have a style. It was still what most people would call long, but it was layered and bouncy, and as I headed home, this new *style* of mine prompted catcalls from several men, and I felt suddenly introduced to the power of hair.

Though I knew I'd never go back to that Upper East Side salon, I did feel that I wanted occasional haircuts. The next time, I went to a walk-in salon on St. Mark's. It was a place below street level with hip music and energetic male and female hairdressers. The first time I went there, I got a good, cheap (and very short) haircut. But after I'd gone there two or three ▶

7

more times, I realized my haircuts were not consistently good. Everyone who worked there seemed too speedy or too spacey, and it gradually dawned on me: they were all using drugs.

Leap now to California. I was working in Hollywood and could not afford to look sloppy. I went to a hairdresser who I'd met at my husband's high school reunion. She was a bleached-blonde former cheerleader with whom I had nothing in common. I sat in the chair feeling horrible social anxiety, trawling for something to talk about beyond my husband's ex-girlfriends and the atrocious condition of my hair.

When I arrived in Eugene, Oregon, my hair had grown wild again without my consent. By luck I landed at a place where my hairdresser (Kelly) was someone who I came to regard as a friend. She was a former special education teacher, but she had suffered from burnout and retrained as a hairdresser. I immediately liked that she wasn't trying to fashion me into someone I wasn't. She didn't humiliate me for trimming my own hair between cuts. She was someone with whom I could discuss movies and books, and I found myself looking forward to my appointments as relaxing mini-vacations. And the atmosphere of the entire salon was—*is*—intimate, almost familial. Like many salons, it's a hotbed of stories. It wasn't long before my fictional mind went to work on a novel set in a salon.

The writing of a novel is, for me, the probing of an obsession. After ricocheting around my subconscious, an idea muscles itself into my frontal lobe. A character begins to emerge,

> " I realized my haircuts were not consistently good. Everyone who worked there seemed too speedy or too spacey, and it gradually dawned on me: they were all using drugs. "

along with a *what-if* situation, and the novel is launched. It takes time to write a novel—a year? two years? ten? It depends, of course, on both the novel and the novelist, but because it is usually an extended period—often including changes of season, changes of mood, sometimes changes of domicile or marital status—one's ideas must have heft and traction and layers that sustain interest. Writing from an obsession more or less guarantees my interest over what can sometimes be a very long haul.

The Stylist wasn't an easy book for me to write because I found myself juggling several elements, and I wasn't sure if they belonged in the same book. The first element had to do with hair and how important it is to us in self-presentation. Then, there was my ongoing gender obsession, which has been with me for as long as I can remember and which figured prominently in my first play, *Mergatroid*. Next, there was this family constellation I'd invented: three daughters, a remote father, and an erratic mother. And finally, there was the thought that had taken root when I was in Costa Rica: What would you do if you traveled with a parent to a foreign country and the parent died, and in the midst of your sorrow, unable to speak the local language, you had to negotiate the handling of the body? For some reason all these ideas were roiling around together in my brain, and finally I had to trust that my unconscious had served them up simultaneously for a reason— they really did fit together, and there was a connecting thread that had to do with people trying to transform themselves in various ways. When I saw that, I realized I had a cohesive novel. ∽

> " The writing of a novel is, for me, the probing of an obsession. After ricocheting around my subconscious, an idea muscles itself into my frontal lobe. "

A Conversation with Cai Emmons

Your main character, Hayden, is a hairdresser who has dropped out of Harvard. How did she come about as a character?

I grew up in a Boston suburb where Harvard casts a long shadow. There was a huge emphasis not only on going to college but on going to the "right" college. If you went to Harvard, people thought you had achieved some pinnacle of success. I liked the idea of a character who rejected this notion and opted to discard the benefits of a high-class/high-brow education in favor of something she could fully embrace and call her own, even if her father—her whole family—would think of it as déclassé.

Emory Bellew appears at the beginning of the book as a "she," and by the end of the book Hayden refers to Emory as "he." What drew you to writing about a transgendered character?

I have always been fascinated by what it means to change one's gender—it is such a complex choice in our gender-bound culture. I never wanted to be a man in quite the way Emory Bellew does, but I do think that I've wanted certain aspects of what we think of as masculinity. Very early on, I developed the idea that things would be better if everyone were androgynous. In fact, the first play I wrote was

> **❝ I developed the idea that things would be better if everyone were androgynous. ❞**

a surreal piece about two women, a couple, who have ten "neuter" children. The children are sent out into the world, and in the course of the play, they come back to tell their stories about being neuter in a gendered society—all pretty horrific stories.

How did you research the transgender aspect of the book?

I did as much reading as I could, particularly the personal testimonies of people who had been through some sort of gender transformation. Amy Bloom wrote a wonderful book called *Normal* that explores the experiences of transsexuals, among others. I loved reading about the experiences of the musician Billy Tipton, a biological woman who "passed" for most of his life—without having had any surgery—as a man. I read books by Jan Morris and Renee Richards and Kate Bornstein and Deidre McCloskey, all of whom went through gender transformations. It was easier to find written testimonies about men who had become women (M-to-F's) than to find stories about women who had become men (F-to-M's). I was also very fortunate to make face-to-face contact early on with two F-to-M transsexuals who were happy to share their stories with me: Ryan Powell and Sunny McHale. Ryan was still in high school when he first had his breasts removed, and at the time we talked he was interested in having access to both male and female personas. I met him through a mutual friend. Sunny I met in a weekend course about gender, taught by Liz Reis. She brought Sunny in to talk to ▶

the class. He had been a man for a long time, and he was married. In fact, his wife came to the class too. It was hard, at first, for me to wrap my mind around the fact that he had ever been a woman. That surprised me, that he could appear so completely masculine. Afterward, in our conversations over coffee, I was impressed with how comfortable he was with his both his gender and his sexuality. I attended the 2004 Gender Odyssey in Seattle, a conference for F-to-M's (and their partners and families) to discuss the issues that arose for them around relationships, surgery, etc. I was warmly welcomed, and I learned so much in the space of a few days. Many of the people had accomplished stunning transformations and were very happy; I also saw a great deal of struggle and pain: there were lesbians upset by having their partners become men, and there were also a few parents who were dismayed by their children going through gender transitions.

66 I attended the 2004 Gender Odyssey in Seattle....Many of the people had accomplished stunning transformations and were very happy; however, I also saw a great deal of struggle and pain. 99

The second part of the book takes place in an eco-resort in Costa Rica. Why did you choose that location?

In 2000 I traveled with my husband and son to an eco-resort in Costa Rica that was very similar to Tranquilidad. The resort was composed of a series of bungalows on a hill in a monkey-and-bird-filled jungle. At the top of the hill was the thatched, open-air *palapa* where we all ate—it had a beautiful view out over the jungle to the water. At the bottom of the hill was the

Golfo Dulce, edged by a beautiful beach. Because there were not many guests, and because we all ate in the same place and took walks together, we formed a loose community and were acutely aware of each other's comings and goings. It seemed a rich place to set a novel.

At the beginning of the book we are exclusively in Hayden's point of view, but gradually, as the story develops, we begin to see things from Emory's point of view, from the father's point of view, from an external narrator's point of view, and even from the viewpoints of some of the characters at the resort. Why did you decide to include those other points of view?

The decision to widen the point of view came to me gradually, as I went through draft after draft. Early on in the writing this was a first-person story, written exclusively from Hayden's point of view, but I slowly realized that we weren't seeing around Hayden's viewpoint sufficiently. I wanted her to be seen more objectively, from another perspective, so I began writing from the third person, occasionally pulling back to an outside narrator's viewpoint. Eventually the point of view became even wider and included Emory, Angus, and even Janine and Perry, who are relatively minor characters. The inclusion of those other perspectives mirrors Hayden's learning curve. As the book moves along, she begins to see that her viewpoint is not the only right one—her ▶

> ❝ I slowly realized that we weren't seeing around Hayden's viewpoint sufficiently. I wanted her to be seen more objectively, from another perspective, so I began writing from the third person. ❞

A Conversation with
Cai Emmons *(continued)*

sister Cornelia has a different view of things, as does Angus, as does Emory, as does Manuela. By the end of the book, Hayden's transformation is to see that all of these different viewpoints are valid, they can coexist, they *do* coexist whether she wants them to or not. ∽

Eyelash Vipers and Snakes in General

IN 2001 MY HUSBAND and son and I went to an eco-resort in the jungle on the Oso Peninsula of Costa Rica, a place very similar to the one portrayed in the novel. It was a small, intimate place, where it was nearly impossible not to be aware of people's comings and goings. One day we noticed John Updike and his wife sitting at a nearby table in the resort's only dining room. I was dying to talk to him, but I was also loath to interrupt him.

The next morning he and his wife were lingering over coffee, and their relaxed posture beckoned me. He was gracious, and as a newcomer to the resort, he was pleased to have the opportunity to ask me questions. He wanted to know what the beach was like and if the path down to it was treacherous. As our conversation meandered from one thing to another, he and his wife mentioned that a friend of theirs had been bitten by an eyelash viper during a visit to Costa Rica. I am deathly afraid of snakes, even garter snakes, yet here were two people who had traveled a great distance to the very place where their friend had almost died of a snakebite. They seemed completely unperturbed by this.

My imagination was instantly ignited. My mother had decided at the last minute not to come on this trip, thinking it might be too rough for her, but what if she had come? What if it had been my mother who'd been bitten? What if she had died from the bite, and I had had to transport her body home?

> " One day we noticed John Updike and his wife sitting at a nearby table in the resort's only dining room. "

Naked Kitties

WHEN MY SON was in kindergarten he was friends with a little girl I'll call "X." One day, about midway through the school year, my son asked if he could have X over to play. I called and spoke to X's father. "We'd like to have your daughter over this afternoon. Could she come at 2:00?" There was a slight but noticeable pause before he said, "I'll go talk to the lad."

Lad?!? I had worked with this child in the classroom, side by side, as I taught her how to use the computer mouse. She was definitely a girl, but—wouldn't her father know?

That afternoon X came over to play with my son, and I hovered close by as they played a game they'd invented, called "Naked Kitties." The game had nothing to do with them being naked, but that afternoon I wished it did. I tried to glean what I could as they leaped around the living room. X had chin-length hair that looked somewhat girlish, but had I really been duped by *hair?*

The father knew, of course. X was, indeed, male, and in the years since then, he has cut his hair and moved into adolescence and developed a whole host of undeniably male characteristics.

I felt a sense of dislocation, caused by my uncertainty about X's gender, and that feeling has stayed with me. The *Saturday Night Live* writers were playing with that sense of dislocation when they invented the androgynous character Pat. It was what I'd been exploring in my first play, *Mergatroid*. It was what I was still exploring when I began *The Stylist.*

66 I felt a sense of dislocation, caused by my uncertainty about X's gender, and that feeling has stayed with me. The Saturday Night Live writers were playing with that sense of dislocation when they invented the androgynous character Pat. 99